THE FIRE WITHIN MY HEART

THE FIRE WITHIN MY HEART

*Scarlet Cherie: Vampire
Series Book One*

Ayshen Irfan

Thank you so much to Emily, for dedicating so much time of your time to work with me and improve my skills as a writer. This book wouldn't be what it is today without all of your support.

Also, thank you to my mum and gran, for helping me with proofing and correcting (some very silly) mistakes. To dad, for the continuous encouragement and making me see that I could take my passion further than just a hobby.

Lastly, to mémé, for spending countless gruelling hours going over this novel with me—without you, it would never have ended up being to a standard I feel so proud of.

I love you all dearly.

THE FIRE WITHIN MY HEART

)CHAPTER 1(

I was only twenty years old when I died.

Walking home the same route I had been taking since I was a child, I had thought nothing of the dark shadow behind me, just another wanderer of the night—until he came closer and closer.

I turned to face him annoyed, and apprehensive, by his invasion of my space. The full moon cast harsh lines across his hooded face, a slash of greasy brown hair and wild, cruel eyes caught the light. He continued toward me. Suddenly too scared to turn my back on him again, I tried to back away. My foot stumbled on the edge of the curb, and I fell to the cold pavement. My hands tried to break the fall, the skin ripping open, burning with pain. Panic rippled through my body. Sick with fear, my heart beat agonisingly in my chest, pounding harder than a wild animal trying to break free of its cage. My legs were numb, failing me when I tried to stand and run away. My tongue was dry and my mouth tasted metallic. Begging for fight or flight to kick in, I tried to rise once again but was rooted to the cold, hard pavement, paralysed in terror.

His footsteps were nearing dangerously close, the sound of his boot violent on the concrete as he picked up speed; I was frozen in agonising anticipation. The first kick was surprisingly light, just enough to push me onto my side. With his short, stocky figure silhouetted by the moon, I could see the rise and fall of his shoulders as he stepped back to swing his foot at me again. Curling my body into a fetal position, my arms instinctively covered my head, trying to protect my face. Despite my attempt at steady breathing, I couldn't help but hyperventilate, each breath shallow and futile. I continued to struggle to gasp for air, but still, nothing came.

Never had I felt like such a coward, I loathed my pathetic self at that moment for not being strong, not being able to fight or run or defend myself. It was quiet. The ground was unwelcomingly cold. Unsure of what to expect, I lay there, curled and waiting for what felt like an eternity. What would be my fate?

For a moment, nothing happened. I could sense him pacing around my body slowly, taking in the sight of me; weak, vulnerable. The movement stopped when the man took up his position behind my back. I didn't dare risk looking back at my attacker, but I could hear his animalistic panting, breathless, excited. The breathing grew closer. I could feel each exhalation on the back of my neck, the smell an offence on the senses.

Time seemed to slow as he stood and a heavy boot thwacked full force into my spine. All the breath was violently knocked from my body; I tried to let out a scream, alas it was reticent. A profusion of kicking commenced, the initial pain bleeding into numbness. I tried to move, but my legs, losing all sensation, no longer seemed to work. The kicking had slowed, at least momentarily. The blunt force of his last punt had thrown me onto my stomach. Cold concrete pressing against my cheek was a welcome sensation after the dull numbness that had spread through my body.

And then it happened, as I lay there face down in the gravel, with the gentle mist of the late summer rain a moment of calm amidst the chaos: the final blow.

It was a different kind of pain than any I had ever experienced. It was what I imagined an electric shock to feel like, one that pulsated through my body, burning every nerve that hadn't already been bruised and battered. The heat was so intense I thought he might have set me alight; until I realised that this pain was internal. There was no way to put it out, no way to escape it.

Infinitude stretched on as the scorching heat trickled into a freezing sensation. I couldn't move my arms to clutch myself, I couldn't breathe or turn to see where or who he was. I began to lose consciousness. I wasn't sure if I had been blinded or my eyes were closed, the only thing I could see was perpetual darkness. The sound of boots smashing onto concrete as he ran into the night made my ears ring. I had been forsaken, left to die alone.

It was at that moment I knew I was seconds away from death. Any release from the pain in my body would be welcome. I thought of my mother, father, friends...of what they would think tomorrow when I hadn't returned home. Who would find my body? What would they do with me? I didn't care; I just needed to be free from the agony.

Death was welcome...

)CHAPTER 2 ((

As if someone had violently woken me from a deep sleep, my brain switched on in a manic awakening, and my eyes burst open. All I could see was infinite darkness. Although the surface I lay upon was uncomfortably solid and damp, it wasn't the concrete that I had lost consciousness on. Someone had moved me. Unwelcome fragments of my attack crashed through my mind, fear making me nauseous. I tried to move, but my limbs were met with a cold, wooden surface. I was trapped.

There was a fleeting sense of gratitude that my body didn't ache and dynamism had returned. Despite the limited space for movement, I tried to smash my fists against the wood, screaming as loud as I could. My hands pounded until they felt battered and bruised; no matter how much I shouted for help, the sounds were lost in the silence of my cage. I sobbed. Begging someone, anyone, to help me. For the first time in my life, I prayed, aggressively imploring Him (or Her) to save me. No one answered. I was abandoned. Abandoned by a God that I had never believed in, by the man who had left me to die alone and afraid.

Adrenaline is quick to wear off; all of my energy depleted in an instant. My body hurt once more. Each limb sore and heavy with profound exhaustion. The bones in my body ached, even my jaw and teeth felt like they were alight with a roaring fire. My consciousness felt disconnected from my body. I was too tired to move, as I fought to keep my eyes from closing, I could sense movement in the box. My body writhed to battle the pain that tore through every in-

4

dividual cell inside of me, but my brain had begun to shut down and, although a part of me knew I was the cause of the loud movement, I couldn't feel it.

Had this been limbo? Maybe I was finally being taken to the afterlife. The pain could finally stop. As my body continued to writhe and buck against the wood, my eyes closed for what I thought would be the final time, then oblivion washed over me.

Unexpectedly, I found myself awake once more. The pain had all but subsided to nothing. If anything, I felt...sturdy, which was a welcome comfort. Stiff-muscled and tired, but undeniably more alert and energised. My eyelids fluttered several times before I realised I could see clearly. My back was no longer rested upon uninviting wood but instead the comfort of a padded seat. I tried to sit up too quickly, my head spun, and the room was momentarily a blur. When I pulled myself up for a second time, it was with caution, and I found I could hold myself up without too much effort.

Looking around, I could see that I occupied what appeared to be a homely library. Three of the walls were taken up with bookshelves of solid oak, almost bursting with the magnitude of their contents. Opposite from where I sat was the only bookshelf-free wall; it was painted a deep red with a black stone fireplace breaking up the solid colour. The charcoal was burning orange as the last embers began to fade. Despite the dim light, I could make out that some of the book spines looked ancient; so old that, with a breath of wind, the paper would flake away. Tucked neatly, contrastingly, in between them sat other books, new and untouched.

Near me was a chaise lounge identical to the one I was slumped against. The legs were short and made of fine, dark oak, elegantly curved to support a fabric body in deep blue. Some areas of the material had worn, fading to murky grey in ugly patches. The wooden coffee table centred between the seats was of an equally sable wood; the corners had begun to disintegrate from years of wear. Everything was gracefully antique, lacking the deep lustre of youth.

The already caliginous room was slowly being entirely swallowed by darkness, the once neon embers now little more than specks of orange, pitifully fighting against the blanket of shadow. I knew I should have been scared, but my mind felt as stagnant as the dust-filled air in the room. I found my mind was vacant, irrationally calm in the warm embrace of comfort that came from resting upon worn furniture, instead of concrete colder than the dead.

My eyes flickered around the room with intense scrutiny, taking in the sight of each object as if my life depended on it, but my body remained deathly still. Static, as though even my blood had slowed to a pacific stream through my veins. There should have been some noise. Something to indicate that the scene I found myself in was real, but there was nothing. The air was too still as if holding its breath, waiting in anticipation for what would happen next. No fidgeting, no whisper of cloth on cloth as I subconsciously adjusted position. Just silence, a quiet so loud it was deafening.

It took me a moment before I realised that I had laid down once again, my body moving faster than my brain could follow. The soft material of the chaise longue was a soothing comfort against my skull, making my limbs feel heavy, and my body tired. The fire had long since dissipated; I couldn't tell if my eyes were closed or the room was such a pure black I was blinded. Sleep coaxed at me once more, but this time

I didn't fight it. I fell into a slumber, shrouded in quiescent silence, grateful for the stillness of my mind after, what felt like, an endless slew of pain and disruption.

My eyes fluttered open at a sound that sliced through the silence, startling me awake. I was unsure whether I had fallen back to sleep or only just closed my eyes. My head felt heavy as though a flood of rain clouds was fogging up any clarity, but at least I still wasn't in pain. The noise that had disturbed me hadn't been loud, but it had seemed deafening. Panic stirred in the pit of my stomach, I tried to look around the room but was still blinded by the endless darkness. For a moment, nothing happened. Maybe I had imagined the noise, had it been nothing more than a dream that I was confusing for reality? I was beginning to feel like the veil between authenticity and imaginary was fragile. Unsure of what memories to trust, confused by my irrational ease, I sat there waiting in frustrated silence. Anxious to see who, or what, had woken me.

Several seconds of nothing passed. Then the sound of a match being struck and the warm smell of sulphur, as flame spluttered into existence and tore through the darkness. I caught a glimpse of a ghostly face as the figure who had lit the match bent down and reignited the fire. Their movements flowed with the grace of water, distinctively elegant in a way I had never seen anyone move.

Before the fire had time to chase the shadows away in their entirety, I glimpsed the silhouette of a tall, slender figure. As the darkness dispersed, my view of the figure expanded, and I felt my heart speed up in my chest. I instantly knew it was not the same man who had attacked me; the anonymity of the figure should have caused crippling panic, but that wasn't why my heart tried to escape from my chest.

Half of his precisely angled face was still cloaked in shadow as if he knew how to manipulate the light and appear only as he wished to be seen. The half I could see was made up of a chiselled jaw, with high and sculpted cheekbones. The defined curves of a strong nose and brow framed deep, slightly downturned, almond eyes. The man's face was whiter than marble, and equally as statuesque, as though he should have been immortalised in stone. The paleness of his face was framed by a stream of glistening, obsidian waves. Viridian green eyes watched me under a cape of long, black eyelashes with a look of derision. Plump, pallid pink lips looked stark against the exceptional whiteness of his skin and were pressed together in a soft line. A triangle of chest was visible between his lazily buttoned shirt; the silk was true black which still wasn't as dark as the tresses of his satin hair. The shirt was tucked into well-fitted dark slacks; he wore black socks over long, slender feet but no shoes.

Resting his elbow on the ledge of the fireplace and laying his chin on top of a curled fist, his eyes fixed me with a look that bore into my soul. I resisted the urge to squirm under the intensity of the gaze, but couldn't bring myself to meet his eye. For a moment, we stayed in silence, my head still turned down to hide under the cascades of my crimson locks. There was a knot in my stomach, anxiety twisting my insides so tight I felt nauseous. I wanted to say something, the quiet was too hot and suffocating, but I thought I might be sick if I opened my mouth. What would I even say? There were too many questions but no words to ask them.

'I am Nikolaos.'

The broken silence was sudden enough that I jumped. Nikolaos's voice rippled through the still space like satin over skin; even from the other side of the room, I could feel the whisper of his words trace my flesh. I shuddered. I dared to look up, and he was still watching me with those cold, vibrant eyes. The golden light of the fire danced along the black of his hair, and, as the flames flickered, orange silhouettes danced across his eyes. Something about the heat was calming, soothing. The crackles of the fire felt like they were whispering to me, telling me it would be okay. I could feel the tender warmth radiate over my skin, reminding me I wasn't alone. I felt stronger.

Nikolaos began to glide towards me, each step perfectly graceful, as if he were floating. Just as elegantly, Nikolaos slipped onto the chaise longue beside me, his elongated, slender limbs falling into a casually seductive pose. Feeling more confident, I met his gaze, staring back into the pools of his eyes.

'You may have some questions,' he announced.

There was an accent of some kind, the faint shadow of a past life. The brain fog had begun to ease, devastating images of the violent attack invaded my mind. I felt ill again, fear and repulsion making my body stiffen. Intuitively, Nikolaos reached out and wrapped a long-fingered hand around my own for comfort. Surprised, I looked up at his face again to see he looked just as uncertain, as though the action had been unexpected even to him. The look was quickly replaced with one of vacant mocking, bordering arrogance. The touch of his skin sent sparks dancing over my flesh, the knot in my gut easing. The room had turned a deeper red as the fire roared.

'But first, may I know your name?'

The question was polite, innocent, but his voice held the promise of sinister pleasures.

'Scarlet.' My own voice was unsteady; high pitched with unease. But at least I could talk.

Nikolaos's head tilted to one side, musing over my

response more than was necessary. I felt the need to elaborate, so used my free hand, the one that wasn't still entwined in his, to trace the line of the cardinal locks that tumbled down my front.

'I see.' His head cocked to one side, following the trail of my hand with his own. '*Ma feu.*'

Was the accent French? He let one of the curls slip through his hand before tracing a cold, smooth finger over the line of orange freckles that danced along my nose. A blush crept up my face, burning my cheeks. I turned my head away to hide it, but Nikolaos used his thumb and index finger to grip my jaw, squeezing tight enough it almost hurt.

'Do not look away from me.' His breath was cold against my burning face. 'You are mine now.'

The way he said it made me believe him. Hidden behind the smooth seduction was a force warning me I had no choice.

'Who are you?' I pleaded, making Nikolaos release his grasp on my jaw.

'I have already told you.'

'*What* are you?'

The question escaped my lips before I had time to think over the ridiculousness of what I'd asked. Nikolaos smiled for the first time, a small spread of lips that warmed his cold eyes. I had amused him.

'What am I?' He seemed to think over the question for a moment. 'I am old.'

As Nikolaos's lips moved I caught a glimpse of pearly-white teeth and sharp canines. Daggers made from the most exquisite ivory, sharper than steel and stronger than bone. So very beautiful. So very, very deadly.

I went to gasp but choked on air as fear sent goose-bumps up my skin in chilled waves. The fire seemed to burn brighter, stronger, as I scrambled backwards in the chair away from the man in front of me. In the deep-red light, Nikolaos's statuesque features were illuminated, like the devil standing in the fires of hell. Alluring, angelic and temptingly pernicious.

Unexpectedly, I found myself by the door beside the fireplace. The speed of my movement made the room spin, and I almost collapsed to the floor, but Nikolaos appeared beside me just as suddenly and caught me in one arm. He held my entire body weight like it was nothing as my knees buckled beneath me. Nikolaos had skin colder than ice but, as I slumped in his grip, a warmth ran through me that made me feel steadier. I resisted the truth that touching him made the fear and anger bleed away. It made no sense. I wanted to be angry; I wanted to fight and thrash and shout, but, as he held me, all I felt was the sensation of static running throughout my body. Pricking at my body almost painfully. It was the feeling of power, something magic and fantastical, coursing through my veins as our skin became one. Niko felt it too, his pupils dilating, drowning the green in pools of black.

'What am *I*?' My voice was unexpectedly steady.

'You are mine—'

'What does that mean, Nikolaos?' I interrupted him, frustration turning my voice dark.

Confident I could stand alone, and as the room had stopped spinning, I pulled free of his support which made Nikolaos smile for the second time.

'I found you several nights ago, *ma feu.*'

'I was attacked.'

Nikolaos gave a curt nod.

'I knew my blood could save you, alas I was too late. As you took my blood you...' Nikolaos searched for the right word, settling on 'Passed.'

I felt myself gulp painfully hard as tears began to sting my eyes, a tightness in my chest made breathing difficult. The sadness was consuming; it made the air so heavy it was suffocating. Unable to breathe, I choked on the pain. I had been under no illusion that to survive my attack would be impossible, but hearing the words aloud made the twisted nightmare an unwelcome reality.

'Scarlet, you must try and remain calm.' Nikolaos's voice sounded strained. He turned his head away from me but not before I caught the dampness in his own eyes. 'When a human dies after drinking the blood of a vampire, they may rise as one of us. It is not something we take indifferently, the connection between master and vassal is one of great power and intensity.'

'Master.' The word was a bitter whisper in my mouth. 'This connection, does it mean you can feel what I'm feeling?'

Nikolaos turned to look at me; there was a damp trail on his cheek where a lone tear had escaped on a voyage of melancholy down his face.

'Yes.'

'I felt calmer when you touched me.'

Beginning to realise what Nikolaos being my 'master' truly meant, the words quietly spilt from my mouth. We were connected, not by emotions, but by blood and power; spirit and soul, if vampires had souls.

'Why did I wake up in a box?' The realisation dawned on me. 'A coffin.'

'New vampires are commonly volatile. Your emotions will be intensified. Few without masters fare well for that reason.' His silken voice was void of emotion, there was no indication of how he felt about making me his vassal, just apathetic nonchalance.

'My parents,' I said, eyes wide with worry, 'they won't know where I am. They need to know I'm safe.'

'You have been missing for days now and they

mourn your disappearance deeply.' Nikolaos seemed uneasy talking about human emotions and mourning. He didn't even try and hide the disdain in his voice. 'But you cannot return. We do not mix our bloodlust with their mortality. Unless we are to feed. I will teach you our ways, *ma feu*.'

The cold reality of what being a vampire meant was sinking in: the loss of my family, of my human life, replaced by the savagery of being undead. I would never see the sun again; I would never age. I was destined to walk this earth as a solitary predator until the end of time.

When Nikolaos had said 'feeding' it had ignited something within me. A deep emptiness like a gaping hole of starvation in the pit of my core. The famine burned like a fire in my soul; the prurient hunger was igniting my body with a lustful yearning. For blood.

I took a step towards Nikolaos to look up into the stream of his eyes. Up close, he was even more perfect, even less human; there was not a single indentation on his face, no indication of age or hardship. Just soft beauty only harshened by the sharp angles of his features. I reached my hand out to wrap around Nikolaos in the same way he had held mine earlier, but this was not for comfort. I willed him, as my master, to feel my hunger. I wanted the fire that was burning me up from the inside to wash over him the same way.

Nikolaos let out a deep breath of air that chased away stray strands of my hair in the breeze, the cool air tickling my cheeks. Where his skin was cold and smooth mine felt like lava at the earth's core. I was ignited, alight with sensation. He withdrew from my hold on him, taking a step back.

'I can feel your puissance, *ma feu*.' His eyes cast down to where I had held his hand; small red marks were on his skin from where my fingers had only gently rested. I had scorched him, slightly damaging his ghostly perfection. 'We must feed.'

)CHAPTER 3((

The first time I fed was a slovenly affair.

Whilst a part of me ached deeply with hunger, the thought of sinking my teeth—fangs—into human flesh filled me with nauseating repulsion. Nikolaos had informed me that as a newly turned vampire, my fangs would have yet to fully develop, which meant an already horrifying process was made worse by the bluntness of my teeth. A dull ache made the bones in my mouth feel bruised as my canines elongated; it was a nuisance more than actually painful.

Nikolaos had explained that, when we were feeding on humans, we must 'allure' them. It was like vampire mind control, putting the target at ease, and then erasing their memory so they wouldn't know that they had spent the evening as vampire fodder. I was too 'young' to master the ability, so Nikolaos took it upon himself to find our victim for the evening and allure her.

The woman, who looked only a few years older than me and had been minding her business taking an evening jog, didn't fight against Nikolaos's engagement. One moment she was shamelessly flirting, twiddling the blond curls in her ponytail with a blush turning her already exercise-flushed face a deep crimson; the next it was as though the life had been drained from her face. Within meer seconds of looking into Nikolaos's eyes, I could see she was under his spell. All the light and personalty bled from her eyes, her face falling into blank obedience as she watched him, waiting with bated breath for his command. It was eerie. And it felt wrong; cruel and exploitative. Nikolaos's own face remained impassive, an unreadable canvas as he manipulated the mind of the innocent woman.

Without looking back at me, Nikolaos held up his arm and moved his fingers in a beckoning gesture. I stepped towards the duo, tentatively tracing the line of her neck where I intended to bite. Underneath the skin was a large vein, slowly throbbing at a steady pace, begging me to taste her. Once again, hunger burnt through me and an ardent heat rippled through my body, igniting every cell throughout me. From behind me, I could hear Nikolaos let out a deeper breath. He could feel it too.

There was no way to avoid feeding on humans; it was the vampire means of survival. Nikolaos had made it abundantly clear that blood was our one true life source, and without it, we could not live. With that in mind, I swallowed back my revulsion and rested my lips against the glorious vein beating steadily in her jugular. Even under Nikolaos's compulsion, I sensed the woman's fear as the vein began to speed up. It bounced energetically up and down as her panic grew, the beating of the movement against my mouth filling me with a sick thrill. I could taste her fear. I had never intended to make the woman scared, but I had to feed. There was no time to feel guilt; I knew that she would be okay, that once I had fed Nikolaos would erase any memory of the ordeal and she would have an ordinary evening in blissful ignorance.

No matter how much I tried to justify it, to tell myself it was my nature as a vampire, I couldn't shake the underlining pleasure from feeling her fear wash over me in turbulent waves.

My teeth were sharper than they had been prior to the attack but paled in comparison to Nikolaos's daggers. It made the biting process unrefined, amateur. I had expected the puncture marks to be small and neat, the way a vampire bite was supposed to look, but instead, the wounds were big and untidy. After the initial pressure of my fangs breaking the first layers of skin, my teeth sunk into the softness of her flesh with surprising ease, and all the insecurity of my underdeveloped feeding skills were washed away as the first drop of blood slid into my mouth.

The taste was like sharp metal, both sweet and salty, warm and thick. It tasted so exquisite, so divine; it belonged in me. Whilst the blood continued to flow into my mouth, I could feel each drop course through my body, giving me power and strength. Without thinking, I had wound my fingers around the bones of her neck in a painful grip, violently gulping down as much of the crimson fluid as I could.

I felt Nikolaos wrap his fingers around mine, pulling me off the woman and then away from her with a strength that made me stumble to the ground. The body of the woman collapsed onto the ground in front of me. Nikolaos, standing in a pearly cloak of moonlight, cast his eyes down at me with a severe look which made me shudder. I couldn't tell if he was angry or mocking me.

'You will kill her.' His voice was low, controlled.

The body lay pale and limp at my feet. The wound was deep and brutal, a mound of crimson flesh against the smooth tan of her skin. The sight made me gasp, instinctively raising my hand to my mouth. My fingers were met with warm fluid, and I pulled my hand back to see it covered with the blood which had begun to coagulate on my face. Still sitting on the ground, I began to scuffle back on my hands and feet, distancing myself from the horror I had caused.

Sensing my anguish, Nikolaos stepped in front of the body, hiding the destruction I had caused, and held his hand out to me. I stopped struggling to move away, taking his hand to let him pull me up. My knees were weak beneath me, but I could stand. Although unsteady, I couldn't deny the rush of power that flowed through me after feeding, which seemed to burn brighter the moment Nikolaos's fingers entwined with mine. I felt sick with guilt. Nikolaos released my hand but remained in front of me as a blockade to the carcass. I could feel his energy radiating over me, the hairs on my arms standing on edge.

I took a moment to compose myself before asking: 'Will she be okay?'

'Yes.' It seemed as though he wasn't going to elaborate, pausing for a moment, before thinking better of it, adding, 'If she drinks my blood, she will heal.'

I let out a heavy sigh that I hadn't realised I'd been holding in.

'I have yet to feed.' As he said the words, Nikolaos's hunger washed over me with such strength I felt my stomach tighten. 'We cannot take any more from her.' He gestured to the woman who lay in a heap behind him.

'I didn't mean to hurt her,' I said, ashamed of myself.

'If I exhibit how I feed,' Nikolaos retorted, ignoring my repentance, 'can you control yourself?'

Underneath the stony silk of his voice was a shred of doubt. I thought over the question, mulling over the possibilities. On the one hand, it seemed logical to learn how Nikolaos had perfected the art of feasting on his prey. On the other, however, I felt unsure of how much more blood I could stomach seeing, and whether or not I would be able to trust myself around it. But, if I was to live as a vampire, I had to learn how to control myself and not keep almost killing people.

'I think it'd be best if you show me—teach me—

how to *feed.*'

I hated how the word sounded. It was so primitive, as though we were nothing more than savage hunters. I was beginning to question how far from that truth that was.

'If you are certain, *ma feu,*' he said, with a small smile.

'I am,' I replied quickly, 'but don't give me a chance to change my mind.'

Nikolaos looked down at me with a curious expression. The look made me uneasy. Despite his stoicism, it was easy to get sucked into the seductive intrigue of Nikolaos's graceful charisma and undeniable sex appeal. It was simpler to fall into the pools of his eyes, drown in his gaze, than think of the centuries of sinister acts that those same eyes had witnessed. Nikolaos was cold and consistently derisive, yet I was comfortable around him. The way our energy flowed over one another, the connection of our spirits, was like nothing I had ever experienced before. It was dangerously compelling.

Shrugging off my disconcertion, Nikolaos knelt down beside the woman whose blood had soaked into the grass, shiny and black in the thick cloak of darkness. Nikolaos sunk his teeth into his own wrist so suddenly that I let out a gasp of air. Lowering his wrist to the woman's mouth, the crimson blood flowed in a steady stream between her lips. For several agonising moments, nothing happened, I was sure I had killed the innocent woman, but then I watched as her chest began to rise up and down. She gripped onto Nikolaos's wrist, sucking ferociously on the wound. Slobbery gulps plagued the peaceful night air until Nikolaos decided she had consumed enough and he stood up from her the body. He darted his tongue over the wound on his wrist, and the puncture marks knitted together instantly.

A black sea of pupil drowned the woman's irises, her eyes rolling into the back of her head and body limp with pleasure.

'She's okay,' I breathed, making no attempt to hide the disbelief.

'As I told you she would be.'

'I can't believe it.'

'You doubt me, *ma feu*?'

The raillery in his voice matched the smile that had spread over his face. I had almost killed a woman, and Nikolaos was mocking me.

'Glad I could amuse you,' I replied dryly. Nikolaos's eyes sparkled with unsung laughter.

Nikolaos and I set out to hunt our next victim for the night. He let me ask questions about what it meant to become a vampire, although only answered the ones he deemed worthwhile with tepid disposition. As a new vampire, I could expect to have intensified emotions and senses. Vision and sounds would have overwhelming clarity, but, after a while, I would adjust to the changes.

'Vampires have been known to lose their way to rage, hunger and lust.'

'Are you speaking from experience?'

Nikolaos ignored the question.

'Vampires were not always creatures of mythology; there was a time when creatures resided amicably with humans. Coteries of vampires with human menials were not uncommon.'

'What happened?' I asked quietly, it was the most Nikolaos had spoken to me since I had woken up as a vampire, and I didn't want to deter him from elaborating.

'Megalomaniacs were not methodical in their killings, and humans did not like to be reminded of the power imbalance. No matter our strength at night, when the sun rises, we are vulnerable. We were exterminated in great numbers during daylight. After years of bloodshed and anguish, master vampires deemed it best to kill off their more volatile vassals instead of continuing to be hunted. It took decades of redress for vampires to fall back into the shadows. To become fantasy once more.'

Nikolaos spoke with poetic elegance that ran like silk over my skin. His words were weighted, when he said 'exterminated' and 'bloodshed' I felt the trickle of pain and resentment. Equally, the way he said 'fantasy' rushed through me as though he were seducing me with whispers of what could be. Each syllable held a hidden story that painted pictures in my mind.

Nikolaos and I strolled through Bolton Park, one of the larger parks in Britchelstone, the stone path illuminated by low orange light that flickered from the street lamps. Tall, ancient oak trees grew like looming giants out of the expanse of grass in the centre of the park, the leaves gossiped in the soft breeze, whispering their secrets into the night. We passed a flowerbed of pink roses and purple hollyhocks, the perfume of the flowers so strong it was suffocating. I choked on the sickly sweet pollen, heightened senses dominated by the floral aroma.

Grateful to be reaching the road at the end of the park and away from any flowers, I sensed movement before seeing the man. He was pushing forty and shuffling around the corner of the street, hands tucked into his jacket pocket and shoulders hunched as a shield to the chill breeze. His brown eyes, behind broad, square glasses, looked surprised to see anyone else out at that time of night. One moment Nikolaos was by my side, and the next he was in front of the man, staring intensely into his now vacant eyes.

I watched with intrigue as Nikolaos reared his head back, mouth wide and fangs exposed, before locking his jaw around the man's neck. When Nikolaos removed his lips from the skin, his mouth glistened red in the moonlight. Once again, he bit his wrist and let his dinner sip at the vampiric life source. It was smooth, clean and quick. Not at all like my attempt.

We had just reached the edge of the forest that led to Nikolaos's house when he pulled a metal case from his pocket, opening it to reveal slender white cigarettes lined up neatly in a row. Nikolaos held the metal wallet out to me in silent offering. I pulled one of the cigarettes out from the metallic strip they were held under and twirled it between my fingers. I had never smoked before. I had never had the chance to properly explore or experiment, to make mistakes, to truly experience the good and the bad that life offers. I had been so young when I died. Opportunity had been ripped from me by one man's brutal crime. Or so I had thought. Placing the cigarette between my lips, I realised a deep irony; becoming the undead didn't have to mean my life was over.

The end of the cigarette sparked deep orange, burning red as Nikolaos took a toke. The smoke trailed from his nose and lips in a blanket of grey. Nikolaos sparked the lighter below the cigarette that rested between my lips. The metal exploded with flame, almost singing my skin, and making me jump back with a surprised *yelp*. When Nikolaos removed his finger from the part of the lighter that triggered it to spark, the flames continued to flutter and beat at the darkness. With a shrug, he dropped the metal lighter onto the damp floor and stood on it. The fire faded into a trail of dark smoke that floated from the ground.

'It was like it had a mind of its own,' I joked, smiling at Nikolaos. He looked at me but didn't respond.

Night slipped into dawn and weariness washed over me in uncontrollable waves. Even in a windowless room, I could feel the sunrise, edging closer into late dawn and making me stumble with exhaustion. Nikolaos had offered me his room until we could find a more permanent arrangement. He told me he would try to make it just as much my home as it was his. After all, I was now destined to be by his side for eternity.

A four-poster, king-sized bed dominated the theatrically grand bedroom. Supporting the bed's ornate canopy, were thick pillars of lacquered wood carved with intricate patterns. Cascading down in luscious waves of red and gold, satiny material acted as an opulent curtain, tied back with a shimmering gold cord. As I lay down, my skin encountered the cold, uninviting touch of dark, emerald sheets in fine silk. On either side of the bed, tarnished, aureate candelabras housing four cream candles sat atop heavy wooden chests of drawers.

Struggling to keep my eyes open, exhaustion took over, sinking me deeper into the unforgiving bedsheets. The room was almost pitch black; with only a slight glimpse of light from one of the dying candles, which was fading fast. I was alone for the first time since finding out I was a vampire, and, without Nikolaos's influence to keep me calm, a rapid flood of emotion washed over me. The fear and trauma that came from knowing what that man had done to me, how he had brutally attacked me and left me to die made my stomach painfully tight and twisted. The loss of my family sliced like a knife through my heart. I had considered ignoring Nikolaos's warning about making contact but knew that to protect them, I had to make them believe I was truly gone. Dead. Never to return.

The silk of the pillowcases soaked up my tears as I curled into a foetal position and wept, clutching at my heart whilst the pain throbbed through me.

When I opened my eyes, I could see that the candle beside me had begun to burn ever so slightly brighter. Just enough to cast baleful shadows into the room, the silhouettes of archaic furniture looming ominously.

Morning broke; I fell asleep in silk flooded with my tears.

)CHAPTER 4(

When I awoke the following night, my hair was stuck to my face in messy tangles from falling asleep in a pool of tears. With Nikolaos nowhere to be found, I jumped on the opportunity to explore my new home; without him watching me like a child in a china shop. But first, I wanted to find a bathroom and wash for the first time in almost a week. I felt grim with dirt.

The hallway was dimly lit. Old tapestries, oil paintings and stone carvings were dotted along the walls. I stopped in front of one particular oil portrait, looking up at it with wide eyes. The frame was thick, faded gold with ornate linework decorating the rectangle. Neatly curled black hair teased at the painted man's shoulders, the obsidian a stark contrast against the pure white of his shirt. The collar was tight and trailed up to his chin, an elaborate cravat of white blooming like the petals of a dahlia at his throat. A fitted velvet coat in deep navy was tightly buttoned, and black thread traced the lapel and collar. Nikolaos's ocean green eyes glistened even in painting form, the condescending glint captured perfectly.

The heavy wooden door beside the portrait was one of the few that unlocked; it led to one of the two downstairs bathrooms. The walls were made of small, neat cerulean square tiles. There was a recess in one wall that contained a triangular bathtub with gold faucets. A grey curtain hung above with golden thread woven in a geometric design. A sink in dull grey porcelain sat below a large, circular mirror the same glistening gold as the bath taps. The ceiling light was dim, covered by a shade the colour of storm clouds, a matching round rug extended on the floor below. A flourish of deep blue towels hung over a metal bar by the bath. The bathroom was coordinated and sultry; I appreciated Nikolaos's flair for detail.

I stood in front of the gold mirror almost not recognising the woman staring back at me. Death had turned my already pale complexion sickly, corpse white. The deep red of my hair burned brighter than ever, flaming against the white of my skin and bringing out the trail of orange-brown freckles on my face. The amber of my eyes had darkened to red pools of ember; stark, haunting and too wide in my round face. I traced my tongue along the bottom of my teeth, watching in the mirror as the tip of my tongue pressed against the point of my upper left canine. Pink flesh turned red with blood, the metallic taste sweet in my mouth.

The jeans I had been wearing since I was attacked were torn at the knee and stained with blood. Most of it was mine, some of it was from the woman the night before. I turned on the bath taps and stripped to nothing. There was blood dried and flaking in patches over my body, but all bruises and wounds had miraculously healed. Not even a scar.

I steeped myself in the boiling water. The steam fogged up the mirror and traced through the room in a cloud of grey. The clear water was quick to turn muddy brown from blood and dirt. I scrubbed the dried blood from my skin and used the clean water from the tap to clean the tear-tangled hair from my face. The towels were soft and warm—luxurious; expensive.

With one towel tied around my head to contain the long, wet locks of my hair and the other wrapped tightly around my body, I left the bathroom to look through the rest of Nikolaos's (not so) humble abode.

The outside was a beautiful stone cottage tucked neatly away between the trees. A flaking green door made of solid wood framed a metal knocker in the shape of a wolf's head. The knocker looked ancient. Ivy climbed the stone walls, the windows were wide and had delicate white lace curtains framing the edges. Inside was decorated with simple, old fashioned furniture. Everything was warm and neutral, giving no hint of the owner. The cottage looked unlived in—because it was.

On one side of the front room was a staircase that led up to a smaller guest bedroom, study and bathroom. A vibrant, red piano stood proudly in the spacious upstairs landing.

Through an archway in the front room was a small but welcoming kitchen. It had faded, pale green walls, old wooden counters and an oven that used firewood to cook. After feeding the previous night, Nikolaos had shown me to the master bedroom, which was just off the front room and next to the kitchen. Hidden away in an old oak wardrobe, under a pile of blankets, was a heavy metal trap door that deadlocked from the inside. Beyond this was a set of metal stairs leading downwards to the real home of Nikolaos.

A collection of archaic ornaments had made me begin to suspect just how old Nikolaos might be. The second downstairs bathroom had cold, stone walls with figures carved into the brownstone. There was no sink, toilet or bathtub. Just a large showerhead that hung from the ceiling and a vent in the floor to catch the water. One of the walls was taken up with a mirror, dim lights glowing orange behind it. Ivy hung from wicker baskets around the room, dark green vines flowing through the air like serpents suspended in freefall. In one corner was a waist-height column holding a vase. The pottery was black with figures painted in faded gold across the body. The room reminded me of what I imagined an old Greek bathhouse to be. Bare and atmospheric.

Other than the library, two bathrooms and Nikolaos's bedroom, the downstairs doors were all locked. I could have used my newfound strength to break in, but I knew Nikolaos would be angry. Besides, did I really want to know what he was so intent on hiding? Although he had tried to make it feel like a home, something about it lacked the human comfort I was so used to. The upstairs kitchen was sparse, the fridge not even plugged in, and the rooms felt paradoxically too large and claustrophobic. Logically I knew the reasoning behind having no windows in the basement, but it made me feel trapped and suffocated.

In the end, I decided it was best to go back upstairs and make myself at home in the cottage area. As long as the sun was down, there seemed little harm in that, besides Nikolaos wasn't there to tell me no.

In the living room, two white wooden bookcases reached all the way up to brush the ceiling and were bursting with books. I found several dating back to ancient Greece and Japan, filtering through to slightly more modern tales from the Elizabethan era. I had just started flicking through the covers to find one I could tuck into when Nikolaos was suddenly behind me.

I could sense him, his presence a pressing weight against me, stirring something internal. I could feel his cool breath on the back of my neck, smell the blood on his lips. He had fed. I turned around to look up at him. I could feel Nikolaos's power flowing through me; feeding had made him stronger. I felt so small compared to him, not just because of how he towered above me, but something about his energy radiated strength and nobility. His eyes seemed to flash brighter, the deep green glistening against his marble skin.

Nikolaos's pupils were significant as he looked at me standing there in nothing more than the navy towel. I didn't need a mirror to know my cheeks were a deep red. As my master, Nikolaos couldn't allure me, but I could still feel the power in his gaze pulsating against me, washing through my veins. It was easy to see how just a human could fall under his spell so effortlessly. Feeling the warmth from the blood he had consumed made me ravenous. Nausea washed over me, causing me to stumble. Nikolaos caught me in a flash, wrapping his arm around my waist. My blush deepened, cheeks burning maroon, which made Nikolaos smile.

'You need to feed, *ma feu*,' he said, still holding me.

'Yes,' I replied, voice high with embarrassment. I knew he was right but with our skin touching a surge of strength had washed over me. I looked up into Nikolaos's glistening eyes and, in an action that surprised both of us, lifted my hand to rest upon his smooth cheek. With wide eyes, Nikolaos released his grasp on my waist and the strength dissolved into ravenous hunger once more. With distance now between us, Nikolaos raised a questioning eyebrow. As usual, I couldn't tell if my surprising act of affection had irritated him or if he was jeering at me.

'Why do I feel so connected to you?'

'I am your master.'

'Do you feel it, too?'

'You need to feed, *ma feu*.'

I could have screamed with frustration at his perfected elusiveness but resisted. I didn't want to seem fractious, even if Nikolaos could sense it radiating from me in waves of irritation.

'I need to get dressed first,' I replied. 'Oh, but I don't have any clothes. They were ruined.' We both knew

29

how the clothes had been ruined without me having to say it explicitly. The unspoken words hung heavily in the air.

Nikolaos showed me his collection of shirts hanging neatly in the dark lacquered armoire, which matched the rest of his bedroom furniture. All of the shirts were dark, expensive silk, save a few which were perfectly white and lacy and vintage.

'Can I borrow this one?' I asked, pulling at the sleeve of a forest green shirt. Green had been my favourite colour as a human; that didn't have to change just because I was dead. Nikolaos, lying on the bed with his ankles crossed and hands folded over his torso, gave a curt nod in response. I pulled the shirt from the hanger.

Turning around to face where Nikolaos was resting, I almost jumped out of my skin to find him standing directly in front of me. I took a step back in shock, knocking against the dark wood of the armoire. He looked down at me, standing so close I could feel the chill of his breath against my skin. Nikolaos smelt of cinnamon and soft florals mingled with the remnants of nicotine. It was a warm, comforting scent. But, underneath, was the unmistakable hint of blood from when he had fed. My stomach tightened. I was unable to discern if it was from disgust at the scent of blood, hunger or the lustful warmth that had spread through my body. Maybe all three.

'I-I'll get dressed,' I stuttered, 'and then we can go.'

Nikolaos reached up to unwrap the towel from my head. My hair fell in a waterfall of damp curls down my body, tips brushing the bottom of my back. Slender fingers teased a lock of my hair, stopping at where the towel was fastened around my body to trace along the line of fabric. Goosebumps rippled over my skin, sending a shiver through me from toes to skull. Nikolaos smiled at me, black hair tickling my cheek as he bent his face down closer to mine.

'In answer to your earlier question, *ma feu,*' Nikolaos breathed against my lips. 'Yes. I feel it, too.'

Heart pounding violently in my chest, I closed my eyes, waiting to feel the satin of his lips against mine. When I opened them, he had disappeared.

The silk shirt hung almost to my knees, which was to be expected considering Nikolaos was close to a foot taller than me, and looked ill-fitting. It was tailored to perfectly fit his slender build, not cater to the curves of my body or rounded bosom. The arms were too long, shoulders too wide, and the buttons around the chest struggled to remain done up. On Nikolaos, the shirt would look amazing. I didn't do it justice. However, it was still better than the blood-stained rags I had worn before.

I fiddled and fidgeted with the outfit as much as possible, looking for any excuse to not go upstairs and join Nikolaos. If I toyed with the buttons anymore, they were going to start breaking free of their thread. I couldn't keep stalling. Besides, I needed to feed. Taking a deep breath, I walked from the room to the metal staircase that would lead me to him.

Nikolaos stood staring out the window, pale fingers clasped tightly together behind his back. He stood stiller than stone, admiring the leaves of the forest rustle in the early autumn air. Like a child, I hid behind the bedroom door frame that opened to the front room, peeking at Nikolaos behind the wood. My heart was in my throat. I didn't know if I was embarrassed about what had just happened or confused by the emotional whiplash. What I did know was that I didn't want to step foot in the same room as Nikolaos at that moment.

Eyes gleaming with amusement, he turned to me

as I gripped onto the wooden frame so tight my knuckles mottled. The jig, as they say, was up. With a defeated sigh, I walked into the front room, pretending nothing untoward had happened.

'Your shirt doesn't really fit me.'

Maybe if I didn't mention it he wouldn't either.

'Is that why you were hiding from me?'

I was wrong. Nikolaos contained his laughter, but barely.

'I wasn't hiding,' I lied.

'You are quite petulant.'

'And you are contemptuous.'

I waited for Nikolaos to be angry, but instead, a chortle flowed from between his lips. It caressed my skin like fur on flesh; plush and sensual. The laughter lit up his face, making him look almost human. At first, I was annoyed that Nikolaos continued to mock me, but, watching the mirth breathe life into his stony composure, made a flutter start deep in my stomach, spreading warmth up my body into my heart.

I had fed without almost killing my meal. It by no means compared to the efficiency of Nikolaos but I wasn't fastidious. I was just glad to have no unnecessary blood on my hands. At least for the time being. We walked back in silence that seemed heavier than usual. Nikolaos's blank face was so controlled, so void of emotion, I could have been looking at a mannequin. The intensity of the quiet was overbearing, but something in my gut told me it would be a mistake to press Nikolaos to speak. The journey home felt painfully long.

'Scarlet.' I had not heard Nikolaos sound so sombre.

'Yes?' Perturbation made my voice high. 'What is it?'

I sat on the sofa opposite Nikolaos, staring with wide, panicked eyes. My nails dug into the flesh of my palm, accidentally drawing blood. Nikolaos looked back with a perfectly blank stare. He was putting excessive effort into being unreadable, which only made me more anxious.

'Whilst you fed, I saw a newspaper article stating there has been another murder.' He studied my face intently, waiting to see how I would respond. 'She was also beaten and stabbed. Much like you were when I found you.'

My mouth gaped open, shock turning my body stiff. I wanted to say something but words eluded me. Nikolaos's accent thickened as he continued to speak, anger turning his voice dark.

'So it wasn't a random attack,' I whispered, the words so soft that if it wasn't for his vampire hearing the words would be lost in the air, 'he's preying on women.'

'I believe so.'

'Why?'

'I do not know.' For a moment the control slipped, a terrifying flash of emotion ripping through Nikolaos's face that made me shudder. He was not someone of whom to make an enemy. 'There was no corpse to be identified after your disappearance, for obvious reasons. Now this young woman has been found they are investigating it as potentially his second victim.'

They weren't wrong. Technically.

Nikolaos continued, 'Do you remember anything of him?'

The question brought back unwanted memories that I had pushed into the back of my mind. The smell of his acrid sweat as he attacked me. The way his breathing had filled the air, burnt against my neck, hungry for my blood. The endless agony that had stretched on with no relief in sight. I had been subjugated and forsaken; left to rot on the side of the road.

Nikolaos reached out across the space between us, placing his hand atop my own but no touch could cool the rage that burnt beneath my skin.

'We will find him, *ma chérie*. You will get retribution.'

The coldness in his voice sent a chill down my spine, the absolute conviction that we would find the man who hurt me. Who killed me. I couldn't bring myself to repent my murderous lust for his blood. I would get revenge. For me, for my family and now for the newest victim.

)CHAPTER 5(

A week had passed since the news of a second killing. Nikolaos had been busying himself with trying to
implement more permanent sleeping arrangements,
leaving me to feed by myself. I had begun to feel more
confident in my abilities; going alone wasn't an issue
for me. I did, however, suspect that Nikolaos was trying to avoid me; arranging my room was the perfect
excuse to not interact. If I thought that Nikolaos had
been apathetic before, I had been sorely mistaken.
The past seven nights, he had barely uttered two sen-
tences to me. When we did speak, I had the distinct
impression my presence was just acutely irritating for
him. So I started staying out until the breaking of
dawn to avoid Nikolaos, the way he was avoiding me.

One night, Nikolaos had thrown a shiny, black
credit card at me with the name NIKOLAOS MIDAS
printed on it. I had been instructed to get myself some
new clothes; there were only so many ill-fitting shirts
of his I could keep borrowing. Using the computer in
the study upstairs, I did as he requested. I mused at
the facade of opening a bank account when you were
a vampire who was older than the British currency
itself. Did I want to know what Nikolaos did to get
money? Probably not.

The clothing arrived several days later, in perfect
time for the grand revealing of my new bedroom. Nikolaos had shuffled upstairs, long hair tied tightly at
the back of his head. The chiselled angles of his face
were emphasised without the cape of black hair to
soften them. There was dust and paint clinging to the
red silk of his shirt; his sleeves were rolled up to show

a trail of dark hair up slender forearms.

'Follow me.'

'Oh, are we talking again?' I said, in my head. Aloud, I muttered, 'Okay.'

Nikolaos probably wouldn't appreciate the sarcasm.

I was grateful to have not been begrudging towards Nikolaos, as I opened one of the previously locked doors. The room that he had created for me was nothing less than interior art. It was large with deep green walls, slashes of gold intercepted the block colour like bolts of lightning striking the night sky. There was a fireplace of white marble built into one wall, with a golden mirror rested above it. The flames were a gentle flicker; protecting us from the shadowy silhouettes that danced in the crepuscular corners of the room.

Opposite the fireplace was a large, plush, deep blue sofa. Cushions of dusky red, blue and green lined up against the backrest, with a gold rectangular cushion resting grandly in the centre. A round glass coffee table with marble legs homed an ornate vase of red roses. In the corner was a black, glass bookshelf filled with novels which spanned a variety of genres.

An archway through the wall was lined with dark chiffon fabric and fairy lights, which hung around the entrance in an ethereal veil. A single step led up through the arch to where the bed sat. A queen-sized bed with four black posters towered up supporting a canopy of dark fabric. The bedsheets were soft and silky, made of the same blue as the sofa and equally covered in matching cushions. Beside it was a white vanity unit and fluffy stool. The top of the unit was bare except a lone red rose in a slender glass vase. A door in the wall opened to reveal a walk-in closet, with the end wall being entirely consumed by a mirror; he had already filled it with the clothes I had purchased.

It was all so strikingly beautiful.

Nikolaos leant against the bed frame, watching me take in the sight of my new room. I wanted to thank him, but there were no words to convey the appreciation I felt. I was eternally grateful. And confused. After days of Nikolaos being icier than a winter night towards me, he had made such a grand gesture. The emotional whiplash was back. I felt my smile wilt.

'You do not like it?' Nikolaos asked, voice smooth, and face unreadable.

'No, I—' I slumped down onto the stool by the bed, the fluffy material tickling my bare thighs. 'I do, it's beautiful.'

'Then, what is wrong?'

'I don't want you to think I'm ungrateful.'

'I do not.' Nikolaos gave a slight shrug. 'I can feel your gratitude.'

I frowned up at him before burying my face in my hands.

'It's embarrassing,' I whispered, into my palms.

I felt his fingers over mine. Nikolaos pulled my hands down from my face. He knelt in front of me, looking up with a watchful gaze, a smile tugging at the corners of his lips.

'You are a beacon of confusion, *ma chérie.* I can feel it throughout my body, your internal conflict.'

'Why can't I sense your emotions the same way?'

'I have put up my guard.'

'Why?'

'I know the turbulence of being newly turned. I do not want to influence the process. You have been emanating bewilderment. If you knew how I felt, it may make it harder.'

'That's why you've been avoiding me?'

'*Oui.*'

'I thought,' I said breathily, cheeks burning scarlet

with a blush, 'it was because you were annoyed with me. That's why you didn't kiss me.'

'I apologise, *ma feu.*' Nikolaos sighed. 'I thought shutting you out would protect you.'

'I already feel so alone.' Before I had time to stop them, tears flowed down my cheeks in a steady stream of melancholy. 'And I don't know if you regret turning me. Sometimes it's like all I do is annoy you, and then you build me this'—I motioned my hand around the room in emphasis—'I'm so lost.' My cheeks were wet with tears, an ache pounding through my temples. Sunrise was not for hours but I was already exhausted.

'You do not annoy me,' he soothed.

'But you *do* regret turning me,' I insisted.

There was a pregnant pause.

'No.' Nikolaos sighed again. 'I have lived in solitude for almost four centuries. It has been an adjustment for me, as well as you.'

I had been selfish to think only of how my transition affected me. Nikolaos was right; becoming a vampire didn't just change my life but also his.

'I resent vulnerability.' Nikolaos placed his hand on the wetness of my cheek. He gazed up at me with a look close to sadness, black hair falling over his face, like a mantle of onyx concealing his features. 'But being close to you, I am.'

'Because you're my maker?'

'I do not know, *ma chérie.*' He paused. 'That would be a convenient explanation.'

'But not the truth?'

'But not the truth,' Nikolaos whispered the words against my mouth.

Satin lips pressed against mine. It started tentatively, a teasing promise. As his breath sped up, so did the movement of his mouth, lips pushing heavily against my own. Nikolaos stood up on his knees, so his face was level to mine, fingers wrapping through my hair, pulling me closer to him. I could feel the lust rolling off him, caressing parts of me never before touched by a man. My newly sharpened teeth clipped him clumsily. A drop of blood spread between our mouths, rubbing into skin as he continued to kiss me. Nikolaos's blood tasted different to that of any human. It was sweeter, richer, like the difference between cheap and vintage wine. The first nip had been accidental; the second was not. I bit into Nikolaos's lip hard enough to make him bleed again, the sweet fluid trickled into my mouth. I locked my own fingers through his hair, beginning to sip at the small wound I had created.

'Enough, Scarlet.'

Nikolaos drew away from me; breath still heavy, but eyes dark with anger and lust.

'I should feed,' I replied, voice low and equally as breathless.

Nikolaos and I hunted together that night for the first time in one week. I had adjusted to venturing the night alone, but I couldn't deny having Nikolaos by my side was a welcome comfort. Nikolaos informed me that when we had kissed, I had been hot to the touch. It wasn't the first time he had noticed my abnormally high temperature. Initially, he had thought it was just the remnants of life still hanging on, but I had been dead too long for him to find a logical explanation. I thought back to the several occasions I had experienced a burning sensation within me, something I had passed off as a normal byproduct of becoming a vampire. I had been wrong.

Another thought couldn't escape my mind. Nikolaos's words from earlier: *'I resent vulnerability, but being close to you, I am.'.* He seemed to think that, by putting the barrier of reticence between us, I would be protected. So far, he'd been mistaken. Would Nikolaos suddenly stop being the epitome of apathy? I doubted it. There had been too many years spent in solitude, too much loss, to change overnight, but it had been a step towards him opening up to me. I could live with Nikolaos being aloof as long as there was honesty between us.

I decided not to tell Nikolaos that he had been my first kiss. The dynamic in our relationship was too imbalanced; he thought my callowness was a liability. In his eyes I was puerile; it was true that Nikolaos had lived a thousand lifetimes, experienced more than I could ever imagine, but it had made him callous and jaded. I didn't think that being trusting and affable made me weak. Nonetheless, I wasn't ready to rock the boat anymore by reinforcing my lack of experience. Not yet, at least. I had to tread carefully or risk him shutting down on me once again. I was no relationship expert, but this seemed a particularly complicated one. It would have been much easier if a less haughty vampire had found me that fateful night. Easier, but far less interesting.

The hypocrisy of wanting Nikolaos to open up whilst I concealed my inexperience wasn't lost on me. But what can I say; no one's perfect—even if they live a thousand lifetimes.

Walking back from feeding in our usual silence, I caught a glimpse of something that stopped me dead in my tracks. Illuminated by a garishly lit newsagent was the front page of The Talus, Britchelstone's local newspaper. The sensational font and bold type sent a shiver down my spine. Another woman had been murdered. There was a picture of her beside the sinister text, standing beside a group of friends beaming up at the photographer. Youthful innocence glistened in her big, brown eyes. Soft auburn hair framed a round face, with fleshy cheeks flushed from laughing. She was eighteen—had been eighteen.

Rage rippled through my body like a stone thrown in water; deep, burning rage and something else: guilt. We had known my murderer was on the loose, we had known he would strike again, and yet my mind had been preoccupied. Preoccupied with my developing feelings for Nikolaos, the lovely new bedroom, the butterflies in my belly, the bloodlust. These had been my focus and now another woman was lying battered and bruised in the city morgue. How could preoccupation by such superficial matters justify more bloodshed? It couldn't. It was unforgivable.

The image of her face blurred and bled to nothing. I saw red.

Nikolaos had warned me that emotions increased tenfold as a vampire, but nothing could have prepared me for the frenzied furore that tore through my body. Through my soul. It started in my stomach, a pounding heat matching the beat of my heart. The warmth proliferated with each pulsation and spread through me. Fire pumped in my veins, igniting every cell in my body, scorching me with poignant rue. I was being cooked alive from the inside.

'Scarlet.' His accent was thick with solicitude; concern amalgamated with fear, rolling off him in metaphysical waves. Nikolaos may have brought down the wall between us, but his feelings could not penetrate me right now.

'You need to calm down,' he commanded.

With our spiritual connection not reaching me, Nikolaos reached out to touch me before thinking better of it. He withdrew his hand, taking a step back to put distance between us.

In the glass window, the reflection of a woman stared at me. Her eyes were wild; wide with a soulless cavern of black where colour had once been. Cardinal hair defied gravity, whipping around her body. Under her skin was glowing like the embers of a fire, the heat in her veins burning too bright to be concealed by flesh. She looked maniacal. Deranged. Powerful. She was me.

I collapsed in a heap to the ground, the shock of my reflection knocking some momentum out of the power.

'It burns.' I gasped for air, voice strained and distant. Nikolaos knelt beside me with discouraging caution, reaffirming that I was a monster. Scary to even an Ancient. He looked afraid to touch me, hand hovering above my skin but not bringing himself to touch me. His dark eyebrows were drawn together in a troubled frown.

'I can feel it, too.' His voice was deeper, I could hear the tension as he held his breath trying to contain the shared pain.

The burning began to subside. I was a blubbering mess lying curled on the ground, hiccuping and crying between gasps of air. I didn't care how pathetic I looked, as long as the burning stopped. Sensing the heat dispersing with my tears, Nikolaos finally placed a cooling hand on my shaking shoulder. His skin was colder than the concrete I lay upon.

Nikolaos helped me to stand. I leant against the shop window, back turned on the newsagents and The talus, my legs weak beneath me.

'I do not recall a newly turned vampire with your degree of power.'

'Why?'

His face contorted at the question.

'What do you mean, *ma chérie*?'

'Why am I different? Why did you even turn me?' I was choking on tears. 'I'm so tired, Nikolaos. Why couldn't you just let me die?'

I spat the words at Nikolaos, each syllable an angry venom directed at him. I resented the man who stood before me, who had doomed me to eternity as this monster instead of letting me rest in peace. Nikolaos stood as straight and still as I'd ever seen him. He tried to hide his annoyance behind an utterly blank face, but the walls had already been lowered and I could feel the anger biting at me.

'I do not know,' he replied bitterly. 'Maybe it was a mistake.'

'Niko—'

'I am fond of you because you are my vassal. Do not be mistaken in thinking I will not humble you.' Nikolaos cast his eyes down at me with a look of heartaching disdain. 'You need me, Scarlet. I do not need you.'

One second he was in front of me, and the next he had vanished into the night, only the bitter residue of his words left hanging in the air. There was an ache in my chest; a river of melancholy streamed from my eyes.

It had been my first taste of Nikolaos's temper. I hoped it would be the last.

Before, the lines had been blurred between master and partner, but tonight he had made my place abundantly clear. A burden primarily, a companion potentially. It had been dangerously easy to overlook a daunting truth: I was destined to spend eternity alone, only mingling with other monsters of the night. My friends and family could not be a part of my life. They were left to think that one day I had just vanished off the face of the earth, and subsequently grieve me. I had to grieve them in my own way. I thought it would be harder for me, knowing that at any moment, I could just turn up on their doorstep, and feel their embrace again. At least they thought I was dead; they had closure. More than I ever would. It occurred to me that I would also get that closure one day. I was sure to outlive them. At some point in the future, they would be just a distant memory, a fog of happier days in my mind. I wondered if Nikolaos could remember his parents, his pets, his lovers from when he had been alive. It seemed I had spent my vampiric existence swimming blissfully in the waters of my developing feelings for Nikolaos, but, now he had withdrawn, I realised I was, in fact, drowning.

There was a part of me that wondered if Nikolaos had bitten off more than he could chew by turning me. He was a ruthless immortal, older than imaginable. He could manipulate the minds of humans and had strength the world deemed impossible. He was not the sort of person to be caught off guard. *I resent vulnerability*; he had taunted me. I had crashed into Nikolaos's life and forced him to become the one thing he hated: weak. His feelings for me, if there were any, would be considered a weakness. He would resent that...he would resent me. My power, our connection and his sentiment for me had brought back a sense of his humanity in an uncomfortable way.

There was something much more pressing than Nikolaos's fragile sense of identity to focus on. My murderer was still out there, roaming the streets at night to prey on innocent women. Neither Nikolaos nor I knew what was special about me, but surely there was a way to harness my abilities and put them to use to hunt the man. With Nikolaos's age and my power, we had to find a way to bring him to justice. What was one measly human against us? Since becoming a vampire, pain and violence came a lot more naturally to me. Vampires are predators; humans are of less significance. It was the food chain, the circle of life—and death. I was trying to hold onto my empathy for humankind, but bloodlust was the dictatorial instinct.

I arrived home to find Nikolaos hadn't returned. Whilst there was an undeniable sadness to find he had left me, I wasn't going to hold my breath for an apology. His words had been a cruel, stinging reminder of my perceived inferiority. Nikolaos was hubristic; a fragile ego is more easily bruised than a fragile heart. One thing Nikolaos did not lack was ego. No, I was not going to get an apology.

I loved the bedroom Nikolaos had built for me, but the dungeonesque warren felt particularly cold and lonely that night. I traced my finger along the set of books lined neatly in the bookcase, trying to find one to distract my mind. I pulled a first edition of Alice's Adventures in Wonderland out from the eye-level shelf. The books beside it released from the tension, collapsing sideways. Wearing a silken pyjama set, I curled up on the sofa and attempted to read. I reread the first paragraph over and over before giving up in frustration, casting the book to the floor with a grunt.

I lay with my back on the sofa, arms crossed over my face, with thoughts racing uncontrollably through my mind. Tonight I had experienced a distressing loss of control. I felt uncertain and vulnerable from the ordeal. There was nothing that could match the fear I had felt the night of my murder. However, the trepidation that came from not knowing what I would do, or what I was capable, of came close. My own anxieties aside, I couldn't allow any more women to fall victim the way I had. I couldn't allow someone else to meet their final moments in the same terror and darkness.

I had been given a second chance at life. I vowed to myself that I would use my revival to seek justice for the women he had hurt, to put an end to the terror that had taken over the city. I owed it to the women. I owed it to myself.

)CHAPTER 6(

Nikolaos didn't return for two nights.

I spent the time feeding alone and exploring some of my new abilities as a vampire. With extreme strength, speed and agility, even the darkest moon shadows in the night were clear as daylight. I jumped to the tops of trees, balancing on the highest branches, leaping from one to another with a shameful lack of grace. I chased the bugs through the grass. Even the smallest ones were magnified and none even half as fast.

I was clumsy; controlling such speed was harder than expected. It didn't come as naturally as I had hoped it would. After two decades of living at one pace, it was like my brain still hadn't been able to come to terms with newfound agility. I had to relearn to control my movements. There had been several occasions when I had accidentally plummeted into the trunk of a tree, bending the solid wood back and sending twigs and leaves spiralling into my hair as panicked birds flew into the night.

As my thrill for hunting humans had increased, so had my appreciation for their fragility. I loved watching how they responded to my fangs in their flesh, to the way my blood healed them after I had fed. The pure, orgasmic bliss as their heads flopped and eyes rolled back. Transported to a joyful realm no drug could match. I relied on humans to survive, without them I would be truly dead, but the way they yearned for my life source as though they needed me was a powerful thrill.

On the third night, there was a knock on my

bedroom door. I was halfway through doing up the buttons of a black shirt when I sensed Nikolaos's dominant presence radiating from behind the wood. The sweet smell of cinnamon and florals floated through the air towards me as I rushed to open the door. It was such a warm, rich smell. Out of place on someone so cold. Something shifted in me the moment I felt him, as though there had been something missing in my soul when he had departed. But now he had returned, I was complete once more. Together, we were powerful. I was stronger, and the possibilities of what we could achieve seemed endless. Alone, the prospect of eternity seemed overwhelmingly daunting.

I resisted the urge to fling the door open and instead took in a deep breath to compose myself before pulling the handle. Nikolaos leant casually against the corridor wall. His tall, agile frame was perfect in its nonchalance. The black of his hair and white of his face looked beautifully stark against the dark green silk of the shirt he wore. It made the ocean green of his eyes seem darker and more mysterious than usual. Between his fingers was a cigarette from which he took a dramatic drag whilst looking deeply into my eyes. I broke eye contact first, squirming under the intensity of his look. My vision cast down to the unbuttoned shirt on my body, torso exposed with only the fragile lace of a bralette to contain my chest. A blush crept up my face.

'Where have you been?' I mumbled, with embarrassing indignance. I dared to look up, finding Nikolaos still watching me. A smile tugged at the corner of his mouth. Stepping closer, Nikolaos reached for the buttons on my shirt. My breath was caught in my throat as his fingers brushed the line of skin on my sternum. His long fingers worked graciously doing up the buttons. I kept my focus on the trail of smoke that danced from the cigarette still between his lips, the grey whisper vanishing into nothingness. I knew the intensity of his look would be burning with promises of seduction, that his lips would be upturned into a mocking smile that begged me to touch them with my own. The smoke was the safest thing to get distracted by.

'You have not fed yet, *ma feu.*'

I could smell the sweet copper of blood on his breath.

'You have.' My voice was a whisper as he took a step closer towards me. A hand, which had finished buttoning my shirt, curled under my chin, turning me to look up at him.

'You avoid my gaze.' The words tickled my face. 'Why?'

'Because I knew you'd be giving me that look and I thought we were fighting.'

A velvet laugh rippled from between plump lips.

'*Ah, je vois.*' Nikolaos's face bent down closer to mine. 'I did not realise you thought of us as in a fight, *ma chérie.*' The air from his lips teased against mine, close enough to kiss. 'If this is the case, I cannot kiss you.'

Nikolaos took a step back with taunt and humour playing over his face.

'No, I guess you shouldn't.' Brave words considering the breathiness of my voice. But I wasn't in the mood to be teased. 'Will you tell me where you were?'

My lack of response to his games seemed to displease him, the humorous light dying to an expression of perfect stillness.

'You must feed, and then there is someone I wish for you to meet.'

I hurried my feeding that night instead of basking in the intimacy of the ritual. When I returned, Nikolaos sat on one of the cream sofas beside an unfamiliar woman. Her presence was distinct, a gentle caress of power that radiated through the air. She wasn't a vampire but certainly not human, either. The power pressed against me lightly as though getting a taste for who I was.

The woman seemed no older than thirty and was of average build and height, almost tall but not quite. She wore a cowl-necked jumper in navy blue tucked into black jeans. Chestnut-brown hair hung in waves to frame a tanned face, pale brown eyes watched me with a friendly, inquisitive look. She was pretty in an understated way, but I knew instantly that she was not as ordinary as her appearance would have you believe.

'Scarlet.' Nikolaos's voice made me turn to where he sat beside her. 'This is Adalia. An old friend of mine.'

Adalia stood from the sofa to come towards me, hand outstretched and a big, genuine smile spread over her face. Around her neck was a silver pendant in the form of a star amidst a circle. Standing in front of me, I realised she was taller than I had originally judged, closer to Nikolaos's six-foot than my measly five-three.

'Oh, it's just lovely to meet you, Scarlet,' Adalia said jollily. Her voice was mellow, and breathy in an almost sultry way. 'Niko has been telling me so much about you.'

Nikolaos raised an eyebrow at the remark but didn't respond. As our skin touched, a spark shocked up my arm as though I'd grasped a live wire. Surprised, I went to withdraw my hand from her grasp, but Adalia placed her free hand on top of mine. Adalia looked down at me, still smiling, but with a look of concentration turning her face more serious.

'I see,' Adalia muttered under her breath, tutting to

herself as she pulled free of me. 'How long ago did you turn her, Niko?'

Nikolaos was suddenly beside us, his finger curling over his lips as he thought.

'Merely a fortnight.'

'That's interesting,' Adalia said with intrigue, voice a whisper as she mused over what Nikolaos had said. The two of them watched me curiously.

'You're not human, are you, Adalia?' It seemed like a rude question, but, under the circumstances, also appropriate. Adalia flashed a coy smile, batting those big, brown eyes shyly. The three of us stood so close I could feel her power brushing against me, entwining with the invisible connection between Nikolaos and me.

'Vampires can't usually tell,' she replied, still smiling, 'but no, I'm not human. I'm a witch.'

I stared at Adalia blankly, mouth slightly ajar, before finally pulling myself together enough to say, 'Oh.'

'Niko stopped by, for the first time in too long, might I add,' Adalia chastised, casting a vitriolic glare in Nikolaos's direction, 'and explained to me your situation.'

'Situation?'

'It seems you have power beyond your vampire age in a way I haven't seen before, and neither has Niko.'

'I have some apprehension regarding your abilities, *ma chérie*.'

'You do?'

I hadn't realised before then that Nikolaos was just as unsure as I was about why I had special skills. I thought back to the other night when we had argued. Maybe that fight hadn't just been out of anger, maybe Nikolaos was genuinely worried and it has come out sideways. Nikolaos was precisely the sort of person who would project his fear as anger.

'*Oui, ma chérie*. Power only grows with age. At this present time, it is too volatile for you to control it.'

'He's right, if you don't learn to manage it now there is potential for it to consume you,' Adalia added, continuing, 'I specialise in reading peoples' auras, getting a taste for their power and essence. I'm hoping if we spend some time together, I can understand what triggered you to have these abilities and help you find ways to control them.'

Unsure of what to say, I stood there in silence between the two of them.

'Scarlet—' Adalia went to continue before I interrupted her, 'Lettie, please.' I smiled. 'It's what people used to call me before.'

'Lettie,' Adalia replied, mirroring my smile, 'if I'm honest with you I thought that Niko was exaggerating when he came to me. But I can feel there is something different about you, and you being able to feel my aura, and I yours, proves it.'

'Can you not feel it, too?' I asked, turning to Nikolaos.

'*Non.*'

'But it's such a conspicuous sensation.'

He shrugged gracefully. 'For you, perhaps.'

Nikolaos and Adalia were quite fascinated by me, but dawn was only hours away and so agreed it would be best to rest for what remained of the night. They both seemed to think that my potential abilities were quite unique. However, I had nothing to compare it to so it had just become another peculiar part of my new normal. After the events of the night when Nikolaos had left, the daunting reality of my lack of control had weighed down on me. I had been utterly engulfed by power, but, however scary it had felt, there had also been intense titillation from feeling so invulnerable; mighty in a way I could never have dreamt. Learning to control the power without it governing me could not only make my life (well, death) easier but also had potential uses to help us track down my murderer. I wasn't sure what those uses were yet, but I'd made a promise to myself to figure it out.

Adalia chatted to me merrily, offering appreciated insight into some of Nikolaos's well-concealed life. Despite looking fresh-faced and young, Adalia was pushing ninety and had known Nikolaos since she was a child. Adalia had been born in 1932 in Bordeaux, where her late grandmother, Brigitte, had raised her. Brigitte had helped nurture Adalia's natural talents as a witch, practising their craft together. During the war, they had used their brews and potions as remedy to the injured.

Nikolaos had befriended Brigitte towards the end of the war and consequently struck up a relationship with Adalia. He had been captivated by a young, pureblood witch with wisdom and charisma well beyond her years.

'Nikolaos had been around for too long by that point,' Adalia detailed, after explaining how Brigitte had died when she was seventeen, 'people were noticing his ways were less than human. With Grandmother gone and my only friend leaving, I thought it best to travel with Niko to London. I've owned my little occult shop there ever since. England feels much more like my home than France. Niko is really the only family I have left now. Not that I see much of him anymore.'

Nikolaos took a long drag from the cigarette resting between his fingers, ignoring the last comment.

Adalia stood up from the sofa, disappearing through the kitchen door frame.

'She's nice,' I said to Nikolaos, who had perched on the arm of the sofa I was sat on.

'*Oui.*'

'I can't imagine you having friends, though.'

Nikolaos raised a dark eyebrow at that but ignored the comment. It hadn't been meant as an insult, more just an observation.

'And you never told me you go by Niko not Nikolaos,' I continued.

'You did not tell me you go by Lettie in lieu of Scarlet.'

He had a point.

'No, I guess there's still a lot you don't know about me. And even less I know about you.'

If Nikolaos was going to respond, he lost the chance as Adalia chose that moment to walk back into the living room holding three crystal tumblers and a decanter. A golden brown liquid sloshed around the glass as she walked, lapping at the rim of the decanter with each sway of her hips. The glasses clinked together as she placed them upon the coffee table.

I sniffed at the honey liquid in the glass that had been handed to me. There was an undertone of woody hues, mostly concealed by a harsh, burning smell that stung my nostrils as I breathed in. Nikolaos had the glass pressed between his lips, watching me as I screwed my face up at the smell. He chuckled at me and shot the drink down in one. Show off.

The upstairs bedroom was perfect for Adalia to stay in for the time being. By the time the night sky was fading from black to deep violet, the previously full decanter had been all but emptied. If I had thought to be a vampire meant immunity to the effects of alcohol, I had been wrong. When Adalia giddily declared it was time for her to sleep, I was swaying in a haze of intoxication.

'Would you please show me to my room, Lettie?' Adalia asked with genuine, almost contagious, warmth.

I obliged and, once we were alone in the bedroom, Adalia turned to me, whispering in a low tone, 'I knew there was something special about you the moment Niko appeared on my doorstep. He's never had any interest in turning anyone, especially not after —' Adalia stopped herself mid-sentence. 'Well, anyway, he's clearly drawn to you. It's nice to see my friend happy.'

I ignored her almost slip of the tongue for the time being, making sure to file it away for a later date. I had already found out a lot more than I expected about Nikolaos tonight and wasn't going to push for more information.

'You can tell when he's happy?' I asked, giggling and hiccuping at the same time to form a very unfeminine sound. 'I can't read him at all.'

Adalia's expression softened in response.

'There's no denying Niko is hard to understand, but I like to think I know him well enough. I just don't let on that he isn't as ominous as he thinks he is. It would damage his pride.'

I couldn't help but laugh at that.

I took Adalia laying back on the bed as my queue to leave the room. Nikolaos awaited me, eyes watching me as I trailed down the stairs. He still sat on the arm of the sofa, what was left of the whiskey pooling like honey at the bottom of the glass in his hand. The look he gave was overflowing with lust. With the barriers between us down, as well as alcohol weakening inhibitions, I could feel the carnal desire rolling off his body. It caressed my flesh, making goosebumps ripple over my skin, seeming to stroke something much more internal. Somewhere no hands could touch. I found myself in front of him without realising I'd taken the final steps into the living room. Nikolaos leant to place the glass down on the table beside him. When he turned back to face me his palm was outstretched, an invitation to bridge what was left of the gap between us

'You are watching me intently, *ma chérie*.' His voice was soft as silk against naked skin, as rich as full-grain leather. The salacious glint in his eyes promised more than just sex—something deeply, passionately sinister. But, underneath the lust, I could feel the embers of something tender beginning to burn through him.

I could feel incipient heat begin to trickle through me; the lapping of power that I had, but couldn't yet control, spreading through my veins. The sensation felt like it should be painful. But it wasn't. It felt good. An internal rush that ran through me deeper than anything physical could go. Along with the alcohol, it made me bold.

Without answering, I laced my fingers through his. His skin was cold, but that didn't make it any less inviting. Even sitting down, Nikolaos was taller than me although not by much. I withdrew my hands from his, stretching my arms up to wrap around his neck. The top of his chest was level to my mouth. I nestled my head into the solidity of his chest, lips brushing against the silk of his shirt. I felt Nikolaos tense in my arms, an unexpected reaction to my affections. The alcohol-fueled confidence dispersed. Embarrassed, I withdrew from his body.

'I'm sorry,' I mumbled, words slightly slurred.

'There is no need to apologise, *ma chérie*.' He inhaled a deep, shaky breath. 'It is not that I do not desire you, but you have been drinking.'

'So have you,' I protested.

'I have over one thousand lifetimes on you.'

The heat that had been rushing through me began to ease, and I heard Nikolaos release a breath of air as if he felt me soothing, too.

'You do not have enough control to risk being intimate.' He said 'intimate' with surprising tenderness. After the prurience of what had just happened the words felt contrastingly delicate.

'The sun is almost up anyway,' I said, casting a glance out the window. Nikolaos followed my gaze to where the solid black was blooming into colour.

'We should retire downstairs,' he replied.

I leant my back against the wood of my bedroom door, breath still shallow from before. Lethargy had taken over my body but not my mind; I could still feel the pressure of his lust pressing through me. Nikolaos stood rigidly in front of me. It felt like the end to an awkward first date, so many things we could say but didn't know how to put into words—the temptation to close the distance like static energy prickling between us.

'Will you stay with me tonight?' The words spilt from my lips before I had time to think of what they implied.

Nikolaos hesitated.

'If you wish.'

Nikolaos kicked off his shoes, placing them neatly by the side of the bed. He collapsed gracefully on top of the sheets. The bedding matched his shirt and eyes. Laying there, he was a picture of perfection shrouded in green and black. He held out a hand to me. I took it and he pulled me to his chest. I lay with my burning cheeks against the cold fabric of his shirt, the buttons pressing against my temples. The steady rhythm of his heart pounded in my ear, loud and consistent. Not what you would expect from the dead. As sleep tugged me into darkness, I felt fingers tease through my hair.

I awoke to find an arm draped over my torso. Nikolaos lay on his side beside me, one arm curled under his head and the other on top of me. Black hair hung like a curtain to conceal his face. His chest rose and fell occasionally whilst he peacefully slumbered, soft snoring a hum in the silence. Nikolaos's head nuzzled into my shoulder, the exhalation from his mouth tickling my arm. For the first time, Nikolaos looked strikingly human. Nautical eyes fluttered open lazily, still half shut in a state of sleepiness. Before personality had time to flood his face, he looked up at me with slumberous tranquillity. It was my first time waking up next to a man. I could see myself getting used to it.

'Good morning,' I whispered, words lost into the thick of his hair.

'*Bonsoir, ma feu.*'

Nikolaos raised his head from where it lay in the fold of my shoulder, propping himself up on one elbow with his head resting on his hand. The other arm stayed around my waist, fingers teased along my side, pushing my top up to stroke bare skin. I shivered at the sensation.

'*Tu es très belle, ma chérie.*'

'I don't understand French.'

Nikolaos's hand was on top of the material again, finger tracing a line up my side, along my neck, under my jaw. He turned my face to his, lips brushing lightly against mine. It was tentative, gentle like the petal of a rose. After the eroticism of last night, the touch was too light. Almost painfully gentle.

'I know you do not,' he whispered against my mouth.

The conversation from a few nights ago was still whirring around my head, an annoying buzzing that wouldn't stop. The cruelty of Nikolaos's words still hurt me, but since he had returned with Adalia there had been a noticeable shift in his regards towards me. Ever so slightly less cold. Bringing it up again seemed counterproductive. It wasn't a fight I was willing to rehash. Some arguments you just have to let go, even if you don't want to. I realised Nikolaos had been saying something to me that I had been too lost in thought to notice. I shook my head, trying to shake the distraction from my mind physically.

'Pardon? Sorry, I didn't hear you.'

'I enquired about your friends.'

'Oh. What about them?'

'Did you have many?'

'I had a small circle of friends. There weren't many of us, but we were fairly close.'

It wasn't entirely a lie. Being short, freckled and a red-head meant I had been bullied for most of my teenage years. When I'd first entered secondary school, I'd been a chunky child which made me an easier target for everyone. When puberty hit, and I came back after summer with more curve and bust, I'd become an easier target for the girls. Boys changed how they spoke to me, but it wasn't much of an improvement. Their lewdness didn't remedy the previous years of bullying. They couldn't understand why being overtly sexualised wasn't that much better than being picked on. Respect was something I didn't get much of growing up. Teenage boys don't seem to realise that undressing a girl with your eyes and civility are not the same thing. By the time college started, most people had fully formed friendship groups, but I was going in alone. It wasn't until my last year of college I really became buddies with a small group of people. It was true we were close, but I was wary around them despite that. Years of being picked on do take their toll.

'Oh? Were you closer to any in particular?'

'Are you fishing?' I joked, grinning at Nikolaos. 'Coyness isn't your strong point.'

He mused over the question before responding with an elegant shrug of his shoulder, a move difficult to look graceful when propped up on one arm but he still managed.

'Fishing.' The word made him smile. 'A peculiar phrase. Yes, *ma chérie*, I am *fishing*.'

'No, I uh...' I sighed. 'I hadn't really had the time to experience much. I guess you could say I was a late bloomer. I hadn't even kissed anyone before. You were my first.'

The last words were muttered almost silently. The proverbial cat was officially out of the bag. Nikolaos kept his face blank and unreadable, but I could feel the sense of pleasure he got from knowing he had been my first kiss, and would, if last night was an indicator to go by, probably be my first of other venereal activities. Once again, there was an evident imbalance of power between us that left me indignant.

Adalia sat on the sofa with her head lost in an ancient book that I recognised from the living room bookshelf. The oak waves of her hair were tied back loosely with strands escaping in soft cascades around her face. Adalia's cheeks were more flushed than last night, sweat making her forehead lightly dewy. I could see the vein throbbing in her neck, beating faster than it should have been. The way it jumped up and down was enthralling; I could smell the blood underneath her skin sweeter than any humans'. Without thinking, my tongue ran over my lips. The duo noticed my reaction, prompting Nikolaos to place his hand on the small of my back. A cool, soothing gesture that didn't quite eliminate the temptation. I had the grace to look embarrassed.

'A warning, *ma feu*,' Nikolaos said from behind me, 'preternatural creatures are much more *séduisant* to us.'

'You two should both go feed.' Adalia didn't sound too discouraged after my undisciplined display. I would have been. 'I can wait here but that's a priority.'

Although I had adjusted to hunting alone it was nice to have Nikolaos alongside me.

'You are learning well,' Nikolaos acknowledged after our dinner. If I were being honest, I would admit that I had been trying to show off just how well I was mastering my skills without him. I liked knowing that I had been able to strengthen my abilities through independent perseverance. *You need me, Scarlet. I do not need you.* Was that true? Maybe in some ways. No matter how much I wanted to protest it, the fact was, Nikolaos was my master and me his vassal. But I refused to let the power imbalance make me inferior. I would not be complacent. I wanted to prove him wrong. It could have been deemed stubborn, but strength born of pettiness is strength nonetheless.

'What are your thoughts on this arrangement with Adalia?' Nikolaos asked, a cigarette bobbing between his lips as he spoke. I took a moment to muse over the question.

'She seems nice, we get on well.' Nikolaos and I slowed to a human pace. 'And if there is any chance it could help us catch the killer, I would do anything.'

'Adalia is an adroit practitioner of magick. She is a witch unlike any other I have met,' he said reverently. 'It may mean she can help us find the man who hurt you. Being close to her will also strengthen the control of your bloodlust.'

'May I ask you something?'

Nikolaos glanced down at me, the end of his cigarette a startling orange in the dark night.

'You may.'

'Did you and Adalia ever have a more, erm, intimate relationship?'

Humour bloomed throughout Nikolaos's eyes.

'Envious, *ma chérie*?'

'No,' I lied.

Envious seemed too strong a word but there was a twinge of jealousy. I was going to be spending a lot of time with someone who had potentially won over the affections of Nikolaos, which was no easy task in itself. I couldn't deny that my feelings for Nikolaos were blossoming more each day. In spite of all his faults, and there were many, I was slowly getting to see a deeper side of Nikolaos. And every time I did, my chest would flood with a warmth of increasing intensity. I thought I knew what those feelings meant, but I still was none the wiser to his true intentions with me. It was a difficult situation to be in. Adalia had been nothing but kind and mature with me, yet I had made it feel like a competition between us. It was irrational. I lost some respect for myself for thinking that way.

'Do not forget I sense your emotions.'

'I don't think I'm envious. I guess I just feel like you two have a bond I can't compete with.'

Nikolaos raised an eyebrow at that. We stopped walking, Nikolaos moved so he stood in front of me. The autumn wind suddenly picked up, sending a strand of black hair whipping across his cheeks.

'There is no competition. Ths is a notion you have fabricated,' Nikolaos said with his usual cold composure. He was more inscrutable than usual, which I had begun to understand was Nikolaos's way of showing emotion. The more he felt, the less he'd show. He was nothing if not complex. 'Adalia is an old friend. I have known her for decades and am fond of her but there is nothing else. The life of a vampire is a lonely one. To fall in love would be a mistake, one I shall not make.' The word *again* hung heavily in the air like a body from a noose. Deadweight, and too painful to explore further, but intriguing nonetheless.

His words stung like verbal thorns piercing my heart, making tears creep from my eyes, to flow down my cheeks. I'd been lying to myself by saying I only thought I knew what my feelings were. I didn't think. I knew definitively. And surely he knew too. As my master, Nikolaos had to know what I felt for him. There was no denying that the connection we had as master and vassal intensified my fondness for him, but it wasn't that alone. I hadn't been sure if Nikolaos felt the same. There were times when his guard slipped that I would feel something close to what I thought was affection from him. I had been misguided. Knowing my feelings were unrequited hurt. Badly.

'I have upset you,' Nikolaos said, sounding close to surprised. 'That was not my intention.'

'I know.'

I believed he hadn't meant to.

'What part of what I said has hurt you?'

'Isn't it obvious?'

'If that were the case I would not ask.'

I looked deep into his eyes, leaving the trail of tears to dry on my cheeks. Looking up at him, I began to question if Nikolaos wasn't just stoic but genuinely socially inept. How much empathy does someone have to lose for them not to understand primary human emotion? It was one of those times where I got an unwelcome reminder that Nikolaos wasn't just dangerous seduction personified, but a creature who seemed to have no regard for anything that didn't impact him directly—although, admittedly, Adalia did seem to be an exception to the rule. Maybe I'd been fooling myself to think I could be, too. It was too hard working out how much of his personality was theatrics and how much was genuine. Every time I thought I was beginning to figure him out he'd throw me a curveball.

'You say you can sense my emotions.'

Nikolaos waited for me to elaborate, when I didn't he responded with a simple: 'Yes.'

'Then'—I took a deep, steadying breath—'you must know how I feel about you.'

I refused to meet his eyes, as my cheeks darkened to red. We stood in silence for a painfully long moment.

'Scarlet'—Nikolaos curled a lock of my hair through his fingers—'I am cautious of my feelings for you. I do not know what part of me being your master affects this.' He paused. 'But I do know that I have not felt this way before.' The lock of hair tumbled from between his fingers dramatically. 'I must be circumspect. For your sake.'

The last remark was so spineless I felt the trickles of anger brewing. I expected many things from Nikolaos but not such a cop-out reply.

'Maybe that's not your decision to make.' I met his gaze again; this time there was no embarrassment or urge to hide. 'Why do you get to call all the shots?'

Nikolaos sighed. It was a tired sigh, sad even.

'I did not know it would be this complicated when I turned you.'

'I'm not sure it's me that's the complicated one.'

'No.' He smiled, but it was morose. 'Perhaps not.'

'I had my life ripped away from me, Nikolaos. I won't lose my independence, too.' My voice was strong, resolute. 'Maybe that makes me a negligent vassal. But if I was given a second chance at life—or whatever it is that keeps vampires functioning—then I won't spend that time giving up my control to you. Or anyone else, for that matter.'

'I do not know what you want of me, *ma feu*.' He sounded exasperated, hands fanning out in front of him as he spoke.

'A partnership.' Nikolaos went to turn his head away from me but I placed my hand on his cheek and forced him to look at me. 'No more games.'

'I do not *play games*,' he said, in a state of pique.

The warmth in his tone hinted at anger. Nikolaos met my eyes with frosty indignation. I didn't remove my hand from the smoothness of his face. In a way, I believed him. To Nikolaos, his haughty disposition and emotional back and forth were less of a game and more just who he was. I was sure he used it to his advantage and got some pleasure from being artfully cunning, but it wasn't just an act.

'Okay,' I replied gently, letting my temper subside. 'Openness, then.'

Baby steps weren't always a bad thing. Nikolaos gave a nod subtle enough I wasn't sure I'd really seen it, like he was agreeing to something, but it wasn't aimed at me.

'I must confess an ulterior motive of Adalia's presence,' Nikolaos said, the anger draining from his face, leaving it familiarly beautiful in it's apathy.

'Oh?'

'I do believe she can help with your exceptional abilities, but I have also asked her for assistance of a different nature. I wish for her to observe our relationship.'

'Why?' I didn't hide the surprise from my voice.

'I thought she might offer additional insight into our dynamic, to see how much of it is related to you being my vassal.'

'And what did she say?' My tone was cautious; neutral. Unsure of what to expect.

'Very little so far, although I am sure she will give her opinion readily,' Nikolaos replied. 'However, after tonight, I can see you are much more stubborn than a vassal your age should be. I am beginning to doubt it holds the significance that would be expected.'

We continued to walk back in silence. There was nothing else I could say that would further the conversation so why waste words? We had agreed to be more open with one another. Nikolaos knew my feelings for him. I had gotten what was as close to a confession as I would get from someone like him. I was content, happy even. Nikolaos had been my first kiss, first love and certainly my first vampire. It was an unsavoury thought that I would never be his first anything. Quite possibly not even his hundredth...or thousandth.

)CHAPTER 7(

Adalia sat waiting for us in placid silence. I could feel the energy of her magick floating around her like a breath of spring air. It wasn't hostile in the slightest, but it was definitely there. How Nikolaos couldn't feel it was beyond me. Adalia seemed content in her own silence as though she could have sat there and waited forever without getting bored—a woman happy in her own company. That didn't stop a smile from blossoming over her face when she saw Nikolaos and me enter the front door. A woman also happy in the company of others.

'You two took your time,' Adalia said, but it wasn't accusatory. Nikolaos ignored her, taking a seat on the sofa opposite where she sat. He lay both his arms elongated against the head of the sofa, legs stretched out, ankles crossed over each other, making himself comfortable.

'Sorry we kept you waiting.' I sat beside Nikolaos, offering Adalia a coy smile. She smiled back, sincere benevolence lighting up her face.

'Now,' Adalia began, 'I've worked with lots of people before, humans and non-humans alike, but none with quite the same brief as this. And, truthfully, with very few vampires. We usually start off with a consultation, but I already know why you asked for my help so I think we should start with trying to get an idea of your powers and the triggers. Does this sound okay for you?'

I nodded. 'Sounds good.'

'I'd also like to witness you having an episode, as Nikolaos calls them.'

Her eyes flicked to Nikolaos in a way that made me nervous. 'Episodes' had always happened circumstantially, usually when angry or upset. I didn't know how they wanted to make one occur, but from the look Adalia gave Nikolaos I didn't think I would like it.

'How?' I asked suspiciously.

'I want to engage an emotional response from you and see how you react.'

It sounded ominous and, if previous experiences were anything to go by, not entirely pleasant.

Nikolaos watched Adalia and I talking intently without making any contributions to the conversation. Adalia reached into her red, leather bag to produce a leather-bound notebook which matched the handbag. There was a loop on the inside to hold a black fountain pen with a gold clip and rim on the lid. Half of the pages in the book were wrinkled and unruly from use. She opened up to a clean page using a red silk string as a page marker and began to write my name at the top of the cream paper. Adalia had impeccable writing; the perfect cursive you would expect from your great-grandmother. Beautiful, but almost illegible.

'I obviously haven't seen your abilities put to use but Nikolaos has told me it's an intense experience, powerful even. What's been the main cause of the episodes so far?'

I thought back to the main event that had triggered Nikolaos seeking advice from Adalia: the night when I'd heard the news of a third murder; the way I had been taken over by rage, guilt, and pain.

I explained that to Adalia, adding, 'I suppose it seems to be in response to more negative things.'

Nikolaos raised his eyebrows at that, a devious smile spreading across his lips.

'That is not entirely true, *ma chérie*. Although factual that most occurrences have been in response to more malevolent situations, I believe you have reacted to *other* events in much the same way.' Somehow he made the word 'other' sound obscene, so much so that a blush crept up my face. I glared at Nikolaos, who smiled back at me, enjoying watching me squirm. Though I had to admit he was right, I had also felt my power stirring when Nikolaos and I had shared brief moments of intimacy.

Adalia didn't rise to the bait, which I was thankful for. Instead, she jotted something down in silence. Female solidarity, maybe. Or she just knew him well enough to ignore the teasing.

'As a human, how would you say your temperament was?'

I glanced at Nikolaos before responding, he had fallen back into his comfortable position with an almost vacant expression, looking just a little bit too pleased with himself for making me embarrassed.

'I've always been quite a relaxed person, I suppose.'

'So you were never reactionary? Quick to get angry?'

I shook my head. 'I've never been one to argue.'

Even when I had been bullied at school I'd never fought. I stood my ground but in complacent silence. That was another thing that seemed to be different about me as a vampire: I was much more confident. It might have something to do with knowing I was invulnerable. Or it might have been having to mature a lot faster after the trauma of being murdered. I either had to grow from it or lose control; the latter wasn't an option.

'New vampires have heightened emotions,' Nikolaos said, sounding almost bored, 'this is not an uncommon phenomenon Scarlet is experiencing.'

'True, I don't know of many newly turned who have steady temper and self-control. But I also haven't heard of many whose abilities come into play so soon.' Adalia turned to me, explaining, 'Usually powers develop with age. Most vampires don't have any at all.'

'Something to contemplate,' Nikolaos added, lighting the cigarette that rested between his lips, 'is how Scarlet was turned. Customarily, we choose humans who can serve us better as the undead. Or those whom we would consider eternal companions. I found Scarlet seconds away from death and was drawn to save her.'

'Drawn to save her? Were you nearby at the time?'

Nikolaos didn't move, instead, he turned deathly still. Slightly frowning eyes watched Adalia with a curious expression.

'No,' he said slowly, 'it is not an area I frequent.'

The two of them shared a knowing look, one that I didn't understand the meaning behind.

'Seems to be a lot of coincidences.'

'Indeed,' he agreed.

'Is there any chance you have a non-human bloodline?' Adalia asked, looking at me as though she'd forgotten I was still there. Nikolaos also watched me. He no longer looked bored. In fact, he looked quite eager.

'No,' I replied cautiously. 'I have a very normal family.'

'Do you have siblings?' Adalia questioned.

'I have an older sister and younger brother.'

'You have a unique look, Lettie. Do any of your family resemble it?'

Nikolaos absently traced a lock of my crimson hair to emphasise Adalia's question.

Luke, my younger brother, had the soft white hair that some children get before it darkens to golden-brown with age. Both my sister and mother had light brown hair, light enough you could almost call it blonde, but not quite. Anna, my sister, had always dyed her hair and tried to pass it off as natural, but even with her fair features, you could tell it wasn't. My father was the darkest of all of us; his hair was a rich brown turning grey around the edges. His complexion was permanently a soft brown, olive they call it, which would darken to light gold in the summer. All of them had dark brown eyes, except for my sister's whose were the same glassy green as my late grandmother. The women on both sides of my family were naturally tall and slender whilst I was short and shapely. The difference in our appearances had never been something I'd paid attention to until that moment when I realised how striking a contrast we were.

'No.' I shook my head slowly. 'I guess not. Not at all, really.'

Nikolaos and Adalia exchanged another look. It was getting unnerving.

'There might be more to this than we thought, Niko.'

'*Oui.*' Nikolaos blew out a dramatic cloud of smoke. 'I believe so.'

'The good thing about having someone who can walk around in daylight, I suppose, is that I can work on finding out more information whilst the sun's up without raising suspicion.'

'I don't understand what this means,' I finally said. They both turned to me looking surprised as if I'd just appeared from thin air. The way they were talking about me like I wasn't there, you'd be forgiven for thinking that was true.

'My apologies, *ma chérie*. I believe you may not have been as human as we originally suspected.'

'I think,' Adalia added, 'that, at this present time, working on your control should be a priority. These are all suspicions for now.'

I gazed at them both with a combination of amazement and frustration. They expected me to overlook that I had, potentially, never been human as if it were a matter to be so nonchalant about. Nikolaos picked up on what I was thinking, saying, 'There has been a lot of change in your life recently, *ma feu*. Until we have confirmation on these suspicions, it is in your best interest to focus your attention on stabilising your powers. Even with immortality, there is a certain fragility that comes with becoming the undead. I do not wish to overwhelm you.'

'Okay,' I concurred. 'I guess I understand.'

My reluctance was not well concealed.

With the sun soon due to rise, Nikolaos and I sought refuge in the light-tight downstairs. Nikolaos glided by my side as we walked to my bedroom door. We walked in silence. Too many thoughts raced through my mind to know how to put into words.

Nikolaos leant against the marble of the fireplace. He watched me as I collapsed onto the sofa with a heavy sigh, flicking the butt of a barely smoked cigarette into the weak trickle of fire that danced off the coals. I bent my knees, calves touching the back of my thighs so that Nikolaos could have a seat on the sofa with me. The tip of my toes brushed against the soft material of his black trousers.

Still in silence, I pushed myself up from the sofa, resting my knees beside Nikolaos. Such a tentative, innocent touch, yet my breath suddenly caught in my throat. Positioned like this, we were the same height. When he turned his head to me, our lips were almost touching. He was still as unreadable as ever but under the deep green of his eyes, I saw the swirling of something as he watched me. Desire. And more than that. Something more intimate but less sexual.

I bridged what was left of the gap between us, my lips tentatively brushing against his as if I weren't sure it was the right thing to do. Nikolaos began to kiss me back. I wrapped one hand around the back of his head, fingers grasping at the velvet of his hair. Turning at an awkward angle, Nikolaos placed both hands on either side of my hips and effortlessly lifted me up onto his lap. I let out a surprised yelp but didn't stop kissing him. I straddled him between my legs, my head raised only slightly higher than his own even sitting on his lap.

Something tightened in my lower body; I ground my hips against Nikolaos's lap in response to the breath-catching sensation. My fingers wove through his hair with more urgency. I took a fistful of the black silk pulling his head sharply to one side. A gasp breathed from his mouth into mine: surprised; pleasured. My tongue traced the edges of his lips, along the side of his cheek, stopping at the earlobe I had exposed. I locked my mouth around the tender swell of his lobe; sucking, kissing, nibbling.

The pale expanse of his neck was next. I kissed the skin so slowly, tongue darting out from my mouth to lick where I kissed him. Until finally, I worked my way back up to his lips. We kissed again and there was nothing tender about it anymore. We kissed with a hunger that had nothing to do with blood and everything to do with flesh. Bare, naked flesh pressed against one another.

Nikolaos's hands ran up my back under the top I wore with haste, the coolness of his fingers sending a shiver through my body as he traced my spine. After his hands had moved, I could still feel the tingling sensation of his touch against my skin like a teasing reminder of where he had caressed me. His hands locked more firmly on the lower part of my hip, pulling me closer into his body. We were pressed so tightly against one another I thought we would merge into one. As my breathing deepened, I felt something else press against me, and an involuntary gasp escaped my lips. I balled my hands tighter through his hair in a forceful grip. Nikolaos breathed out against my mouth.

Still kissing him, I moved my hands from his hair to the lower part of my top. As I began to lift the material up over my torso his hands caught mine. We sat utterly still, staring at one another in near silence with nothing but the sound of lustful, ragged breathing.

'What's wrong?' I asked, eyes flicking to where his hands still encircled my wrists.

'We should be cautious,' he said, face guileless, almost uncertain.

I felt the warmth stir in me, sending a salacious fire that burnt behind my eyes as I looked at him. Nikolaos saw it, eyes widening just a touch, but his hands unwound from where they held me in place.

Leaning against his lips, I whispered, 'Fuck caution.'

He didn't take much convincing. The uncertainty had bled to prurience. The desire burnt through me. Through us. I felt it wash over our bodies in scalding waves. It felt amazing. So right in all the wrong ways; wrong in all the right ways. Rich, decadent power that was born of love and desire spread over us like a guilty pleasure.

As our bodies merged to one, so did the power. I felt it flow through me the way Nikolaos's body flowed through me. More than just physical, our auras entwined in a blaze of strength and bliss. Each thrust of his hips into me sent a spasm through my body, every crush of lips against mine brought a sound I'd never heard myself make. Our bodies found a rhythm working like dancers in perfect, rejoicing unison. Aura, power, energy, magick flowed through us with such an intensity it almost hurt, but the line between pain and pleasure had been blurred. I wanted that fine, uncertain line of eroticism and pain to be tested further. I cried out, begging for more. Nails shredded down the perfect smoothness of his back, and I felt the trickle of his blood run along my fingers so warm and tantalising.

His power thrust into me, reaching places his body couldn't. It was such an overwhelming pressure I screamed out. A different pressure was building. Primitive, physical and nothing to do with metaphysics. It was a heat in my body starting low and spreading further through me, building up like a hot, scalding wave getting ready to burst through me. I ground my hips harder into Nikolaos, slowing our rhythm, so each thrust was slow and deep and caressing. Either he took the hint of what was to come, or he was close too. His ferocity picked up; each rotation of his hip teased at my G-spot and then, as he moved, stroked my clitoris. The pressure built up more, more, more. I was crying out for more. And he gave it. Gave me everything I cried out for. Until that pleasure burst through my body and my fingers ripped down his arms, back, buttocks. As the pleasure flowed through my body, his speed picked up until he was a blur working inside me, hard enough to keep stimulating the orgasm but tender enough not to hurt me.

Nikolaos cried out too, his own body spasming between my legs. He pushed himself up enough to uncurl my hands from the marks in his skin, pinning them above my head as his body continued to flinch in mine. Finally, he collapsed on top of my body. Neither of us could catch our breath. We lay in a heap of ragged breathing; damp, sweaty flesh, and the trail of red from the wounds I had made on his skin flowing freely around us.

The sun rose with me entwined in silk sheets and

Nikolaos's bare body. My fingers stroked the line of hair that trailed down from his belly button. It looked like it should have been coarse yet felt plush against my fingers. My other arm curled under my head, Nikolaos's outstretched hand entwined his fingers with my own. His free hand made slow circles over my skin, a slender finger tracing the crease in my waist and belly from where my knee was at an angle over his lower body. His touch had always made my hairs stand on edge, but knowing those same fingers had explored a whole new part of me made the touch seem obscene, titillating.

The fading fire burnt brighter. A trick of the golden glow made Nikolaos's skin look darker, he no longer was deathly pale but instead a rich brown. The colour breathed life into him, making the strong features of his face seem more at place. Despite Nikolaos's accent and penchant for the Gallic language, I could see then he was not of French origin. He was something much older, more exotic. From a distant land across far seas. From a time so very long ago when myth and legends were still fact. I still wasn't certain of Nikolaos's true age or origin but at that moment I knew it was older than I could have imagined. My energy flowed over him, basking him further in the light. I could feel his age in his skin. All that he had seen, all that he had done. There was such deep pain there. So much loss, sorrow. I gasped as his dismay flowed through me; tears burned behind my eyes. Nikolaos tensed in my arms. I could feel the hairs on his body standing upright to attention. Just as quickly as it had appeared, Nikolaos felt the intrusion of my power and shut himself down, pushing me out.

'I'm sorry...' My words trailed off. I was unsure if I was apologising for entering his mind without consent or for the turmoil he felt. I hadn't achieved an exact reading of Nikolaos's true age, but he was old. Old enough to have seen more than any one man should, old enough to cause so much anguish. I didn't know if Nikolaos knew what had just happened; I wasn't even sure I knew what had happened. I doubted Nikolaos wanted me to know just how much he suffered from his existence, so I didn't say anything. We continued to lie in silence.

'In all my years,' Nikolaos finally whispered against my hair, 'I have not met anyone as bewitching as you, *ma chérie*.'

I felt the break of dawn. If sleep hadn't washed over me, I would have blushed.

)CHAPTER 8(

Nikolaos wore a silk shirt in blood-red tucked into leather trousers. On most people, it would have looked histrionic. On him, it was mesmerising. It made him look less human, more like what he was: vampire. Seductive, powerful and oh so deadly. I had pulled on a black silk shirt with long sleeves buttoned tightly at the cuff. Clinging to my curves was a faux-leather skirt riding down to my knees in the same deep crimson as Nikolaos's shirt. The red of his shirt matched the flames of my hair, the black of mine only a touch lighter than his true onyx locks. It hadn't been intentional coordination of our wardrobes, but as we stood beside each other, we looked like the perfect match. After the intimacy of last night, something had opened up between us more than just master and vassal. I could feel my energy flowing over Nikolaos in ways it hadn't before. It floated around him, curious and enthralled.

Adalia returned not long after dusk. She came through the door less settled than usual, her calm demeanour replaced by hyper anticipation.

'Niko,' Adalia said, almost slamming the door behind her, 'can we talk for a moment?'

Nikolaos didn't respond. In silent agreement, he sauntered past her to the bedroom that led downstairs. As Adalia trailed behind, I could practically see the excitement buzzing around her skin.

I watched them disappear down to the cave-like warren where they knew I wouldn't be able to hear the discussion. The connection between the floor of the cottage and the ceiling of the downstairs was lined with thick silver making it soundproof to vampires. I'd been curious to why Nikolaos felt the need to soundproof the area before realising I probably didn't want to know. I wasn't happy that Nikolaos and Adalia were keeping something from me, but my energy told me it was safe, that we could trust Nikolaos. It was fascinated by him, clinging to him like the residue of sweet perfume. It also knew to be cautious; trust only extends so far without being earned, and I was under no illusion of his potential for danger. For now, I listened to that magickal gut instinct. We could trust Nikolaos. As my master and, as of last night, my lover.

The two emerged from the downstairs close to an hour later. I sat in anxious anticipation for them to return, wide-eyes watching cautiously as they walked into the living room. Adalia was smiling secretively. Nikolaos looked at me with a cross between fascination and amusement. He floated over to where I sat with rhythmic grace. When he was close enough for the leather of his trousers to brush my knees, he held his hand out to me. I took Nikolaos outstretched hand, letting him pull me to my feet. The flow of energy ran up his arms, down his shoulders, into his chest. It was a gentle caress, a comfort to know he wasn't alone anymore. Nikolaos's pupils grew large but other than that he didn't respond. Letting my hand fall from his, Nikolaos raised his fingers to the lock of hair that curled down the front of my body. He let it slip through his fingers tentatively like it may dissolve if he were too rough. We stared at each other for a moment in silence, me craning my neck up to look into his eyes, and Nikolaos tracing his fingers lightly over the back of my wrist where it rested at my side.

'Are you quite certain?' Nikolaos asked, turning to Adalia. She nodded. '*Fascinant.*'

'What is?'

My question knocked him out of the trance. He looked at me normally for the first time since they had joined me upstairs.

'I think,' Adalia interjected, 'I have found out what makes you special. It would explain your abilities and why Niko was called to save you the night of your attack.'

'We believe you are a nymph, *ma feu.*'

'A what?'

'A nymph,' Nikolaos reaffirmed, as if saying it a second time would make it any clearer. I rolled my eyes over to Adalia, who shook her head lightly at Nikolaos.

'They are elemental deities,' she said.

I laughed out loud. Such an abrupt sound it made even Nikolaos tense.

'You're joking!'

'No, Lettie,' Adalia said. 'We're quite serious. I visited your family today.'

Instantly the humour drained from me.

'My family.' It came out as a strained whisper. 'How are they?'

My heart ached. With the knowledge that I could never see them again, I had done all I could to try and shut out the memories of my family. But Adalia had visited them, and by doing so, it had reopened a wound that was beginning to scar. One moment I was standing and the next my knees buckled below me. Nikolaos caught me by the arm, lowering me back onto the sofa.

'Adalia found an abundance of history regarding your lineage. It may be a lot for you to process.'

'Maybe you should both feed first?'

'No,' I said, too quickly. 'Please, I need to know how they are. Please, Adalia, I can't wait.'

The two of them exchanged a cautious look, weighing up how to respond to my plaintive pleas.

'It is a risk.'

'Please, Nikolaos. I can control myself.'

Maybe it was my piteous beseeching or the raw need as I turned doleful eyes up to him, but Nikolaos gave a slow nod.

'If you are certain.' He looked at me like he didn't really believe me. 'I will find us a human whilst you talk.'

'Thank you.'

'I shall not be long. Do not lose control.' The warning in his tone wasn't lost on me.

Nikolaos had fled into the night to bring us a meal leaving Adalia and me to talk alone. We had taken up position beside each other on one of the sofas. I was hungry, so hungry. Sharing power with Nikolaos last night, and then the emotional turmoil of Adalia seeing my family had drained me of energy. Vampires don't eat food, or sleep to rest as humans do, so all that was left to regenerate that depleted energy was human plasma. I could see the vein throbbing in Adalia's throat, begging me to taste her. With my own heart in my throat, I swallowed down the hunger. I had to control it. Fueled by my need to know how my family were, I let my love for them overpower the disquietude.

Luke, my little brother, was so young. I doubt he understood what my disappearance meant. He must have thought I had abandoned him one night, never to return home. In some ways, him thinking I had disappeared and left him was better than the truth. I'd rather he hated me for relinquishing the family I loved so dearly than knew that I had been torn from their embraces against my will. That thought alone was enough to slice through my heart. I hoped the adults of the house were staying strong for him. Anna, my sister, was two years older than me. We had never got along well; she had a sharp tongue fueled by unjust resentment for my existence. I still would have done anything to see her face again.

I was grateful my siblings could be there when I couldn't, especially young Luke. He would give my parents something else to focus on. They still had a family unit. They weren't alone. I hoped Anna could put aside her selfishness for once to support our parents. I wasn't overly optimistic, but it was a nice thought.

'I know you'll have a lot of questions about your family,' Adalia said gently, 'so I'll answer those first and then tell you what I learnt when Niko comes back.'

Adalia was faithful to her word, letting me ask frantic questions with seemingly endless patience.

'Why did they let you in?'

'I'm a trained grief counsellor.'

My eyebrows furrowed into a wordless question; Adalia responded with a sheepish smile.

'I may have used some magick to coax them to seek my help. Pro bono, of course.'

She continued, 'Your mother was very gracious, she's a hospitable woman. A kind aura.'

Adalia explained to me that she had sat with my mother in the bedroom I had grown up in. My childhood home. She had shown Adalia the collection of metal and china figures I had collected since before I could walk, all lined up on the same wooden shelves my dad had built for me when I was four. Now they were nothing more than senseless memories sitting there collecting dust. It made me sadder than I would like to admit knowing they would have to be thrown away. Sentimentality is a peculiar thing.

My mother had wept on Adalia's shoulders for over two hours. They'd had no closure. Whilst what had happened to the other victims had been truly dreadful, their families at least had a body they could lay to rest. My family didn't get the same closure, and they felt it was impossible to give up entirely because of that. They were still holding on to pitiful shreds of hope that I may return; that I wasn't really gone.

Heartbreak isn't just felt emotionally, there is something very physical about it. I bent over, clutching my chest, feeling my heart slice in two for my family. The pain was like a dull ache that tore through my body. Slices and bruises blossomed over something that wasn't physical but hurt all the same. I pulled my knees to my chest, burying my head into the skirt and just sat there, letting the pain consume me. At that moment, I knew how people could die from a broken heart, and how, in many ways, death seemed like the ultimate relief so such oppressive sorrow. Adalia placed a hand on my shoulder but said nothing. We both knew there was nothing she could have said to make it stop. I stayed huddled into myself mewling, endless tears turning my face from damp to wet. A dolorous whimper escaped my mouth before I could stop it—the sound of a wounded puppy; weak and pathetic.

The door slammed open, making Adalia jump. I peered over my knees to glance at Nikolaos kneeling in front of me. Moonlight illuminated the lone tear that slid down his face, a woeful diamond down white marble.

'I can feel such immense pain. Your pain, *ma chérie*.'

Whilst my parents grieved I had been bathing in the blood of humans and floating on the high of the power that rode Nikolaos and I. I had become a monster; they were left to deal with the desolation of my death. For the first time, I truly understood why I could not see my family anymore. They still may still have clung on to the last shreds of hope, but their daughter was dead. I may be there in presence, but the Scarlet they knew was gone. Their hope was misplaced. No matter what, I could never return.

If Nikolaos had left me to die, then they would have at least been able to get the closure they so desperately needed. The closure they deserved. I wasn't ungrateful to be given a second chance at life, but it suddenly felt so selfish. Heat began to swirl up inside me. It started in my heart, following the sorrowful ache that ran through my body. It felt my pain, knew my grief, and it wanted to help me. With each tear trailing down my cheek, each crack in my heart, the fire trickled through me. It soothed me in a way I'd never experienced. Pure, complete comfort that ran through my mind, body and soul. I didn't so much see as feel the aura encompass me. We worked together to build a barrier between the world and us. In the impenetrable ball of comfort, we would be safe.

'Scarlet?' Adalia's voice was distant, unreal, like she wasn't really there. I didn't look up.

'She is experiencing it,' Nikolaos whispered, voice low and breathy. 'I can feel it inside of me. But it is not like before.'

His words drew some of my focus back to the room. It had never occurred to me that Nikolaos would get the drip back of my powers in such a way. I knew my energy surrounded him, clung to him like a lover, but I hadn't known he felt it inside the way I did. I felt Adalia's hand touch the skin of my back in an attempt to soothe me. As her skin made contact, she pulled back with a yelp, rubbing her left hand over the right as if wounded.

'Careful,' Nikolaos warned, albeit too late. 'Scarlet burns to the touch during these moments.'

I felt like a mirage was between the real world and

me. I was safe behind the shield of warmth; everything else was too distant to harm me.

'Are you well, *ma chérie*?'

I ignored him. Adalia must have said something to Nikolaos to make him nod at her, but the words were too muffled for me to hear. Nikolaos disappeared from where he knelt in front of me. I stared at the space he had occupied as if I could still see him. Or maybe I hadn't really seen him sitting there in the first place.

Nikolaos returned with something that chased away some of the haziness. A woman was clasping to his arm, staring up at him like he was the white knight who would rescue her from the monsters. Little did she know he'd dragged her willingly into the monster's lair.

A black dress so short it left little to the imagination clung to a body made for the catwalk. Long, long legs were elongated by high, black heels that sunk into the carpeted floor like voguish knives. Hair dyed so blonde it was closer to white, framed a fake-tanned face. Large blue eyes drank in every ounce of Nikolaos without paying any heed to Adalia or I. Full, plump lips painted neon fuchsia were pursed in a pout meant to look seductive but instead made her look surly, resembling a child who had been told no and wasn't happy about it.

Under the sickly scent of expensive perfume was a smell I recognised. Sweet, metallic and entrancing. Bloodlust kicked in instantly, swatting away any remains of the fiery fog. My power was hungry, too; we didn't need safety anymore—we needed blood. Under the white of her hair, I watched the vein throbbing up and down, calling me to taste her like a siren calls to a forsaken sailor. My tongue brushed over my lips, tasting salt from where the tears had fallen. Her dress was so short other main arteries were visible, beating under the flesh of her slender thighs. Prudish hesitation at the thought of sinking my fangs into her scantily clad body was quickly overtaken by the pure need to feel her blood flow through me.

My breath was heavy. The rapacious yearning for her plasma sent the internal warmth through my body in a blaze that made me stagger. Nikolaos and Adalia both turned to me as though they'd felt it too. Nikolaos's eyes were all pupil, the beautiful colour swallowed by black. I could feel his hunger. Not just for the blood but for the power he knew we could achieve together. Adalia, still sitting, looked up at us both with distaste turning her face sour.

She stood. 'I will leave you both to...eat.'

Nikolaos and I both observed her stalk from the room, eyes following the movement the way snakes study mice before delivering the coup de grâce. Seeing her watch me with such distaste was almost sobering. I didn't know Adalia well yet, but I cared about what she thought of me, I even considered her someone with whom I could become close friends. Expecting to be destined to solitude for eternity, finding a friend was a precious relief. Alas, the hunger was ultimately too strong to fight off. She'd known Nikolaos for close to a century, she knew what we were, surely she wouldn't resent me for my natural instinct as a vampire?

'What part of her would you like, *ma chérie*?' Nikolaos asked, tracing a finger down from her neck to just above the top of the woman's navel. Her eyes fluttered at his touch, a small gasp escaping between overly full lips. I opted for the artery I knew best: carotid. I watched Nikolaos sink slowly between the woman's legs. His hands wrapped around her waist the same way they had held me last night. His pink tongue traced along her thigh, eliciting a soft moan from the woman. Her head was flung back making the stretch of neck clearer for me. The vein continued to throb with increasing velocity as her pleasure grew. I felt a twinge of emotion very different from lust bubble up in my stomach: jealousy.

Nikolaos closed his eyes and bit down on the woman. She drew in a deep, shocked breath and then let it out in a slow, shuddering release. The pleasure rolled off of her, wrapping over Nikolaos and me. I saw her hands wrap through his hair as he rested his head between her thighs. I bit down, fangs sinking into the flesh harder than necessary. Petty and not my most decorous moment. I felt her body tense up at the pain, but soon she eased into the sensation of two vampires feeding off of her. The blood was warm; thick, treacly, and piquant. It tasted like the apple in the garden of Eden, the air after sex, decadent treats you know are fattening but still crave. It was pure and primal, the rush of a beast tearing into flesh; seductive and sensual, the feeling of the fingers from someone you love caressing your bare skin. Venereal, pure, sinister; everything you so deeply desire that you know you shouldn't have. Humans tasted so good it was easy to forget their transience and even easier not to care. But Nikolaos had taught me well, and I knew when it was time to release her.

Nikolaos bit into his wrist, sharing some of his own life source with the woman. The holes we had made on her body knitted themselves together like magic. In some ways, it probably was.

I could see the blood breathing life to Nikolaos in front of my very eyes, the same way I could feel it spreading warmth and animation through my own body. Although still pale, a flush was coming to cheeks and lips. His face looked fuller; the blood seemed to chase away some of the shadows which had made him seem gaunt. The whites of his eyes shone brighter, the green was more startling. Black obsidian locks flowed like water as they thickened, shining in the light with an intense radiance. How could the epitome of grace and beauty be made even more perfect?

With blood flowing through me, I was beginning to sober up from before. Conflict was brewing in my mind. I couldn't deny the eroticism of us feeding together, and the thrill I got from the pure, carnal pleasure of it. But had Nikolaos really needed to find the skimpiest dressed woman in Britchelstone? I couldn't help but feel it was intentional.

'I can taste your displeasure,' Nikolaos said, pink tongue darting over his mouth to lap up a stray drop of blood. 'What is wrong?'

I did not, for one moment, believe that Nikolaos was that oblivious. I gave him a dry look. It was a conversation I already felt awkward having; the main focal point of the issue slumped on the sofa beside us didn't make me feel any more comfortable. Nikolaos, seeing my eyes flicking to the dazed woman, gave a tepid shrug.

'She will not remember this night, say as you wish.'

Logically, I knew he was right, but it still felt cruel to use her for blood and then discuss her as though she weren't there.

'Nikolaos,' I began, and then sighed, not sure how to put the deluge of feelings into words. He stood there with a stillness only the dead can master, watching me with vacant, waiting eyes. Even with the flush of colour in his cheeks, it was impossible to mistake him for a human. 'I feel like each day more of my humanity slips away, and I'm terrified that soon I'll have nothing left. I want to savour the last of my humanity, but I think you're trying to rush it along.' I motioned to the lady as an example. She still hadn't caught her breath from the climax of us feeding on her.

'I am inclined to disagree, *ma chérie*. I do not wish to rush this process for you. I am merely easing your transition to the ways of a vampire.'

'You could have chosen anyone for us to feed on, yet you chose the least dressed woman in the city. I don't enjoy seeing your head between another woman's legs, playing with her in that way.'

The first rousing of annoyance bubbled under the surface from both of us. Nikolaos's face slacked to the utter vacancy reserved for the times he wanted to keep everyone from seeing the truth. It was too late for that. I had felt the warning of his anger lapping at me the way waves stir before the current becomes deadly. He could be annoyed; so was I.

'You will remember my age, Scarlet,' he said with forced indifference. 'Humans have been my toys for longer than you can imagine. They are more than just food to me. They give me undivided pleasure, entertain my every desire. As they will for you, too, once you have truly embraced what you are. I will not forfeit my ways because of your petty jealousy.'

'I'm not jealous,' I protested, but even to me, it didn't sound believable.

Nikolaos scoffed. 'I saw the marks on her neck, Scarlet. You punished her for my actions.'

Nikolaos took a step towards me, so close our bodies almost pressed against one another. I could feel the tension radiating from him despite his blank expression.

'I do not think it is me you are angry with, Scarlet,' Nikolaos continued. 'I think it is the resentment you hold for yourself for enjoying it.'

That one statement knocked all the fight out of me. He'd taken the blade of my insecurity and sunk it home. How do you argue with the truth? You don't, not if you want to keep your dignity. Nikolaos was not mine to claim. I didn't have to like everything he did, but we weren't committed to one another by anything other than magick. Yes, I had been jealous. But I had also enjoyed it. That scared me much more than anything else. It wasn't Nikolaos who was forcing the last of my humanness away. It was me.

'You're right.' I sighed. 'I'm sorry.'

Nikolaos pulled me into his arms. Although a surprising response from him, I softened into the embrace, grateful for the comforting warmth of his arms around me. I could hear how his heart beat steadier against his chest after feeding.

'If you embrace your instinct,' Nikolaos whispered, turning my face up to him so his lips could brush against my own, 'it is an unrivalled pleasure.'

However much I hated to admit it, I knew he was right.

☽CHAPTER 9☾

Nikolaos had dropped our dinner back into town. The three of us sat together on the sofas, Nikolaos back into his casual stretch against the sofa which left him looking both nonchalant and seductive. I felt much less relaxed than him; I still didn't know what Adalia had found out.

Despite the intensity of the subject matter, over the days that our trio had spent together, we had formed a dynamic that complemented one another well. I enjoyed Adalia's company; she made me feel sure of myself amidst so much uncertainty.

Realising I was a novice in regards to mythology, Adalia had to explain the history of nymphs to me. They were most commonly known to be from Ancient Greek mythology, although we had established that myths and fairytales tended to be as equally true as history books. Nymphs were known to be the personification of nature, considered elemental deities. I did not, in any way, feel spectacular enough to be considered a deity. Fire nymphs were the least commonly known, at least when it came down to Greek mythology. They had preferred to hide in the shadows whilst their earthly cousins frolicked in light.

'I had my suspicions when we first met, fire is elemental, and there are very few creatures still around with these particular proficiencies. Elemental beings are some of the eldest and most powerful creatures to exist,' Adalia informed.

'To be born of elemental origin is celestial—a great rarity. Most creatures are created or cursed, so few are truly natural,' Nikolaos added cryptically.

'I wonder,' Adalia continued to speculate, 'if Niko's origins have something to do with why he was drawn to save you.'

'What do you mean?' I asked. And then I realised. Watching the realisation dawn on me and shock spread over my face, Nikolaos's lips curled up into an amused smile. 'No way.' I looked at him then, really looked at him, as if the memory of his face needed to be imprinted on my mind forever. 'That's impossible.'

'Is it, *ma chérie*?'

I thought back to the last night. The way the golden firelight had illuminated the strength of Nikolaos's features had hinted to something old and exotic but never had I imagined he was *that* old. Suddenly it all fell into place: the robust and shapely jaw; thick, dark hair and eyebrows; the prominence of his nose which saved him from being beautiful, instead making his features handsome and masculine. Nikolaos looked like he had been carved from the same marble as statues I'd seen in the history museums. In particular, the ones I had visited as a child with my grandparents when a museum had been doing a special exhibition on Greece in ancient times.

'You didn't know?' Adalia sounded surprised.

'I can't believe it.' I shook my head. 'Say it out loud. Tell me how old you are.'

'Will you believe it true if I confess my age?'

'Maybe.' I stared at him, eyes wide, not sure I *could* believe him.

'I was born two thousand, four hundred and ninety-four years ago.'

Trust Nikolaos to be so precise.

'But who's counting?' I said, grinning at him.

Adalia laughed; a warm, rich sound which chased away some of my shock.

'My grandad studied history at university. He would

have loved to have met you.'

The thought of my family quickly dampened the mood. The humour suddenly drained from the air, replaced with something sad and wistful. Adalia reached across the sofa to lay a hand across my own. It made me look over to her but seeing the gentle sorrow in her eyes, the pity, was enough to make me turn away.

'There's something else I found out about your family, Lettie.'

'What?' The word came out too quickly, shrill with panic.

'I believe you may have been adopted, Scarlet. When I met your mother and was shown around the house, I was sure of it—there is nothing supernatural in the house, it was a mystical null.'

Adalia continued to speak, but the words sounded like she was speaking underwater, distant and contorted, as I processed the information. 'I took an item of yours and one from each of your family members —just small things that won't be missed—and took them to an old acquaintance of mine. He's an energy reader, of sorts. He can get a reading of peoples' species when given an item of theirs. He confirmed my—our —suspicions.'

'You did not tell me you went to see Gwydion.' The evident disdain in Nikolaos's voice was enough to draw my attention back to them. Adalia watched me with solicitous eyes, doing an excellent job at ignoring the intensity of Nikolaos's gaze on her.

'He was very interested in your situation. He would like to meet you.'

'No, Adalia.' The calm composure had slipped to show the hintings of anger, the words prickled at my skin like thorns of ice. 'I do not want her entwined with the likes of him.'

Everything was moving too fast. My mind was delayed, still coming to terms with my family not being who and what I thought they had been. Whilst the cogs in my brain continued to whir Nikolaos and Adalia had come to an impasse.

'He could really help us out, Niko. My abilities are limited—as are yours. He is more knowledgeable of the arcane than either of us combined,' Adalia said calmly, but the glare she shot Nikolaos was hostile; it aged her, made the softness of her face seem harsher. The darkness in her expression made her surrounding energy swirl aggressively, almost extending out enough to touch Nikolaos and me. It was still shocking to me that he couldn't sense it.

The walls slid back into place over Nikolaos's face, leaving his expression unreadable once again. His stiff back once again relaxed against the sofa. To anyone else, he would seem utterly at ease, but I could see the tension was still there, making him more rigid than before. Adalia smiled to herself, taking his silence as a victory.

'If we drive there tonight, we will risk hitting daylight, so I suggest we go tomorrow at dusk.'

We'd fed in begrudged silence. If I didn't know any better, I'd have said Nikolaos was pouting. Adalia was leaning against the door of her 2009 Audi waiting for us. Nikolaos slid into the front passenger seat, leaving me to ride alone in the back. After an hour of taking chaotic twists and turns off the main road leading out of the coastal city of Britchelstone, we started driving down a woodland track. An adumbral forest shrouded the dirt track. Autumn was setting in fast, the branches of the trees stark and bare. They entwined with one another like skinless serpents creating a canopy of darkness to drive down. The true blackness swallowed all light making the lights of the car a blinding beam of white.

After almost another hour of driving down the dirt track, the tunnel of trees broke off into a sudden expanse of green. A building stood in the centre, an aphotic monolith amidst the sea of trees and shadows. It was one-story, made of stone so old it had fractured and crumbled. The once light-coloured walls had been stained black and dark grey from years of weathering. Windows had faded to a dismal, cloudy grey; some of the thin glass had cracks shooting through them like cobwebs. Built into the centre of the stone was a door of solid wood. The worn wood was decaying; patches flaked off onto the grass below. A thick, metal knocker clung to the door, the surface beneath chipped where it had made contact over the years.

The residence was ample, stretching back far into the night. Ivy and moss clung to the stone like a glove of green refusing to release the building from its grip, and bracken grew from the dirt in waves of green. They looked like a shocking breath of life blooming from the ground littered with dead twigs and brown, decaying leaves. Adalia parked the car, and we began to crunch through the graveyard of forestry which made up the ground. The almost full moon cast a beam of white that fought against the darkness. Shadows loomed like giants waiting to strike.

I felt a pressure build-up as we edged nearer to the building. It was gentle at first, nothing more than a tender stroke with each breath of wind, caressing my skin and whispering to me. By the time we had reached the door, the pressure had built to a suffocating level. I struggled to catch my breath; my chest was heavy and tight. I could feel my internal blaze trying to reach out to me. It called my name, wanted to engulf me, but something was stopping it from flaring.

The power tasted of death. Cold, icy and unliving. It

called to the part of me which no longer lived; whispering promises of life once more, of light in an existence shrouded by darkness. A chill rushed down my spine making goosebumps ripple over my flesh. It felt like someone had walked over my grave—disturbed my peace.

I gripped onto to Nikolaos's arm, nails digging into the flesh beneath his shirt. My breath was shallow and deep, each inhalation a sharp, almost painful gasp. Nikolaos turned his head down to look at me clinging to him. Through the shadow of his black hair, I could see the green wells of his eyes had been consumed by pure black. He watched me with those cold, dead eyes and for a moment it wasn't Nikolaos looking at me. It was like looking into the eyes of a shark; pure endless pools of black that glistened with danger. Hunger. I wondered if my eyes looked like that. It was almost enough to make me let go. Almost. Nikolaos saw the fear in my face and shook his head. His whole body shuddered with the effort of it, but when he turned back to face me, his eyes had bled back to normal.

'This was a mistake, Adalia.' Nikolaos's voice was breathy and strained. His arm slid around my waist. My hip was so tightly pressed into his body, I thought it may bruise us, but the comfort of his body against my own made me feel more solid. The flames licked through me stronger than before, chasing away some of the ice.

'I can't breathe,' I whispered to Nikolaos, finally steady enough to get the words out.

'You can, *ma chérie*. Rune—Gwydion—is a necromancer. He is taunting you, testing his strength against yours.'

Adalia slammed on the metal knocker. The sound echoed through the darkness, carrying through the damp air into the night.

I had expected the door to creak, but it was opened silently by a massively tall man. He huddled in the door frame with a height pushing seven-foot, maybe more. He was as spindly as the broken twigs lying at our feet, with skin paler than Nikolaos's stretched so thinly over bones I could see the blue of his veins underneath. High, angled cheekbones gave shape to his gaunt, cadaverous face. Eyes such a pale apatite they were almost white stared at us guilefully out a forest of pale lashes. Ivory hair hung straight to brush the tips of his bony shoulders. In the moonlight, the white of his skin emanated a translucent glow. He was grotesquely beautiful.

The man flashed a sinister grin at us, making me gasp. Every single one of his pure-white teeth was a sharp, pointed dagger. Deadly. My reaction made his icy blue eyes flicker to me. His painfully thin lips spread into a wider smile.

'Adalia, welcome.' The words came out as a soft hiss; a long v-shaped tongue flickered between his lips as he spoke. When those strange, blue eyes met the gaze of Nikolaos, I could feel him tense up around me. The man's power flowed over him to encase us both. Cold energy pricked at my skin with a sensation more irritating than painful.

'Nikolaos.'

He nodded curtly in Nikolaos's direction and the power disappeared so suddenly I would have stumbled if it wasn't for his arm still around my body. The air came back to my lungs, and I could breathe again, but there was still a residue of energy that made me want to be closer to the man. To hear the whisper of his offerings for life and power.

I instinctively moved away from Nikolaos, putting myself a step closer towards, who I assumed was,

Gwydion. Gwydion held his hand out to me, and I closed the gap, threading my fingers through his own. His hands were perversely skinny. Just bones with skin stretched so tightly it looked as though it might tear. Long, long fingers curled around my own and I felt instantly calmer. The pressure was released. I was safe. Gwydion could make everything okay. His power called to me, caressed me, sent bountiful waves of tranquillity through my body with such ferocity I gasped. His power felt like the line between pain and pleasure; good and evil. There was a sinister twinge to it which made me cautious. My own energy reared its head once more to warn me against Gwydion. That fire roared through my body to chase away his cold, internal touch. Together we worked to fight off against the mendacious assurances. We cast out his energy with a force that knocked me backwards. I stumbled, letting go of Gwydion's hand and falling against Nikolaos.

'A superfluous display of your power, Rune. Do not toy with her,' Nikolaos warned, wrapping his hands over the tops of my arms with painful force. Tension rang through his body, almost like an electrical current that would shock me if I stayed too close. Gwydion's mouth opened to laugh, but the sound that came out was not human enough to be considered humorous. The hiss sent a chill through my body.

'I am just getting a feeling for the young one's aura,' Gwydion replied. He didn't look much older than me, but the experience in his eyes was not that of someone young. For that reason, I let the condescension go. 'But she occluded my own.'

I rolled my head back to see Nikolaos's face, but it showed nothing.

'It's okay. He wasn't hurting me.'

'I intended no harm,' Gwydion added, looking smug.

'It really is okay, Niko.'

I squeezed his arm in reassurance.

Nikolaos sighed. 'Then you are naive, *ma chérie*.'

Gwydion's apatite eyes bore into me.

'Forgive my impertinence.' Gwydion picked up my hand and raised it to his lips. The kiss was chaste, formal, but insincere. 'I am Gwydion, although most call me Rune. Please, do all come in.'

Gwydion stood back from the door, gesturing his long arm out as an invitation to enter the stony abode. Adalia, who had remained very quiet since we arrived, followed through first. I went to trail at her footsteps, but a hand gripped me around my arm.

'Stay by my side, Scarlet,' Nikolaos hissed into my ear.

The first room we stepped into was small, dark and bare. The walls smelt damp, faintly mushroomy. The smell of moss blooming from graves when autumn grows damp. Even as a vampire I could feel the chill from the stone, for humans it must have been unbearably cold. I doubted being human was something Gwydion had to trouble himself with. Candles flickered in the darkness, the golden light turning the white of Gwydion's hair orange in the glow. Shadows weaved like lovers throughout the room dancing to music no one else could hear. The heat from the flames was a soothing touch against something deeper inside me than skin and bone.

'What an inhospitable room,' Nikolaos muttered rudely. I may have been thinking it too but would never dream of saying it out loud.

'It is cold and dark, Nikolaos. I would presume your fondness for it,' Gwydion retorted with a sly smile.

Nikolaos grabbed my hand, squeezing it between his fingers so hard I could feel the tension in his body spreading into my own. Annoyance radiated from him. I squeezed his hand back both as a comfort and an urging to release his death-grip on me. The quip shouldn't have riled him up as much as it did; it didn't take a genius to pick up on the feeling of unpleasant history between the two men. I resisted the urge to sigh. I got the impression it would be a long night.

'Please follow me,' Gwydion said with a harrowing smile. 'I will take us somewhere more inviting.'

We trailed through the monolithic corridor with Gwydion leading the way. Even hunched over, his white hair stroked the ceiling. We passed a collection of cracked wooden doors sunk into the stone before finally stepping through the threshold into the final room at the back of the building. Or perhaps cave would be more appropriate.

The room we found ourselves in was undoubtedly an improvement but not by much. Whilst still dark and cold, a candle chandelier filled the space with beautiful, golden light. The warmth echoed off the stone, hunting the chill in the air and winning. I could feel the heat building up in the room. In me. I shuddered, but it was a pleasant sensation. Nikolaos looked at me, and I shrugged. Could he feel it too? My control was still so erratic I didn't know if we always shared the sensations.

It was a sparse space. Two chesterfield sofas made from worn, patchy leather took up one side of the room. Most of the buttons pressed into the backrest had come loose whilst the few that remained barely held on. Appearing to be carved from the same old stone as the walls, a coffee table was positioned in between the sofas. Gwydion had thrown a red sheet over the table for a splash of colour. There was a bookshelf close to the door, the dark wood rotting consistently with the rest of the house. The final pieces of furniture came as a small, oak table with worn leather chairs tucked underneath, and another shred of murky red cloth strewn over the table like bloodstained linen. A variety of potted plants had been dotted desultorily around the room offering some muchneeded life to the stony desolation.

Gwydion didn't seem like one for grandeur. Quite the opposite of Nikolaos.

Adalia and I sat down beside each other on one of the sofas. My body sunk into the worn leather giving me an unobstructed view of Nikolaos leaning against the bookshelf with a cigarette resting between his lips. An unfamiliar smell filled the air—the scent of...wet animal.

The smell accompanied a man I hadn't met before. He strolled with a languorous air. Each plod was taken sleepily further into the room but underneath the sluggish movement was the sinuous grace of something more than human. The gait of a predator. He almost made Nikolaos look clunky, which was no easy feat. Gwydion grinned when he noticed the man; a smile that he reserved for the man in front of him. It was no longer a roguish smile framed by cunning eyes. His whole face softened, warmth and light filling his eyes to bring a youthful joy to his expression. Even the hollow pits of his sunken cheeks seemed less fearfully gaunt in the new man's presence. It was a look of pure, unabashed love.

The man had black skin darker than any I had ever seen. His head was completely bald besides the thick line of his black eyebrows along the smoothness of his face. Half closed eyes blinked sleepily, his short frame reaching up to stretch like a cat awoken from a nap. When his eyes opened fully, I couldn't help but stare.

There was no white to surround the iris. Instead, small black pupils floated in a sea of pale amber and orange. Where Gwydion was tall and scrawny, he was only several inches taller than me but what he lacked in height was made up for in muscle. Shoulders three times the width of mine were barely contained by the white t-shirt clinging to his body. The top stretched over his front revealing defined muscles rippling over his abdomen; the white fabric glowed against the darkness of his skin.

When Gwydion turned his back to us to face the new addition, I noticed his loose-fitting top was mis-shapen over the expanse of his back as though it were concealing something. I automatically assumed Gwydion had a weapon at his back. Not a comforting thought. Not that I was an expert, but on closer in-spection, it seemed like the wrong right shape for a weapon. I had no idea what it could be.

The new man glided over towards us with Gwydion close enough at his back they were almost touching. It was a protective stance with the potential to look possessive but didn't. A tension I hadn't noticed in his shoulders had released. The same could not be said for Nikolaos, who had also come closer to the sofas. He stood straight-backed and still, watching me closely like he wanted to see my reaction to something. The closer the man got, the stronger the scent. When they were standing behind the sofa in front of us, my nose wriggled involuntarily. I think it was what Nikolaos was waiting for as he let out a thunderous roar of laughter.

'She can smell your pet, Rune.'

The man laughed in response, white teeth flashing in his swarthy face. His top and bottom canines were neat, pointed fangs. Subtle enough that some people may not notice, but I had enough experience with fangs by now to tell the difference.

'Mind your tongue in my home, nightwalker,' Gwydion hissed at Nikolaos, not finding the humour in it. I shot a warning glare in Nikolaos's direction. I got a perfunctory shrug in response.

'As charmin' as ever, I see, Niko.'

He had a honey-rich voice with a deep American twang. The man closed the distance between us and reached his hand out to me.

'Pleased to meet ya, the name's Kai.'

Kai reached up to place his lips over the skin of my hand much the same as Gwydion had done when we first met. If Kai had had a hat, I'm sure he would have tipped it. Gwydion had made the action seem derisive, but Kai managed to make it gentlemanly in a down-home sort of way.

'And it's always great to see you darlin',' Kai said to Adalia, a drowsy smile playing along his lips.

Gwydion slunk over with his graceful, reptilian walk to sit opposite Adalia and me. Kai collapsed beside him, curling around himself with his head on Gwydion's lap. Gwydion's hand absently trailed over the smooth baldness of Kai's head the way you would stroke a cat. It was odd, but not the strangest thing we'd seen so far, and I doubted it would be the last. I tried not to focus on Gwydion's long, bony fingers tracing Kai's skin as he began to speak.

'Adalia, it is you who asked for my assistance, do you wish to enlighten me on why you have all come?' Gwydion turned to Nikolaos, who had taken a seat beside me. 'I must confess, I am surprised to see you, Nikolaos. It has been a long time.'

'It has,' Nikolaos replied apathetically. At least the taunting had stopped.

'Too long.'

Nikolaos didn't respond. Gwydion flashed the grin

of a trickster, but there was a sadness in his eyes not quite concealed in time to miss. I realised Gwydion hadn't been sarcastic when he had said 'too long'. The air was thick with tension; no longer weighted by snide quips and callous remarks but a heaviness soured by loss.

'I think we can all agree that Scarlet has unknown potential,' Adalia said, finally breaking her silence, 'and I don't know of any cases of vampirism and nymph being a comorbid condition. I think we all bring a certain expertise to the table. But, honestly'—she sighed —'now I'm not so sure us working together was such a good idea.'

'If Nikolaos deigned to solicit my help then he should have come to me himself,' Gwydion said with eyes locked on Nikolaos. It was not a friendly look, nor one aimed at strangers. No, there was undoubtedly a history between the two men.

'Rune, please. It's not him you're helping, it's Scarlet. You said yourself the situation has sparked your interest and this may be your only time ever to meet another nymph, let alone one who's also a vampire. Would you really throw that away because of an old feud?'

'I have heard bruits of elemental deities being near extinction,' Nikolaos added, I think trying to help our case. The cigarette he'd had in his mouth had disappeared back into the box unsmoked.

'So did I,' Adalia said enthusiastically, grateful for Nikolaos's input. 'You have a magickal sagacity unmatched by any of us, but we can find a way to make this work without you. I thought you would want to be a part of exploring the unknown.'

'I will help you, Adalia. I am quite intrigued by your little nymph.' Gwydion's lips curled up into a grimace. 'You should not have been able to shut me out earlier,

Scarlet. I got a taste for your power. It is strong but capricious.'

'Thank you, Rune. I'm grateful for your help,' I said, with sincerity.

'I cannot deny the amusement of not one, but two, vampires seeking aid from a necromancer. There would have been a time such things were unheard of.'

'You have always slithered your way into vampire business, Rune.'

'Is that so, Nikolaos?' Gwydion spat back bitterly. The words themselves were innocent, but the tone was not. Nikolaos, surprisingly, backed down.

'I don't actually know what a necromancer is,' I said quietly, trying to change the subject.

'I apologise, *ma feu*. We forget ourselves.'

'Indeed. A necromancer, young nymph, is someone who can communicate with and animate the dead.'

'Which means Rune has some influence over vampires, as well,' Adalia added.

'That's what you were doing to me earlier. I could feel your power whispering to me promises of life.'

'You tried to raise her, Rune?' Adalia sounded shocked; I could feel the rage seeping off Nikolaos.

Gwydion shrugged. 'I cannot raise any deceased without a ritual, especially the walking dead. However, I confess to getting carried away earlier. For that, I do apologise. It will not happen again; you have my word.'

I really wanted to ask Nikolaos if we could trust Gwydion's word, but he had eased at the pledge, so I had to trust that it was safe.

'Vampires do not often affiliate themselves with those who can control the dead, *ma chérie*. But if Rune gives you his word you can trust it will be kept,' Nikolaos said, as though he had heard what I was thinking. I risked a peep at his face, but it was still perfect and blank.

'If I were merely a necromancer, my expertise would not have been sought.'

Adalia answered the question I hadn't yet asked, leaning in to whisper, 'Rune has both demonic and magickal parentage.'

'A mongrel,' Nikolaos sneered. I hit him lightly with the back of my hand.

A small sound escaped from Kai's lips which drew my attention back to him. He was still lying curled on Gwydion's lap, with the taller man's fingers stroking the smooth skin of his face. The sound had been a low growl whilst he slept. Suspiciously similar to how an animal sounds during an exciting dream. As if he could feel me watching, Kai blinked up at me slowly, strange, orange eyes watching me with lethargic curiosity. I could feel the energy radiating off Kai, but it was nothing like what I felt from Adalia or Gwydion. Nikolaos had an aura, but it wasn't quite to the same extent the others did. Whilst Gwydion's energy made death feel seductive, Kai was like a ball of life and warmth. I couldn't explain it.

Kai felt so different in my head I couldn't help but say, 'Kai's energy feels different to anyone else. I don't know what he is.'

'Can you not decipher his species from the smell?'

Everyone in the room glared at Nikolaos. He had the grace to feign embarrassment.

'You're not human, either, are you Kai?' I asked the man who had now woken up from his catnap.

'No ma'am.'

'My husband is an ailuranthrope,' Gwydion said, running his thumb over Kai's eyebrow and down the bridge of his strong nose. A low, gravelly purr came from Kai's throat.

'She won't know what that is, Rune,' Adalia said, and

then turned to me. 'He means a werepanther.'

Ah, of course. Kai was a giant pussycat; it was the most logical explanation. The fact I was now considering wereanimals to be logical was concerning in itself, and indicative to just how far down the arcane rabbit hole I had fallen.

Two vampires, a demon-necromancer, a witch and a werepanther walk into a bar...I wondered what the punchline would be.

)CHAPTER 10(

We were back in the barren room at the front of the building. This time Nikolaos had made no scathing remarks, but I wasn't holding my breath he'd stay quiet. Gwydion and Kai had collected every candle they owned and were placing them around the room. Gwydion made an inferno circle in the centre of the floor. Other tealights were slotted into gaps in the crumbling walls. By the time they had finished, hundreds of candles had been lined up, the darkness being chased away fearfully by the flames. The candles slotted into the cracked walls were enough to begin heating up the stone room like an oven. It didn't take long for Kai and Adalia to begin sweating. I found the growing warmth comforting; the fire beautiful and inviting.

I obliged Gwydion asking me to sit within the circle of fire. The room wasn't large enough to have made the circle too big, which meant the flames licked at my skin. I sat on top of my knees, skirt smoothed out under my legs, with the fire tickling the back of my bare feet. In the hue of the orange light, Gwydion looked Mephistophelian. The shadows were dark in his hollow cheeks and eyes so sunk they were black pits burnt into white flesh.

I closed my eyes, deeply inhaling the warm scent of smoke.

The warmth grew inside me, mirroring the increasing heat of the room. The candles felt energising; the fire was empowering. At that moment, I knew I could take anything in my stride. The warmth ran through me like the soft flow of a river, gently filling my veins with the enchanting glow.

'How do you feel, Scarlet?' Gwydion's voice broke my meditative state. I felt my eyes flutter open.

'Peaceful,' I replied, my voice distant and soft. I could feel my words floating through the air, stroking the faces of the others. I think Adalia shivered, but I wasn't paying enough attention to be sure.

'Anything else?'

'Yes,' I replied. 'Powerful.'

I focused my attention to see all of them watching me with equally intrigued looks. Usually, I would squirm being the focus of such intense scrutiny, but I was safe in my shield of flames. No one could penetrate it unless I allowed them. Gwydion whispered something in Kai's ear low enough for me not to hear. Kai edged around the circle to the door, careful not to step too close to the fire. He returned with an even bigger candle in his hands. He had also removed the white shirt which had begun to turn translucent from perspiration. Beads of sweat clung like spring dew to his skin; the liquid caught the light to form amber drops over his face and body. The beads trickled down the front of his stomach following the walls of his abs like river banks of muscle.

Gwydion quickly reached into the circle to place the lit candle in front of me. I felt a distortion in the air that surrounded me, but it was okay, we let him in. He was safe. And if he tried to harm us, we could protect ourselves. My power and I worked as one. Separate entities to form one consciousness.

The candle, wider than both my palms, was contained in a red-painted wooden case with six wood wicks standing to attention. The flames on the wicks merged to form one mighty, orange flame.

'Could you place your hand in the flame?' Gwydion asked. Not realising they had closed again, I opened my eyes. There was a part of me that felt hesitant to do as he asked. I had spent my entire life being warned against touching naked flame. Every instinct in my brain was telling me *no*. Every instinct in my soul told me it was safe. The internal warmth was luring me into making the abstract heat physical. I obliged willingly, giving myself over to the beguiling power.

I wasn't sure what to expect; pain, agony, a deep burning that would maim me for life? Only one way to find out, I suppose. I closed my eyes again, took a deep breath in and started for the flame. At first, it lapped at me tentatively, almost teasing. A cautious greeting to let me know it was safe. I moved my hand further into the fire, and it still didn't burn. The fire spread through me, reminding me of the summer days under the burning sun when I lay in tall grass. Of the fireplace at my grandparents' on Christmas day. Camping as a child and roasting marshmallows on the bonfire. The longer I kept my hand in the fire, the more the warmth spread up my hands, arms, shoulders. It no longer was just the heat from a fire; it was the warmth you feel in your heart after a day of bliss. It was spectacular.

'Open your eyes, *ma chérie*,' Nikolaos suggested gently.

The room was cast in golden light as though the sun had burst between the stone walls. It took me a moment to adjust before realising where the extra light had appeared from. My hands and arms were a trail of fire. It wasn't an intense flame, more like the dwindling embers of a fireplace, but my skin was alight all the same. The second my brain registered what was happening, I had a moment of panic and every candle in the room distinguished to nothing. We were suddenly shrouded in darkness, cooking in the stone walls, and with the smell of smoke thick enough to choke on.

'*Fascinant*,' Nikolaos said, sounding breathy.

'Fascinating indeed, Nikolaos.'

I saw Nikolaos walk towards me with his arm outstretched, felt the cool touch of his fingers against the arm of my skin and then, suddenly, we were no longer in a cage of stone.

Uneven cobblestones stretched on into the darkness. The mist of the evening rain dampened the stone, leaving it to shimmer under the glow of the moonlight. Stretched high up in the air were cables connected to the tops of buildings. Iron-framed lanterns hung from the rope cable like small suns flickering in the night. In the distance, I could hear the faint clipping of hooves on stone. It was the only sound in the otherwise still silence. I took a step towards a tall, slender silhouette hidden in the shadows.

A mass of black hair hung in tight curls around the paleness of his face and blended into oblivion against the sleeved cape he wore thrown over one shoulder. An elaborate doublet with the bodice tight over his torso was black with dark grey patterns woven into the fabric and had a line of round, shiny buttons down the front like Tahitian pearls. The sleeves were bulky yet still tight at the wrist, leading up to the inflated upper sleeves and protruding shoulders. Large, puffy breeches in the same dark, stiff fabric thrilled around his thighs almost reaching down to his knees. White tights consumed his calves with a black ribbon tied around the bend of his knee, and buckled leather boots stretched up to mid-calf. A cavalier hat made of black felt flopped over his head with one long, white feather sticking up.

Nikolaos turned a pale face and striking green eyes to look at me, adorned in all black and grey his skin glowed ethereally, and his eyes shone like burnished chrysocolla. I began to move closer, wading through a fog that was growing thicker to get to him. The *clip, clip* of heels sounded on the cobblestone behind me. I stepped out of the way to let the stranger come through, and Nikolaos's eyes stayed where they were. He hadn't been looking at me. He'd been looking straight through me towards the woman he awaited.

She looked like a china doll brought to life. A pale, round face housed a small mouth with plump lips set into a permanent pout and lustrous, green eyes framed by white silk lashes. A small, black freckle dotted under the outer corner of one eye made her seem older somehow. She would have looked entirely innocent if it weren't for those eyes. They held something deeply nefarious; a promise of sadism, sex and pain as if she would tear your heart out and eat in front of you but you'd enjoy every moment of it. Beg her to keep doing it. Plead with her to never stop the torture until you were hollow and bloodied. She made evil look seductive.

There was an uneasy feeling in my stomach, and it wasn't just from the sight of the woman Nikolaos was waiting for. The fog in the air was growing plentiful enough to choke on. I could feel the thick greyness of it beating against my body as if it would suffocate me.

I watched the woman walk past me, high heels delicately striking the stone. Tight, white-blonde ringlets bobbed around her upper body as she glided with confident elegance. The black corset of her bodice looked painfully tight, accentuating the tininess of her waist. A low, broad neckline showed off the bounce of her bust as she continued with her sultry gait towards Nikolaos. The large skirt of her dress swayed with her movement, barely high enough off the ground to stay dry against the damp pavement. A large ruby ornamented her neck like a splash of blood against the whiteness of her chest.

Nikolaos gave a low, graceful bow, removing the hat from his head to sweep against the ground in an old fashioned gesture.

'*Mon amour*,' she said in a rich, mellifluous voice thick with French.

The woman had reached Nikolaos; even in heels, she had to reach on tiptoes to wrap her arms around his neck. Her pouty, pink lips crushed against his own with a violent passion.

The fog was thickening fast. I fell to my knees, gasping for air as the greyness swam down my throat like water drowning me. I went to scream for Nikolaos to help, but it was too late. I was choking on the haze. My vision of the two of them faded. Specks of white danced in my eyes like fireflies in the darkness.

The last thing I could make out before the blackness consumed me was one word. One name.

Camille.

)CHAPTER 11《

I woke up alone tangled in the silk sheets of my bed. My head was pounding so hard I could hear the blood rushing through. It felt like someone was hammering my head from inside out, trying to crack my skull. It took several failed attempts to sit up before finally mustering the strength to lean my back against the wall. Sitting up, I realised it wasn't just my head that hurt. My bones ached deeply. The blood in my body felt like it was moving too slowly, agonisingly trying to push its way through the veins. Someone, Nikolaos I presumed, had changed my outfit so I was wearing an oversized t-shirt which smelt vaguely mossy. Nikolaos didn't own anything like this in his wardrobe, so I assumed it was either Gwydion or Kai's. The short sleeves and mid-thigh cut off gave me a clear view that none of my body was physically damaged, and yet it felt like every inch of skin was swollen and bruised.

I had debated changing into a different outfit but even the light fabric of the t-shirt hurt against my skin so I decided against it. Nikolaos was nowhere to be found in the downstairs dungeon—sorry, vampire living quarters—which left me painfully shuffling up the metal stairs to try and find him. I walked through the door into the front room, finding three faces watching me. None of them was the one I really wanted to see.

Rune sat tall and poised on the sofa with Kai beside him. A dark arm was thrown over the taller man's shoulders. Kai's upper body nestled into Gwydion's chest with his knees curled tight to his own body. Adalia sat opposite them both sipping from a steaming mug. I wondered who had bought the tea. And the mug, for that matter.

'She has finally arisen,' Gwydion said.

'Evenin', darlin'.'

'Hey, Kai,' I replied, with a genuine smile. Kai and I had only met once, but I had an irrational fondness for him. Like Adalia, he was sort of impossible to dislike. Even if I did find his smell...distasteful 'Wait, what do you mean *finally*?'

'You've been asleep for several days, Lettie,' Adalia chimed, in between a sip of her tea. I could smell peppermint. My body felt like a ten-tonne truck had smashed into me and no one had lifted the weight, not the well-rested one would expect of someone who had slept for half a week.

'Do not look so surprised, young nymph. I am unsure what you did, but it fatigued Nikolaos as well as yourself.'

'Nikolaos? Is he okay?'

Gwydion looked thoroughly amused at the question.

'Yes, Scarlet. Nikolaos arose safely from his slumber yesternight.'

Gwydion had mastered apathy and mocking better than even Nikolaos. Something I would have thought impossible.

'Have you all been here this whole time?'

'Yes, Nikolaos has been the most genial host.'

'You're joking.'

Gwydion grinned at me.

'He did not have a bad word to say about our stay, up until last night.'

I sighed, but even that small action made me wince. I rubbed my fingers in circles over my temples. Gwydion was, somehow, making my headache worse.

'You are in pain,' he observed. I gave a brief nod, fingers still massaging my head futilely.

'I'll make ya some tea, darlin',' Kai offered, uncurling himself from his husband.

'Tea sounds lovely, but I don't think that's what my body needs right now. Besides I don't think I can even drink it anymore.'

Kai looked momentarily uncertain, his body awkwardly half-raised off the sofa from where he had begun to get up.

'You have drunk liquor, have you not?' Gwydion asked.

'Yeah, I guess that's true.'

'Just because Nikolaos has distanced himself from his human self does not mean you must give up all your small pleasures. But I must agree, there is only one liquid that will remedy your ailments, and I do not think you will find that from anyone here.'

Kai nestled back into the welcoming embrace of Gwydion looking docile and content once more. It was sort of endearing.

'Before you feast, I must ask if you remember anything of what happened?'

Images of old cobblestone roads and suffocating fog flooded back into my mind. It all felt like a distant memory or a dream I couldn't quite recall. Then I remembered the beautiful woman, with her malicious gaze, kissing Nikolaos under the moonlight with a passion we had never shared. I wished I hadn't remembered that part. My head was pounding again so hard I swooned. I leant against the doorframe for balance, leaning my head against the solidness of the wall. I was very close to flashing the room wearing nothing but the t-shirt; nevertheless, I was past the point of caring. Whilst not a priority, I would have liked to know who had changed me out of my clothes and why. I'd get to those trivial questions later.

'It's sort of hard to explain. One moment I was in the room with all of you and the next it was like I was transported somewhere I'd never been. If I passed out, then maybe it was a dream. I saw Nikolaos there in some strange clothes, and he was with a woman—Camille, I think—but they didn't see me. I felt out of place; it was all so strange. The world felt distorted.' I shuddered.

'Camille,' Gwydion said with piqued curiosity. He rolled the word on his tongue and then spat it out like it was something unpalatable. Kai and I exchanged an equally puzzled look. It was that moment Nikolaos appeared through the door.

'You are awake, *ma chérie*.'

He placed a cautious hand on either side of my face, turning my head around for closer inspection. I winced again.

'Are you hurt?'

'No, not really.'

He leant his face down to mine, placing the chastest of kisses against my lips. When I contorted my face again, it had less to do with the pain and more the memory of his lips pressed against Camille's. I was under no illusion of Nikolaos's colourful sexual past but watching it up close and personal hadn't been a welcome reminder. Gwydion cleared his throat dramatically. With slightly hunched shoulders, Nikolaos stepped back from me, turning to the room.

'You are still here I see, Gwydion.'

Scooting Kai off his lap, Gwydion stood. The superior look on his face was enough for me to know what he was about to say next would rile Nikolaos up more.

'I admire such astute powers of observation,' he retorted, spiked tongue flickering between teeth of swords. 'Your little nymph, Nikolaos, appears to have uncovered an *interesting* chapter of your life.'

Nikolaos kept his gaze surely on Gwydion.

'How very cryptic, Rune.'

'Please,' he said, gesturing to me with a sweep of his hand, a smile feigning innocence playing along the line of his lips, 'do ask her yourself.'

I flashed Gwydion wide, confused eyes. Nikolaos turned to me with a face that showed nothing. His body was very still; every part of him controlled and cautious. I struggled to meet Nikolaos's gaze.

'Camille,' I mumbled, part of me hoping he wouldn't hear it, and all of me knowing he would. I didn't know the significance of the name, but I could read from Gwydion's reaction that it meant something to Nikolaos. Something unpleasant. Nikolaos stood inert against my words. So still he didn't look real, a statue of captured perfection but no life held within. Finally, Nikolaos turned back to Gwydion.

'What have you told her?' Nikolaos said, voice low, and surprisingly restrained. The voice was calm, but I could feel the anger coming off of him in waves of ice that washed over me, making me stumble against the door once more. I felt his anger spiral through the room towards Gwydion, crashing against him. Gwydion didn't stumble. He smiled, with a laugh slithering from his lips.

'Oh, *mon vieil ami*, I have not breathed a word. Any uncovered history is not my doing. After all, it is not I who bound myself to a deity.' Gwydion grinned. 'I can see the temptation, though, Nikolaos. Your own strength is certainly bolder now.'

'I don't understand any of this,' I interjected, hoping to distract the two men.

'Psychometry, a degree to which even I do not possess.'

'In Layman's terms, Rune,' Adalia said, with a sigh. She was the only one who remembered I was new to the arcane.

'You appear to be able to read memories, Scarlet.' Gwydion looked over at Nikolaos again. 'Have you not told your lover of your many ventures, Nikolaos?'

Even standing away from Kai, Gwydion's hand reached out to absently stroke Kai's head. His face rubbed against the hand, nustling into the palm, taking in a deep breath of his scent.

I could still feel the icy air of rage that rolled off Nikolaos like a mercurial wind. I reached down into myself, looking for the heat. My fire was as tired as I was, whatever had happened at Gwydion's had depleted both of us, but we also knew Nikolaos needed something to soothe him. The heat rose. We made a blanket of metaphysical warmth, comfort, and sent it out to Nikolaos. We enveloped him, stifling his cold vexation. We sent him the love we felt, the power we could share, and the knowledge he was not alone. I could feel his anger instantly dissipating. It was this that made me realise I was more powerful than Nikolaos. It wasn't the first time I had felt his emotions, but before it had been through our connection as master and vassal. This was the first time his own energy had solidified and been cast out towards someone he was not metaphysically bound to. But it hadn't been enough. If I hadn't already been weakened, it wouldn't have made me stumble. Gwydion had laughed it off. My own fire dampened it easily. He had only a hint of possibility, and it wasn't strong enough against Gwydion or I. Nikolaos was many things: ancient, charismatic, strong. But he was not powerful.

Everyone was silent. The blood pounding through my head was thunderously loud. Gwydion and Nikolaos both watched me as if I'd done something interesting. Maybe I had. At least it meant I had their attention.

'I don't know what has gone on between the two of you but could you put it aside for just one evening.' With a deep sigh, I added, 'Please.'

Gwydion did a small bow, eyes twinkling with unsung humour. He was laughing at me. I could handle being mocked as long as it meant the petty bickering stopped. I still had a lot of questions to ask Nikolaos, but we had more important things to pursue.

'As you wish, Scarlet.'

'You must feed, *ma chérie*.'

'Once you have fed, I wish to explore your psychometry. I believe it came from the simultaneous touch of naked flame and flesh. Presently, however, it appears to not only exhaust you but the focus of your ability, also.'

'It might be because Niko's a vampire,' Adalia said, coming to stand with us, still with the empty cup wrapped in her hands. 'That would be harder for anyone no matter their experience or training. Maybe if we were to try it on someone with human blood, it would be easier and have a less adverse outcome.'

We all watched Adalia expectantly. She, as the most human of us all, had indirectly volunteered herself for the job.

)CHAPTER 12((

Gwydion and Adalia theorised that, if we took some additional precautionary measures, we could ensure a safer experience. We were going to be somewhere I was familiar with and felt safer; with someone who was close to human, and, finally, going in with some expectations instead of blind. With all of this in mind, I found myself sitting in my bedroom besides Adalia. I had already gone and fed alone. On my return, I found the three men busying themselves around the bedroom. Adalia and I had to try and keep our heads clear and at ease which meant we sat sipping tea on the sofa whilst the men gathered an enormity of candles to place throughout the room.

Ever prepared, Gwydion had brought some of his own candles from home in the form of simple, white tealights. Nikolaos had found some, too; they were taper candles in matte black and red, housed in ornate golden holders. Beautifully gothic, much like the man who owned them. As I watched him strike the match to light his cigarette and one of the black candles, I couldn't help but feel a sense of sadness. The first time I'd find myself in bed by candlelight wouldn't be with Nikolaos. He would be in the room with me, watching, with the other two men but it wouldn't be romantic.

I pulled my knees to my chest, the top covering my legs and body like a glove, and rested my head on top of my knees. Adalia followed my gaze to where Nikolaos was standing. His black silk shirt was tucked into black suit trousers with a leather belt. The golden candelabra had metal thorns protruding from the arms, the tops carved into blooming roses to hold five candles. Dressed all in black with nothing but the gold of the metal and green of his eyes for colour, he was a picturesque ghost.

'There was a time,' Adalia whispered, leaning into me, 'when Niko would have simply refused to be in the same room as Gwydion. It took a lot for him to agree to meet with him.'

I switched my gaze from Nikolaos to Adalia who had shuffled so close our faces almost touched. I could smell the peppermint on her breath as she spoke. She underestimated the hearing abilities of a vampire, even speaking so softly I knew Nikolaos would hear. I didn't know if the same could be said for Gwydion or Kai.

'Do you know why they dislike each other?' I asked in an equally hushed tone. Feeding had made me feel much better; I wouldn't have been able to hold down a conversation before. My body still had the ache of a thousand bruises, but the headache had mostly gone. I was just grateful for some of it to have eased. Thank god for small mercies, as they say.

Adalia sighed.

'Yes, I know why. Some of why at least. Neither of them has ever told me the full story, but I know enough to put some of the pieces together.'

'Is it something to do with Camille?'

'Yes and no.'

'I expect the men to be cryptic but not you.'

Adalia smiled, but it wasn't happy.

'I think Niko would say it was. Gwydion might think otherwise.'

'You don't believe Niko?'

'I believe he would like it to be that simple. I don't know, Lettie. I get the impression there's more complexity to the situation than they let on. Something I don't know.'

'I want to ask you what you know, but I think it's one of those times I just need to let him come to me when he's ready. I don't want to push him. Or you.'

'I agree.' Adalia beamed at me. 'But you may be waiting for a long time.'

'Luckily we have time on our side,' I said, smiling back at Adalia. 'If I can learn anything from being a vampire, it will probably be patience.'

'Being with someone like Nikolaos will *certainly* teach you patience.'

We both burst out laughing. For one wonderful moment, all the peculiarity of my life faded to something wholesome and normal. Adalia and I were just two women, sitting in my bedroom, talking about the men in our lives. The laughter carried through the room swatting away any building tension as it carried. When I raised my head from my knees, the three men were staring at us curiously.

'What is so amusing?' Gwydion asked.

Adalia waved him off. Nikolaos turned back around without giving any hint he had been listening in. I knew he had. Kai, however, was trying to contain his own smile, which made me wonder if, like vampires, wereanimals also had extra sensitive hearing. Kai and I made eye contact. The more he continued to try and contain his smile, the more it made me laugh. In the end, the three of us were in a fit of giggles. Kai's laugh was more a low rumble, or a purr, than a human sound. Joyous nonetheless. We ignored Gwydion's frowning.

Adalia sat crossed-legged on the bed. With all the candles and fireplace lit, the room was a casket of heat. As I walked past Nikolaos to join her, he grabbed my arm softly. He bent his head down, satin lips brushing the line of my earlobe. Even that small touch sent a warmth through my body.

'*Ma chérie*,' he whispered.

'Yes?'

Black hair tickled my cheek, the musk of cinnamon strong and enticing. I could smell the smoke from the fire and cigarettes clinging to him.

'When this is all over,' he continued, 'we will arrange some time for Adalia and you. If you can just be *patient* with me until then.'

'I knew you were listening!'

Nikolaos gently nipped on the soft flesh of my lobe. I shuddered, a blissful rush of air escaping from between my lips.

The light of the fire brought out gold and auburn hues in Adalia's chestnut hair. Orange glow danced around her eyes like pools of honey swirling through the rich brown. We sat crossed-leg opposite one another. Gwydion and Kai leant against the wall beside us, Kai's back pressed against the door of the wardrobe, his arm circling Gwydion's waist. Nikolaos sat on the fluffy, white stool on the opposite side to Gwydion. He looked casual but I could sense the concern and intrigue he felt. I needed to focus on Adalia without getting wrapped up with Nikolaos's feelings. For the first time, I wished he could close the walls between us temporarily. Better yet, I wish I could. I was getting distracted.

I took a deep breath in, let it out slowly, and closed my eyes. Gwydion had placed the same large candle I had used at his in between Adalia and me. I picked it up, careful not to touch her, and held the weight of it in my hands. I could feel the heat building up in the room; it beat against my skin like the midday sun. Magick stroked inside me. The aura began to rise within, spreading through my veins. I willed the fire to stay on an internal passage without igniting my skin. The heat streamed through me; up to my sternum, dancing around my heart.

'I think I'm ready,' I said, without opening my eyes.

I placed the candle back down in front of me, holding one hand palm out to Adalia. She responded by curling her fingers around my own. Her palm was clammy. I willed the heat to channel through into Adalia and heard her gasp as my aura rushed through me into her. Our two energies embraced like old friends, swirling around one another. I could taste her aura in my mouth. She was also an elemental practitioner to some extent; her bond as a witch to the earth made her energy taste like spring grass, the sea air, damp ground ready to burst with life. I could feel her reverence for the earth and all that She blessed us with. I knew I was ready. That we were both ready. With our energies still swirling, I cast my free hand into the flames of the candle. There was no hesitation this time.

It was much less jarring than with Nikolaos. Even with my eyes closed, I could feel the room fading around me. I could still feel Adalia's damp hand in my own like a distant memory, yet, somewhere in my mind, I knew it was still a real, solid weight. A grounding reminder of the room in which we sat.

I blinked my eyes open.

We were no longer sitting on my bed surrounded by three watchful men.

The sun beat down on my skin. I looked up into the blue sky watching the white clouds blow like mammoth phantoms through the vast cyan. The sun was a blaze of yellow and gold that blinded me. With closed eyes, I could feel the pressure of the light turning my eyelids deep red. I stood with my arms wide by my side, basking in the heat. It was the first time I had seen the sun in almost a month. Humans aren't meant to go that long without feeling the embrace of sunlight. But I wasn't human anymore. I never really had been.

A bell chiming knocked me from my reverie. I turned round in time to see the man who had set off the bell as he walked out through the door of a shop. The building was painted a soft pastel blue with large, arched windows. Herbs and flowers grew out of a long planter resting on the window sill. A weathered sign read, '*Bordeaux Botanicals*', in white lettering, imprinted in a strip of wood painted light green near the top of the building. I moved closer to the door, painted the same green as the sign, peeking through the large window in the wood. A lacy curtain still fluttered behind the glass from the breeze of the wind flowing through the window.

The walls inside were fern green with dainty teal flowers climbing up the wallpaper. Rows and rows of wooden shelves covered the walls, on which glass vials in varying sizes and colours were neatly lined up. Towards the back of the shop was a counter; a blackboard hung on the wall above. '*Aura Readings and Botanical Healing*', was written in white chalk on the sign, with prices and ingredients listed underneath. The cursive handwriting swirled in a familiar fashion. Behind the counter, there was a rectangular archway, a veil of blue chiffon fluttered down from the top of the arch. Green vines had been woven into the fabric in delicate trails.

Blue and green swirled as a body walked backwards through the arch, getting tangled in the fabric. Adalia, looking fresh-faced and only a few years older than me, unwrapped herself from the material, letting a large wooden box down onto the counter. The glass vials in the wood clinked together in an ariose chorus.

Umber hair was curled around her head, leaving her olive-skinned face bright and bare. Her loose white shirt was tucked into dark denim jeans stopping mid-calf. With red kitten heels on, she was close to six-foot. The shiny red of her thin belt matched the shoes and vibrant lipstick.

I went to open the door, but my hand glided through the brass handle like it was some strange illusion lacking physical form. After several failed attempts, I finally gave up with a frustrated sigh. It was disconcerting, but I made my way into the shop by walking through the closed door as though it were air.

Adalia was arranging the vials on the counter by size and colour. I left her to fuss, walking up to the shelves on the wall to get a closer look. Inside, there was an accumulation of smells wafting through the air; herbs, florals, spices—all with earthy undertones that mingled with the cool breeze to almost overwhelming levels. The bell on the door went off again, drawing both our attentions up to the entrance.

Doe-eyed, Adalia watched a man close the door softly behind him, her lips spreading into a huge, scarlet-painted grin. The punter in question had tanned skin the dark gold of someone who had spent a lot of time working outside. He lifted the battered, grey flat-cap off his head, using his free, rough, and calloused hand to run through hair thick with concrete dust. A cloud of grey puffed around his face as the fingers traced through dark brown hair beginning to turn grey. The hair didn't match the age of his face, he looked too young to be greying, but he still managed to pull it off. It added more character to his rugged handsomeness. Kind olive-green eyes lit up when he saw Adalia looking in his direction, his own grin bringing a glow to his face that had nothing to do with the dark tan.

He slapped the cap onto the counter lightly, reaching over the wood to kiss Adalia with passion. Her hands trailed up the solid muscle of his forearms, fingers playing with the rolled cotton of his off-white shirt at the elbow. When he pulled back, a blush had crept up Adalia's cheeks.

He and Adalia began to talk. The words were muffled; a static noise that I couldn't understand. A familiar cloudy fog had started to spread through the room, distorting my view of the lovers. Fatigue hit me like a tidal wave and my knees buckled below me. I went to grab for the shelf to steady myself but my fingers went through the wood, and I collapsed to the floor. Not wanting a repeat of last time, I grounded myself in the knowledge that this wasn't real. Unsure of how to control it, I took a leap of faith that imagining myself back in the bedroom, surrounded by people I knew, would be enough to pull me from Adalia's mind.

The sensation of fingers wrapped around my hand was getting stronger. I closed my eyes, focusing on the solid feeling. The cool breeze circulating through the shop, the feeling of the sun heat beating through the window, began to grow fainter. A fiery warmth took the place of them; I could almost feel the weight of three pairs of eyes watching me.

Adalia sat slouched opposite me. The thick mass of her hair hung in a curtain of oak satin framing her face. I could smell the distant scent of fresh blood. Drops of red trickled from Adalia's downturned face, turning the blue silk sheets black where they pooled. A warm liquid ran down my own face onto my lips. I darted my tongue out to lick away the blood that trickled from my nose. I released Adalia's hand, which was still resting on mine, to wipe away the crimson stream. The moment I let go of her, Adalia jolted upright like she'd been shocked, wide eyes blinking frantically. She raised a shaky hand to clear the blood from her own face.

'Are you well, *ma chérie*?'

Nikolaos went to touch me, but, thinking better of it, drew his hand back. I dismissed his question with a wave of my hand, focusing on Adalia who looked dazed and confused.

'Yes, yes, I'm fine,' I reassured. 'Adalia are *you* alright?'

Adalia nodded at me, too slowly, and then suddenly her body collapsed backwards onto the sheets. Her body shook lightly against the bed, eyes rolling into the back of her head. Her sockets were a sea of white and red veins as the steady stream of blood quickened to a fast flow pouring down her cheeks.

'Niko!' I shouted, rising to my knees. The three men rushed closer to the bed. I turned panicked, pleading eyes to Nikolaos. 'What's happening?'

Adalia's right hand clutched around the left, the one I had been holding, as though she was injured. I uncured her fingers as gently as I could; the sight of her hand made me gasp, horrified. Adalia's palm was a mass of yellow blisters spread over red, pink and white mottled flesh. Olive skin had burnt off in charred patches of black leaving layers of raw flesh open to the air. I gasped again, swallowing back the bile burning in my throat. Kai saw the wound, letting out a hiss of air.

'Feed her your blood, Nikolaos,' Gwydion instructed calmly.

For once, Nikolaos didn't argue back. I didn't need to look at him to know he had bit into his wrist as I heard the sound of fangs puncturing layers of flesh. I could smell his blood mingling with the scent of Adalia's; the smell of both their blood awoke something in me. Monstrous bloodlust tried to overpower my concern for Adalia. For a fleeting moment, I didn't care that my friend lay convulsing and injured on my bed with wounds I had inflicted. Her blood called to me. I swallowed hard enough to be painful; I would not let the hunger control me. I could not let the hunger control me.

My hand reached for Adalia's. I tried to inspect her injury without touching the wound, but my fingers accidentally brushed one of the charred edges of her palm. Nikolaos's bleeding wrist had almost reached Adalia's blood-stained lips when, to my shock, and relief, the black begun to fade. Blistering bubbles of damaged flesh deflated; a flow of skin consumed the raw reds and pinks of the open wound. Within seconds, Adalia's palm looked perfect and untouched. She lay still against the bed, no more spasming or blood flow. Just the slow rise and fall of her chest as she breathed normally. My own breathing was ragged with panic and the effort to not feast from the fountain of blood on Adalia's face.

Nikolaos failed to mask his confusion. He stood with his wrist above Adalia's mouth hesitantly. He looked over to Gwydion, asking a silent question with his eyes. Gwydion gave a nod and Nikolaos plunged the semi-healed bite marks in between Adalia's half-parted lips. I could feel Gwydion's eyes on me. I turned my head up to him, knowing I looked crazed with shock. Hunger. Disgust. Disgust at myself for coming so close to draining Adalia.

Knowing Adalia was going to be okay, the adrenaline was wearing off. The bile I'd been holding down was pushing back with a vengeance. I could still smell the seductive sweetness of Adalia's blood where it was drying on her face.

It was suddenly all too much.

I didn't make it to the bathroom in time. Merlotcoloured vomit pooled onto the stone floor of the hallway. I stayed on my hands and knees panting and retching until nothing was left to throw up but my guts. My throat and nose burned like acid. My eyes were puffy and bloodshot from crying and retching. Exhausted was an understatement. The draining of energy it took to go into Adalia's memories aside, my body was heavy with resentment. Just touching me had left Adalia so severely burnt that, if it weren't for my esoteric magic and Nikolaos's blood, she would have needed to be hospitalised. It was a wound that would have required a skin graft at least. And, in spite of the horror of seeing Adalia's layers of flesh bared to the world, it had taken an almost painful level of self-control not to drink from her. I had been so focused on denying that I was a monster, I hadn't noticed it progressing right in front of my eyes. Gripping so hard onto what I thought was left of my soul, malevolence had spread like a tumour through me.

Adalia had showered and changed into new clothes courtesy of my wardrobe. It's incredible how much of a healing property vampire blood has. Under different circumstances, it would be groundbreaking for the field of medicine. If I asked Adalia if she was okay any more times, it would be pestering instead of solicitous, so I finally took her reassurances as truth. Sunrise was less than an hour away, and out the window, I could see the sky fading from true black to deep blue. I was very grateful that Adalia had scrubbed herself clean of all the blood. I wasn't sure how much control I had left to exhaust.

We'd only been sitting upstairs for half an hour, and I was already on my fifth cigarette. Nikolaos, who seemed to be getting frustrated at my constant asking him for another, had just handed me the pack and a lighter. I sat huddled into the corner of the sofa with Nikolaos in the middle between Adalia and me. My body was pressed against the fabric, curling over the arm where the ashtray rested, to put as much distance between them and me as I could without being obvious. Or more obvious. In a state of shock, I had yet to speak. I wasn't even sure I had blinked yet. Adalia had let me use some of her mouthwash but the taste of blood and bile left my mouth tasting foul.

'Scarlet,' Gwydion snapped impatiently.

I'd been lost too deep in thought with my eyes fixed thoroughly on the crystal ashtray to realise he had been speaking to me. I turned wide, red eyes up to look at him.

'Yes?'

'Did you hear any of what I said?'

I shook my head. Nikolaos wrapped his arm around my shoulders. With his other hand, he took the cigarette from my shaking grasp, reaching over me to stub it into the crystal cigarette cemetery. He pulled me closer into his body. I curled in his arm, resting my head against his chest. Whether I wanted to admit it or not, Nikolaos, as my master, grounded me. Especially when we touched. It was just another way, on a long and rapidly growing list, that I was no longer human.

'Can you repeat yourself, please? I'm sorry.'

'You healed Adalia with your touch,' he said slowly, like I was a frightened child who didn't grasp the situation. That didn't feel too far from reality.

'Yes.'

'Do you understand what that means?'

I shook my head again.

'I shall explain it once more. Please focus, Scarlet. The sun will rise soon.'

'I will. Sorry.'

Gwydion didn't look entirely convinced. Nikolaos's thumb stroked along the line of my waist. A tender touch meant to soothe.

'Most practitioners can either heal or destroy, to varying degrees. Few can do both to the extremes you displayed by inflicting that level of damage and then remedying it.'

'Does necromancy fall under healing or destruction?'

Gwydion flashed a beguiling smile but didn't answer.

'It is a rare skill, Scarlet. What did you see when you went into Adalia's memory?'

I told them what I had witnessed.

Adalia stood up from the sofa abruptly. We all watched in silence as her figure disappeared into the kitchen. Kai and I exchanged a puzzled look. Nikolaos softly patted my side as an indication to move. I uncurled myself from him, and he stood in one fluid movement to go after his friend. The three of us waited for them in silence. I could feel the pull of dawn tugging me into a sluggish state, but we still had a little while before Nikolaos and I would have to flee from the day's awakening. Adalia returned with a ghostly trail of white down her face from where tears had dried in salted tracks on her cheeks.

'Forgive me,' she said, sitting back down in her original spot.

'Are you okay, Adalia?' I asked.

I wanted to reach out to comfort her, but the fear to touch her again after the pain I had caused was too intense.

'The man you saw, Scarlet'—Adalia turned to me, Nikolaos stayed standing rigid beside her—'is my late husband. Henry.'

'I'm sorry, I didn't know. I'd have been more tactful

if I had.'

Adalia was the one who reached out to me first. Her hand squeezed my own as if I were the one who needed comforting. I resisted the urge to flinch or pull away.

'No, please don't apologise. That day, in the shop, it was the last time I saw him before he died. It had always been a hazy memory, one I could never recall to the detail I wished. When you spoke about it just now, it all came flooding back, and clearer than before, as if you brought it forward in my mind. I suppose it must have always been there, I just needed your help to really see it again. For that, Scarlet, I am eternally grateful.'

Adalia's eyes distorted with tears quivering on her lower lids. And yet, despite the tears, the look she gave me was not one of sadness. It was a look blooming with love for Henry, loss at his passing, and gratitude that, for the first time in so long, she could recall their final moments once more. Seeing her look at me like that almost made the physical pain I had caused her to seem worth it.

'When I tried to open the door, my hand went straight through it. I couldn't pick anything up or communicate with Adalia,' I said to the room, but directed it towards Gwydion.

'You are witnessing the situation from an outside perspective, but it is not a physical circumstance thus, you are unable to alter it.'

'So if I opened the door it would change the entire memory for Adalia?'

'Yes.'

'What would happen if I did?'

'I do not know. There are those who can do such things, but they are unique. It is a dangerous phenomenon to alter and manipulate something as personal and as deep as a memory. I have heard of those who have lost control. It left them unable to withdraw from their subject. Others have been left stuck in a perpetual loop of remembering one event. It can cause damage to the brain of both the reader and the subject. The potential for detriment is far too high a risk.'

I shuddered at the thought of being stuck in a trance of one event for eternity. Or worse, evoking it in someone else and being imprisoned in their mind.

'As a vampire,' Gwydion continued, 'you will have an eternity to progress and govern your abilities. There is potential to grow and become puissant. I do not know of a time in history where a nymph has been turned into the undead. We simply cannot anticipate potential outcomes.'

'It is a historical anomaly,' Nikolaos added, suitably vague as usual.

'Unfortunately,' Gwydion said, looking out the window, 'night hastily slips away.'

Nikolaos and I barely made it down in time to miss the first beams of sunlight slice through the darkness. With my bed still tainted with the blood of Adalia, we sought refuge from the day in his bedroom.

I fell asleep perturbed with the knowledge no one knew the true extent of possibilities, even with their combined experience. But I also couldn't deny a part of me felt exhilarated. Unparalleled, we were all a part of history in the making.

)CHAPTER 13(

Two weeks of training had passed. The five of us worked for all hours of the night to explore the depth of my abilities. In that time, there had been another murder. This time the woman had been the same age as me. She'd recently been accepted to university to study law. In the paper, there was an image of her smiling next to the very contrasting photograph of her parents and younger brother grieving. The boy was only a few years older than Luke. Thoughts of my own family's bereavement were overwhelming, no matter how hard I tried to push them to the back of my mind. There was no time to get hung up on sorrowful sentiments.

We all sat gathered around the newspaper that lay upon the coffee table. A gruesome monochrome reminder that my murderer was still loose.

'It's been a while since he last struck. I wonder what triggered this,' Adalia mused aloud.

'We should not have lost focus,' Nikolaos said. 'We cannot let him strike again.'

Gwydion raised a white eyebrow so light it was almost invisible against his pale face.

'It is unlike you to be altruistic, Nikolaos. Has your little nymph plagued you with benevolence? How very human of you.'

Nikolaos looked as though he were about to respond, but I spoke first. 'Has Adalia not told you?'

Gwydion's disappointed eyes flicked to me; he had been looking forward to Nikolao's retaliation. The antagonism fell on deaf ears.

'He murdered me, too, Gwydion.'

'I see,' Gwydion said, musing over the news. 'Adalia failed to mention this.'

'I'm sorry, Lettie,' Adalia said. 'We've all been so absorbed with your ancestry and what that means for you as a vampire. I didn't tell Gwydion why you initially sought my help.'

I wasn't annoyed that Adalia hadn't enlightened Gwydion, although maybe I should have been. In some ways, I could understand how she'd forgotten. It wasn't her vengeance to claim, wasn't her priority.

Over the weeks we'd spent as a quintet, neither Adalia nor Nikolaos had left my side. They seemed to be waiting with bated breath to see what I would do next as if I were a magician with never before seen tricks. Gwydion kept more of a distance from me, but I would often look up to find glassy blue eyes watching me with an intensity that made my skin crawl. He had a perpetual cunning glint in his eyes like he knew something no one else did. It was a look I neither understood nor trusted. Gwydion's face was a painting of secrets, ones he wanted everyone to know he had but not what they were. Kai was the only one who didn't seem to want anything from me. He was just along for the ride with no investment in the situation. A slothful presence which was calming amongst the chaos. I think he was just happy to be a part of the action.

I could admit to myself that I loved Nikolaos. I felt confident enough in myself to know it wasn't just to do with our vampiric bond, although that definitely played a part. It seemed that I had a certain immunity to the intensity expected from the relationship between a master and vassal. In fact, Nikolaos being my maker was about the only thing still warranting that label. Masters were meant to have a certain degree of control over their vassals. It was more than just a label; vampires were essentially owned by their creators. Even if a vassal created their own vampires then those vampires would, technically, still belong to the original master. Like some macabre family tree of the undead. Short of killing them, there was almost no way to break free of that bond. And killing the master vampire could fatally weaken the vassal unless they were strong enough to withstand it. The only other way was for a master to release their vassal and sever the bond between them. Unsurprisingly, they were generally reluctant to do that.

All vampires have the ability to make more. Only some have the strength to be a master. At almost two-thousand-and-five-hundred years old, Nikolaos should have had that strength. If I tried to be a master, it would be a very different story. Then again, I was full of surprises.

Nikolaos did not have the control he was supposed to over me. We shared a bond which meant we were sensitive to one another's emotions and physical touch was mutually calming, but it didn't hold the depth it should. Neither Nikolaos nor I knew why that was, it was another vampire anomaly we didn't have an explanation for, but it felt like a good guess to say it had something to do with me being a nymph. I suspected Gwydion might have more theories on it than he was sharing, but it would be futile to push him. I wasn't into playing mind games with the demon.

I think that Nikolaos not having control over me the way he ought to bruised a part of his ego. It defied his vampire abilities, something he would almost certainly see as a weakness. I, however, was much more content with holding onto my independence.

'I was hoping that by getting more control over my abilities maybe I could use them to find the man doing this. To stop him. So far the police don't seem to be doing enough to help, matters need to be taken into our own hands. I just don't know how we can do that yet,' I said.

'Do you also wish to hunt down this man, Nikolaos?' Gwydion asked, humour dancing plainly over his face.

'*Oui*,' he replied cautiously.

'After all the blood spilt at your hands, all it took was one woman to tame you. Millenia of sanguinary ruthlessness is lost to a conscience. It is almost a shame.'

Over the past couple of weeks, tensions between the two of them had been running high, and I still didn't know what had happened between them to warrant it. Nikolaos had managed not to take the bait. Up until now. He had bitten his tongue for as long as he could. It had actually been a lot longer than I, and probably everyone else for that matter, had anticipated. Gwydion was finally going to get the retaliation he so desperately desired.

'I was made a monster against my will, Rune,' Nikolaos spat, temper swirling through the room like a storm of ice. I saw Adalia shiver as his words slashed through the air. 'At least I was not born one. Evil runs through your half-blood veins.'

The words carried like a tidal wave of resentment. Goosebumps trailed up my arms, chilling me to the bone. I glanced at Kai and Adalia to see the same had happened to them. I knew that it was expected of me to get the trickle of Nikolaos's emotions, but this was the first time it had affected others as well. Even Gwydion and Nikolaos both looked surprised at the physical bite his words held.

I stood between the two men with my arms reaching out on either side of me towards them. I was caught in the middle of two contrasting energies, both trying to fight their way through me to one an-

other. On one side, the stirring of Gwydion's necromancy pounded against me like a strong wind in a
cemetery, fighting to knock down all the graves with
its ferocity. On the other, a stream of icy rage beat
against me like a blizzard storm. I stood inert as their
two energies tried to break through my own barrier.
I could feel my fire trying to mediate them both; with
Nikolaos, it reached to soothe and caress, and with
Gwydion, it was a voice of reason like talking someone off a ledge. I knew Nikolaos was no match for
Gwydion. But I was. We'd proved that the first time we
met. So I focussed most of my attention on keeping
him away from the brunt of Gwydion's force.

Despite my best attempts to control the situation,
they were both relentless. I knew I wouldn't be able
to stay between them for much longer without being
overpowered by one of them. Or both. My own fire
was reacting to the disturbance. It felt my frustration
and fed on it. It fought against Gwydion's call to the
undead, leaving only his demonic aura trying to tear
through me to the real focus of his anger: Nikolaos.
We stood in silence for several agonising minutes.
Breathing was becoming harder and harder. It felt like
standing in the sand between a tidal wave and the
rocks of a mountain. If it carried on for any longer,
the wave would crash into me and cast me into the
rocks. It would drown me, would smash me into the
rocks until my body lay bent and broken. Nikolaos still
wasn't strong enough to cause enough damage on his
own, but the two of them combined was enough to
hurt me. I knew that. My fire knew that.

I couldn't take it anymore.

The combination of their power trying to tear
through me and my own clawing to break free was too
much. I felt like a balloon filled with too much hot air;

soon, I would explode and fall crashing to the ground.

'Enough!' I shouted.

As I did, without meaning to, my invisible fire carried with the words. The force of it flew from my hands in a wave of heat to destroy the frost of their energy, sending both men stumbling backwards. Gwydion caught himself against the wall, but Nikolaos ended up on his knees on the floor. When he looked up at me, his pupils had been consumed by pits of black, the beautiful green swallowed by oblivion.

I also collapsed to the floor. The air in the room had returned to normal so suddenly, it was hard to remember how to breathe regularly again without power crawling down my throat and choking me. Nikolaos stood back up, only his slightly ragged breathing indicating that something had upset his equilibrium, and held out his hand to me. I ignored the gesture.

'I'm going to bed,' I said, picking myself up from the floor.

My knees felt weak, but I forced myself to stay standing. The night was still young; dawn was a distant rumour in the darkness. We all knew that, no matter how drained I was, I physically was unable to sleep so early in the night. I didn't care. I needed to be curled up in my own space away from the catalysts of chaos with whom I'd shared a home with for the past two weeks. I could feel tears burning my eyes. I would not let any of them see me cry.

I fled. Running away from the choking tension in the room. From the flabbergasted looks of everyone in the room. From Rune's cunning smile as if I'd done something to make him proud. From the knowledge that there were so few parts of my humanity left, I didn't know who I was anymore. I ran with tears streaming down my face, flying like pearls of sadness in the air as I flashed from their watchful gaze.

I slammed the bedroom door behind me, sliding down the wood with tears still streaming down my face. I clutched my knees to my chest and buried my face into the fabric of my jeans. All I wanted was to go home. Like a child, I wished for nothing more than the comfort of my mother tucking me into bed and telling me it would be okay. I wanted to feel my father's lips against my forehead, his hands ruffling through my hair, as he said goodnight. I would do anything, *anything*, to be wrapped in the safe embrace of my parents' arms once more.

Letting go of my humanity to live as the undead, as a monster, had been monumental. Finding out I had never truly been human, never really had any humanity to lose, made life, death and everything in between so much harder. Everything I thought I knew about myself was a lie. I had spent twenty years floating through a distortion of reality. I yearned for the blissful ignorance I once had.

Several hours of solitude passed before Nikolaos knocked on the door. I could feel the sun beginning to rise, not quite dawn yet but soon. I didn't tell him to come in. We both knew I'd heard the knock, that I could sense him like a burning presence behind the door. I also knew he would come in whether I wanted him to or not.

Sure enough, the door opened despite my lack of response. I pulled the covers up over my head, clutching them with a tight fist so I was contained within a cocoon of silk. Silk is sensual but not soothing. It's a material made to be felt by bare flesh in the throes of passion, not to soak up the tears of a broken heart. Nikolaos took a seat at the end of the bed by my feet, the mattress declining under the weight of him. His hands ran up and down the fabric over my legs.

'May we talk, *ma chérie*?'

'If I say no, will you accept it?' I asked, voice muffled by the tear-soaked silk.

'I have asked the others to leave,' he said, indirectly answering the question he ignored. 'They will not return until you grant it.'

I didn't reply.

'Tomorrow, if you are well, I wish to tell you of my history with Gwydion.' He hesitated, and then added quietly, 'With Camille.'

That got my attention. I lowered the sheets, peering at him with half my face still concealed.

'Really?'

Nikolaos nodded. I could feel how hard it was for him even to say her name. The loss, regret, repentance, was such a burdensome weight of emotion it made me tear up once more. I held my hand out to Nikolaos. After a brief moment of hesitation, he laced his fingers through mine. I pulled him down so his head rested by my chest.

'Thank you,' I whispered into his hair, breathing in the warmth of him. He lay very still in my arms. 'Niko?'

A pale face turned up to me.

'*Oui, ma chérie*?'

'We have to put a stop to these murders,' I said, my voice quavering with unshed tears dangerously close to escaping. 'I just don't know how.'

'We will find him, this I vow to you.'

He sounded so sure it was almost enough to believe him.

☽CHAPTER 14☾

Day was swallowed whole by night; the world was lost to a blanket of darkness. The night was cloudless and clear, out the window I could see stars blinking in the sky like diamonds catching the light. Darkness brought something unexplainable and primal out in humans, a fear of the shadows and what they concealed. Humans feel safe during the day. Guided by the sun, they are free to roam and rule the lands. But when the sun gives way to the light of the moon, it's the monsters time to come and play. Nikolaos and I were two of those monsters. Of course, people didn't really believe in creatures of the night anymore, and not all monsters were imprisoned by the sun, but it was a feeling seemingly shared by most of the world. And feelings don't always adhere to logic.

When I came upstairs, the cottage was clear of anyone else. A weight that I hadn't even realised was there had been lifted. Even the air felt cleaner, easier to breathe in, without the constant humming of multiple peoples' power.

I felt a figure come behind me and leant back against Nikolaos's chest in response. For a moment, we stood in silence, staring out at the deep blue night sky. I reached back to take his arms that hung loosely by his side, wrapping them around me. I held his hands tightly against my sternum, stroking my thumb over the cold flesh of his fingers. Nikolaos leant his chin on the top of my head, softening ever so slightly in my embrace. His skin was so chilled it made the silk of his royal blue shirt feel warm.

'Are you ready, *ma feu?*'

We still had yet to feed, but I knew that wasn't what he was asking. Tonight I would finally be finding out why Nikolaos disliked Gwydion so, and what part Camille played in it.

'Yes.' I squeezed his hands, which were still wrapped between my own. 'Are you?'

I felt his chin brush against my hair in a nod.

After we had fed, Nikolaos told me there was somewhere he wanted to show me. We walked through the thick woodland, silver light from the moon slashed like a knife through the trees. We had been trailing through the forests towards the back of the cottage for miles before we finally stumbled upon the intended place. Britchelstone had at least three parks I knew of with a rockery, all of which were spectacular in their own way, but none compared to the one which Nikolaos lead me to.

The trees formed an erratic circle around a hill which steeped upwards suffocated by the embrace of nature. Royal blue columbines and soft, almost baby, pink dahlias bloomed amidst darker ones looking more like the colour of old blood in the night. Blue and pink hydrangeas grew wild and bushy around the edges of the space. But, mostly, roses a deep, pure scarlet rolled over the grass. The thorns of the roses glinted menacingly in the silver light. Tall, old trees of pine, oak, copper beech, and silver birch lined the hill. Some grew like soldiers standing tall to attention, others were curved and wispy and growing to the rhythm of the wind in its wildness. The moonlight illuminated the deep green of the grass appearing from under the trees and flowers. Large, ancient rocks looked out of place where they sat in between the grass as if they were too solid for the fluidity of the greenery. Grass rippled like an ocean of jade in the breeze of the wind.

The small hill was cut in half by a stream of water. Mossy rocks and stones stuck up from the water, obstacles in the constant flow. The water rushed and tumbled down to meet another, larger strip of water, so they created a T-shaped stream, disappearing into the trees. Four wide, flat stones, two to the left and two to the right of the downwards stream, formed a makeshift bridge onto the other side of the bank. I leapt from the last stone; my black boots were met with a cobblestone path. The pathway led to a stone bridge across the water that danced down the hill. Moss and weeds grew like green hands reaching from the ground between the gaps in the stone on the ground.

We crossed the bridge, following the path until it curved up into stone steps carved into the small hill. The steps were lined with big rocks and flowers of all colours in untamed masses like a bannister grown from the ground. The steps were curved up to the left and then stopped abruptly giving way to flat ground. A huge pine tree grew on the flat ground but other than that this area was free of any other plants. Even the grass had faded to nothing, just dry brown dirt. Ashes of the dry mud picked up in the wind getting carried away into the night air. Under the pine tree sat a weathered iron bench. It was positioned perfectly on the flat ground at the peak to look out over the forest with no trees disturbing the view.

We sat down, the bench was unexpectedly cold against my legs, with a canopy of pine above. Some of the green spikes fell in the wind, landing in my hair. Nikolaos reached over and, with a tender touch, pulled them from where they rested. I looked out at the lights of Britchelstone twinkling in the distance like the stars in the sky had fallen and landed somewhere far off on the ground. Behind the pine, the steam rippled. The constant sound of water lapping over the rocks like a clumsy lover was an echoing chime in the darkness, only the whisper of the breeze rustling the leaves of the trees to rival it. We were far enough out of the city for the air to have that cool, clean feeling that you only find in nature where there's no pollution to dirty it. The air that the whole earth once had until humans came along and started destroying it.

'This is beautiful. How did you find it? I never even knew this was here,' I asked.

'It is private land.'

'How come we're allowed on it?'

'It is my land.'

'But we've been talking for miles. How much land must you own?'

He ignored me. No point wasting breath on questions he didn't think were worthwhile, I suppose. A lot of what I said to Nikolaos was left without a response, but I was used to it by now. In fact, sometimes I would purposely ask him things I knew he'd think were obscure or ridiculous just to see if I got a response. It was a little game I enjoyed playing. So far, he hadn't caught on. At least, I don't think he had. Of course, it also meant I was getting better at knowing what was considered important questions. Knowing what to ask and how to phrase it wasn't always easy but, slowly, I was cracking the code. I had enough time to master it; time wasn't exactly limited to a vampire. Being a vampire made everything seem less frustrating and tiresome. Having eternity to grow and learn took away the burden of mortality; the fear of missing out, the constant rushing, the competition and striving to be better than the other mortals with whom you share your short stint on earth. I found that relief of pressure cathartic.

We sat in silence for several still moments. There

was an unfamiliar tension in the air, almost nervous. It took me a second to realise it wasn't me who was nervous. It rolled off Nikolaos in waves so strong I could feel my own anxieties brewing. The sound of the water and wind had become a sort of background noise, so I jumped when Nikolaos's lighter burst into life with a thunderous roar. He passed me a lit cigarette. I took it from him, breathing in the grey smoke like it was the air I needed to breathe. If neither of us spoke soon, the tension would get overwhelming. We were feeding off each other's nerves; two becoming one in shared trepidation.

It was Nikolaos who had invited me to talk so I wouldn't break first. I continued to let the silence grow until it was deafening, watching the rise and fall of his chest with each unnecessary breath. He only breathed like this, like a human, when something was making him tense, or if he was too caught up in emotions to remember. It was one of the few tells I had noticed Nikolaos had that something bothered him or made him emotional. I was learning to read him as though we were playing poker; any small tell, or detail, to give away his hand. The smoke trickled from his mouth and nostrils like a grey ghost escaping his body, swirling through the air until, finally, it vanished into nothing.

I broke first. 'Niko,' I said, touching his hand lightly with my own.

'I have known Gwydion for a long time,' he said, voice soft with nostalgia. 'Centuries, in fact.'

Nikolaos spoke, but he didn't look at me. I got the impression that, although the words were intended for me to hear, he wasn't really speaking to me; a soliloquy bitter with sorrow. I stayed silent, waiting for him to continue.

'We were first introduced over four centuries ago.

I was a different man back then. I had lived in solitude for many years. A shadow in the world, travelling mindlessly with complete discretion and never staying anywhere long enough to call home. I found myself in Paris, not for the first time, but there was something different in the air. A certain indecorous hedonism. Seducing to a vampire, it called to me. The seductress came in the form of another vampire, as you know, by the name of Camille.'

I stayed reticent, scared that if I spoke, it would deter him from continuing. This was the most I had ever heard Nikolaos speak. His accent got thicker with nostalgia, his voice becoming richer and velvety.

He continued, 'It was the first time I had let go of my inhibitions in aeons. She had the key to the cage of propriety in which I had imprisoned myself. I was introduced to a lifestyle of decadence. We lived amongst humans and vampires alike, the humans willing donors of their blood and bodies. In exchange, we would offer them our own blood. It is like a high to humans; they were addicts, and we were their drug. Though it was rare they would live long, like most addicts with a ceaseless supply. We would often wake at night to find human carcasses lining the floors. It was bothersome, but they were easily replaceable.'

Pensive eyes glazed with memories turned to me finally. He was looking at me, but he didn't see me, not really. He saw something far off from long ago, imprisoned in a trance of remembrance.

'Camille had me at her every beck and call. She was the most sadistic woman I have ever encountered with an unparalleled skill for cruelty. She had a penchant for keeping her victims alive as long as possible as she tortured them. She ruled her *ménage* with an iron fist tainted by blood and brutality. And yet, with me she was forbearing. There was a time when I thought we would spend eternity together.

'Opium and alcohol were used by many across the globe. Thus Camille would find servants to bring it to us in influx. She had always been a vicious woman but it changed her. For the worse, I would say. She would disagree. Her methods of torture became increasingly perverse. The house in which we resided would be plagued with relentless pleas of mercy as she chipped away at their bodies and souls. The only justification being her pleasure at their torment.

'Camille saw my age and strength as something of tremendous potential. With our combined skills and experience, she sought dominance and power. Of what, I do not know, I do not think she was certain either. Blood, sex, death. Love, hate; power thrives in the throes of all passions. And power is notoriously enamouring.

'I had been bewitched by a culture of blood, intimacy and stimulation. After so long of being alone, sex and companionship felt like love. I had an endless stream of companions, all of whom swore their adoration. I spent my nights riding a never-ceasing wave of thrill. An elixir of blood, death, sex, and devotion ensnared me. United with my growing affections for Camille, I was trapped by my own heart. Camille sought reverence through fear. I was the man sent to distil such terror, and then together we would bathe in their blood. With each passing night, her demand for tyranny would prevail, and I would find myself sent to undertake the most egregious of endeavours. It did not take long for my own sanity to abandon me.'

Nikolaos cast a glance in my direction. I could feel him searching my face for any hint of reaction, but I was doing the best impression of my stoic lover.

'There was not a waking second Camille and I were not feasting on a cocktail of substances, which would be enough to kill any human. Or most supernatural creatures, too, for that matter. We survived in body but not in mind. Alas, we had grown careless in our actions; our ways were gaining notoriety. The whispers of what we were had travelled further than neither Camille nor I could have anticipated. Gwydion, who resided in London, heard rumour of *Camille la Cruelle* and her coterie of vampires and human menials.'

'Camille la Cruelle. That means Camille the Cruel, right?' I asked, finally breaking my vow of silence. It didn't sound even slightly as silken when I spoke the words. I lacked the grace he had even linguistically.

'*Oui.*'

'Who coined that name?'

'I do not know. It would not surprise me if she spread it herself to exaggerate her prominence. Nonetheless, it was a fitting title, and it spread throughout lands.'

'Sorry I interrupted,' I said.

Nikolaos took another drag from the almost finished cigarette.

'I did not expect you to stay patient this long; it is unlike you to lack curiosity.'

'I'm just giving you a platform to speak without interruption. It's a rarity for you to open up, one I'm not ungrateful for.'

I was rewarded with a minute smile.

'I anticipate the questions you undoubtedly have,' he said mockingly. 'Rune travelled to us out of mere curiosity. Appearing whimsically on our doorstep, he passed no judgement, instead accepting our invitations of hospitality. He was not so fond of the women Camille purveyed, but it did not take long for a young gentleman to catch his eye.'

The desire to ask questions was so strong I had to

contain the urge to bounce up and down in my seat. Had the man been Kai? Was Kai over four-hundred years old? I resisted, letting him continue uninterrupted.

'It would be understated to say Camille was fascinated by Gwydion. A woman driven wild by her appetence for power now resided with a necromancer of demonic lineage and a vampire older than any she had ever encountered. To her, the possibilities were inexhaustible. It did not take long for her to realise her machinations of seduction would not work on Rune. The failed attempts, I suspect, damaged her amour propre, as well as being an embarrassment to witness. She quickly changed strategies requesting I be the one to bed him—'

'Did you?' I blurted out, interrupting him.

'*Non*,' he replied. 'I was fond of Rune, and he of I, but there was no sexual desire between us.'

'So you didn't sleep with him because you weren't attracted to him?'

'*Oui*.'

'Not because he's a man?'

That earned me a glance.

'I did not expect prejudice from you,' he said, but his voice held amusement.

'I'm not prejudiced, just surprised.'

'When you have lived as long as I, *ma chérie*, you realise there are much more important things to seek in a lover than gender.'

'You're a sapiophile?'

'I do not know this term,' he said, brows furrowed into a confused frown.

'Someone attracted to intelligence.'

He shrugged gracefully. 'If you wish to categorise me, then do as you see fit, but I have no need to define myself. May I continue?'

I nodded.

'Gwydion and I became close friends. Finding comradery amidst the chaos. Camille thought it best we flee Paris. Too much attention had been drawn to our escapades. We journeyed to rural France with an entourage of vampires and humans in tow. Gwydion joined us, but Camille had grown suspicious of our bond. Entwined in gluttony, he had become the balance I needed to see reason once more, much to Camille's dismay. After close to two decades of cohabitants, he was banished from our home. She forbade me from his company, but her clutch on me was weakening. She was losing her control over me, and Camille feasted on control as though it were blood. Realising this, she only intensified her endeavours. Every night I would awake to find increasingly beguiling men and women appearing at my bedside. They would beg for me to feast on them, not just their blood, but on them as a whole. They offered mendacious promises of gratuitous love and their souls. I had grown repulsed by Camille's malevolence but, alas, a lone mans' will is only so robust. I could not forsake my attachment to her no matter how much I wished to.

'I believe humans have the term to, fall off the wagon. I did not merely fall but plummeted. And Camille was there to catch me, condemning me to a harrowing fate. The two of us were monstrous in our carelessness. She had become so lost in her desperation to capture me her own hedonism drowned her. We were a capricious force of terror and pain.

'What we did not know was that pandemonium was brewing like a ferocious storm. The good people of Paris who had lost their sons, daughters, siblings, to the throes of vampires sought vengeance. This was a time of great superstition; suspected witches were still burnt alive at the hands of humans. Many of which were no less human themselves; conjecture was trial enough. They did not know we were vampires, but they suspected a play fouler than witchery. For this reason, a plan was devised to extinguish the life of all who resided with us.

'Rune had returned to Paris. He knew of the plan and travelled to warn us. I laughed in his face when he told me of their machinations. I had lost my sanity, my grasp on reality, to such an extent in the embrace of Camille that I truly believed we were Gods. Indestructible.' Nikolaos shook his head lightly. 'I was sorely mistaken.'

He continued, 'Gwydion obliged my instruction to leave and not return. Or so I thought. I spat those years we had spent together back at him as though they meant nothing. I was too blinded by the darkness that ate me away to see the light Rune offered me in his friendship.

'The people of Paris formed like a pack of wolves, travelling to burn our abode in daylight.'

'What about the humans?' I interrupted, again.

'The humans who lived with us were also considered witches. Thus, their murders were justified.'

'You don't really believe that justifies it, do you?'

'I believe to them it was enough. Their hatred for magick was enough to burn their own children alive. I do not waste my time questioning the logic of such formidable loathing.'

I frowned but stayed quiet.

'Gwydion endeavoured to travel with them and escape with me whilst I slept. When I awoke the following night, it was to find myself chained in silver and caged. Gwydion kept me there until I was relinquished of my addictions, but there was a rottenness inside me even he could not cleanse. The repentance for my sins against morality was enough to blacken my soul. I realised that Camille was not to blame for the suffering I caused. The only true power she had ever held over me was my love, or what I thought to be love at the time, for her. She had never been strong enough to overpower me if I had wished to desert her. The blood was ultimately on my hands and my hands alone. I do not doubt Gwydion got a great deal of pleasure from my suffering.

'He has left me cursed with an eternity of suffering. The weight of remorse at what I have done is....' He waved his hand through the air in search of a fitting word, finally settling on, 'Devastating.'

Nikolaos's eyes were distant. He was seeing a place that was not sitting in the rockery with me but somewhere of dark, evil things. I touched his hand lightly, bringing his attention back to me. Green eyes turned to me painfully slowly as if he were still trapped in a dream he couldn't entirely escape from. No, not a dream, a nightmare. Nikolaos's pupils had shrunk so small they looked like black pins lost in a sea of viridian.

'Niko?'

'*Oui, ma chérie.*'

I placed my hand on his cheek, turning his head to focus on me firmly.

'Why do you really hate Gwydion? It seems like all he's done is to try and look out for you.'

That caught his attention. A look not too dissimilar to anger flashed over his face but, underneath the anger, I could see something else. Pain. Nikolaos could be annoyed with me all he wanted, and I would nurture his frustrations as they were valid to him, but if he expected me to just lap up the tales of his heinous past without questioning it, he had the wrong woman.

'He let Camille die, Scarlet,' Nikolaos said, pulling my hand from his cheek. I let it fall limply onto the iron bench. 'I do not believe Rune did it from the benevolence of his heart. He wished to punish me. I now live forever with the knowledge that Camille is gone and I am still here. He has damned me to an eternity of mortification. A punishment bred out of malice, not love.'

He stood suddenly in anger, staring out through the forest, so all I could see was the hair on the back of his head slither against the blue of his shirt.

'You loved him, didn't you? Maybe not romantically but a deeper connection; intimate, without the intimacy. That's why it hurt you so much what he did.'

Nikolaos was silent.

'But love can be blinding, Niko. You've let your own self-hatred cloud your judgement. You resent yourself so much for what you did, you can't see that he truly cared about you despite it all. Cares for you now, too, probably.'

He turned to me then.

'You speak of love and intimacy like you know what they mean. What, in all your twenty years, gave you the profundity to lecture me?'

I rolled my eyes. The response seemed to knock some of the annoyance out of him like he'd expected me to concede or retaliate with my own anger.

'Okay, fine. I probably don't know enough about the situation for an informed opinion. But I'm still going to give you my uninformed one. Besides, I don't think you're telling me the whole story.'

A look not too dissimilar to amusement spread over his face, washing away the anger entirely.

'And why would you believe such a thing?'

'After over two-thousand years of life, it seems like a petty resentment. You're many things, Niko, but you don't seem like one to hold a grudge.'

'You do not seem too dismayed by my confession of torture.'

'I'm under no illusion that you've done a lot of nefarious, even downright evil, things, Niko. But you spared me the details. Did you do it on purpose?'

'Perhaps,' he said.

'Why?'

'Maybe, Scarlet, I do not wish for you to judge me.' He sighed a deep, defeated sigh. 'I thought I knew what love was when I was with Camille. Now I realise that it was something far more sinister. I condemned myself to solitude as punishment for my sins. Until I met you. I have already spent a hundred lifetimes alone, and what long lifetimes they have been.'

I stood so we were only inches apart. So close that if either of us took a deep breath, we would be touching. Nikolaos was that much taller than me that, even standing, I had to crane my neck up to really see his face.

'So what else aren't you telling me? I just can't believe this is all about some girl who's been dead for four hundred years.'

Nikolaos threw his head back and laughed. The sound trickled down my skin thick and sweet like honey. For the first time, the laugh did not hold sex or seduction but real, genuine humour. I preferred it. It felt real, like the glimpse of the old Nikolaos showing himself after years of hiding behind a perfected facade. The Nikolaos before he lost himself.

'Oh,' he said, still laughing, 'if only Camille were here to hear you call her *some girl*! You would have been far too stubborn to have fallen into her embrace the way I fell.'

'I would also never have done her bidding the way you did,' I said silently in my head, and then thought better of saying it out loud. Maybe after millennia of life in the shadows, alone and exiled from society, I too would have sought companionship and comradery with such desperation no matter the cost. I hoped I'd never had to find that out. I thought my strength of will would be strong enough to never give in the way Nikolaos had done to Camille, but I'd never truly had it put to the test. It can be very easy to look down on your high horse when you've never experienced that same debilitating pain that so often leads to such damning desperation.

To my surprise, Nikolaos planted his hands on either side of my face and kissed me. Deeply. It was a kiss we had never before shared. One of great passion and comfort, as though I were medicine he had to drink to completion. I realised that his fear had been of my judgment. That I would reject him the way he had rejected himself. I kissed him back just as deeply, putting all my passion and care for him into that kiss. When he pulled back, we were both breathy.

'I said there was a rottenness inside me that Gwydion could not cure,' he said.

'Yes?' I replied, voice a lot less steady than his.

'Have you ever questioned how someone as old as I lack the powers one would expect?'

I thought about the answer and then shrugged. 'It's crossed my mind. But you're the only other vampire I know so I don't really have much for comparison.'

'I once had a great deal of power, one paralleling my age. I grew so fearful of my own capabilities, I asked Gwydion to take it from me. It is not a feat many could accomplish.'

'But Gwydion could?'

'And he did.'

'Can you get it back?'

'No,' he said, almost too quickly.

'Do you want it back?'

He did not respond.

'Why are you so sure you can't, have you ever asked?'

'Rune and I have not spoken in centuries until you needed his aid. Adalia knowing him is nothing more than an unhappy coincidence.'

Somehow, I doubted that Gwydion meeting Adalia was that much of a coincidence. I got the impression Nikolaos didn't think so, too.

'That's what Gwydion meant when he said your strength is bolder now. I felt it last night, too, when you argued. Your aura has a stronger presence than before.'

Nikolaos raised one arched eyebrow at me.

'It took both him and me by surprise last night,' he said.

A realisation dawned on me.

'I've assumed my resistance to you as a master was because I'm a nymph. But maybe it's because Gwydion stole your power.'

'I suspect both play a part,' he said cautiously, face beginning to shut down again.

'Does that mean if you get your power back, then I'm going to be at your whim?'

'Somehow, *ma chérie*, I do not think you are so easily restrained.'

'I'm being serious.'

'As am I,' he said, almost woefully. 'In all honesty, I do not know. I have thought over this after the events of last night; if I am getting my powers back due to you, then I doubt my ability to use it to master you. Even if I wished to.'

It was my turn to sigh. I really, *really*, didn't like the idea of Nikolaos becoming a true master. I was only just beginning to find a more balanced dynamic in our relationship. It would knock me back fatally.

'I think we're going to need to talk to Gwydion about this. I have a sneaking suspicion that he knew about this already and just didn't say anything,' I said.

The sky above was melting from deep blue into dark violet. The stars looked even brighter somehow against the paler sky. Nikolaos and I had been engaged in the conversation so thoroughly we had both lost track of morning eating into the night. Nikolaos had given me a lot to think about. I was glad that when the sun rose, I would be able to sleep without mulling too much over the knowledge he had spent the good part of a century torturing people. And that was only one century I knew about out of so many. Yes, sleep sounded good. I didn't want to think about it anymore tonight; this was a problem for future Scarlet to deal with. Compartmentalising at its finest. Was it cowardly, or all I could do to stay sane?

)CHAPTER 15(

Four nights after the divulgence of Nikolaos's dark past, there was a knock on the door. I had only just come upstairs, still wearing the black silk pyjama set and with sleep tousled hair wild around my torso. I peeked out the window, catching a glimpse of ice and frost gracing the canopy of trees. We were barely into the first week of October, but already the autumn was giving itself over to winter like a submissive lover. The icy air whistled and whipped against the old windows of the cottage, making the glass shudder as if it were cold. A figure cloaked in red stood huddled on the porch. As though she had sensed me watching, Adalia turned her face up to me and smiled. It was a smile warm enough to melt away some of the wintery ice. Her woolly hat was too big for her head, slipping half-way down her eyes.

I opened the door. Adalia rushed in from the cold, running her hands up and down her arms. Her cheeks were so red they were only a few shades lighter than her maroon winter jacket. Nikolaos chose that moment to drift into the room. His hair was also an untamed mass from sleep and other less virtuous activities. He was still shirtless but had at least pulled on a pair of black trousers. A black velvet robe billowed around his body like a cape, framing the sculptured alabaster of his torso. Adalia looked at Nikolaos, and then her eyes flickered to me. I felt my own cheeks turn red.

I dressed and showered whilst Nikolaos entertained our guest. In my haste, I had just donned black jeans with a black t-shirt that fell halfway down my thighs. It had a red dragon climbing up the front looking ready to attack. My hair would take too long to dry, so I left it to hang wet and heavy down my body as I went to join them upstairs. With the water to weigh it down, my hair hung almost the same length as the top. Had it grown since I'd become a vampire? Surely not.

The two of them abruptly ceased talking as I entered the living room. I had a suspicion the topic of conversation had been about me. I slunk down beside Nikolaos.

'I've had an idea of how we might find your killer,' Adalia said, skipping all pleasantries to dive straight into business. My ears pricked. Before I had time to say anything, Adalia continued, 'It would require necromancy, which isn't my field of magick. I would need to discuss the plausibility of it with Gwydion, but I wanted to get your permission first.'

I saw Nikolaos tense minutely at his name. A reaction so small no one else would be able to see it.

'What's the idea?' I asked eagerly but with caution.

'I don't know if I should say without knowing if it's actually a possibility,' she said, with a sigh. 'I just didn't want to go behind your back if you weren't ready to continue working with us again.'

I was hyper with anticipation to know what her plan was. It was the first shred of hope I'd had that we may be able to hunt down my murderer. No matter how small the possibility it may work, I couldn't help but get my hopes up.

'Please ask him, Adalia,' I said, with surprising composure. 'There are some other things I want to ask Gwydion as well.'

Adalia slightly furrowed her brow at that but didn't comment.

'I will go there tonight, but I don't think we'll be able

to make it back in time for sunrise. As I said, I can't make any promises.'

I reached over the coffee table to place my hand over Adalia's. Staring intensely into her eyes, I said with sincerity, 'Thank you, Adalia.'

My eyes welled up with tears of hope and fear.

As promised, the following evening, as the day faded into dusk, three figures appeared on our doorstep. Gwydion's tall, sickly silhouette glided through the darkness like a serpentine shadow. The moonlight danced off the black cape hiding his figure so slashes of milk-white skin would appear in the blackness suddenly as he neared. He blended with the trees and the twigs eerily well.

Kai braved the frost in a white T-shirt that clung to him like a second skin. Muscles under his herculean arms rippled as he moved in a very inhuman way. Even in the distance, I could feel an intensity to Kai's energy which hadn't been there before. It undulated around him, emanating from his skin like waves of heat. It was an energy that felt very alive. Orange eyes shone like neon lights in the shadow as he stalked forward almost predatorily. Silver light gleamed on his perfectly smooth, bald head.

When Kai's foot was halfway onto the first step of the porch, Nikolaos's body rippled with an involuntary shudder. I could feel Kai's power riding over me; it was definitely stronger than before, but I had adjusted to the feeling of it. Nikolaos, however, hadn't felt it before. I cast my eyes up to where he stood beside me.

'You okay?' I asked.

He cast large-pupiled eyes down to me.

'*Oui.*'

I was about to reply when Kai bridged the gap between us and scooped me into a hug. His body was so hot I thought, if I weren't a fire nymph, the touch might have actually burnt me. The second our bodies touched his power rushed over me with such a ferocity I gasped. I heard Nikolaos echo the sound; he was close enough that Kai's arms brushed him as well. Kai's shoulders were just that broad. I scrambled free of Kai's grasp, pushing him a bit too hard, so we both ended up on the floor, staring at each other. He looked confused, hurt even, as if I had offended him. Goosebumps still lined my skin, making the hairs on my body stand so upright I thought they might pull off. I was shivering, and it wasn't from the cold.

Gwydion looked down at us both with an entertained smile playing over his lips. Adalia had stopped at the bottom of the stairs, distancing herself from the sudden influx of power, but her eyes were wide as she huddled further into the wine-red jacket.

'What was that?' I asked. 'We've touched before and that didn't happen.'

Kai's pure orange eyes watched me strangely. Gwydion held out a long, bony arm to point at the moon. I didn't know how someone could be that skinny and still have muscle. He looked like skin barely stretched over an abnormally long skeleton. The moon in the sky was edging perilously close to full. It shone like a huge, white halo in the sky emitting a blinding beam of silver light.

'It is five days until the full moon. Kai forgets himself,' Gwydion said, lowering his hand to hold out to his husband. Kai took it and stood, brushing off the back of his dark jeans.

'Sorry, darlin'.'

'It's okay, Kai,' I replied, smiling.

Accidents happen, and it wasn't like I had enough control over my own power to throw any stones at his. What had been surprising was Nikolaos's reaction. He'd felt Kai's energy as strongly as I had, if not more. That was certainly a new development.

'Therianthropes are tactual by nature,' Gwydion explained.

'What does that mean?'

'It means they are less decorous in relation to physical touch. It is not uncommon for them to greet through physical embrace.'

Kai had the grace to look embarrassed.

'I forget you ain't used to it,' Kai said, his voice was such a deep, resonating sound it was almost a growl. That rich honey tone I was so used to had been taken over by something animalistic. If he were human, I would think it would hurt to talk so throatily. Of course, he wasn't human. None of us were.

'Just be lucky it was a hug,' Gwydion said, baring his teeth in a disturbing grin. 'Some greetings are much more intimate.'

With that cryptic comment, he pushed past me still sitting on the floor and into the house with a confidence that was dangerously close to being arrogance. Nikolaos actually took a step back from Kai when he passed, not wanting another brush of that power again. With Adalia still waiting at the bottom of the steps, Nikolaos held his hand out to me. I watched Adalia as he pulled me to my feet, giving her a confused look. She looked tired but offered a weak smile and shrug.

'Did I offend Kai when I didn't hug him back?' I whispered to her, leaning in close enough I hoped he hadn't heard me from inside the cottage.

Adalia patted my arm gently.

'He'll get over it; you weren't to know. It can be a'— she paused momentarily, searching for the right word —'an adjustment getting used to therians.'

'But I've basically spent the last two weeks living

with Kai and I've never felt his power like this,' I said, rubbing my hands up and down my arms as if I could still feel the burning heat of his energy on my skin. 'I've even hugged him before. Lots of times, in fact.'

'Physical touch is very important to wereanimals. Kai doesn't have a shadow—a pack— like most so he controls himself better but this close to a full moon...' she let the words trail off.

I guess that made sense. As much as any of the arcane made sense to me. I hadn't meant to offend Kai, though. Adalia seemed to read my thoughts as though they were written on my face for all the world to see.

'If you were pack or another wereanimal it would be seen as a rejection. But Kai knows you don't understand any of this. Honestly, Scarlet, in the grand scheme of things do you really have the time and focus to be prioritising Kai's hurt feelings?' Adalia said, sounding uncharacteristically impatient.

She looked tired again. A certain lethargy clung to her, dragging her down. But she was right; we had a lot to discuss tonight. Panther customs were not on the agenda.

Nikolaos had disappeared into the kitchen, returning quickly with a crystal decanter. He poured the whiskey into five copita glasses. They had long, slender stems blooming into a bowl shaped like the bud of a crystalline tulip. All but Kai picked up their glass. He just sat there eying up the glass as though debating with himself if it was a good idea. Noticing me watching he looked up at me, his eyes an almost identical shade to the amber liquid, and grinned. The fangs of his canines seemed to look longer, sharper, somehow.

'This close to the full moon,' he said, 'I can't risk losin' control.'

The energy buzzed around him like a swarm of bees gearing up for an escape. I wasn't sure I wanted Kai to lose control. Not when he was like this.

'Has your convalescing left you well, Scarlet?' Gwydion asked in a way that made me think there was a right answer. It was a fifty-fifty chance, I suppose.

'Yes,' I replied cautiously.

Truthfully, more time would have been ideal to recoup my strength more thoroughly; however, the murderer wouldn't wait on my exhaustion, and I had some questions for Gwydion.

He accepted the partial-truth with a nod. 'Good.'

And so Adalia explained her plan to us. In theory, if Gwydion could raise one of the recently deceased victims with his necromancy, then I could use psychometry to read their memories and finally put a face to the unnamed killer. Theoretically, it wasn't the worst idea. But we didn't know what it would be like in practice. I did have some qualms with the plan. Most importantly, it would mean having to wait for him to strike again, which was far from ideal. But as well as that, in a deeply selfish part of my mind, the thought of having to relive that harrowing experience once again through the eyes of another victim, another woman, filled me with a dread so ferocious my body vibrated with it. I wasn't allowed to be selfish. Not about this, not when more lives were at stake. Which only left the problem of having to wait for another dead body.

'Waiting for him to strike again,' Gwydion said, playing devil's advocate with my moral dilemma, 'will mean more time to strengthen your skills. We do not yet know if this is even a possibility.'

'As plans go, I have heard worse,' Nikolaos added.

'I think we'll need to test the theory on another corpse,' Adalia said.

'We must take into consideration the very real possibility that to read the memories of one who has been murdered, especially in such a brutish manner, may come with some complications.'

'What sort of complications?' I asked.

'The memories will be distorted and emotional. It may make them unreliable,' Gwydion replied.

'So we could try just for it not to work?'

'It is a possibility. But is it not better to have tried and failed than do nothing?'

'Do you think it will work?' I asked, feeling suddenly apprehensive.

Gwydion gave a tepid shrug.

'I do not know. If the soul can survive the trauma enough to stay, at least relatively, unmarred then I believe it has potential. I cannot say for certain.'

'The night's still young. We have time to try it out tonight,' Adalia said.

Something rippled through the air coming from the direction of Kai. His eyes were staring out the window towards the moon shining almost blindingly in the sky. The hot energy washed over all of us, pulling out a reaction from everyone; we sat in a sudden mirage of power. Nikolaos and I shuddered in unison. I could feel his own energy curling over the surface of him like a gentle spring breeze. It wasn't strong, but it was there. And it hadn't been before. Gwydion raised an almost invisible eyebrow at Nikolaos.

'There's something else we want to talk to you about, Gwydion,' I said.

Gwydion turned those icy turquoise eyes to me and smiled a sinister smile.

'I have a feeling, young nymph,' he said, 'that I know what you wish to discuss.'

'Nikolaos told me about your past together.'

That got the attention of everyone. Adalia and Kai both turned surprised eyes to me. I guess no one had expected Nikolaos to open up. It had been a shock even to me.

'I am sure he has told you some fable of the truth.'

'No,' Nikolaos said harshly, 'I told her all. I do not wish to hide from my past any longer.'

'I cannot say I am not surprised,' Gwydion said, and then turned to look at me. 'I am more shocked by your acceptance, Scarlet. I question why you have not fled your master if you truly know his past.'

I shrugged and then gripped Nikolaos's hand. He was very quiet, very still, beside me. I think he was wondering the same thing.

'I guess you don't really know me.' I smiled at him. 'I don't spook that easily.'

The truth was, I was scared of what Nikolaos had done. It shocked and horrified me in a way which made my stomach knot with disgust. I just had to keep reminding myself it was four hundred years before my lifetime. I could sense Nikolaos's emotions; I knew the deep resentment he felt for himself, for what he'd done. The repentance had to count for something. Nikolaos hadn't gone into detail for this exact reason. We both knew that my own imagination would never be jaded enough to come up with any imagery close to what he had done. The worst I could picture would never be as abominable as the reality. I knew that, and I wanted to keep my blissful ignorance. Because I knew that if Nikolaos had told me in detail the sins he had committed, I wouldn't be sitting here now with his hand laced through mine.

'Perhaps not,' Gwydion replied. 'Ask your questions child, if you think we have this much valuable time to squander. I'm sure the murderer will wait on your curiosity.'

I didn't appreciate the sarcasm, but he had a good point. I sighed.

'You're right, this can't be the focus until he's caught. But I just want to know one thing for now.'

Gwydion nodded his head in encouragement, sending the white tips of his hair slithering over his shoulders like albino serpents.

'Is this why Nikolaos doesn't have the control over me he should? If he gets more powerful, will he get more control?'

'That is two questions. However, the answer to both is the same: I do not know. I have suspected that your lineage has played its part in creating a natural resistance to the dictatorship of master over vassal.'

'You didn't think to tell us?'

Gwydion shrugged, again. There seemed to be a lot of that going around tonight.

'I do not see why I would waste my words on something I merely suspect. If I told you every time I have an idea not necessarily plausible, we would never have the time to do anything.'

Gwydion and Nikolaos were so much alike at times it was eerie. I could see how they both were once so close. I could also see how easily they would hold onto resentment for one another. It would be like arguing looking in a stubborn mirror. They were both frustratingly dogmatic.

'I—we—have more questions. But not tonight.'

'Nikolaos's power may cease to augment. If this is not the case, then I will do what I can to answer your queries.'

That would have to do. For now.

'We will await you at Bear Grove Cemetery. Feed and then join us. The night dwindles,' Gwydion said.

He stood and walked out the door with the other two in tow.

Bear Grove Cemetery is spread over twenty-one

acres of land. Opened in 1857, it is one of the oldest cemeteries in Britchelstone, and also one of the only ones which still has spaces for new graves. After the war, a lot of cemeteries in the area got too full or were opened specifically as memorials. The grounds close to the public in the early evening; when we arrived at nightfall, there was very little chance of us being disturbed.

The entrance to the cemetery is a large, black wrought iron fence with *Bear Grove Cemetery* twisted into the metal and painted gold. Adalia and Gwydion were waiting for us outside the gate. Adalia sat up on one of the tall brick planters blooming with more weeds than actual flowers. The flowers that did make it through the strangulation of weeds were light-pink, yellow and baby-blue. Gwydion stood tall and straight just a bit in front of her watching us approach.

A pub towards the end of the road to the left of us filled the night silence with drunken chatter. A punter stepped out into the street, bringing the sound of heavy rock out with him through the door. He spared a glance in our direction as he planted his pint on one of the wooden tables, the cigarette between his teeth bobbed in his mouth as he nodded in our direction. I turned my head away. As far as the good people of Britchelstone were concerned, I was supposed to be dead. Getting noticed wasn't on the plan for tonight.

'Where's Kai?' I asked.

'It is too close to the full moon to be around the freshly dead,' Gwydion replied.

I could feel his power thrumming in the air more potent than usual. It called to me in a deceptive, secretive way. Even his words seemed to hold a new enticement to them.

'Are you testing me again?' I asked him.

Gwydion looked confused for a moment and then grinned at me.

'I am a necromancer; the energy of the dead surrounds us. It cannot be helped.'

We couldn't risk entering the graveyard until there were no people around to witness the intrusion. Finally, the man from the pub flicked the butt of his cigarette onto the ground, downed the remnants of his pint in one swig, and opened the door to go back inside. Once again the night was suddenly awash with the beating of drums and guitar music. When the door closed behind him, it swallowed the sound whole, making the night seem almost too quiet all of a sudden.

With the streets clear, we all hopped up onto the planters and walked up to the iron fence. The trees behind the fence loomed above hiding us in shadows so dark they seemed solid. Other than Adalia's jacket, we were all in black. The shadows consumed us into their embrace and made us invisible.

Gwydion and Nikolaos were the first to jump the fence. Nikolaos vaulted it with his usual grace and Gwydion, being almost two foot taller than me, was elongated enough that the drop-down seemed a lot less for him than anyone else. Adalia went next. She climbed up with her feet flat on the wide tops of the gate, using one hand to steady herself on the thick spikes and the other to hold Nikolaos's hand. I followed in her footsteps, lining the soles of my boots firmly on the metal and clinging onto the metal spikes on either side of me in an awkward crouch. Gripping Nikolaos's outstretched hand, I hopped onto the concrete ground beneath. As I touched the ground, my balance went. I ended up landing on my backside, looking up at the three looming bodies in front of me. Nikolaos didn't say anything, he just held his palm out to me to help me stand, but the look he gave was enough. Both he and Gwydion were silently laughing at me. I stood without his help.

The concrete path was long and wide through the cemetery, wide enough for at least two large vans to drive comfortably abreast whilst still having enough space on either side for pedestrians to walk. About halfway up, the path narrowed into one only suitable for people on foot, half of the concrete being consumed by an old stone chapel. Flowers and bushes grew around the stone, climbing up the walls. There was even a little pond beside it with water lilies and broad green leaves floating on the water top. In daylight, it was probably very serene. Not that I would ever get a chance to see it. That was a sad thought. Eventually, I had to come to terms with never seeing daylight again; I thought I was doing okay mourning the sun, but then small things like this would remind me and I would feel a sense of loss all over again. I sighed; the sound made all three of them turn to face me. I waved them off. It wasn't the time to get pouty over being undead. It felt disrespectful whilst trailing through a graveyard. I may be dead, but I was in better shape than any of the other deceased people here.

We continued up the narrower stone path. The flowers surrounding us had been consumed by the beginning of frost. The stems were icy and contorted with wilted petals dying in the grass below. Brown, decaying leaves flooded the ground. The graves looked like stones growing from a foliate sea with only the frost slowing the death of the shrubbery. Bare branches loomed from the trees above us like brown, deformed bones. The air was thick with desolation. I could almost feel Gwydion's energy growing with each grave we passed, every crumbling headstone building his power to overwhelming levels. Eventually, we stopped at a fresh grave.

The headstone was white marble. It looked stark and out of place in the river of old stone and debris. Brown earth was overturned in a rectangle about six foot long in front of the marble. The grave was very fresh—as in, buried today fresh. I felt a twinge of guilt that we would be upturning the corpse of someone whose family and friends still freshly bewailed. Had their tears even had time to dry yet? Gwydion took a deep breath, eyes closed and face peacefully slack.

'This one,' he said, 'will suffice.'

The headstone read:

Gillian Grace Withnail

1978–2019

Loving mother and wife, gone too soon

Lilac coloured hydrangeas, pink and white gerberas and darker purply-pink chrysanthemums formed a wreath spelling 'mum'. It leant against the white marble a bright, beautiful and morbid reminder of the life that had been lost. Everything suddenly felt much too real. The cold autumn air was harder to inhale. Death turned the air thick and stale.

Gwydion produced a knife and a candle from seemingly nowhere. He handed the taper candle to me. It was white and untouched. Our skin accidentally brushed as he passed it to me, sending a shiver up my spine.

'Stand back unto I say otherwise,' Gwydion instructed.

The hilt of the knife was made of dull, red stone. There were four carvings with two on either side. One side of the handle was carved into a sort of trident. Below it were two long triangles on their side with the top points touching one another, similar to an infinity symbol or a crudely drawn hourglass. On the other side of the hilt was the same angular symbol below a geometric 'C' shape made by two joining lines

'What are those symbols?' I asked.

Gwydion opened his eyes with a look that wasn't friendly.

'They are runes,' he said.

'What do they mean?'

'These two,' Gwydion said, pointing to the trident and triangles, 'are Algiz and Dagaz. They mean life and dawn.' He flipped the handle. 'This is Merkstave Kenaz and Dagaz. It means destruction, darkness and dusk. They represent the two sides of necromancy. The light of reanimation and the darkness of death.'

'So necromancers use runes?'

'No, not commonly.'

'Gwydion studied rune magick,' Adalia added, from behind me. Her voice was so sudden I jumped. I guess I was nervous tonight.

'That's why you're called Rune,' I said, making it a statement. 'What is the hilt made of? It's a lovely colour but I haven't seen a stone such a pure red before which is this matte.'

'Is she always this curious?' Gwydion asked rudely, looking over my head at Nikolaos who was standing at my back. I felt him shrug behind me.

'*Oui.*'

'Very well.' He looked back at me. 'It is cinnabar, or dragon's blood; it represents manifestation and immortality. The metal is lead. Lead is malefic; the carrier of immortality and destruction. It symbolises both life and death. May I proceed?'

'I won't interrupt again,' I said.

'That would be preferable. Light the candle when I say,' he instructed, adding hastily, 'Please.'

Both his hands wrapped around the hilt. The moment his long, sickly fingers curled over themselves, I felt the connection he made to the knife and his power like a jolt of electricity through my body. I gripped the candle so hard my knuckles mottled. I forced myself to loosen my grasp, worried that the wax may snap under the pressure. The weight of his energy pulsated against me, making it hard to breathe. I could feel it like a second heartbeat in my body thudding wildly. It took me a moment to realise it wasn't his power causing that sensation. I could feel the pounding of Nikolaos's heart in my own body like we were one form. Bound by death, love and magick. I gasped and felt him gasp too as Gwydion's power washed over us in bountiful waves of power. My own energy fought against his necromancy. It drew on my bond to Nikolaos for strength. We were caught in a triad of power. I struggled to gain control of myself and let the fire in me breathe through Nikolaos and me as protection. He gasped again, but I didn't. I gulped down his new, more substantial energy. Breathed it in like it was air and used it to shield us both.

'Most necromancers require a living sacrifice to perform their magick. Rune is both old and powerful enough not to need death. His power bypasses the ritual most require. A lone drop of his demonic blood holds enough influence to raise one hundred bodies.'

The words washed through my mind like a silken wind in Nikolaos's voice. A seductive intrusive thought that was so unexpected it made me dizzy. I whipped my head around to see Nikolaos smiling at me. He raised a slender finger to his upturned lips.

'They cannot hear me, ma chérie. I am speaking to you as your master.'

I wasn't sure how to respond telepathically to Nikolaos. I tried closing my eyes and sending him the thought as a mental letter.

'Could we always do this?' I asked silently.

'Non. Few master and vassals have this particular fac-

ulty. It would be more expected after a long period of connection.'

'Then how?'

'Gwydion's necromancy may have expedited the process. I expect it may have something to do with my own power returning. Our situation is sui generis.'

'It could be useful.'

'Oui,' he replied.

'Are you ready?' Gwydion asked, his voice breaking me out of my trance. I nodded.

In a precipitous, harsh movement Gwydion sliced the lead blade down the palm of his hand. Blood turned black by the darkness poured in a steady stream from the wound. With closed eyes, Gwydion began to mutter something in an ancient language long lost to history. The words beat against my skin like the wings of a bird trying to escape. I didn't know whether I wanted to swat the power away until it was no longer touching me, or move closer towards Gwydion and let the wings of his energy engulf me. Without realising, I had taken a step closer to Gwydion and the grave. I felt a hand wrap around my shoulder. Nikolaos pulled me back into his arms. We were whole once more, and just like that, the power was less intense.

'I know it is burdensome. Despite his many, many, faults there is no denying Rune's power.'

'Light it now, Scarlet,' Gwydion said.

I closed my eyes, gripping the candle tighter, and willed the wick to light. When I opened my eyes, an orange flame sneered at the blanket of darkness that hung like a weighted cape over us.

I focused my eyes back on Gwydion and the gravestone. The mound of earth shuddered by his feet. The blood from his hand soaked into the dirt, turning patches of it black. The earth continued to shake and ripple before my very eyes. The brown began to part like the ocean around a ship, and the ground regurgitated a corpse. It was like the flow of dirt spat out the body before settling into unanimated stillness below the corpse once more. It looked like what it was: magick. Confusing, illogical, wondrous magick.

Gillian lay pale and unmoving on the bed of dirt. Her long, brown hair was tied in a plait that fell over her chest. Her body was clad in a white sheath dress with three white buttons over the chest area. The fabric was so pristine it made the white of her skin glow with a green tint. Makeup had been applied lightly to a gaunt face. It must have been an open casket funeral. Gillian's fragile body remained very still like she was slumbering peacefully in the middle of her grave. If I hadn't known she was a corpse, I wouldn't have thought she was anything other than a woman lying serenely in the dirt.

The thought was wiped away when her green eyes fluttered open. The eyes were too wide as though the eyelids weren't doing their job at protecting the eyeball, and the skin and bone around the eye couldn't contain the weight of her eye the way it was intended. There was no life in those eyes. They were dull and glazed and almost unreal like the eyes of a realistic doll. That's what she looked like; a peaceful, blinking doll.

'This, ma chérie, is your very first zombie.'

)CHAPTER 16(

Gwydion knelt down beside the blinking corpse. He used a long finger to catch some of the blood still wet and gleaming on the lead blade, and then stuck the bloodied finger between Gillian's thin, rose-pink-painted lips. Blood was lapped up at increasing speed by a dry, cracked tongue. Eyelids stopped fluttering, wide eyes focusing on Gwydion as though he were the only thing in the world that mattered. To her, at that moment, he probably was. He stood, pulling Gillian by the hand with him. Her bones cracked as she stood. Her head flopped to the side as though her neck wasn't strong enough to hold up its weight. A scarlet-stained tongue licked the remnants of the blood around her mouth. Slowly, her spine and neck straightened with more cracks. Gaunt cheeks filled out, and the lifeless glaze of her eyes was replaced with a joyous light which hadn't been there before.

Staring at Gillian's soft face and figure made me realise she must have been beautiful in life. The wrinkles around her mouth and eyes showed her age, but they were the lines of someone who had spent more of her life smiling than frowning. As Gwydion's blood breathed life into the corpse, it also paved the way for something else. Fear. She looked at us all with confusion and panic so plain on her face she may as well have had it branded on her forehead for all the world to see.

'Do you know your name?' Gwydion asked, in a surprisingly tender tone. Gillian, who had still been clutching on to Gwydion's hand, dropped her grasp on him. She looked down at the hand as if it had been touching something corrupt. Crescent moon imprints were filling with blood on Gwydion's hand where her brittle nails had dug into his flesh. I could see her uncertainty, the internal conflict she was facing fighting over her expression. She gazed at Gwydion like he was God himself standing before her, but even under that devotion was overt fear and fierce will. As Gwydion's zombie, she was at his command, but she didn't have to like it.

'G-Gill,' she spluttered clumsily, each word getting caught in her throat. Her voice was hoarse and so dry, it sounded painful.

'Do you have a last name?'

It seemed an odd question. We had all seen her gravestone; we all knew what her last name was. This may have been my first zombie, but it wasn't Gwydion's, so I just had to trust this was a part of his process and served a purpose.

'W-Withnail. Gillian Withnail,' she replied.

Gillian sounded surer of herself as if saying her name brought back some of the personality she had lost to the grips of death. Gillian's eyes stayed on Gwydion's tall frame as he stepped away from her to come towards me. He was careful not to touch me with the live candle still in my grasp. Bending down, he whispered, 'She is sentient. Take heed, zombies suffer from malaise and are quick to agitate.'

'Is she ready for me?' I asked, staring all the way up into Gwydion's ash-blue eyes.

He nodded, stepping back so Gillian and I could stand in front of one another unobstructed. Her eyes stayed on Gwydion; I cleared my throat to get her attention. Murky green eyes stared down at me reluctantly. She looked surprised as if I had just suddenly appeared. Gillian was a similar height to Adalia, so she had to crane her neck down to really see my face.

'Hey Gillian,' I said softly, with my best affable smile. 'I'm Lettie. Do you mind if I call you Gill?'

The look she gave me was suspicious. Gillian fidgeted nervously, picking at the skin around her nails. Dried flakes of skin were peeling off, fluttering to the ground below like fleshy snowflakes. The skin around her nails was pink and raw. If it hurt, she didn't show any indication. Gillian's eyes kept wandering off behind me to where Gwydion stood. Without thinking, I used my free hand to reach out with the intention of bringing her focus back to me. I had a moment to think of how cold and clammy her skin was, like uncared for leather, and then the world around me faded to somewhere strange and unfamiliar.

Grey fog swarmed around the room, blinding any peripheral vision I may have had. I was standing in a kitchen; out the window, I could see a small lane with a wall on the other side, and wooden doors built into the crumbling chalk and stone. Fresh green vines clambered up the stone weaving their way through the bumps of the wall. A part of me recognised the lane, it was one of the smaller residential roads which veers off directly from the main street into town. The houses were all two stories and small with low ceilings like old-fashioned English cottages, but, despite their size, the prime location made them cost a pretty penny.

The kitchen was light and airy; pale-yellow walls, off-white curtains and light-wood counters gave the illusion that the room was larger than it was. The front room and dining room were in the same space as the kitchen, with only island counters to divide the kitchen from the rest of the room. There was no hallway or downstairs bathroom, just the front door beside the television to the far right of the space and a staircase opposite. All the walls were done in the same fresh, spring yellow. A white tablecloth was strewn across the pale oak dining set with a bouquet of daffodils housed in a glass vase on top. In front of the television was a cream sofa with yellow and green cushions lined up neatly. Between the sofa and television was a coffee table in the same style as the dining set with a collection of unopened letters strewn over the wood. That which had the potential to be cramped and claustrophobic managed to be instead cosy and bright.

I walked over to the eggshell-white fridge with uncertain footing. The fridge was sparkling clean, with four pictures held in place by animal-shaped magnets. On closer inspection, I could see that three of the four pictures were drawings done by children. One was of a blue, scaled dragon breathing red and orange flames. *James, age 7,* was in the bottom right-hand corner. The middle drawing was a clumsy river scrawled over with turquoise pencil, and bouquets of yellow flowers lining the river bank. The artist in question was a two-year-old called Lucy. The final drawing was shockingly good considering Ava, who I assumed was the eldest of the Withnail children, was only twelve years old. Her style was refined with neat lines and perfectly contained colours forming an anime-style school girl with long brown hair and large dark eyes.

The fourth image on the fridge was a photograph. Three children and two adults stood in the middle of a field under a grey sky. Despite the dull weather, they all grinned at the cameraman, their faces so joyous it gave the still photograph life. Gillian held a toddler on her hip. The little girl had curls a perfect honey-brown and round eyes gleaming with elation. All of them stood in muddy wellies and colourful rain jackets. A perfect, happy family. Seeing Gillian like this made my chest tight. My sorrowful musings were interrupted by a sound behind me.

A man in his mid-forties clambered through the door with a golden-haired toddler clinging to his leg. Wrapped around her father's leg, she let out a dulcet giggle. It was a mellifluous sound that chimed through the air like a flute spreading joy wherever it touched. The father was balding and greying. As his hairline receded, his waistband expanded but there was a jubilant air to him that chased away the ageing and made him seem youthful and charming.

Clinging to his back like a monkey was a young boy with hair a darker, but no less rich, brown. His arms were so tight around his father's neck, it looked like he was choking him, although that didn't stop them all from laughing. The last through the door was a girl who looked older than in the photograph on the fridge and much more sullen. She slammed the door behind her using her foot and leant against it with crossed arms and a look of scornful embarrassment at her family. The girl must have been about fourteen, and teenage angst was kicking in with a vengeance. I remembered what it was like to be fourteen and fueled by hormones and unjust vexation but soon this girl, young woman, would also be half orphaned. Just from looking at her, I knew that the loss of her mother would destroy Ava in a way the other children wouldn't experience. A teenage girl lost in a confusing world needed her mother, and soon that would be ripped from her. Watching her pouting face trying so hard not to join in the laughter with her parent and siblings reminded me of the women who had fallen victim to my murderer. Not that long ago we'd all been the same sulking teenager unsure of everything and feeling angry about it all, and now all except me lay extinguished in the dirt like her mother.

Gillian came rushing down the stairs to greet her family. Her green eyes were red and puffy with white streaks down her flushed cheeks from where she had been crying. Still, when she saw her beautiful clan, her face lit up with pure adoration and pride. Those green eyes, the same shade as her eldest daughter's, held a kind intelligence. A look of knowledge and acceptance like she knew the world could be a dark place, but she would still search for the good in all of it.

Ava noticed the phantom tears before her father did. The faux-anger gave way to concern and loss. I got the impression Gillian didn't show weakness in front of her children very often. She was a rock they could rely on who took their pain in her stride and built them up to be resilient and empathetic. So why was mummy crying?

Gillian walked into the kitchen, turning her back on the family to wash an already clean mug in the sink. We were so close I could have reached out and touched her. Narrow shoulders shuddered with the attempt not to shed any more tears. Not now, not in front of her children. The people she had sworn to always be there for; to always protect.

It didn't take long for the husband to catch on. He placed his son gently down on the floor, ruffling his dark hair with a large, square hand. Ava seemed to know what she needed to do. Swallowing her own concern, she forced an amiable smile and led the toddler and young boy upstairs away from the distress. The moment the door closed upstairs, Gillian turned around with a blotchy face soaked with tears. She collapsed into her husband's arms, clinging onto his body like he was the last surety she had left. He wrapped those big, fleshy arms around his wife in a solid embrace.

'Ed,' she whimpered, into his chest. His hands smoothed over the back of her hair, lips whispering quiet promises of safety into the top of her head. 'The doctor...' She hiccuped, unable to finish the sentence.

The unuttered words hung heavily in the air. I watched as understanding dawned, his face crumpling into a distraught picture. My own eyes were damp with unshed tears as his began to fall. Ed buried his head further into the nest of his wife's hair. For a moment they stood in anguished silence, holding one another tightly, bodies shaking with their silent sobs.

Grey fog began to take over my vision. The sorrowful scene was washed away by storm clouds until all I could see was darkness. The last thing I heard were the lover's shuddering, heartbroken breaths...and then nothing.

I blinked up at the star littered darkness. The grass was cold and damp under my back, the frost which had melted under my body soaking my top with icy water. My cheeks and eyes were still moist with tears. Gwydion's face appeared above me so close I had to blink a few times to readjust my vision. His blue eyes were burning with scorn.

'You broke my zombie.'

It was my time to scowl up at him. I sat myself up, forcing Gwydion to either step back or risk me head-butting him. He moved out of the way. Sitting up wasn't much of an improvement. Now I could see Gillian's lifeless corpse lying crumpled in a heap beside me. The pure white of her dress had been stained with mud and Gwydion's blood. All that life had vanished, and she looked definitely dead now.

I fought back the tears, but seeing the corpse of a loving wife, mother, and friend lying broken and contorted was overwhelming. I lost the battle; tears fled my eyes like a river of misery breaking free of the dam.

)CHAPTER 17((

One zombie a night meant, after ten nights of tireless working, we had raised close to a dozen zombies. I was learning to read the memories with less jarring effects and in a way that didn't drain me or leave Gwydion's zombies lying in boneless heaps by their graves. Gwydion and I had fallen into a natural flow with one another, and I couldn't deny that by day ten, I felt significantly more confident in my abilities.

A quickly realised inadequacy in the plan was that, although I had no trouble going into the memories of the recently deceased, we had no way of knowing what that memory would be. It was an interesting discovery of my power, but not very helpful when it came to catching the killer. Adalia, who was full of bright ideas, suggested Nikolaos tried alluring the zombies. As Gwydion's zombies, they were expected to do as he commanded but instructing them to remember something didn't necessarily mean they could or would. Zombies are surprisingly disobedient; it's like they try to hang on to the final shards of their independence with such a ferocity it makes them stubborn and unobliging. So Nikolaos had started to allure the walking dead enticing one specific memory from their past for me to read.

The memories I found myself in were always rapturous; a first kiss, wedding, once in a lifetime experience that had brought the zombie pride and joy. Nikolaos never admitted it, but I think he allured the zombies into the more pleasant memories to make the experience less harrowing. Zombies seemed to fixate on the negative if Nikolaos didn't encourage something less mournful; there are only so many times you can see someone's darkest fragments of life before it becomes too distressing. I had made a mistake getting engrossed in Gillian's family. They had reminded me too much of my own family; Ava had been too close in age to the latest victim, and it had bothered me so much I had been fearful to attempt reading another zombie. Luckily, or maybe unluckily, Gwydion and Nikolaos were both experts in apathy, and I was beginning to understand why putting up barriers between the world and me wasn't necessarily a bad idea. I was either going to need to toughen up or put up an impenetrable self-defence of the mind.

Gwydion and I's efficient duo flowed into an equally effective trio. The three of us drew from each other's power like we were feeding off it, and it had become very complimentary. I wasn't the only one with newfound skills; Nikolaos was also evolving into someone of more energy depth. Even Kai, who had rejoined us once the full moon had passed, was picking up on Nikolaos's power evolution. He seemed more uncomfortable around Nikolaos now. Gwydion, Nikolaos, and I had agreed to discuss his growing power more in-depth once the murderer had been caught, something we were growing increasingly confident would happen.

On the eleventh day, our training was put to the test. Nikolaos and I arose for the night to find three eagerly awaiting faces. The air was tense with mournful anticipation.

'I might as well get you a key if you are to break in every night,' Nikolaos said disdainfully.

Gwydion, looking unamused, tapped his finger against a copy of The Talus which lay waiting on the coffee table. It had today's date written above the headline detailing another murder. The murderer had been affectionately named *The Britchelstone Barbarian*, which I, personally, felt lacked a certain decorum.

We all huddled solemnly around the paper. There was a photo of Detective Martin Todd, the lead detective on the case, looking abashed and tired beside a team of police from the Specialised Crime Unit. Todd wanted to assure the public that, whilst they currently had no leads, they were working on this case as a top priority. The reporter in The Talus had not tried to hide their scathing opinion regarding the abilities of the task force. I couldn't really blame them for not staying impartial. People were scared, and fear is quick to turn to anger. With no perpetrator to point the finger at, the lead detective had become the easiest target for peoples' unease. The latest victim, Sophie Jenson, was one year older than me and had been murdered in the same brutal way. The Britchelstone Barbarian suddenly seemed a lot more fitting a title.

Unlike in our training, we wouldn't find this body in a graveyard. Instead, we were making a trip to the local morgue. Becoming a vampire had meant adjusting to very abnormal situations becoming my new normality. Living solely off human blood, my arcane entourage, and watching Gwydion use his necromancy to reanimate the dead wasn't exactly how I had planned to spend the first year of my twenties. Still, when Gwydion told me we were going to have to go to a morgue for this particular ritual, the strangeness was overwhelming. I was almost beginning to forget what an average night had been for me before becoming a vampire. Something very dull comparatively, but I'd take mundane and monotonous over the macabre. Of course, to go back to my life before ludicrous morbidity took over would also mean having to give up Nikolaos, Rune, Kai and Adalia. Put like that, the tedium of human life seemed less appealing.

The seaside city of Britchelstone has one medium-sized hospital at the top of Elm Hill. It seems ridiculous to even consider Britchelstone a city considering the size. In fact, we'd only been given city status in 2001, and most adults still didn't accept it as one. I had only been to Britchelstone hospital twice in my life: the first time had been when I was born twenty years prior, and the second when I had dislocated my shoulder playing with my dad as a little girl. Other than that, I had always been healthy and managed to stay clear of hospitals for most of my life. Even when I had died, I'd not ended up in one.

It was three a.m, and the streets were deadly quiet. The waning moon was hidden behind a blanket of tenebrous clouds swallowing the moonlight and stars in their solid darkness. Streetlights were dotted along the road offering a faint orange glow which cut through the darkness in small, futile segments. Other than for Adalia, the darkness didn't obscure our vision. The five of us had all made the journey to the hospital, but Adalia and Kai had opted to stay outside. Their delusive reasoning had been that three breaking into the morgue would be a lot less conspicuous than five. The logic was sound enough that none of us could argue, but we all knew the real reason they didn't want to come with us. Not that I could blame them. I also would have jumped on any alternative to breaking into the morgue, but short of waiting for Sophie's funeral that wasn't much of an option and time was of the essence. Sneaking into moonlit graveyards where the dead lay at peace was one thing, breaking and entering into the city morgue was a whole new ballgame that I hadn't prepared myself for.

So I cast no stones at Kai and Adalia's reservations. The idea perturbed me and I was already dead. The same could not be said for Gwydion and Nikolaos.

In fact, they seemed quite thrilled at the thought of breaking into the morgue. Behind their equally impassive masks was an eagerness. I frowned at the two of them.

'Why do you scowl at me, *ma chérie*?' Nikolaos asked, with a tasteless smile.

'She scolds us, Nikolaos,' Gwydion said, sounding amused.

'Whilst it's nice to see you two being pally again I get the impression you're enjoying this.'

That wiped the grin off Nikolaos's mouth.

'When you have been around as long as I,' Nikolaos said resentfully, 'you find pleasure in the small adventures.'

'Nice to know catching the man who murdered me is your idea of fun,' I replied, the bitterness in my tone almost tangible and scathing.

'If you two are quite done bickering we only have several hours before dawn,' Gwydion added.

'That's rich coming from you,' I muttered under my breath, knowing full well they could both hear me. Gwydion glanced coldly in my direction but didn't respond. I glowered back feeling justified in my grumpiness.

Like most of Britchelstone, the hospital is built into the top of a steep hill. The entrance to the morgue is around the back of the main entrance, down a series of concrete stairs melded into the earth. With no reason for the public to be going to the morgue area in the wee hours of the morning, there were no lights down the steps. Only suffocating darkness. If it weren't for having night vision, I'd have been scared of falling and breaking my neck.

There was one dim, white light flickering above the heavy metal door which led into the morgue. Huge red waste bins were locked safely behind a mesh fence with barbed wire gracing the top of the fence. Metal spikes caught the light like silver fangs shining menacingly. I was trying very hard not to think about what had been discarded in the bins. Gwydion picked the look with suspicious expertise. All of us were strong enough to break down the metal door with one push, but we were trying to be covert and ripping a solid metal door clean off its hinges seemed a good way to draw attention to ourselves.

In one easy movement, we were through the door. The hallway was dimly lit, as would be expected for a morgue during witching hour when no one was working. The walls were painted a sickly green that's meant to be serene but manages to be anything but. There were three doors in the wall on the right and two on the left. At the bottom of the hallway were two gym lockers, one of the doors was half-open, showing a white lab coat peeking through. One of the doors to our left was heavy and metal with hefty handles. Beside it was a very outdated thermostat showing us it was two degrees. Under closer inspection, I could see stickers on the metal. One was black and yellow with a menacing symbol warning of biohazard. The other had a black silhouette with a big red line through it saying *no unauthorised personnel* and the last was white with blue text reading *protective clothing is provided for your safety and must be worn.*

I hadn't realised I had had any expectations until I found myself mildly disappointed at the sight of the very normal hallway. I wouldn't have exactly liked blood-stained walls or ghostly shadows but at least some flickering lights or unexplained noises. If it weren't for the looming metal door closest to us giving away something was different, we could have been standing in any part of the hospital. It was all dull, plain and sterile. So far, the most ghastly thing I had found was the putrid miasma of sickly sweet death and suffocatingly harsh chemicals. I was under no illusion that this would change shortly. If the worst thing we experienced tonight was a throat-burning smell, then I would be content. But I wasn't that naive. In an attempt to shield my already heightened senses from the scent, I covered my mouth and nose with the sleeve of my black jumper. It did very little.

'We will need to go in here,' Nikolaos said, into the echoing silence so unexpectedly I jumped. He gestured to the smaller of the two metal doors, the one closest to us. 'It is where the bodies are stored.'

'What are the other rooms?' I asked.

Gwydion responded, 'It will be offices and showers for staff. Most likely a bathroom, too, I imagine.'

Clearly, this wasn't his first trip to a morgue.

Harsh luminous lights looming overhead reflected on the sparkling-clean white tiles lining the floors and walls. There was a metal drain in the corner of the room and a huge stainless steel fridge consuming the whole of one wall. We stood with our backs to the door exiting onto the hallway, to our right was another door leading to the autopsy room. Other than the drain, fridge and doors there was nothing in the room except gleaming tiles and the faint yet distinct smell of bleach. The looming metal monstrosity of a fridge had three long rectangular doors mounted in the metal.

Above the handles on the doors were small metal wallets holding paper labels with the names of the deceased. Two of the three were empty, but the third read, *Jenson, Sophie*. In that long, metal fridge was the body of the woman who was the potential key to finding the Britchelstone Barbarian's identity. My killer's identity. *Our* killer. Her death, although an unintentional sacrifice, could be all it took to stop any other young women going through the same torment we had faced.

We all stood in unmoving silence. When I looked up, both men were watching me.

'Are you ready, Scarlet?' Gwydion asked.

I fished the candle out of my pocket, clutching it tightly to my chest. Even unlit, it was soothing. Was I ready? No. Did I have a choice? Also no. Working with Gwydion to control my powers so they were no longer as debilitatingly capricious had given me a newfound certainty in myself. Right then, I was feeling far less confident. With every cell in my body screaming at me to turn, run, and hide somewhere warm and safe, I forced myself to stay standing in between the two men.

'Yes, are you?' I asked, with badly concealed uncertainty making my voice wobbly.

Gwydion and Nikolaos shared a look before nodding.

Much like the room containing the chambers of the deceased, the autopsy room had blinding, fluorescent lighting and was tiled from top to bottom with tiles so white they looked vaguely unreal. There was another drain in a break in the floor tiles. In the centre of the room was a table made of stainless steel large enough to hold a body of significant height and width. However, much like me, Sophie was short, although much more slender than I was. She looked shockingly small lying on the autopsy bench; frail and childlike despite being older than me.

The walls were bedecked with metal cabinets. Some had glass windows offering a peek into the contents of the cabinets, and some were just solid metal leaving it a mystery. I was quite happy not knowing any more than I had to. Morbid curiosity can only extend so far before it turns from interesting to repulsive. The dead body of the woman who still looked prepubescent lying feebly in front of us had already pushed the night into deplorable grounds without needing any more insight into the autopsy process.

Chemicals and fumes circulated through the air mingling with the sickly sweet staleness of death. It took a lot of willpower to resist gagging. Even Nikolaos was deterred by the scent, bunching his nose up just enough for me to notice. If Gwydion found it unpleasant, he gave no indication.

There were a total of six sinks in the autopsy room. Four of them were massive and square with multiple taps in each. Long plastic tubing coiled from some of the taps like pliable rubber serpents. The fifth sink was silver and neon yellow with a round basin and two heads reaching out the metal like mechanical sunflowers. There was a sign beside the sink saying, 'Emergency eyewash', and a big yellow button pad that, when pressed, would trigger the water. Cardboard boxes of surgical gloves had been placed substantially through the room for ease of access.

Above the autopsy slab was an adjustable light hanging from the ceiling and beside it was a big scale like you'd find in a supermarket to weigh fruit and vegetables. This one was used for weighing organs. Beside the autopsy bench was a steel table on wheels. It had been wiped down and cleared save some waxy thread and a box of thin, curved needles. The sixth and final sink was attached to the head of the autopsy table with two slender faucets. On one wall was a large whiteboard that had been all but wiped clean of any markings except some words scrawled illegibly in green marker. Red bins sat below the cabinets, some had been mounted on the walls, whilst one had been placed at the head of the autopsy bench. I was very grateful the bin bag had been changed before we came.

Actually, I was grateful everything had been cleaned before our arrival. I just wasn't sure how much gore and guts I could stomach. Living off blood did not make me immune to the unease of carnage.

Sophie Jenson had been found less than twenty-four hours prior to our illicit visit and appeared not to have been dead that much longer. The pathologists had yet to do her autopsy; I said a silent prayer of gratitude that we wouldn't be looking at her body sliced up and stitched. It had been maimed enough without needing to see anything else gruesome. Sophie's fair skin had dulled to an ashen grey except for her toes and feet which had purple-red blisters forming under the skin. Her skin was cold and stiff from more than just the freezer. Rigor mortis had long since come to freeze her body in her state of death.

Without the handy work of the embalmers and morticians to bring deceptive life to the corpse, Sophie looked definitively more dead than any of the zombies Gwydion had raised in the cemetery. Sophie's eyes were open and wide, staring off into nothingness. Large black pupils swallowed any colour from the iris, her eyeballs sunk deep in their sockets. Rippling through the sickly grey of her skin were purple, brown and green bruises from where she had been beaten. Through a gap in the hospital gown, I glimpsed the sight of her brutal wound. Like me, Sophie had been stabbed from behind. Unlike me, she had put up a fight. Her fingernails were bloody and raw from where she had fought off the attacker in a desperate bid to escape.

We were both redheads. Her hair was a softer red than mine like silken copper still shining against her lifeless body. Brown freckles embellished the softness of her face like constellations. Nikolaos, also noticing our similarities, absently traced a finger through my hair. I could feel his anger turning his body as stiff as the corpse in front of us. He leant down towards me, lips brushing my earlobe as he whispered, 'I will kill him.'

A chill ran through my body that had nothing to do with arousal and everything to do with fear. Fear, not for me, but for the victim of his wrath.

Of all the skills I had started to grasp, flame configuration on a small scale was the easiest. It signified the development of pyrokinesis, but I still had a long way to go—being able to light the wick of a candle wasn't quite as impressive as true pyrokinesis. Both Nikolaos and Gwydion had been surprised by the swiftness of my magickal advances seeming every bit as concerned as they were pleased. They could tell I had significant potential but the extent of which was unknown. I found the unknown troublesome; they thought it was exciting. I used the ability held within me, the power that Adali and Gwydion were helping me tame, to bring life to the candle in my hand the way he gave life to zombies. Fire spluttered and licked from the wick weakly at first then blossomed into a strong orange flame.

Once again, Gwydion produced his sacred blade and sliced the palm of his hand. Blood flowed from the wound; power washed through the small, contained room with such aggression I stumbled. With nowhere to go, the power of Gwydion's necromancy blew through the room vanquishing all the air. Nikolaos gripped onto my free hand to steady us both. I had enough control to hold onto his hand without going into his mind. The two of us stood as one against the battle of necromancy over the will of a vampire. Nikolaos and I, master and vassal, used our bond to rivet ourselves against the true force of his undiluted power.

Gwydion continued to chant in his ancient tongue, each word calling on something arcane and sinister. His power tasted of life and death, good and bad, light and darkness. It was the promise of immortality and life to the deceased, the knowledge that he could extinguish the life of any undead he touched. It was godlike and fierce.

I could feel Gwydion guiding that force into Sophie's stiff corpse. He shoved all of that conjured life-force into her petite frame. Gwydion's blood trickled down from her forehead in a crimson river drowning brown freckles in blood. Sunken, pitless eyes blinked up at us all crowding her on the table, white, cracked lips parting in shock.

☽CHAPTER 18☾

'Nikolaos, you must allure her quickly. She is exceptionally vulnerable. We do not need to prolong her terror,' Gwydion said.

Scrambling to sit up, Sophie's panicked eyes flickered from side to side. Restrained by rigor mortis, her feeble attempts to sit were unsuccessful. The rigor mortis would wear off eventually, once Gwydion's necromancy had breathed more life into her body and soul. Until then she was unable to move anything besides those scared green eyes sunk too far into their sockets. Nikolaos stood over the poor girl looking deeply into her eyes. Almost instantly, the allure washed over Sophie, her body and face went slack with ease but even allured I could see the panic in her eyes. Nikolaos continued to soothe Sophie, long fingers stroking through her hair the way you would comfort a distressed child. Gwydion turned to address me.

'Scarlet,' Gwydion said, 'you must prepare yourself, this will not be like your other experiences. The physical and mental trauma of the event will obscure her memory. I do not expect this to be easy for you.'

I looked up into his solemn face, unable to think of a suitable reply. I didn't want to do this. I didn't want to relive these horrors. But I had to. There was no other way. It had to be done no matter how difficult. The damage it would cause me mentally could be addressed in the future when the hunt was over.

Nikolaos had his cheek rested against Sophie's ear. Pale fingers continued to work through the rich silk of her copper hair as he whispered sweet French lulls.

Serenity made Sophie look younger, even more child-like than she already had.

'Is she ready?' Gwydion asked.

'Yes,' Nikolaos murmured. Turning his face back into the line of Sophie's jaw he added: *'Je suis navré.'*

Gwydion's face was a mask of regret and pity; the dark knowledge of what we had to do chasing away any remnants of humour or excitement. When we had first raised Gillian, Gwydion had said I had broken his zombie. Now I had the feeling his zombie was about to break me.

'Do it now, Nikolaos.'

Sophie's calm demeanour shattered into writhing and screaming on the cold metal. Her eyes closed, back bucking up and down violently. Harsh thwacking sounds were drowned out by the wetness of the skin on her back breaking against the ferocious slamming.

Watching her struggle on the table sent a deep fear through me, making my stomach knot and nausea burn my throat. Nikolaos had to make her relive the moment incessantly until I had the information we needed. If it even worked. We still weren't sure it would. Either this torment would be fruitful, or the distress we were causing Sophie would all be for nothing. Gwydion and Nikolaos had done all they could do; now it was time for me to do my part. But I found myself hesitating, unable to move against the fear.

'Hurry, Scarlet. We do not need to torture the girl any more than is necessary.'

I took a deep, shuddering breath. Eyes closed, I reached my hand out to touch the exposed flesh of Sophie's arm.

Nothing could have prepared me for just how different going into Sophie's mind would be. I opened my eyes finding myself at Sweetheart Lane off from Bolton Park. If it weren't for the sign at the bottom of the concrete staircase, I wouldn't have recognised it. Sweetheart Lane is actually just a long, steep stairway made of concrete nestled deeply between two walls. Usually, the crumbling stone walls are decorated with slender, curling vines and small colourful flowers. When you reach the top, the view looking over Britchelstone and Bolton Park is worth the lung-aching steepness of the stairs. At the top, large Victorian houses stretch on in rows; a sea of attractive architecture lining the rolling hills that Britchelstone is built on. Moss blooms in the cracks of the concrete, small green patches of damp softness against the stone. Lavender and roses appear with sudden beauty from the patches of dirt between the wall and stairs—human developments futile against the force of nature. It is a very attractive, if not underappreciated, part of the city usually. This was not the case in Sophie's mind.

The sky was a sable void whirling hysterically with menacing grey like the beginning of a hurricane preparing to smite the ground below. Part of me knew it was night time although the pirouetting darkness had drowned the stars and moon. Thick, hoary fog made seeing anything past the length of my arm impossible. There was a dampness to the air, a promise of a catastrophic storm brewing; one to bring destruction and misery. Muddy red hues tinted the air, the night shrouded in a mist the colour of old blood. It was like the red sands of Riyadh filled the air; scratching at my eyes, skin, the back of my throat.

I started up the concrete stairs. Black sludge oozed from the slits in the stairs and walls where life and greenery had once bloomed. The floral vines were rotting and dying, strangling the metal railing set into the wall. When I was halfway up, the sound of footsteps from behind made me stop walking. They started off slow and steady, soon growing increasingly frantic. Shoes slammed onto the concrete as Sophie started sprinting. Copper hair whipped me in the face as she ran past me in a surprising blur of motion. Sophie's desperate panting was loud in the gloomy night whilst she tried tirelessly to flee up the endless steps. All I could hear were the sounds of her painful pants, shoes striking concrete, and my own pulse beating wildly.

Sophie's head turned back over and over again, making sure he wasn't nearing her. Sweat dripped down her burning red face. Looking back over her shoulder once more, the toe of Sophie's dirtied trainer slipped on an eroding edge of the concrete. Sophie's knees hit the ground with an agonising thwack. Bone cracked excruciatingly loudly as she collapsed. She pushed her forehead against the concrete in a silent scream refusing to make any noise, to draw any more attention to herself. Tears squeezed out from her balled up eyes; her red eyebrows were furrowed so hard they merged to one. Sophie gripped her hand to her mouth, letting the piercing wails of her scream get lost in the fabric.

There was nowhere to run. Nowhere to hide. Unable to move, she was stranded alone on the cold stone waiting for her attacker to appear. I would have done anything to make this a reality. One where I could save her from the torturous fate I knew awaited her. Instead, we were both caged in the fragments of her decaying corpse's memory. If I still had a soul, I would have sold it right then to be the protector she so desperately needed. My blood could have healed her; my strength could have rescued her.

All I could do was sit beside Sophie with her body shuddering from silent sobs. Fog thickened like the smoke of a burning house around us, blinding us from what we both knew was coming. The silhouette of a figure was approaching, a blackness against the grey. It grew larger, more menacing until a small hunched figure sliced his way through the fog.

Panting and wheezing, murderous red eyes set on Sophie wild with hunger. They were just as crazed as I remembered, but he hadn't worn a hood when attacking Sophie as he had with me; I could finally get a proper look at him. The man, who must have been under five foot and heavily set and square, spat and sweated over both of us as he tried to regain his breath. Looking at the man in front of me knotted my stomach, nausea washed over me from fear and disgust. Acrid breath blew over us with each pant. Decay, and something much more familiar. Blood.

Where my eyes were more amber than true red, his were a dark sangria like demonic garnets set deeply into a beefy face. Those red eyes were void of all humanity. He watched Sophie like she was a piece of meat, leaking with sadism and a barbaric hunger for something more primal than food or sex. Flesh. I'd spent the last few weeks terrified I was becoming a monster, that I was sharing my bed with one, but, looking into this creature's eyes, I realised we weren't. This was what true evil looked like. I was staring it right in the face.

Other than the eyes and height, or lack thereof as the case may be, there was nothing particularly extraordinary about the man from what I could see so far. Greasy, brown-red hair hung in strands down to his shoulders. The top of his head was covered by a red cap so tight to his skull it looked like a second skin, the redness was dull in the strange murky light. Red, scarred cheeks brought an extra harshness to his already off-putting face. The rest of his body was enveloped by dirty black clothing, his hands stuffed into the tattered pockets of the black jacket he wore.

Sophie, who had been watching the man with a disgusted intensity, turned her head away from where he loomed above her. It was difficult to be so short and still have a presence considered looming, but he managed it. She whispered between her sobs into the concrete begging anyone, anything, to save her. I knew no one was coming. I think she knew it, too.

With horror-filled eyes, I watched his hand shuffle around in the jacket pocket, reaching for something. Somehow I knew what he was reaching for, and what was to come. Taloned fingers pulled out a knife dull with rust. He had made no attempt to clean it. Murky flecks of dried blood clung to the tarnished blade like macabre paint. Was my blood on that knife? I swallowed back bile.

Sophie must have sensed the movement behind her. She flipped herself around and stared up at him. Fear turned her eyes into almost full pupil, black swallowing the green like black caves of terror. Horror and fear had drained from her eyes. She was suddenly animated by rage-fueled determination. Without the use of her legs, she couldn't do much in the way of fighting, but Sophie gave it her best attempt. In a move catching both the murderer and me by surprise, Sophie leant out and wrapped her arms around his stumpy legs. Using all of her adrenalised strength, she yanked her arms back sending the monster stumbling, but his grip on the railing stopped the fall from becoming detrimental. He stood half crouched with a look of surprise quickly turning into pure rage. The man licked his lips, showing a black tongue held in a cage of brown-stained teeth almost as knifelike as Gwydion's.

I had retrieved what I needed to identify the man as much as possible. But I couldn't abandon Sophie here to die alone. She wouldn't know anyone was here with her; I could admit it was a selfish comfort. I needed to be by her side as she died the same way I had needed someone to comfort me on that fateful summer night.

It didn't take long for the brutal deed to be over but the minutes stretched on endlessly. Enraged by her audacity to retaliate, the man grabbed Sophie's slender wrist with his claws digging into her flesh. He yanked her arm so harshly I heard the wet pop of the joint dislocating from the socket. Her scream sliced through the air like a knife in the silence. Even with the pain, Sophie used her free hand to slash and claw at him but he dodged the movements remaining unharmed. He snarled at her, bearing those sharp, dirty teeth.

Flipping Sophie around so her back was facing the blanket of darkness, and her face was pushed into the concrete with painful force, he shoved his boot forcefully into her spine, pinning her to the ground. Battered, bruised and without the use of almost all of her limbs, all Sophie could do was wriggle weakly against his weight and use the least harmed hand to claw at the ground. Concrete soaked up her tears and the blood from her raw fingers. Swallowing down pained whimpers, Sophie pleaded piteously for him to stop. It was futile, and we all knew it.

Raising the blade above his head, he grinned diabolically before slamming the knife into the side of her back with the full force of his heavy frame. Sophie attempted to scream one final time, but it was silent as the air fled her lungs and blood gushed from the wound at an alarming pace.

Trembling with revulsion, I watched death glaze the once sparkling emerald of her eyes.

)CHAPTER 19(

We were no longer in the morgue when I came to. Gwydion, Nikolaos and I all stood in the expanse of forestry by our cottage. The two men had put some noticeable distance between myself and them. Kai and Adalia were nowhere to be seen. Surprisingly, I was already standing up. If I had lost consciousness, which was the only logical explanation I had for blacking out, then why wasn't I lying down, or at least sitting? My eyes adjusted more to the surroundings. Grey smoke rose thick and heavy in the sky behind the men like ashen ghosts dancing into the darkness. My body was hot, burning hot. But that felt good.

I thought it was raining until I realised the would-be raindrops weren't wet. Flecks of ash and dust swirled through the air like powdery rain, so fragile it disappeared into everything it touched in a little puff of grey. Embers of leaves, branches and shrubs lay on the frosty ground glowing red and orange against the charcoal debris. Confusion gave way to worry. What had happened?

I took a moment to take in the sight of the two men stranded in the destruction I had caused. The silver light of the moon looked ethereal and out of place in the chaotic blazing. Gwydion was still watching me with a look not too dissimilar to amusement. It was such an infuriating smugness. Gwydion had the face of someone who should look wizened, but his skin was smooth and clear like the perfect flesh of a child stretched too tightly over a skeleton. The moonlight reflected off the pure alabaster of Gwydion's skin, paler than even I, and his lifeless, white hair like spun silver. The shadows made the emaciated hollows of his cheeks look cavernous. Red and orange light danced off his skin, crimson shadows swimming over his face like the silhouette of wavering flames before being swallowed by the darkness. Gwydion, at that moment, looked very demonic; it seemed almost shocking anyone could think of him as human, but people found comfort in familiarity and would only see what they wanted to make sense of.

Whilst Gwydion looked perfectly demonic, Nikolaos was a dark angel brought to life in the fiery glow of dying embers. The two men so very disparate, and yet, oh, so similar at the same time.

Rune watched me with his usual blankness, eyes glinting with familiar hubris like he knew all the sordid secrets of the world. Surely if things were that bad, Gwydion wouldn't have been so calm, right? Nikolaos, however, was a mask of concern with his face contorted into lines of worry. That, more than anything, let me know something was really wrong. Cautiously, Nikolaos stretched his hand out to me. Forearm outstretched, facing outwards, I could see the black, peeling skin of Nikolaos's singed flesh. Puddles of blisters and raw, open flesh looked particularly gruesome in the barrier of charred skin.

'Niko?' I asked, voice high and panicked. 'What happened?'

I began to rush towards him, through the rainfall of calcined debris turning the air chokingly thick. Nikolaos, visibly recoiling, took a step back from me as I neared him. Standing amidst the inferno destruction, Nikolaos looked as ghostly as ever; hauntingly beautiful, perfect everywhere except the black, marred skin on his arm, so dark against that pure, pale flesh.

'Stay back, Scarlet,' Gwydion warned, his tone was soft, but the element of threat had not been lost on me.

I stood totally still, hands held out in front of me trying to show I meant them no harm. Gwydion's power stirred through the air. He was shielding himself with an invisible force of magick that weighed against me. Something truly bad must have happened for Nikolaos to look so unnerved and Gwydion to take these precautions. The problem was, I still had no idea what I'd done in the time it had taken us to leave the morgue. I tried to remember so hard it gave me a headache, but there was nothing but blankness. I had lost time; how much, I didn't know.

'Where are the other two?' I asked.

Logically, I knew that if I had hurt Adalia, Nikolaos would not be this calm. And if I'd hurt Kai, Gwydion would release the fires of hell over me, and Nikolaos too probably.

'They are safe,' Nikolaos said, and a tension released from my shoulders I hadn't realised was there.

His face was slipping back into one of familiar reticence. It seemed he no longer thought I was a threat.

'We thought it best they distance themselves from you temporarily,' Gwydion said, adding, 'As the most mortal.'

'How do you feel, *ma feu*?'

Gwydion glanced at Nikolaos. 'A fitting sobriquet, Nikolaos.'

Nikolaos cast a glare at Gwydion. The phrase, if looks could kill, came to mind.

'I'm fine, I think. I just don't know what's happened.'

The two looked at each other once again, this time with a mutual understanding. They both seemed to relax like a shared held breath had been released.

'Will you two stop looking at each other and just tell me what's happened?' I demanded brusquely. I sounded tired and suddenly felt it, too.

'Certainly, as you beseech so politely,' Gwydion replied dryly.

It was my turn to glare at him.

Nikolaos and Gwydion finally got around to telling me the succinct version of what had happened after my blackout at the morgue. Neither of the men had been able to wake me as I had writhed and mewled trapped in a horror-filled trance on the tile floor. Nikolaos had tried soothing me, Gwydion had attempted to use his Necromancy to bring some control over me, but both were to no avail. Both Kai and Nikolaos had struggled to contain me on the journey home. On the way, I had begun to burn increasingly hotter. Eventually, my screaming had subsided and they thought I had woken, but when my eyes had opened, they had bled to pits of pure, drowning black. I had stood there non-respondent until Nikolaos tried touching me.

Fire had soured over the flesh of his arm as I gripped onto his bare skin, burning him red and raw. Using all of that supernatural strength built up over millennia, Nikolaos had finally been able to unweave himself from my grasp, but the damage had been done. Not even his vampire blood had been able to heal the wound entirely. Kai and Adalia, the more vulnerable of the group, had sought safety in the cottage whilst my rampant fire roared and I proceeded to burn and torch the forest surrounding us.

I wasn't certain how best to respond; it felt inappropriate to gape at them in disbelief, and I was too tired to think of an intelligible question. Luckily for me, Gwydion knew just what to say.

'It seems you have more potential than I originally thought.'

Gwydion's lips twisted into a sinister grin that leaked scandal the way Nikolaos's smile could promise sex.

'She is not to become your personal weapon, Rune,' Nikolaos hissed, taking a step towards me. The uncertainty had all but dissipated, he walked with his usual elegant gait as if the earth would part like water yielding to his movements.

'Oh, on the contrary, Nikolaos,' Gwydion said, unphased by the other man's reproach, 'I am quite certain your little nymph's magickal endowments will surpass us all. I do not expect her to be anything of mine, and I would urge you to relinquish your dreams of dominance. Scarlet has shown her disdain for control, ostensibly even her own at times.'

Gwydion ignored our louring.

'I didn't mean to hurt you,' I said weakly.

'*Oui, je sais.*'

Nikolaos and I took a step closer to each other. Grey ash clung to the rich darkness of his hair like the fragile ghosts of all I had torched.

'You could,' Gwydion said, 'attempt to remedy the wound on your master.'

Gwydion said '*master*' with such derision it made the word sound obscene. Was he being particularly gruelling tonight or was I just extra sensitive?

'How?'

I cared more about healing Nikolaos than attempting to chastise Gwydion's impertinence. I took the final step towards Nikolaos, grabbing his wounded arm in my hands. Yellow blisters bubbled over shiny pink skin and raw flesh. Up close, the wound was much more gruesome. I hissed, tears welling in my eyes. I had never meant to hurt anyone. I looked up, still clasping his arm in my hands, and Nikolaos met my gaze. Unshed tears quivered in my eyes perilously close to breaking free. Nikolaos's face was as indecipherable as I'd ever seen it. It felt selfish to cry. He was the one wounded by his lover, and yet still he stood beautifully blank and unmoved. I had no right to cry whilst he stayed so calm. Of course, I knew Nikolaos's blankness was at its best when he was trying to hide his true feelings. The shield he had put up so I couldn't sense his emotions spoke volumes within itself. I had hurt him; the question was: was it just physical pain he was trying so intently to conceal?

Gwydion still hadn't answered. He just stood there watching us with a wistful look on his face—no, not us; Nikolaos. When he turned his focus on me, a smile played on his lips I hadn't seen before. Guileless; a smile that spread to his eyes, filling them with sorrow instead of mirth.

'Forgive me, I lost myself in deep reverie,' he said, turning to Nikolaos. 'You may not be the master of her soul the way one would expect, Nikolaos, but, the way she looks at you'—he shook his head gently—'it is clear you have captured it by other means. It does not appear unrequited.'

A look was shared between the two men I didn't quite understand. It held a wealth of emotions far too intimate to be shared with anyone other than them. But the weight of their history was palpable. A friendship once so pure had been soured by woe and loss. Loss, not just of one another, but of themselves. Of Camille. And their virtues.

Gwydion shook his head again, more aggressively this time, as if trying to shake the thoughts, the memories, away physically. I wanted so desperately to reach out and comfort Gwydion but I also knew that he would take my concern as pity; a grave insult. So, I stayed silent, waiting patiently for Gwydion to fall back into that perfect taunting blankness, almost an identical reflection of Nikolaos's own mask.

'You have healed Adalia of damage once,' Gwydion

said.

'I don't know how I did it, though,' I said. 'I don't seem to know how any of this really works. I feel like I'm winging it most of the time. And then stuff like tonight happens'—I wafted my free hand through the air—'and I'm reminded just how little control I have.' I tried not to sound as tired as I felt and failed miserably.

'Do not be a cynic. Magick is not linear, nor is it black and white. You can only understand how it works as much as you understand yourself'—he touched a long, bony finger to my chest—'it comes from your heart, your soul and your intentions. You cannot expect yourself to truly grasp that which is unfathomable. Magick is not about knowledge or the mind but senses and metaphysics.'

'It is arcane, Scarlet,' Nikolaos added, not exactly helpfully.

'Has our working together taught you nothing?' Gwydion asked, sounding frustrated.

'I thought I was getting better at learning, but tonight has made me feel so unsure of myself.'

'Magick is not so much learned as it is natural; most are just unaware they have a raw ability to unlock. It is the downfall of most who think they are human but truly are not. We live in a society that stunts our senses and our connection to ourselves,' Gwydion said disapprovingly. 'I do not know how you healed Adalia, but you did. Think not of it as knowledge to remember, but an instinct to call on. Doubt, Scarlet, is the scourge of magick.'

I sighed deeply. Gwydion had a tendency to speak in poetic riddles; pretty to hear, but not entirely helpful.

'Okay,' I took a deep breath. 'I'll give it another go.'

Magick is this epic, weighted, invisible force like the air, or oxygen, or heat. No matter how strong the presence, how much it pushes and beats against you, it is also silent and unseen and impossible to capture. Control is only as strong as the will of the practitioner, and it can very easily become wild and untamed like a rogue beast. I'd proven that on several occasions, although admittedly none had been quite as catastrophic as tonight. Humans have been raised to rely solely on the five basic senses, but no matter how out of touch we fall with our inner selves, that sixth sense will always be there. We will always get those gut feelings that turned out to be right, or that peculiar feeling you're being watched by something or someone who isn't a physical presence in front of you. Not all humans are magick, but we—oh, they—all have the ability to unlock that sixth sense. The one we relied on for survival for so many years until we fell out of touch with the Earth and the energy we share with Her. Gosh, all those lessons with Gwydion and Adalia were really beginning to rub off on me. I was beginning to sound a lot like my witch friend.

Magick, like seeing or breathing, is easier to do when not focusing on it overtly. Much the same way breathing suddenly seems unnatural when it's noticed, magick has to be guided but not overthought. I gripped Nikolaos's forearm in my hands, one clutching underneath for a tight grip and the other letting a finger tentatively trace along the raised, blue vein in his wrist just below the wound. Nikolaos was very still in my grasp, his fingers lightly curled, unmoving. I closed my eyes, still caressing the smoothness of his unmaimed skin.

Visualisation is one way to send magick out with a direct intention and purpose. With closed eyes, I tried to picture the wound healing. Familiar warmth curled through me like the caress of a lover. My fire recognised the feeling of Nikolaos; the smoothness of his skin, floral and cinnamon musk, the feel of the coolness of his strengthening power which caressed my own intimately. We, my magick and I, didn't want him to be hurt. I felt the heat trickle from my fingers. It wound up his skin like a fiery serpent coiling over the damage, whilst also entering into him somewhere intimate and reserved for power, energy, aura, where no hands could touch. My fire flowed through his veins, circulating with the stolen blood which gave him life, and danced through the aura surrounding him.

Tears had escaped my eyes without me realising. When I opened them, a lone tear dripped from my chin onto the healed flesh of Nikolaos's forearm. I chuckled, sniffling at the same time, not the most attractive of noises but one so evidently joyous it made the snort less embarrassing. Lowering my head to Nikolaos's arm, I placed the chastest of kisses on top the once again perfect smoothness of his skin. Nikolaos used his free hand to slip a finger under my chin, raising my face to his. The soft warmth of his lips kissed away the salty residue of tears on my cheeks.

Deep, dark blue had washed over the cloudless sky like an unobstructed, drowning ocean promising dawn soon to come. Adalia and Kai had seemed cautious of me initially until Gwydion assured them I was safe to be around. Nikolaos had tried to reassure them as well, but the other two seemed more trusting of Gwydion. If I were being perfectly honest, I also took Gwydion's word as more credible when it came to magick.

It had hurt to see two people I cared about wary of me in that way, but I couldn't blame them for being cautious. If I'd seen either of them torch a forest in an almost possessed state, I'd have probably been reluctant to sit in a contained room with them too. But here we were, all sitting beside each other on the cream sofas which had probably seen more action in the past few weeks than since they were bought, who knows how long ago. Most of the tension had eased, if you didn't count the constant agitated air between Nikolaos and Gwydion. It was so familiar it had become a comfort in some ways.

Gwydion traced a cadaverous finger along the line of his painfully sharp jaw stewing over the information I had just relayed. All four of them had sat in utter silence whilst I had detailed my experience in Sophie's mind. Having Gwydion and Nikolaos silent this long with no witty—insulting—remarks could be considered a minor miracle.

'Could you explain to me once more what this hat looked like?' Gwydion asked for the third time. I sighed.

'I do not see how this is of relevance,' Nikolaos said, sounding just about as tired as I felt. Dawn was pushing dangerously close, and I was having to explain about my murderer's fashion choices.

'You know swimming caps? It kind of looked like that. But like it was attached to him permanently.'

'Like he was scalped,' Nikolaos added very matter-of-factly.

'How am I supposed to know what someone looks like after they've been scalped? Torture is your area of expertise, not mine,' I snapped, and immediately regretted it.

The silence that fell in the room was crushing. I was exhausted and frustrated, but that had definitely crossed a line.

'I'm sorry,' I said, placing my hand on top of Nikolaos's. 'That was cruel.'

Nikolaos failed to hide the anger in his eyes, the tight press of his lips, as he looked at me. I withdrew my hand.

'I am unfamiliar with a swimming cap,' Gwdydion

said into the hostile silence. 'Besides this peculiar hat, you also say he has pointed teeth, a short frame and red eyes, is this correct?'

'Not exactly. *I'm* short; this man was less than five foot. Dwarf height I'd say. But other than that, you're correct.'

I had wanted to say the murderer had teeth like Gwydion's, but it seemed like it may be rude. I'm not sure why, it was a fact, but pointing it out seemed uncouth somehow.

'I see,' Gwydion replied for the hundredth time tonight.

The only noise in the room was the sound of Gwydion's bony finger rubbing over the paper skin of his jaw. Adalia and Kai seemed to barely be breathing. Even with the open windows, the late-night wind was hushed as if holding its breath with the rest of us.

Gwydion suddenly clicked his fingers together, the snap so startling in the silence it made both Adalia and I jump.

'I've got it!' Gwydion announced, a grin lighting up his whole face. It would have been beautiful if it weren't for those dagger teeth. 'Did this creature also happen to have small, pointed ears by chance?'

'I didn't get a good look to see.'

The smile didn't waver as he shooed my misinformation away.

'Ah, that is no matter. Yes, I am quite certain I know of what creature we have averred a foe.'

'Which is?' Nikolaos said, at the same time Adalia and I chorused, 'What?'

Adalia was suddenly sitting upright, eyes gleaming with anticipation.

'A Redcap.'

)CHAPTER 20(

'Ludicrous!' Nikolaos blurted, failing to hold back a laugh.

Kai and I exchanged equally bemused looks. Adalia had slumped back onto the sofa looking both defeated and tired.

'This is no time for jokes, Rune,' she muttered.

'I never joke, Adalia,' Gwydion replied, glaring at both her and Nikolaos in turn.

Gwydion never joking was something I believed entirely.

'What'sa Redcap?' Kai asked in his thick southern drawl.

'It's a goblin,' Adalia said unenthusiastically.

Nikolaos stifled a laugh once more. 'You cannot expect me to believe in Britchelstone we not only have a vampire-deity hybrid but now a goblin. You are demented, Rune.'

Any reconciling of friendship I thought may have been initiated when it was just the three of us outside was wiped away. The look that Gwydion gave Nikolaos would be enough to scare armies out of battle. I thought Nikolaos had an excellent glare, oh, boy, had I been mistaken.

I hated to admit that I couldn't disagree with Nikolaos. Britchelstone may be known for its diversity, arts, and culture but it is a tiny city. To think a goblin of all things had decided to set up shop here was, as Nikolaos eloquently put it, ludicrous.

'I am many things, Nikolaos,' Gwydion said, 'but mad I am not. I do not profess to share your knowledge of the ways of vampires. However, this is my area of prowess. I can assure you, I am much more educated on the matter than anyone else in this room. If you think otherwise then I do not know why my aid was requested.'

Considering it was a very valid argument Nikolaos didn't have much to say in response. He stretched his back against the sofa and crossed his arms against his chest. It was a very graceful way to pout. And this man had actually had the audacity to call *me* petulant once.

'Okay,' Adalia said, 'we'll go with the theory that it's a Redcap.'

I wanted to say, 'You don't sound convinced either,' but thought better of it.

'If my *theory*,' Gwydion said resentfully, 'is correct, and I am quite certain it is, then we are fortunate.'

'How so?' I asked.

'As Nikolaos so wisely pointed out'—the words were dripping with derision—'there are likely very few other goblins in your precious city. I should think it will make him easier to seize.'

'And how do we *seize* him?' I asked.

'That I do not know.'

Nikolaos let out an exasperated sound felicitously mirroring my own discouragement.

'Dawn creeps nigh too quickly. Whilst you slumber for the day I shall research methods of entrapment,' Gwydion said, and then turned to Adalia. 'I request you join me, Adalia. What is it they say: two minds are better than one.'

'How long will you be gone for?' I asked.

'I should think no more than three days. We shall aim for less.'

'I have been thinking,' Nikolaos said, 'I must journey to the Empress to alert her of my growing powers. If you are to be gone for the forthcoming days, I shall arrange my travels to coincide.'

'The Empress?' I asked, sounding as confused as I felt.

'You are being temerarious, Nikolaos,' Gwydion admonished. Both men ignored me. If I didn't know any better I would have said Gwydion sounded concerned. 'We do not know if your powers will continue to evolve. If they do not, you would have brought attention to yourself for no purpose.'

I cast a glance in the direction of Adalia and Kai. Both of them shrugged in sync.

'I bargained for safe passage and residency in this country, for I was no threat to her throne. If she discovers I have lied to her then it will be treason. I must go soon or face the consequences.' Nikolaos shuddered minutely. 'I do not wish to feel her wrath.'

'You are, at present, still not strong enough to threaten her reign. It is in your best interest to wait.'

Nikolaos said, simply, 'I cannot.'

Gwydion shrugged. 'If you will not heed my advice, I shall not waste energy belabouring the discussion further.'

I was going to ask who the Empress was once more but pink stroked the edges of the trees like the brush of a paintbrush on the edge of the earth. If Nikolaos and I didn't retire to the, what I not so affectionately called, oubliette, soon then we would have two fried vampires.

)CHAPTER 21((

Water beat against my skin in a gentle thrum. Nikolaos had still been deeply entrapped in sleep when I'd arisen for the night, so I took this time of solitude to shower. I turned my face up to the shower with closed eyes, running my hands through the long, thick tangles of my hair.

Hands traced the line of my bent arms. My eyes flew open, an embarrassingly high-pitched *yelp* escaping my lips. I whipped around, foot slipping on the wet stone floor. If it weren't for Nikolaos grabbing me around the waist I would have fallen onto the stone. My heart pounded against my chest; Nikolaos's bare arm held my body suspended in the air like a dancer being dipped by their partner.

My moment of anger at the disturbance was quickly distracted by Nikolaos's totally nude body. The water sluiced over his body like liquidized crystals trailing down the pale definition of his torso, clinging to his skin as though they stuck to his body too scared to be free from a touch of his beauty. Stray droplets trickled further down getting lost in the tangle of hair on his stomach, dripping along the curve of his hip bone and thighs. Obsidian hair lay wet down his back, pushed back from the carved angles of his face. Droplets of water dripped from the wealth of his black lashes and thick, dark eyebrows.

Green didn't do justice to the actual colour of his eyes. They were the swirling malachite of deep Mediterranean seas. In some light they were more aquamarine than true green; dark verdigris. In this room, modelled like the bathhouses Nikolaos knew from times of old, he looked exactly like what he was; a picture of ancient Greek pulchritude immortalised.

I swallowed back the pulse in my throat. It wasn't the first time I'd seen Nikolaos fully exposed yet every time my reaction was like it was brand new. Still equally enchanting, haunting, and terrifying in all the best ways. My breath caught in my throat, blood rushing to my cheeks and turning them scarlet. It was hard to blush with no blood circling in my veins, but Nikolaos managed to make it a possibility.

Nikolaos raised me slowly, bringing me into the circle of his arms. The water flowed over both our bodies; I could feel the hair on his lower belly like satin against my upper stomach. My head nestled into the curve of his chest. I traced my fingers over the wet smoothness of his back, lower and lower, caressing the dimples in his back and the swirl of his derrière.

'You scared me,' I said, turning my face up to his.

Nikolaos obligingly turned his face down to me.

'Forgive me, *ma chérie*, I did not mean to frighten you.'

He flashed a licentious smile at me. I frowned back.

'Why do you scowl at me?'

'Last night you mentioned something about an Empress. Gwydion seemed worried. I've never seen him anything but smug before, it was...disconcerting,' I said, partially-lying.

Truthfully, I didn't like it when Nikolaos smiled at me like that. It wasn't the look for someone you love, or even really lust for. It was a reminder of the libertine modus vivendi Nikolaos had sworn by for over two millennia. I had, indirectly, forced him into a life of monogamy and restraint. Not that he had ever overtly complained but I didn't think Nikolaos was entirely satisfied with these changes. I got the impression he was still waiting for me to come around, give in to the whims of vampire desires and relinquish my morals. I was still constrained by youthful diffidence; the same could not be said for my lover.

However, the events of last night had genuinely confused and concerned me. So we'd focus on that instead of trying to explain to a seasoned Lothario why I didn't want him to debauch my moral compass.

'There are certain politics in the vampire world. Rules we must adhere to,' he said with a look making it clear he didn't believe that was what was really on my mind.

'So we have a government? And vampire laws?'

Nikolaos thought over this for a moment.

'*Oui, et non.* It is more like a monarchy and a council. Laws would be a fitting terminology.'

'So, how does it work?' I asked, water getting caught in my lips.

Nikolaos traced his hands through my hair, getting his fingers caught in the wet tangles.

'We have seven monarchs, one for each continent. Each Emperor or Empress has a Prince and Princess, a vampire whom they have made and a human as a servant.'

'So we also have seven councils?'

'*Non,* we have many.'

'Are you being intentionally elusive?'

'Perhaps.' He shrugged. 'We do not have a local council as I was the only vampire in Britchelstone. Vampire politics are notoriously corrupt. I wished not to involve you if it could be helped.'

'Ignorance is bliss kind of thing. Human politicians aren't exactly known for being honourable.'

The look he gave me was a clear indication of how naive he thought I was being.

'Vampires must request permission from the Emperor or Empress to move territory.'

'But you moved from France, which is also in Europe.'

'*Oui*, but there are few vampires as old as I. Many do not make it this long, and those that do have immeasurable power. In France, I was far from her throne. To move to England would be seen as a threat.'

'So you had to prove you weren't a threat to her. How?'

'The Empress may not be as old but she is powerful in her own right. She could feel that I do not possess the power I should. Nonetheless, she forbade me from a home in London, instead granting me permission to reside here. We have no other vampires in Britchelstone; there is no council for me to corrupt or overpower down here. It weakened my ability to stage a coup.'

I thought over what he said for a moment, still wrapped in his arms with the warm water beating over us like liquid silk.

'Would you have staged a coup, or tried to take over, if you had been around more vampires?'

'*Non*, certainly not. My lack of power was no deception. She needed to see it as reassurance, although I believe she suspects I found a way to lie about my power. To show this weakness to others would be a death sentence. I am happy residing alone. It is safer.'

'Do you have to tell her you're getting more powerful? Surely she has no way of knowing.'

He gave me another look showing just how ignorant I was being. I scowled back.

'I fear the consequences of mendacity would be much more severe than honesty. It would be seen as perjury if the truth were discovered.'

'I don't understand these vampire politics. Before last night I didn't even know they existed.'

'We do not adhere to the laws of humans, but even vampires must be policed.'

'I guess that makes sense,' I said. Nikolaos was shielding from me hard, but I caught the sense of his discomfort. Nearly fear. It was not reassuring. 'Won't that mean she needs to meet me, too? If I'm the one who's helping you gain power?'

'Rune was right'—I raised my eyebrows at that unexpected admittance—'it would not only be rash but foolish to visit her so soon. I do not wish to involve you. Your abilities, *ma chérie*, are so very unique I do not know how she will react. You will either be seen as a great weapon or a significant threat. Which is worse, I do not know.'

Again I got the thread of fear.

'I have a bad feeling about this, Niko.'

'Me too, *ma chérie*, which is why I must think over this for longer. I have been alive, if you can consider this existence one of life, long enough to understand the politics of vampires. But even I cannot foresee how this may go.'

This was the second time Nikolaos had willingly opened up to me. I decided to exploit it further and ask something I'd been wondering for a while now.

'Why, if you're from Greece, do you have a mostly French accent and a penchant for the language?'

Nikolaos rested his chin on top of my head forcing me to turn my head and press my cheek into his chest or risk being suffocated by his flesh. He was silent for long enough I was sure he wasn't going to answer.

'I have lived in Europe since my rebirth as a vampire whilst only a mere twenty-seven years were in Greece. Most of those later years have been spent in France, although I have left periodically. I have resided there since before it was known as France.'

It took me a moment to realise what he meant.

'You mean when it was still Gaul?' I asked, failing to hide the shock. Of course, I did know how old Nikolaos was but it was easy to forget that the man I was sharing my bed with was *that* old. Sometimes the age gap did make me feel a bit strange. Other times it seemed so absurd it was hard to feel anything.

'*Oui,*' he said, humour in his voice. 'I settled in Massalia, known today as Marseille.'

'Oh,' I replied, because what else was I meant to say?

By the time we were out of the shower, my fingers and toes had shrivelled to fleshy prunes. I threw on an oversized men's t-shirt in dark charcoal and black jeans. I was short enough and the top was large enough that it was actually longer than some of the dresses I owned. I felt more confident flashing a bit of flesh as a vampire. Some days it was nice to feel sexy. Others, like today, I would have been happy in trackies and a jumper, but we needed to venture into town.

Besides, I still had that new relationship insecurity where I wasn't quite ready for Nikolaos to see me that slobby yet, especially as he was such a foppish man. Relationship? It felt too presumptuous to think of what we were doing as a *relationship* in the traditional sense. I wasn't putting money on Nikolaos being the sort of person to ask me to be his girlfriend and, if I were being honest, I think we were too complex to define in such a black and white way. We certainly had a type of relationship, I just wasn't entirely sure of what that really meant. I sighed and shook my head. It was all too complicated for me. There were much more pressing matters to attend. Like catching my murderer. That definitely took precedence. I could worry about my complex lover and our future together later.

Nikolaos walked out of his own room at the same time as me. He wore a silk shirt only slightly lighter than my own tucked into black trousers. The silver of his belt buckle matched the silver pin in his shirt collar, done up to the throat, with a glinting black stone set into it.

'Well one of us needs to change,' I said, grinning at him. Nikolaos gave me a blank gaze back. I sighed. 'We're basically matching outfits.'

He still didn't seem to get the joke. Over two thousand years of life and Nikolaos had never mastered humour. Or I'm just not that funny.

'Well, I look like the pound land version of you.'

'Pound land?'

'It's a shop where everything is a quid or under. Like a budget store kind of thing.'

'You could wear the rags of a peasant and still be bewitching.'

Comparing me to a peasant seemed like an outdated compliment, but it was a sweet sentiment. I wrapped my arms around his waist.

'Self-depreciation is the way of a millennial's humour,' I said, gazing up from below his chin.

Both Nikolaos and I were surprised to hear the shower running upstairs when we walked into the living room. We exchanged a puzzled glance.

'Adalia and Gwydion?' I asked.

'They are more intimate than last I saw them to be sharing a shower,' he said, sounding very monotone.

It took me a moment to realise Nikolaos had just attempted humour. That was actually distracting enough for me to stare at him even more bemused than some potential intruder taking a shower in our house. I fought not to gape at him. The water turning off made me turn back to watch the stairs.

'Should we be worried someone's in the house?' Nikolaos looked behind him to the front door. I followed his line of sight.

'I cannot see forced entry,' he said.

I shrugged. 'I can't imagine an intruder taking a shower.'

The sound of feet plodding down the stairs drew both of our attention back. A muscular body sauntered down the stairs with languorous grace like the way a contented cat would stroll into the room. Kai grinned at us, one of the white cotton towels stored in the upstairs bathroom wrapped around his dripping waist. All of the cottage was done in cream, white and muted greens and blues: nondescript, unassuming, and definitely not the surreptitious lair of a vampire. Or at least that's what Nikolaos wanted people to think if they did so happen to stumble onto the cottage tucked away in miles of forestry. The woods were a fort in their own right. A sort of maze to deter potential trespassers.

Muscles rippled under skin as he flowed down the stairs. Kai's grin widened when he properly looked at us both.

'You two always dress like his and hers when we ain't here?' he asked. I felt Nikolaos stiffen beside me.

'Maybe,' I said, grinning back. Kai always could make me smile. 'Or maybe we walk around in the nude with no company. You really missed a show there.'

Kai laughed, a deep, rich sound like a strange combination of brassy growl and feline purr.

'Why are you here?' Nikolaos asked rudely. I nudged him, none too gently, in the ribs with my elbow.

Kai's grin wavered slightly as his pale orange eyes flickered to Nikolaos. He was always tense around him. I wanted to ask why but no matter how well we got on I simply didn't know him well enough to start intruding on his personal life. I could ask Nikolaos, but I wasn't sure he would be honest with me about what was up with Kai. He hadn't seemed this tense before Nikolaos started displaying more power. Hopefully, I'd find out sooner rather than later.

'Rune 'n' Adalia were gettin' on with their magickal research. I dunno a thing about magick.' He grinned again. 'I'd just be gettin' in the way back home.'
'You're welcome to stay here, Kai.' I rolled my eyes back up to where Nikolaos stood incredibly still behind me. 'Right, Niko?'
'Yes, you are always welcome here kitty cat,' he said with sarcasm thick enough to choke on. I elbowed him again. Kai brushed off the sarcasm with ease.
'That'sa relief'—he let out a mock exhalation of air —'cuz I've hunted all the animals near us. I was hopin' I could use your woods.' Kai sniffed the air. 'You're far enough out to get deer 'n' all sorts here.'

Nikolaos finally relented after some persuasion to come with Kai and I out into the woods to hunt. We had to go out and feed first. When we returned, Kai was wearing nothing but a pair of blue jeans almost entirely faded to white. The knees were patchy and frayed, not in the way that was fashionable but just from being worn that often. He'd had to roll up the legs on them. Jeans aren't really made for men as short and bulky as Kai.

Even as a vampire I could feel the hostile bite of frost in the air. I huddled into myself not because I was actually cold but because I felt like I should be. Nikolaos said it was a very human mannerism. I'd just glared at him. It did make me wonder why Kai was able to walk through the night in nothing but those old jeans without freezing. He'd told me therianthropes ran much, much hotter than humans. When I'd asked why they were so warm-blooded he had shrugged and queried why vampires are always cold. Direct and uncouth, Nikolaos had replied 'because we are dead' and that had quickly put an end to the conversation.

I'd never seen a shapeshifter—oh, sorry 'wereanimal' was the PC term apparently—actually shift before. If it weren't for his peculiar eyes, to think Kai was human would be easily forgiven. I even forgot at times. Tonight I was going to be shown up close and personal just how not-human he was. I was excited, if not a little bit nervous.

We broke out into one of the few expenses in the forest not consumed by thick trees and shrubbery. I hadn't actually explored that much of the forest that surrounded our cottage. Other than the direct path down to the main road and the recently discovered rockery, I hadn't really known just how big the area of land is. Again I wondered where Nikolaos got the money to buy this much land. It still felt rude to ask. Money is just one of those things I always feel awkward talking about, and demanding to know where Nikolaos got his income was simply too far out of my comfort zone no matter how curious I was.

Kai asked Nikolaos and me to step back from him. We both obliged. I stepped backwards still keeping my eyes firmly on Kai's form and stumbled on a log fallen from one of the trees above. If Nikolaos hadn't caught me I'd have ended up on the floor. I felt like I was single-handedly battling the stereotype that all vampires are creatures of poise and elegance. Becoming the undead may have made me agile, but sophistication wasn't automatic, unfortunately.

Kai turned his face up to the sky with closed eyes. His nose twitched as he took a deep breath of the cold night air. Clouds ripped through the sky like dark grey explosions shielding the display of stars in the blanket of endless darkness.

I wasn't sure what to expect. How does a human body morph into one of an animal? Painfully, I found out. At least it looked painful from where I was standing. For a moment, nothing happened. Kai stayed with his face turned up to the sky staring up as if he could see something in the clouds Nikolaos and I couldn't. Kai's back began to arch. It was only a slight bend at first and then I heard the bones start to crack.

The muscles and bones began to ripple, bone stretched under his skin like they were trying to break free. The sound of multiple bones breaking is a haunting sound, much louder than I could have ever imagined. It was as if the sound of his spine snapping echoed through the night.

Kai collapsed to his knees with his back bowed outwards. He panted so heavily I thought he was hyperventilating. I turned wide eyes to Nikolaos who looked back at me blankly. Was it meant to be this way? Surely this wasn't right. Kai bayed, a high-pitched, deafening sound which caused birds to flee from their homes in the trees. I turned back to look at him. Kai's bones continued to break and crack. He fell onto his stomach with arms and legs outstretched. The bones grew, elongating his limbs. As he stretched and contorted the skin on his body was rippling, black fur began to flow and spread over his body.

It wasn't graceful or particularly quick. I had to turn away when the bones on his face started trying to fight free of their fleshy prison. Human faces just aren't meant to stretch the way his did. Looking away the sounds of bones cracking seemed even louder.

Another shrill shriek forced me back around. A huge black cat stood staring at me. His body was covered in a thick, bloody fluid which he shook himself free of like a wet dog. Kai's body stretched about six-foot long with a thick, soft tail trailing behind him curling at the end. Short and silken fur, which would have looked pure black if it weren't for the ebony rosettes rippling through the darkness, covered his body.

Kai plodded over to me on large paws. He nuzzled that broad, feline face into the softness of my belly rolling pale amber eyes up to look at me. It was almost disconcerting seeing the same eyes he had as a human in the face of a predator, but they also seemed more at home in his feline face. Faded blue denim lay in tatters on the frosty ground.

I stroked tentatively along the wide bridge of his nose. Kai's eyes closed as I brushed my hand down the fur. It was unbelievably warm and soft. So comforting, like heated velvet against my skin. A sonorous purr rumbled from Kai's throat vibrating against my stomach. I giggled.

I turned my head back to Nikolaos using my free hand to signal him over. He looked hesitant but came to stand beside me. He stood very still by my side. Still stroking Kai's head with my left hand, I used my right to take Nikolaos's hand and place it on top of Kai's head. Kai opened his eyes and looked up at us, cocking his head just slightly to one side. Nikolaos kept his hand on Kai's feline face but didn't make any move to stroke him. I sighed, placing my palm on top of his, using it to guide his pale fingers down the black satin of Kai's fur.

I removed my hand from Nikolaos's, and his fingers continued to stroke slowly down the fur. It was such a tentative gesture, cautious, like stroking a nervous lover for the first time. Just as I turned my head up to smile at Nikolaos, Kai snarled and whipped his face out of reach from Nikolaos and I. Nikolaos pulled his hand back quickly, letting it fall loosely to his side. His posture straightened and the softness of his face faded to the usual cold amusement he showed the world. A look that made it seem like he was quietly mocking everyone, but I was learning came from a place of self resentment, not outward disdain. I turned back to glare at Kai. Nikolaos rarely softened around me let alone in the company of others. For him to do so was a rare display of affection, vulnerability. And Kai had ruined it.

I strutted angrily past Kai, flicking him, lightly, on the nose as I went by. He growled again, although it was a lot less threatening this time.

'You said you wanted to hunt so let's hunt,' I said grumpily.

His response was another deafening shriek. The hair on my arms stood to attention. Primitive fear washed over me, like the part of me still nothing more than a hunter-gatherer knew that sound meant danger.

Kai began to plod towards me. He walked like a lazy predator. Knowing full well the world is his prey so he can savour the hunt, take his time. It would have been scary if it weren't Kai. Nikolaos stayed standing taut away from us. I turned to him and held out my hand with a smile.

'C'mon. We don't have all night.' I wiggled my fingers encouragingly.

Nikolaos looked uncertain, and, for a moment, I wasn't sure he would join us. I let out a sigh of relief when he stepped forward, lacing his fingers through my own. I beamed up at him, resting my head on his shoulder and holding his arm against my body.

Kai zipped through the night like a black shadow. He was used to being the fastest of both predators and prey but he'd never run with a vampire. Don't get me wrong, Kai was fast. We were just faster. When it came to jumping, however, he had me beat. Kai lept ten feet off the ground into the trees above landing with perfect grace. It was breathtaking. I followed, clumsily, with Nikolaos behind me. Together we galloped and flung through the trees like a perfect dance.

We did eventually stumble across a deer. Kai spotted her first. The doe was small, fragile and beautiful. I'd actually never seen a deer up close before. She huddled in a cage of browning bracken on feeble, slender legs. Her fur was a light oak, with a white underbelly and a scattering of ivory dots like freckles over her back. The doe looked around urgently as if she could sense the danger but didn't know where it was.

Kai braced himself in the trees, watching her with eyes shining with primal delight. I could almost feel his craving for her flesh rolling off of him. It reminded me of the bloodlust of a vampire but this was less about blood and all about meat. Vampire hunting is erotic, sensual, the blurred line between pain and pleasure; life and death. That is not the case with a beast. It was all about suffering, death and the thrill of the conquer.

It may have been hypocritical, but I had to depart when he pounced on the stunned doe. Deer caught in headlights took on a whole new, much more literal, meaning to me. Suddenly feeding on human blood seemed a lot less barbaric as I watched his huge, yellow canines tear into the throat of the deer. I hadn't eaten meat as a human, becoming a vampire hadn't hardened my stomach that much apparently.

I pointed to the lightening sky, using the whisper of dawn as my pass to flee the slaughter.

)CHAPTER 22(

Adalia and Gwydion sat at the pale oak table set tucked under the window at the back of the front room. It was so rarely used I usually forgot we even owned the set. It was nice to see someone putting the furniture to good use. Adalia clutched a white mug between both her hands, the steam rose and curled through the air. Chamomile, this time. I knew for a fact Nikolaos did not have a secret stash of herbal tea hidden somewhere in the cottage. Adalia was having to bring her own supply. We were terrible hosts. I'd ask Nikolaos to get some for her, although truthfully now I knew I could also still enjoy such simple pleasures it would be nice to get some in for me as well.

Gwydion was wearing his usual loose black fabric trousers, tunic-style top, and jacket which was actually more of a cloak. A huge, onyx cat lay curled under the table with his wide face resting on top of Gwydion's lap. Gwydion traced his fingers over the fur on Kai's face tenderly.

The few days they had been gone had felt lonely in some ways. I knew Nikolaos didn't like having his personal space invaded but I had grown quite accustomed to the company. Nikolaos appeared behind me the moment I thought of him. It wasn't intentional, at least I didn't think it was, but it was still strange timing.

We exchanged the expected pleasantries. It was all very amicable and civil, despite the fact I was bursting with anticipation to know what they had discovered. The table only had three chairs, Nikolaos had said he didn't mind standing whilst I sat but I ushered everyone to the sofas so we could sit communally without him lurking like a displeased shadow behind me. The table and chair set went back to blending in abandoned and forgotten once more. Oh well, it had been nice whilst it lasted.

'I am still not convinced of this theory,' Nikolaos said from where he sat beside me.

'That may be, but what harm does it do to indulge me, Nikolaos?'

'It is a waste of valuable time.'

Gwydion shrugged. Kai was curled at his feet watching me with his lovely eyes the colour of a summer sunrise.

'You are not a necessity to the plan if you do not wish to participate,' Gwydion cajoled. 'However, I can only imagine how your little Nymph would feel if her lover played no part in helping bring this monster to justice.' He made the word *'lover'* sound dirty, and *'monster'* ironic.

I rolled my eyes. Suddenly those three nights of peace without bickering seemed a lot less lonely. Gwydion really was the master of subtle manipulation. The words he had said had been hissed with indifference like it didn't matter either way to him, but we all knew he was right. If Nikolaos chose not to help us, I would be hurt. Not just hurt, angry.

Nikolaos looked at me. I responded with a coy shrug making him sigh defeatedly.

'Thank you, Nikolaos,' I said silently.

'Anything for you, ma chérie.'

It turned out Redcaps aren't a species with a lot of documentation. Gwydion had compiled the resources he could to find out as much as possible but it still hadn't been a lot of information. Still, with what the duo did find, they felt confident that their plan might work. Feeling optimistic that something *might* work didn't exactly fill me with the same surety. But I didn't have any better ideas so I forced myself to share their hope.

'Most scriptures,' Gwydion explained, 'seek only to repel a Redcap. Under such extraordinary circumstances, this is not what we wish to do.' I didn't say he was pointing out the obvious, though it was tempting. 'They're such a rare creature, you see. One of highland folklore; the last recorded sighting was over fifty years ago. Of course, no one believed it to be a Redcap but I am quite certain it was. According to the fables, the way to repel a Redcap would be through holy scripture or paraphernalia. Such as a crucifix.' Gwydion cast a look I didn't understand at Nikolaos and me. 'Theoretically, if holy items are a repellent, then impious scripture will attract him.'

There's nothing like relying on *fables* and *theoretics* to fill someone with confidence. Again, I kept the sarcasm to myself. Nikolaos was less innocuous.

'Your plan is fatuous.'

I tapped my knee against Nikolaos's leg, warning him to stop being vexatious.

Gwydion ignored him, continuing, 'Adalia and I have found an ancient sacrilegious scripture. It is not quite demonic but close enough for me to be able to use my own powers to more of an advantage. I believe between this diabolic text and my blood we will be able to ensnare this pesky goblin.'

Adalia sensed my uncertainty.

'I know it doesn't sound like a definitive plan but we wouldn't have come to you with it unless we were confident that this'll work.'

I had no choice other than to trust them.

)CHAPTER 23(

Gwydion had accumulated heavy chains woven from solid silver. On some of the thick loops of the chain, he had begun to attach a variety of wooden and metal crosses. It looked like a giant charm bracelet for a zealous Christian. Nikolaos actually backed away, his back hitting against the wall, when Gwydion produced the chains. Nikolaos pushed himself so hard into the wall it looked as if he were trying to disappear into it. Gwydion instructed me not to go anywhere near the metal, so I went to stand by Nikolaos. His skin had paled, if that was even possible, so he was translucent, glowing. Green iris had been consumed almost entirely by blackness, and the whites of his eyes looked very, very white.

'What's wrong?' I asked quietly, touching Nikolaos's arm tenderly.

He turned wide black eyes to me.

'The crosses, *ma chérie*.'

Oh.

'Do you not feel it?' he asked.

'Feel what?'

Nikolaos failed to hide the astonishment.

'If Gwydion is a demon, how come he can touch a crucifix without getting hurt?' I whispered.

I aimed the question at Nikolaos, but the answer came from across the other side of the room.

'It is a common misconception that objects of religion would hurt a demon. We are descended from divinity, much like angels and deities. Thus we are immune to such things. Demons are hard to hurt, let alone kill.'

236

'So, how do you kill a demon?'

Gwydion grinned at me, flashing all of those razor teeth.

'That, young nymph, is not information I would share so readily.'

I shrugged, smiling back.

'Seemed worth a shot. There is one thing that still confuses me about all this.'

'What is it, *ma chérie*?' Nikolaos asked, at the same time, Gwydion said, 'Which is?' The two men shared a less than friendly look.

'You say I'm a deity and I, like you, am descended from divinity. Does that mean God exists?'

Kai, who was sitting beside his husband back in human form, gave us a leaden blink, shaking his head at me. Gloves cloaked his hands to shield him from threading the last of the crosses through the silver. It turns out silver isn't just harmful to vampires but therianthropes too.

'You explain this one, Rune, I ain't gettin' involved,' he muttered under his breath.

'That certainly is a laden question, *ma chérie*.'

'Does that mean you don't know?'

'I have been alive long enough to lose my faith.'

'But holy water and crosses still hurt you—us?'

'Any blessed item will hurt a vampire,' Gwydion interjected. 'It is the strength of the belief that correlates to the damage, not the religion itself.' He fixed his gaze on Nikolaos. 'There is such wondrous irony in declaring the perish of your faith, Nikolaos. How does one lose their heart to a creature of divinity and lose their piety concurrently? You never cease to perplex and fascinate me, Nikolaos,' he said the last so softly it was a reverent whisper.

Nikolaos was momentarily taken aback.

'I had not considered this,' he said.

'Scarlet,' Gwydion continued, 'life and death are not linear. The world is not so black and white. Humans are simplistic creatures, lacking both wisdom and resilience. The flaw of humankind is that they have still not tapped into the knowledge of their own power. It makes them weak. A pitiful waste of species.'

'What do you mean?'

'I mean,' he said with patience, 'that faith is, in essence, magickal energy. When humans have faith, they are creating a sort of power which they should be able to control.'

'*Should* be able to?'

He smiled at me.

'This is where they have gone wrong, you see. This energy which *should* be their own is fed into the power of others. Throughout the centuries man has found themselves manipulated by non-humans. Of course, gods and goddesses exist. As a nymph, your lineage is of divinity. Being a god does not, however, automatically equate to omnipotence. Some creatures have been artfully cunning,' he said woefully, as if he were envious of their deception, 'and shown themselves to humankind thence evoking worship. Human faith, instead of being used to strengthen themselves, has been breathed into others and empowered them. This is how religion was born and why it has continued to change throughout the ages. Different entities have shown themselves at different times.'

Adalia's head popped up from behind the sofa.

'No matter what you are, we all feed off the universe and nature. It's why Pagans' belief feeds into the earth. Our reverence for Mother Nature feeds into her power,' she said piously.

'Indeed, Adalia,' Gwydion said. 'This is why celestial beings and elemental deities are superlative. It is true they are not always of the strongest or most dominant disposition, but their ties to the earth and all that it, or She, offers makes their power wholesome. Pure. They are the earth personified, Her children sent to walk this world and share Her fertility with those who reside on Her.'

'In my experience,' Nikolaos said resentfully, 'those who believe they are celestial are nothing more than priggish fools.'

Gwydion shrugged listlessly.

'If they are truly as they claim, then it is a rightful temperament. We are talking of creatures born of light and vitality. They are rarely fond of vampires, as creatures bred from death and darkness.'

I looked at Nikolaos to see how he would respond to, what I would have considered, the insult. He looked back with contented blankness as if it were just a fact, one he neither liked nor resented but simply accepted as truth. This was the longest Nikolaos and Gwydion had gone without arguing. I may have disliked being compared to nothing more than death and darkness, but in the name of keeping the rare peace, I kept that opinion to myself. If they weren't going to argue then I wasn't about to start.

'Most religion is derived from creatures of light who have shown themselves to humans. When a human prays to these beings, humans are also drawing from the earth's virtuous energy and feeding into the light. This is why items blessed this way will repel creatures of the night.'

'Like vampires,' I said.

'Like vampires,' he agreed with a nod.

'But Mother Nature is also neutral. She cannot be all good as what is life without balance,' Adalia elaborated. 'It is just most religions are based on the creatures who have shown themselves as beneficent. If you were to pray to, say, a religion based on a malevolent demon, then those holy items would be harmful to creatures of light. Like all magick, the intention is key.' She grinned at us. The sudden theological discussion was interesting if not moving too fast for me to process. I was getting a headache.

'So creatures of darkness are harmed by blessings of light? And visa versa?' I asked.

'Exactly,' Gwydion said. 'Though that does raise the question of where you stand as both a creature of darkness and light; good and evil.'

'But, as far as I'm aware, no one here is Christian. So won't the crosses be duds?'

Gwydion and Adalia exchanged a penitent look. Well, Adalia looked repentant, Gwydion didn't change his expression.

'We may have had to acquire them'—she appeared to be struggling for a word—'unethically.'

'You stole them,' Kai stated, a smile playing along his lips, humour shining in his eyes, making them glow like golden fires.

'You stole crosses? From a church?' I asked, aghast at their confession.

Adalia had the delicacy to look ashamed.

'Well, if there is a hell you're definitely going to it now,' I said, but even I couldn't withhold my stunned amusement.

'I wonder if a cross would still damage Scarlet,' Nikolaos said quietly, more musing aloud than directed at anyone in particular. He didn't seem bothered by their blasphemous crime.

Gwydion's paper-thin lips stretched into a villainous grin. At speed no human could match, he shot across the room to where Kai was still sitting ignoring us. Gwydion reached down, picked up one of the wooden crosses and lobbed it at me harder than was necessary. The wooden cross landed on my chest, my hands instinctively reached up to clumsily save it from falling to the floor.

Two things happened at once: Nikolaos, who had been standing abreast to me before, disappeared in a flash to halfway up the stairs where he cowered from the cross; at the same time, both Kai and Adalia shouted, 'Rune!'.

The carpet muffled the clang of the chains hitting the floor as Kai dropped them, rushing with Adalia over to me. Kai grabbed my hand so aggressively it forced my palm open, letting the little wooden cross tumble to the floor.

'Ow!' I exclaimed. 'What are you doing? That hurt.'

I snatched my hand back from Kai's grasp, rubbing my wrist. Even wearing gloves, Kai had grabbed me tight enough I was sure it would bruise. Everyone stared down at the cross, lying dark and bare on the cream carpet.

'You are not burnt, *ma chérie*?' Nikolaos asked from the stairs. He'd stopped cowering from us but stayed as far back as he could without being partly in the upstairs landing. His back was extended provocatively along the stairs, lying long and stretched with his upper body propped up on his elbows.

'Burnt? No.' I was still rubbing my wrist. 'My wrist hurts, but I'm not burnt.'

'Sorry 'bout that, darlin',' Kai said sheepishly.

Chuckling, Gwydion slithered over to the other side of me. It was a sinful laugh; serpentine and seductive all at once.

'Now this is fascinating,' he hissed, licking his lips with that viper tongue. The look in his eyes was hungry, eager.

I suddenly felt like the mouse staring into the eyes of a snake; frozen, scared, small.

Gwydion wrapped long, skeletal fingers around the

wrist of my hand that had released the cross. I had always known Gwydion was pale like the undead but seeing his skin on mine was startling. He was so very pale, as if not only the life had drained from him but all the colour that comes with it. Only those icy-blue eyes saved him from being entirely achromatic. Gwydion's skin was surprisingly warm; warm, dry, and smooth like stretched leather. He was close enough for the heat of his breath to blow over my cheeks. His breath was a cloying musk; again, it reminded me of old leather, and vaguely piscine. Not exactly unpleasant, but distinct.

'Why would I be burnt?' I asked of no one in particular.

'Do you not know what happens to a vampire at the touch of a cross?' Gwydion asked like he already knew that I didn't.

To look into his face, I had to look up, stretching my head back as far as was comfortable. He was just so tall. I shook my head still looking up at Gwydion towering above me.

'I know it hurts. Or is meant to hurt us.'

Gwydion released my wrist to bend down. He picked up the cross from the floor, twirling the dark wood through his fingers absentmindedly.

'It burns us, *ma chérie*. It is an agony worse than silver,' Nikolaos replied.

He was beginning to look quite silly all the way up the stairs away from the four of us. I was feeling almost claustrophobic so closely surrounded by the others. Suddenly sitting far away from the crowd seemed like a better idea.

'But I'm not hurt.' I held both palms out in front of me. 'See. So can I have some space, please?'

Kai and Adalia backed up. Gwydion, unsurprisingly, did not. I sighed, stepping into the now free space beside me away from his looming presence.

'You could have hurt her, Rune,' Adalia said softly.

'But I did not. The risk of pain was worth such an intriguing discovery, was it not?'

'Because you weren't the one riskin' pain,' Kai replied, sounding as close to annoyed as I'd ever heard him.

Gwydion dismissed us with a waft of his hand through the air.

'You are both being dramatic. If we were only to dwell on what could go wrong, then humans would still be nothing more than men in caves. Besides, she would have healed. I would never permanently maim such winsome beauty.' Gwydion flicked the cross he had still been twirling between his fingers in the direction of Kai, who caught it effortlessly. 'I would very much like to see how you respond to silver, Scarlet'— he sighed disappointedly—'natheless, we have more pressing matters to attend tonight.'

The lines between which parts of me were nymph and which were vampire seemed to be becoming blurred. I also wanted to see how I would react to silver if I were immune to crosses, but Gwydion was right, there were so much more important things to focus our energy on tonight. If all went to plan, we would finally catch my killer. That, however, was a big if.

Clouds dominated the sky above; a blanket of steel eclipsed the moon and stars. The five of us had settled into a small break in the woodland closer to the main road and city than the cottage. Trees loomed like spindly giants above us; stark and bare, only a handful of leaves still clinging to the branches with pitiful desperation. The woodland floor was a quilt of decaying leaves. Soft, plentiful rain tumbled from the clouds in a grey mist. The sort of rain which is so fine you can barely feel it touch your skin but soaks you quicker than a heavy storm. It didn't take long for my dark top to cling to my skin from the wetness. My hair was a cascade of wild, wet tangles down my back, stray strands clinging to my soaked cheeks.

Gwydion was drawing a sigil I had never seen before in the leaves. It looked like an elaborate upside-down triangle; the bottom point curled up, with a gothic 'V' caught between the curling lines. The two top points had lines crossing over each other in the middle and coming out the sides. When I had asked what it was, he had explained it was the sigil of Lucifer. Gwydion used a combination of snake blood, ground goat bone, his own blood, deadly nightshade, and garlic to draw the sigil in the leaves. Oh, and thistle. As, 'it's the national flower of Scotland and he is from highland folklore, of course'. Of course, because it was silly I didn't know that.

Adalia kept a lot of distance between her and the mark on the ground. She was really only with us to act as a sort of power buffer for Gwydion, but she had refused to take part in the ritual.

'I subscribe to the belief in the threefold law,' she explained.

'Which is?' I asked.

'That all energy you put into the world will come back three times as strong.'

'But won't sharing your power with Gwydion impact that indirectly?'

Adalia sighed.

'Yes, but it is for a good cause. I'm hoping that will count for something.' She sighed again. Adalia seemed weary, some of her usual joyous verve swallowed by mental exhaustion. 'If it weren't you asking, I would not do this at all. But as we said before, magick is about intention. I'm hoping the righteousness of my intent will countervail the depravity of this magick.'

Until then I hadn't realised how much I was asking of Adalia. Gwydion had no qualms about the imbalance of his magickal moral compass. I had assumed that it was the same for Adalia, without understanding just what this meant for her.

Kai, wearing nothing but a pair of pale blue jeans identical to the ones he had worn the other day, was resting under one of the larger trees. He was slouching against the trunk, denim-clad legs stretched out with one ankle crossed over the other. He ushered me over with a wave of his hand.

I didn't really want to sit down on the cold, wet ground with him but staying standing seemed like too aggressive a stance, so I ended up crouching down beside him, one hand resting on his shoulder for balance. Even in the late autumn night, Kai's bare skin was feverish.

'Are you okay?' I asked softly.

Kai looked over to me with sleepy eyes; a lazy half-smile played on the dark skin of his full lips. A stray lock of my crimson hair escaped with a gust of wind, and Kai used the arm I wasn't supported on to reach over, tucking the wet tangle behind my ear. His warm fingers lingered above my cheek a moment too long, not quite touching. It was a sensual caress, although not sexual. I was learning that intimacy to therianthropes doesn't mean the same thing as it does to most. Intimacy to Kai was about shared warmth, touch, and comfort, not sex or seduction. Even long past the full moon, I could feel the power radiating from him like a scalding pressure. It was languorous energy, but I knew Kai was so much quicker than he seemed. Astute and dangerous was our Kai.

'It ain't me I'm worried about. Are *you* okay? This'sa big night for you.'

'I just want it to be over,' I said with a cracking voice. The first tear escaped silently, the ones that followed flowed like an army of sorrow down my face. Kai pulled me down into his arms, so I rested like a child in his lap. I burrowed my face into his chest, letting his warm body engulf me. It was a comforting embrace, like being wrapped up in your favourite childhood blanket; toasty and safe. Kai's heart beat strong and fast against his chest. I hated to admit that Kai's embrace offered much-needed solace in a way Nikolaos couldn't. I knew he loved me in his own way, but Nikolaos's touch brought the serenity of death. There was something that felt very final about his skin on mine, the haunting touch of seductive demise, each kiss an offering of quietus. Kai felt like life. More alive than any human. The life that comes from being a creature who feeds, hunts and lives off the land.

'Y'know I've been married to Rune a long time,' he whispered into my hair, "n' I ain't never seen him take a likin' to anyone the way he has with you. You're family to us, darlin'. That won't change when this bastard's caught.'

'You're like family to me, too, Kai,' I said, adding hastily, 'To us. Niko, as well.'

Kai laughed his rich, growling laugh; sweet as honey, dangerous as venom.

'That man sure is lucky to have you.'

I shrugged, which is harder to do when being held tightly by someone.

As if summoned, Nikolaos was suddenly standing in front of us looking down. The rain had plastered his hair to his face making it look like a sea of black trying to consume his pale face. With no light to illuminate him, the green of his eyes looked stygian.

The night air abruptly went from autumnally cold and wet to jaw-chatteringly freezing. Not the cold of winter or rain but a chill that felt lifeless, as if all nature's essence had drained from around us and we were surrounded by death. My eyes flicked beside Nikolaos. The shadows in the forest looked more menacing than they had before; growing, stretching upwards like angry giants uncurling from their bodies to loom above us.

All three of us shuddered in unison. Goosebumps rippled up my arms, all the hair on my body standing up so tightly it felt as though they were trying to tear from the follicles. I gasped.

'What was that?' I asked, voice breathy.

'Rune has completed the sigil,' Nikolaos replied.

'Wow,' Kai said. 'I don't usually feel his necromancy, but this feels...' He had let me go to run his hands up his arms. There were goosebumps all over his bare chest. 'Sinister.'

'I have been dutied with embattling us.' Nikolaos's delusive black eyes narrowed just slightly. 'Unless I am interrupting something,' he taunted, trying to hide behind a sardonic smile. It wasn't an overly convincing performance, especially as I could get glimpses of what Nikolaos was feeling. Not jealousy; insecurity. It wasn't that he didn't trust me, even wrapped in another man's hold, but he knew Kai could offer me something his arms never could: warmth, life.

Still sitting on Kai's lap, I stuck my hand up to Nikolaos. He pulled me to my feet hard enough that I stumbled, having to steady myself against his chest. I wrapped my arms around his waist, resting my ear against where his heart beat slow but steady. Nikolaos felt so cold compared to Kai; it was like hugging Azrael after being wrapped in the arms of Ariel for too long.

Gwydion completing the sigil had stirred not only my own fire but Nikolaos's power, too. We stood in an embrace of arms, hearts, and energy. Intense heat, the living warmth of the earth, one of the five elements, frolicking mystically with Nikolaos's cold brush of death. Him drawing from me as master and I from him as vassal. It should have been that he mainly drew strength from me as the supposed dominant; instead, we mutually feasted from one another. We stayed standing together until, finally, the overwhelming weight of the eldritch energy Gwydion had conjured was background noise to the strength of our bond.

The plan was, in theory, straightforward. Gwydion was to read the impious text whilst drawing on Adalia's own power for leverage in the hopes that it would lure the Redcap to us. Kai, in his kitty-cat form, would prowl through the higher branches of the trees waiting to pounce. To be honest, Nikolaos and I weren't really needed so we took refuge about half a mile away to watch from the distance without getting in the way. Even if I couldn't help, I wanted to be there to watch.

The cross adorned chains would have only deterred the goblin from coming to us so those had been left at home, waiting limply for their purpose later on. Nikolaos hadn't exactly been thrilled with us leaving the silver and crosses in the cottage, but I think he was also relieved to be free from them for a while. It was the lesser of both evils to him. Personally, it made no difference since they didn't have any impact on me.

I rested my back against the rough bark of an old oak tree with my hands pinned behind my back. My fingers rubbed nervously against the trunk, playing with the harsh edges until the flesh was raw. Nikolaos stood utterly still in front of me. If he were nervous, it didn't show—Nikolaos wasn't one to fidget. Kai's piceous fur was camouflaged somewhere in the treetops closer to where Gwydion and Adalia stood. We'd lost sight of him a while back but still, I knew he was there. Watching, on guard; waiting.

'Come closer,' I whispered.

Nikolaos blinked at me slowly as if he had forgotten I was there. He closed the short distance between us, resting one hand on the oak tree beside my face, the other lower down by my hip. Mere inches kept his arms, hands, face from brushing against me. The wet tangles of his hair teased along my cheeks.

'Do you think this'll work?' My voice had dropped so low if it weren't for his vampire hearing the wind would have carried the words away to nothing.

'I do not know,' he whispered back, 'but even if not tonight, we will find him.'

He was so earnest it was nearly convincing.

'I love you, Niko,' I said, almost just a movement of lips with no sound.

Nikolaos hesitated for long enough for my heart to speed up, all my own insecurities reared their ugly heads making my stomach knot.

Finally, he replied, 'I love you, too, *ma chérie*.'

)CHAPTER 24(

From behind the trunk, I could see Gwydion beginning to read from an unrolled scroll made of brown parchment older than Nikolaos. Even if I hadn't seen him, I would have known when the spell—if that was what you could call it—started. The air was growing colder, denser, like trying to swallow ice instead of oxygen. Ice so cold it burnt going down my throat.

Adalia stood further back from the sigil than Gwydion. Chestnut-brown hair whipped violently around her face. It wasn't that windy out, but the power Gwydion was conjuring charged through the night like an invisible blizzard. I had a moment to worry about Kai's safety up in the trees before I got another bolt of power through me, driving me to my knees.

Nikolaos fell beside me, making even that motion graceful in a way I never would be. He held a slender hand out to me. I took it. Together we fought against the building pressure which felt like it would explode with us consumed by it, raining death, destruction and our physical bodies through the forest. My heat tried to battle the cold. The battle was lost. My teeth chattered against each other so violently I thought the bone would break. The dark hair on Nikolaos's arm looked like it was pulling away from his skin. I had felt Gwydion's necromancy before on so many occasions. This was different. Oh, so different.

The magick felt old, older than life itself, from a time when there was nothing but darkness. Before even planets burnt in space to bring light; when all that existed was a cold, black void. The nothingness was suffocating. I couldn't breathe, because there was no need to breathe when the air didn't exist. For a moment, all I could see was that perfect eternal blankness; I was suspended in that growing, smothering nil. Nikolaos's grip tightened painfully on my hand, crushing the bones in my fingers. It hurt, but at that moment the pain was more welcome than the tormenting nothing.

'Fight it, Scarlet,' he wheezed through gritted teeth.

I squeezed his hand back, let the feeling of his skin ground me to the here and now. I could see again. Like bones sticking from the grave, the canopy of leafless trees stretched above me where I had collapsed. Nikolaos's usually cold skin felt like fire compared to the ice of the air. Fire. That thought brought me back to myself. Flames we knew; the only true warrior against ice was fire. It was enough to let my power blossom within me, flowing through me, and into Nikolaos where we touched. We gasped in perfect unison, drawing in breath with the urgency of a drowning man.

The air was still heavy with an ancient evil, my stomach and chest were still tight with a knot which made me feel nauseous and weak, but we were safe. Or as safe as we could be in the battle against such heinous power.

Good and evil are meant to be subjective. We have laws, morals, ethics, but there is no single authority to determine the difference. Gwydion and Adalia were teaching me that there is no black and white, not really. The world moves in shades of grey. Some people see that grey as black, some as white, and some see it as a whole new colour entirely. Life, death, and everything in between simply are not linear. I had truly begun to believe they were right until that moment. There was nothing good about this power. It was the evil that corrupts good, consumes morals—a tsunami of sin. Grey did not exist to this magick.

Had Adalia known what she was signing up for before Gwydion had started the ritual? Guilt twisted my stomach into an even tighter knot. She'd wanted no part in this, and now I knew why. Because, even with all the good intentions in the world, this magick did not care. There was no virtue strong enough to fight this evil.

Gwydion stood caught in the gust of his own power. Ivory hair flew around his face like seaweed floating in choppy water. Adalia stood behind him clutching onto the trunk of a tree for dear life. Her knees were bent, trembling beneath her, threatening to collapse. I wanted to run to her. I wanted to stop this. Murder no longer seemed like a sin, not comparatively. I would have rather looked down on the decaying corpses of one hundred women than face this power anymore. Death, even violent, terrifying death, was a virtue compared to this.

I realised I had been crying, the tears carried away in the wash of the rain. Only the stinging of my eyes betrayed the secret weeping. Nikolaos looked at me with wide, bloodshot eyes. He looked at me with such woe, as if this evil power were eating him up in ways I didn't understand. Was he more affected? We were both vampires, but we had also established I had ties to the earth that kept me a creature of light. Did the darkness consume him more than it did me? That was a truly terrifying thought.

If I could have asked I would have but a sound brought reality crashing down around us. A silhouette began to crash through the distant trees until a short, stocky figure stormed into the opening, breathless and wild-eyed. The Redcap paid no attention to his surroundings, stumbling over his own feet with a crazed urgency until he fell into the circle of power Gwydion had created. The moment the Redcap centred himself in the sigil, Gwydion stopped chanting. Both he and Adalia collapsed to their knees. Gwydion panted aggressively propped up on all fours, long white hair brushing the ground. The silence was so sudden I thought I had gone deaf.

The silence didn't last long.

Standing directly in the centre of the sigil, the Redcap let out a shrill cry. The noise ricocheted through the forest, bouncing off the trees in a thunderous, penetrating squark that vibrated through my body. What happened next was instantaneous: Kai lept from the tops of the trees in a blur of black, rolling through the sigil on the floor with the Redcap caught between his teeth; at the same time, Nikolaos and I rushed the half-mile down to meet the others. We arrived within mere seconds, branches sliced my cheeks as I ran carelessly but the pain only fed the adrenaline I was currently thriving on.

We appeared beside Kai and the Redcap, screeching to a sudden halt. Gwydion had used the seconds we had taken to break the line of the sigil. The air was still heavy with woeful evil but it was dissipating. Kai was pinning the struggling Redcap to the floor, claws teasing at the damage they could do if he continued to struggle. The goblin didn't take the warning. Kai let a baritone growl trickle from between huge, discoloured fangs as his claws dug deeper into the meaty flesh of the Redcap's arm. It made the hair on my arms stand on edge and it wasn't even aimed at me. It would have been wise of the goblin to cease struggling. Wisdom eluded him.

Struggling even harder against the claws, blood began to pour from needle-like wounds in his arm. Kai was letting out a deep, rasping bark and I realised he was enjoying the struggle. Kai was feeding off his fear the way a vampire feeds off blood. It excited him. Fear made the vein in his throat pound against his icteric flesh. Just as Kai was about to plunge his canines into that throbbing pulse, Gwydion bellowed, 'Enough!'. Kai responded with a displeased growl but released the pressure of his paw from the goblin and moved his muzzle back.

We all turned to look at Gwydion. He held a black rope loosely in his hands like a long, limp serpent. I didn't remember him having a rope before. I was losing time. Too much power in such a concentrated space was leaving me confused. Or maybe watching a giant predatory cat lock his jaw around the goblin who murdered me was distracting. Maybe.

Using the black rope, Gwydion expertly bound the goblin's limbs. The rope knotted around his ankles, thighs, lower and upper chest, waist and in his mouth to act as a gag. It pinned his arms at an awkwardly painful angle behind his back, with the rope extending in one line from the gag to the ankles to make it easy to carry him like some obscene handbag. It looked vaguely erotic in a torturous sort of way, which was actually closer to the truth than I cared to know.

Gwydion, entirely too pleased with himself under the circumstances, explained with a haughty grin that it was called the *Gyaku Ebi* tie. It was once used as a torture position in Japan. It was also prominent in the bondage scene. That was more than I had wanted to know about Gwydion's fetishes. I wished I'd never asked about it; some questions are best left unanswered.

Residue of the goblin's blood from where Kai's claws had sunk into flesh stained the ghostly white of his hands. Gwydion rubbed it onto his clothes like he was trying to wipe off something nasty, distaste contorting his face.

We all stood in silence for several moments watching the Redcap thrash against the constraints, trying to swear through the gag. The wind beat around us with a fury, carrying away some of the gagged profanities. The fine autumn rain had picked up, slashing against my skin like liquid daggers.

I'd seen the Redcap before, most clearly in Sophie's memory, but never with such a clear, unobstructed view. Now I knew he was a goblin I could see all the characteristics which should have made it glaringly obvious initially, as if now I knew, it felt stupid to not have worked it out sooner. He was at least half a foot shorter than me with grey-green skin mottled with yellow. His eyes were the colour of weathered copper sunk deep in a decrepit face. Even in the limited light, the grease glistened in his dirt-brown hair. Half of his head was still hidden by that peculiar red cap, which his species was aptly named after. I had never seen anyone scalped before but Nikolaos's analogy now seemed nauseatingly fitting.

Long, yellow talons curled from his stumpy calloused fingers. I was unable to contain my disdain, abhorrence contorting my face into something ugly. I knew, without seeing, that my face was a picture of hatred at this grotesque creature. This was the man who had been the cause of so much pain, so much suffering. Those discoloured claws had been the last thing to touch my living flesh before life was ripped from me.

The Redcap had stopped struggling enough to turn wide eyes to me.

'A know ye,' he spluttered through the gag almost unintelligibly. Even through the gag, I could hear the thick Scottish accent. 'A killed ye.'

The gag wasn't able to hide his surprise. I felt my lips curl up into a depraved smile, flashing my oh-so-sharp fangs. I bent down to his level, pushing my nose against his own. I swallowed back the bile as his mephitic breath wafted into my face—the acrid smell of rot and death. Up close there was another scent I recognised: blood.

'And yet,' I whispered into his mouth, with a voice I barely recognised as my own, 'here I am.'

I noticed for the first time slashes in the trunks of the trees on the trek back towards the cottage. Kai had marked these woods as his own territory. I was actually surprised it had taken me this long to notice, but I'd been understandably distracted over the last few days. The goblin spat lewd remarks through his gag aimed at Adalia and I. We both did our best to ignore the increasingly vulgar comments. Realising he was not going to get the desired reaction through salacious obscenities alone, the goblin changed approach. In excruciating detail, he elucidated how he wished to kill me once more and in what manner it would be done. He wanted to make Adalia watch so she knew what would come next.

The murder was one thing, but when he started detailing the gruesome acts he wished to perform on our corpses I began to lose my composure. Unsure whether I was going to cry, scream or vomit, it took all my resolve to hide my disgust. I would not give him the satisfaction of my response. I would not let him see that my knees were weak and eyes shiny with unshed tears. Tears that begged to fall. But I knew that once I started crying that would be it. If I let myself begin to crack then I would shatter into a million pieces. I couldn't break. Not yet. Not when he could see me weak. I swore I would give myself the chance to break when this was over. I needed it. At that moment

I realised just how broken I truly was. Without the opportunity to mourn all that I had lost I would eventually become consumed by this pain. A pain that, until then, I hadn't even known was decaying me. If I didn't give myself the kindness to heal then I would rot. Death perishes the body; pain perishes the soul.

Nikolaos walked beside me like a silhouette of cold rage. I could feel the tension in his body build with each word that was spat into the air. All of that usual composure was lost to wild fury so unlike my reticent lover. I had suspected that Nikolaos softened his demeanour around me. He was, at times, complex and infuriating but I had never been afraid of Nikolaos.

Nikolaos finally lost his composure. It was as if two millennia of unresolved rage, disdain and self-loathing shone in a harrowing nimbus around him. Nikolaos glowed with nefarious power. Black satin hair whipped around his face in a wind of his own rage, those arrogant aquamarine eyes bled to a fearsome green fire. Nikolaos turned to face the goblin like a fallen angel risen from infernal ruin to force retribution on all those who had wronged him. My heart pounded against my chest, throat turning so dry to swallow was painful. For the first time I looked at Nikolaos and my pulse did not speed from his beauty, or love, but from absolute terror.

In an abrupt movement, too fast to be anything more than a blur even to me, Nikolaos raised his hand and struck the goblin full force in the face. I winced at the loud crack from his nose bone shattering. I risked a glance at the Redcap, having to turn away quickly at the sight of his mutilated nose. The bone was twisted entirely to one side, skinless in patches from where Nikolaos's hit had taken away some of the flesh. Blood poured from his nostrils in a stream of black, not the colour of a humans' blood. Where the skin had been ripped off more blood pooled, quivering on the edge of the wound as if uncertain of what it would do next, before finally trickling down his face. White glinted where his bone caught the dim moonlight.

We finished the expedition in tense silence. The only sound was the occasional wet gurgle of the Redcap attempting to breathe through his mutilated snout.

Kai, now in human form, bound the goblin in the cross-bearing silver chains with help from Gwydion. It subdued him, slightly. At least, the struggling stopped being as aggressive. The pained grimace that had contorted an already mangled face squeezed tighter together as if he had tasted something bitter.

The goblin forced his squinted eyes open enough to look up at me. I stared back into his dirt-red eyes as he pushed a dry, black tongue through pursed lips, licking away some of the blood that had dried black and sticky around his nose. The skin around the open wound on his nose was already blossoming into deep, purple bruises. His face was a mish-mash of purple, red, grey, yellow, green, and black like the abstract painting of a deranged artist. The grin that tried to spread his lips left his eyes sparkling with malevolence like tarnished jasper.

I knew some of the atrocities Nikolaos had committed, I was under no illusion that Gwydion had a dark, heinous past, and yet I had never bore witness to such a sickening lack of humanity. There was no rational thought process to reason with in his hostile eyes. The lights were on, but no one was home.

Usually seeing blood made me hungry but watching the Redcap lap away at the black plasma with slow, deliberate movements of his tongue made my stomach churn. If I didn't need it to survive, I would be put off for good. Making the sight of blood sickening to a vampire could almost be deemed impressive.

'What is your name, goblin?' Gwydion asked, drawing the prisoners attention back to him with a light tap of his foot against his arm.

The Redcap did not respond. With an impatient sigh, Gwydion kicked his booted foot into the Redcap's face with more force. The goblin let out a pained growl, all of that dried blood being washed away in a fresh stream.

'Maglark!' he cried out.

'What brought you to Britchelstone, Maglark? You are quite far from home.'

Even through the pain of his mutilated face, Maglark tried to grin at us again. The flowing blood pooled between his lips turning his mouth a red so dark it was almost black. He spat some of that blood onto the clean, white carpet.

'Am no gone tell yous that,' he gurgled through a blood-filled mouth, spraying more onto the carpet. Red seeped into the cream like a morbid inkblot on paper. Gwydion dropped his shoulders in frustration. He was not a patient man at the best of times, tonight even less than usual. I could feel his agitation growing with each passing moment like water filling up the room, drowning us in seething irritation.

Maglark spat more deliberately, spraying Kai and Gwydion with blood. A brassy growl trickled from between Kai's lips. It was not a sound made for human throats, so deep it sounded painful squeezed from between human lips. Nikolaos flashed behind Maglark, gripping a handful of all that greasy hair and pulling Marglark's head back at a painful angle. Nikolaos's other hand traced along Maglark's forehead so gently it was an eerily sensual touch, a caress reserved for lovers not enemies. His index finger played with the line of the red cap and his head and I realised then that, although it wasn't exactly flayed, that hat seeming shape was actually an extra layer of skin on top of his head. I had a moment to wonder how, why, it was red when Nikolaos's finger sunk into the flesh like it was squidgy making a thick trail of blood ooze down from his forehead.

The room spun, I had to steady myself on Adalia to not collapse to the floor. She turned to look at me with a pale, almost green, face. She looked clammy, beads of sweat clinging to her forehead and hairline. I felt like I was going to pass out, Adalia looked like she was either going to faint as well or vomit, or both. Maglark whimpered. I couldn't tell if it was a sound of pain or pleasure. I didn't know which I preferred. Pain. I would much rather that Nikolaos had hurt him by touching that loose, bloody flesh than pleasured him. I wanted to turn to look at the two men again but Adalia caught my attention.

'Lettie,' she whispered, voice hoarse and breathy as if even just those words were too much effort. 'I can't watch this. I'm sorry. Please understand.'

I did. I didn't want to watch it either. But, although Adalia had been a significant part in capturing Maglark, this wasn't her vengeance to claim, so she was allowed to flee the scene. I was not. I could not. No matter how much all the parts of my brain were screaming at me to run away.

'It's okay, Adalia,' I replied softly, forcing a smile which was meant to be reassuring but came out more as a grimace. 'Please make yourself at home in the guest room. Thank you for all you've done tonight.'

That earned me a smile although it never reached her haunted eyes. Everyone in the room had blood, flesh, and death as a part of their nature—including me, however much I hated to admit it. All of us except for Adalia. She had compromised more than just her magickal ethics to be a part of this.

Adalia left as hastily as she could without running up the stairs. I watched her go, turning to the other men only once she was completely out of sight. Nikolaos had moved his fingers away from the rim of the soft, moist flesh. His fingers were stained with dark, bloody sludge, it looked more the colour of dirty water than the bright crimson of fresh blood.

Seeing the blood on his fingers repulsed me beyond words. Those same fingers which held my hand, stroked my hair, made love to me, were now coated in the sticky residue of my murderer's blood. I stared into the menacing eyes of Maglark, looking at the face which had forced my demise. Even bound and wounded he showed no remorse, he watched me back with arrogance instead of fear. It was not the face of a man who knew he faced impending doom. Looking into his eyes brought back the unwelcome memories of my last night amongst the living. I thought of the determinative moment I had laid on the cold ground awaiting death to end the suffering at his hands. I thought of Sophie, and the other girls, who had died just as forlorn and afraid because of the man in front of me.

Maglark had robbed more from me than just a beating heart. He had stolen from me life in more senses than just breath and blood pumping through my veins. I had been raped of all opportunities. All the good and the bad I would have experienced had been extinguished by a fate determined by him; the scourge of my potential. I would never age, have children, find a career, watch Luke grow old, make an impact on this world besides stealing the blood of humans. Twenty is the age where life has so many paths, your future is undetermined and new and dauntingly filled with possibility. Now the trajectory of my life was pathed with living in shadows and darkness, feasting off the blood of humans or facing true death. My heart would never beat without the stolen life source of strangers.

Of all his victims I had been the 'lucky' one. Nikolaos had given me a second chance, and although the transition into the preternatural world had been burdensome, I was beginning to find my feet. It was only chance, or maybe fate, as Adalia would say, that had brought Nikolaos and the others to my side. He had found me seconds away from the final sparks of my life dissipating, turning to ash. If he had been any later, then I wouldn't be standing here staring into the unrepentant face of my murderer.

There were times when it felt like maybe facing true oblivion would have been easier than this strange half-life I was trapped in. But I also was grateful. With immortality on my side, I still had the opportunity to prosper. The other victims did not have such a luxury. They had had their chance at life violently ripped from them. It felt entirely too selfish not to be thankful for my second chance. I had an obligation to them to achieve all that I could as the undead, even if it wasn't the life I had anticipated for myself.

With all the images of mine and Sophie's final nights flooding my mind, a rage I had never felt before washed over me like a tsunami of anger. My flames had always been scalding and wild, an untamed fire flickering through me. This was different. It was a wave of cold, calm anger. I could feel the fire within my heart stir and flicker, burning bright the way all the hottest flames do—a pale blue, the colour of frost, not flame.

I was overwhelmed with the knowledge that this would be Maglark's final night. He would never be free to hurt or hunt again. The burst of emotion that came with the thought sent an unfamiliar lust through me. It was the lust for blood. But not to drink. To drown in; luxuriate and coat myself in. I wanted to watch his blood drip from my hands into the earth below and know that I had done to him what he had done to me and so many others. He deserved to hurt. He would, for he was ours—my fire and mine. And we would get our retribution.

I let all of that burning, disdainful rage permeate my eyes. Without looking I knew they burned with a black flame swallowing all the colour. I forced the heat of my wrath into that flame. I wanted to wipe the smugness of Maglark's face, and for the fear he deserved to feel twist his insides and spread through him like rot spreads through the dead.

Nikolaos made no movement, but for some reason, I was drawn to look at him. His own eyes had turned pure jade, flickering like ocean coloured flames. Our power flowed through the room, reaching through the air to entwine with one another. It soothed some of my rage. I knew that my own power was feeding his, he feasted off the energy I created until it breathed life into the power he thought he had once lost forever. Nikolaos had given me a second chance at life, but I had also given him a second chance to live up to some of his lost potential. I didn't know how, or why, as it shouldn't have happened this way, but it had and at that moment I felt high of the thrill of our energies flowing through each other as though they were making love.

Kai and Gwydion had stopped watching Maglark to stare at Nikolaos and me in turn. Goosebumps ran up their arms as our power washed over them as well. I heard Maglark gasp as it hit him, it recognised him as hostile. I had gotten my wish; arrogance had been replaced by caution. Not fear. Not yet. But the night was still young.

'I shall not ask you again,' Gwydion said, bringing Nikolaos and I back into the present. He visibly shifted, regaining his steel composure, eyes returning to normal as he swallowed back the power we had conjured. 'What brought you here, Maglark?'

Maglark let out a maniacal laugh, a mix between the haunting roar of a crazed scientist and the resounding growl of a dangerous animal. He would not answer our questions without a fight. Gwydion shrugged apathetically, saying, 'Whether you answer or not, this night shall be your last.'

The words were uttered with such cold conviction even I shuddered. If Maglark still wasn't scared it had nothing to do with arrogance and everything to do with foolishness.

⟩CHAPTER 25⟨

Despite my rage, I did not want to watch Maglark be tortured at the hands of the man I loved, which was perilously close to happening. It seemed as though the touch of Nikolaos's power against mine had calmed me but had had the opposite effect on him. He knelt behind the man, one arm wrapped around his neck and the other around his broken, bloody nose. Nikolaos had to keep enough distance to stay clear from the silver chains or crosses touching his bare flesh, but the deterrent they had been to his closeness earlier seemed to have vanished in the fit of rage that had overcome him. Maglark's eyes were beginning to pop with the inability to breathe, as well as pain from his butchered nose being crushed against Nikolaos's arm.

Half an hour prior, I had wanted nothing more than to cause him the pain he had inflicted on so many. Now, I wasn't so sure. I was certain he had to die, but wishing for pain and actually witnessing torture are two very different things. Gwydion didn't want him dead yet. He wanted answers. This was the first Redcap he had ever met, thinking for so long they were extinct; a species lost to legend. Gwydion needed answers that had nothing to do with Maglark's reasons behind the senseless killing but just trivia of why he had travelled all the way from the Highlands, alone, to seek refuge in this particular city.

If I were being honest with myself, Gwydion gruelling Maglark was an excellent distraction to the inevitable: killing him. So far, the questioning had been to no avail. Nikolaos cutting off his blood flow to the brain and any chance at getting enough oxygen to breathe wasn't exactly helping either. Gwydion instructed Nikolaos to stand by me, away from Maglark. He obliged reluctantly. Maglark took his retreat as weakness, eyes glistening with that rage-inducing arrogance even as he coughed and choked, gulping the air like a drowning man.

Gwydion explained to me that Redcaps were notoriously ruthless with barbaric instinct running through them like blood through veins; it was exceptionally rare for them to come out of hiding from the Highlands. To stay alive, Redcaps had to murder and use the blood of their victims to keep their caps wet, or they would shrivel and die as it dried. Most small villages surrounding areas rife with the goblins had been deserted, and they would rarely wander far enough out to get their kills. It had eradicated a lot of their species, although a few rogues had still roamed hunting human blood. Long ago, when they were more common, the Syndicate of Occultists had decided they were simply too dangerous to let breed so had murdered all the females. It meant the goblins, who had a long life span, could live on but never reproduce. I'd asked who the Syndicate of Occultists were. Gwydion had responded with a coy smile saying he was sure I would find out sooner or later at the rate my powers were growing. Gwydion did not do coy well, but ominous, that he had mastered.

Maglark's cheeks began to fade from the breathless maroon back to his usual ashen green. He thrashed and beat against the chains whilst still gasping for the air he had yet to regain fully. All that haughtiness was replaced by seething rage. Maglark shot Nikolaos a murderous glare, Nikolaos returned it with perfect blankness. Not raising to his bait was a more powerful retaliation. When people are angry, they don't like that anger to be ignored. It either makes them feel silly and mutes the rage or pisses them off even more. In this case, it was the latter.

We were at a standstill of sorts; I forbade torture to be used, and Maglark was refusing to answer our questions without the incentive of pain. For a short while, we stood in a tense, uncertain quiet. The only sound to save it from being silent was Maglark still thrashing against the chains. His ragged, gurgling breath hinted that he was growing weary from the battle of flesh against metal. I'd never been one who was able to stay angry long, and standing in silence had cooled my temper. I watched Maglark struggling against the metal with a strange vacancy, a distance between the others and myself as if there were a glass pane between them and me. It had nothing to do with magick, and everything to do with my brain shutting down. Without anger, I was numb, lost. Overwhelmed to the point of nothingness, an out of place serenity left me floating and feeling illusory. It wasn't a pleasant calmness. It was the calm before the storm; my brain, unable to cope, preparing for the inevitable horror.

Maglark struggled and thrashed against the chains until he had no fight left. Realising he had no way to break free, he switched tactics to shouting and raging. It didn't phase the others, and, at that moment, nothing could phase me in my not-so-real reality in which I was suspended. The problem was, Maglark already knew how to rile Nikolaos up. He was the only one of us who had lost their composure already, reacting with violence and rage. It was his last bullet in the chamber, and he would not waste it.

'I remember ye well,' he said, about me but looking at Nikolaos, 'your fear was sweeter than the others. Ye tasted of prey. The stench of terror'—he tried to inhale dramatically through his broken nose—'like fine wine on my tongue.' He licked his lips again, slowly, as if savouring the flavour of his own blood.

Maglark continued to explain in agonising detail the pleasure he had received from murdering me. How much weaker I was than the others; I had simply collapsed and waited for him to finish the job, the other women had put up some sort of fight. I had acquiesced in his decision to kill me; laid down in silent complacence awaiting my terminal fate. Unlike the others, I had given up before the fight had even begun.

Maglark speculated how I was the least deserving of a second chance. Why should the weakest of his victims be given the opportunity of immortality? I would just waste it. The words stung like a knife slicing through all that quiet peace, each syllable cutting to the bone. Deep down, I agreed with him. My silent assent to the statement made the words hurt even more because he was putting into words all the thoughts I had been too afraid to let myself think. Maybe it was irrational, but I was also scared that now the others had heard it so openly they would also agree. Nikolaos would regret turning me instead of the others. Gwydion, Kai and Adalia would know they wasted their time on someone pitiful, but not worth pity.

I was too wrapped up in my sorrowful self-pity to notice Nikolaos's anger growing like an untamed physical presence. Emotion radiated off of him in bountiful waves, but they could not penetrate my dissociative state. I was so distracted that when Nikolaos moved in his vampire speed, it was a startling blur. The world already felt slow, my brain lagging behind the flow of everyone else. Usually, I could register his movements at a normal pace; tonight, it was as though he had not just run in a blur of speed but disappeared magically. One moment he was beside me; the next, *poof,* he was gone. And so was Maglark.

It took me several dumbfounded moments to process what had happened—seconds ticked by at the speed of hours. My brain simply was not working the way it was meant to be. This was not a very good defence mechanism in times of crisis. The front door slamming to the floor of the porch in a deafening thud helped pull me from the trance. Wood had scattered in chaotic splinters all over the porch and front room from the impact; brown and green stuck up from the carpet like tiny pikes. Nikolaos hadn't even bothered to open the door, just crashed straight through it in his fit of fury.

I turned startled eyes to Gwydion and Kai, not sure if they were back to their usual colour or still an ocean of black. Gwydion swore loudly in a language I had never heard before, I don't think it was a tongue known to humans. Adalia almost fell down the stairs, catching herself on the bannister in the wall just in time to save herself, as she rushed to see what the commotion was. Everyone turned their heads to look at me and, for the first time, I really registered what had just happened. Nikolaos had levanted with our hostage. Without fully processing the information, I was speeding out the door to follow them. It felt like my body was working faster than my mind. It knew we needed to go, but my brain still hadn't thought that far ahead.

Trees whipped past me in a blur, like running through a brown nebulous with hints of green slashing through from the final determined leaves refusing to give themselves over to autumn. Branches hit my face, slicing the skin. Just as the first trickles of blood began to fall, the wounds knit themselves back together. The pain was an abrupt, eye-watering sting.

It didn't take long for me to find them both. Nikolaos held Maglark by his throat against the bark of a large oak tree. Maglark's face was turning a deep, plum-purple with his beady red eyes bulging out their sockets from the strength of Nikolaos's grasp around his throat.

A twig snapped below my foot, crunching into the frosted grass, which made Nikolaos turn to me slowly. His eyes were large and wild, burning like a green ocean alight with flame, but they did not hold anger. The look on his face was one of perfervid hunger. The moon appeared dramatically from behind the wall of cloud casting white light on the dark blood around his mouth. Moonlight illuminated the black fluid as it fell in thick droplets from his lips, hands, and down Maglark's unmoving body. I could smell the acrid stench of rotten blood, nothing like the sweet alluring blood of a human or the even more enchanting plasma of other supernatural beings. The smell was so intense I knew the wound would be significant. The problem was I still couldn't see the extent of the damage.

Nikolaos was always such a neat feeder. To see his face and shirt covered in blood in the sudden harsh light of the moon made him look far from human. Still hauntingly beautiful but monstrous. Steam spilt into the air from where his hand touched the crosses that bound the goblin. I knew he must hurt, but Nikolaos paid no mind to his wound, keeping his hand firmly in place with the smoke and fumes of burning flesh seeping into the damp air.

The night was alight with the most bitter of scents. So much so I fought with myself not to cover my mouth, nose and eyes. Everything in my body screamed, *danger, run*. All instincts kicked in that this was not safe, that nothing should smell of so much repugnant blood. Tears quivered against my eyes. I wasn't sure if they were watering from the burning smell or from seeing Nikolaos watch me with such a crazed expression I no longer recognised him.

What made it all so much worse was I could feel his emotions stronger than ever before. The shields between us had been truly shattered; Nikolaos had spent more energy than I had ever realised to separate us from the potential of our bond. Now I could feel his hunger, the thrill he got from seeing blood taint the perfect whiteness of his flesh after so long being reserved and, deep down, the pleasure of my fear. I smelt vulnerable, the way so many women had before me. They, like me, had all seen him as an animated statue of beauty and grace. They had all thrown themselves at his feet, begged him to take them in every way imaginable, except none of them could honestly know what that meant. He relished in watching their eager, lustful gaze turn to dread as he showed them the monster he concealed so well. He never truly hid it, the monster always lurked below the surface like a leviathan in the depths of the seas, but humans only see what they want to see until it's too late. He looked at me the same way he had countless others. I was just another besotted woman who did not know the true him, and could never accept him for what he was: the undead; a monster.

Nikolaos had told me of some of his addictions when he was with Camille. The drugs, drink, stream of bodies for sex and blood. What he had not told me was the one addiction which had been the hardest to kick. Not the trickle of blood for feasting, but the rivers of it that come with murder. Enough to bathe in, which he did, with Camille. Nikolaos hated that she was evil, but worst he hated her for showing him that he was, too. No matter how much the torture and death had repulsed him, it had also always satisfied a craving he could not escape. Camille was the only one who had ever nurtured this side of him. He despised her for it; he loved her for it.

He knew I would never be able to accept this side of him, the side he had spent years running from after her death. Nikolaos had been waiting for me to either flee from him in disgust or horror. And now I had fulfilled the latter prophecy. I was just another person who resented him when he revealed all the parts of his soul, not just the pretty bits. The only person who had never run had been Gwydion, but Nikolaos had been so caught up in hating himself he couldn't accept the embrace of his friendship. Instead, he had been the one to flee. For four centuries he had hidden from Gwydion until I had come along and forced all those heavily guarded memories wide open.

I stumbled, falling to the ground gasping for air. Tears were now trailing my cheeks in a burning stream. I had fallen so deep into the mind of Nikolaos it took me a moment to adjust to the reality of here and now. The reality had not gotten any better in the moments I had been transported to the dark, hidden corners of Nikolaos's psyche.

'Is that truly how you see me, Niko? Just another infatuated woman in love with the parts I want to see and not the whole package.'

'I can taste your fear of me like sugar on my tongue.' His voice was strained.

I did my best not to let my eyes flicker to Maglark's limp body still pinned to the tree.

'How could I not be scared? I'm overwhelmed, Niko,' I said, my voice cracking, 'so very overwhelmed. Did you want me to rejoice in watching you kill? I don't have to love every part of you to accept it.'

The look on his face was clear that my words alone

would not suffice. It seemed like a peculiar time for Nikolaos to parade his abandonment issues on full display; all that anger, and fear, that I would hate him as much as he had learnt to hate himself. Or maybe I wasn't the only one who had reached the end of their tether. Adalia had crossed a line she never wished to cross, the consequences of which we did not yet know. I had faced the man who had murdered me, all of the trauma I had been hiding from slapping me with a staggering force I couldn't ignore any longer. What had Nikolaos given up to help me?

With the shields between us obliterated I did the only thing I could do to try and ease the burden of his insecurity.

I let him into my mind, body, soul. I allowed him to see further into me than I truly ever looked myself. It was intimate in a way that no hands, tongues, words could ever be. I let myself be vulnerable, so very vulnerable. At that moment, he held my heart and mind in his hands and I knew that once I opened up this way there would be no returning, because I was scared, too. Scared, like him, that he and the others would flee from me if they truly knew who I was.

I did not feel likeable, let alone loveable. For the first time in my life, I had people I truly loved, who I would do anything for, and I was terrified of them casting me aside. I didn't know how to let myself be happy with them without bitter insecurity plaguing my mind. I waited with bated breath for the day they would all realise I was not worth their time. The love I felt for Kai, Gwydion and Adalia was wholesome and gentle but paled in comparison to the tender fondness I felt for Nikolaos.

I let him see the purity of my love. Not because he was beautiful, or seductive, or ominous in a way that made me want to uncover and analyse him. I loved him for his frustrating reticence; the very human way he played with my hair when he was musing; the gentleness he had with Adalia after years of friendship; the way him opening up slowly, in his own time, filled me with not only happiness but honour that he trusted me enough. I accepted his complexities because, without them, he would not be Nikolaos. Even the ugliest parts of his past, present, and future would never make him any less spectacular to me.

Truthfully, even if I had wanted to run from him we were too tightly bound as master and vassal. I may have been powerful in some ways but we simply did not know if I would survive severing that connection. I might not be able to stand alone even if I wished to. Vampire magick aside, I was also bound to Nikolaos by my fondness for him. I did not want to part his side. I let him see all of this. I willed him to see how earnest my heart was. I forced him to see himself the way I saw him. Not as a monster, not really, despite what he was—what we were.

If what Nikolaos did then, after I had let him see further into me than anyone before, had the desired intention to shock me, he succeeded spectacularly. Eyes locked on me, Nikolaos released his fingers from their grasp on Maglark's throat. I heard the two *thuds* before my brain made sense of what I had seen collapse in a lifeless pile to the ground. Maglark's stocky body lay crumpled on the grass. Beside it lay his head; face now colourless, eyes still bulging and glassy with death. There were ragged edges around the stump of his neck where Nikolaos had ripped his throat away with bare teeth, tearing through flesh and bone to finish the barbaric decapitation.

Spine caught the light, so pure and white in the mounds of raw, red flesh and black blood. The smell was stronger now, not just the smell of blood, but of flesh and bodily functions giving way to death.

Nikolaos had lifted the wall between us so high I didn't know how to shut it down. Before then I hadn't even known he was doing it. Before I had a chance to stop them, thoughts of repulsion, disdain, horror swam through my mind. I felt his twisted satisfaction as if he were going, *See, I told you.* He thought he had been right, that I was disgusted by him. The game had not been played fairly. Nikolaos had used the theatrics to coax the desired horror from me. That, more than anything, was what truly broke me. On top of the horror of Maglark's corpse lying in pieces only a foot away from me, he had decided it was the time to play such ridiculous, petty mind games.

If I weren't already on my knees I would have collapsed. As it was I fell to my hands and knees and wretched. Bloodstained vomit poured from my mouth onto the grass. I threw up until there was nothing left. Somewhere along the way, the other three had joined us. Warm hands pulled my hair back from my head. Kai stroked his palm around my back in comforting circles. So warm, so alive. I needed life right then.

Kai helped raise me to my feet with one arm under my elbow, the other around my waist. I steadied myself against his body, knees shaking so hard I would have fallen again if he hadn't wrapped his arm tighter around me.

I had wanted Maglark dead. Yearning for vengeance, consumed by rage, I had desired to watch him suffer. Now, watching the blood trickle through the grass, creeping towards me like a macabre river, I felt empty. That awful emptiness that comes with shock when your body and mind no longer knows how to cope. There was no denying we had needed to put an end to Maglark, to punish him for his atrocities, but

this was inhumane. We had not achieved the right-
eous justice I had sought but become as bad as the
monster we hunted.

My attention was caught by something held in Nikolaos's unbloody hand. Small, white squares were
held loosely in his palm. I couldn't work out what they
were. I turned my head to one side, trying to focus
more on what he held. Anything to focus on other
than the dead body or the blood that coated Nikolaos
like an obscene shield of liquid armour. So much
blood. The world began to spin again. I tightened my
grip on Kai to steady myself. If I just focused on whatever he was holding it would be okay, nothing else was
real except what was in his hands. Nothing could be
worse than what was scattered around us.

'What is in your hand, Niko?' I asked, voice shaky
and distant. It sounded like my voice echoed through
the woods as though we were in a hollow, dark space. I
was pretty sure I was imagining it.

I flinched at the movement of Nikolaos reaching
his hand out to me. I curled into Kai's chest, turning
my back on him. I knew that by hiding further into
Kai's embrace I was only reinforcing Nikolaos's skewed
ideas of how I saw him; I needed the comfort more
than I needed to tend to his sensitivities.

I peeked from where my face was nuzzled into Kai's
chest in time to see Gwydion walking over to Nikolaos. He took the squares from his hand with a hiss.
Gwydion was usually as good as Nikolaos at hiding his
emotions, but as he flipped through the squares, he
was unable to stop the horror leaking onto wide, pale
blue eyes. I pulled out of Kai's hold to take a closer
look at what had left Gwydion so shocked. He hadn't
even reacted to the carcass lying at our feet. This had
to be unimaginably bad. I didn't want to imagine it; I
wanted to see for myself. Gwydion, seeing me turn,

clasped the squares to his chest to shield me from the sight of them.

Kai walked away from me to take them from his husband's hands. He let out a deep, shocked exhalation. Kai slammed them back against Gwydion's chest hard enough he stumbled backwards, catching them just in time to not fall into the blood-soaked floor. My toes had begun to grow warm from the blood seeping into my boots. I'd been trying my best to ignore the sensation. It wasn't too hard in my state of shock. Sometimes the mind shutting down has its upsides.

Usually mild-mannered and demure, Kai pushed his stocky frame against Nikolaos's taller body, staring up at the slender man with a burning rage. The air was ignited with energy: Kai's heated therianthrope power trickling into the air, prickling along my skin like tiny, feline claws; and Nikolaos's cooler, damper power responding. Kai's fists were balled up so tightly the veins on his arms stuck out like blue vines running up his dark skin. Violent tension was so thick around him it was palpable. If this was a test of wills, I was sure Kai would win. If it became physical, I was less confident.

'Why,' he began, voice a strained growl, all of that honey-sweet accent lost to something predatory, 'the —fuck—would—you—show—her—this?' Each syllable was squeezed out painfully. It hurt just to hear, let alone be the speaker.

'Step away from me, pussycat,' Nikolaos retaliated, seemingly unphased.

Gwydion took a step towards the two men, wrapping his free hand over Kai's shoulder, pulling him back from Nikolaos so Kai rested against his husband's chest. Some of the aggressive tension left Kai's body, his hands were still balled into fists, but they were looser now.

'Do not talk to Kai in such a manner, Nikolaos,' Gwydion said calmly, but his power began to wash through the air, targeting Nikolaos. 'This is not a battle you wish to lose.'

Adalia and I shared a look. This was potentially getting further out of hand. Testosterone filled the air like something drinkable; the display of power becoming petty male dominance. Adalia had paled to something sickly, her light olive skin green. Beads of sweat formed around her forehead and upper lip like morning dew. We were both doing our best to ignore the decapitated corpse at our feet. Something much easier said than done.

Gwydion wafted the squares in front of Nikolaos's face just enough for me to make out that they were dark, grainy polaroids. What possible reason would Maglark have polaroids horrifying enough to shock two of the most stubbornly stoic men I had met. A daunting, sickening thought occurred to me of just what they may show. No, surely not. I had heard of killers keeping trophies of their victims but no one would be sick enough to have photographic evidence. I would have asked, but my throat was thick with something bitter.

Gwydion spoke before I had the opportunity to clear my dry throat enough to get the words out.

'Maglark truly was a vile little creature.' He pointed to the body, my eyes followed the movement before I had a chance to think better of it. The world swooned again. I moved back enough to rest my body against the solidness of a tree. 'Yet' Gwydion continued, 'that does not grant you carte blanche to cause such disarray.'

'Are they what I think they are?' I asked, voice small and hoarse. I sounded afraid, like a child who finally found out the monsters in the closet walk amongst us. I was one of those walking nightmares.

The men all turned to look at me as if they had forgotten I was there. At least Nikolaos seemed calmer now.

I pushed myself away from the tree to walk closer to the three of them, stepping around the body on the floor. Gwydion used his grip on Kai to pull him further back, giving me the space to stand in front of Nikolaos. His eyes were back to their calm, unreadable beauty as normal. Nikolaos reached his hand out to me. I did not take it. Raising that same hand further, he traced his fingers through my hair, tucking it behind my ear. The temptation to rub my face against his palm like a cat which felt safe and content was overwhelming, but I did not feel safe, nor content. Usually, I would have fallen into his embrace, given myself to him readily. Tonight, there was a tension in my body which left me rigid against the tentativeness of his touch.

'What is it you think they are, *ma feu*?'

I swallowed hard enough it hurt; choking back words, tears, screams. What came out my mouth was steady when what I really wanted to do was fall apart.

'I don't want to play a guessing game. I don't want any more games at all tonight. Just tell me.'

'Maglark kept photographic souvenirs of all his victims once he had murdered them. I discovered them in his pockets before I killed him.' He said the last so matter-of-factly without a shred of remorse.

I had guessed that was the case but hearing Nikolaos say it out loud made me feel faint. If Nikolaos had killed Maglark after he had found the photos then the brutish murder seemed considerably easier to defend.

'You were his first victim, *ma chérie*.'

'I want to see.'

'No, Scarlet, savour your sanity. It is so easy to lose, and almost impossible to regain once lost,' Gwydion said gently. 'Trust me when I say you do not need to see such horrors. I speak only of what is best for you.'

'Are you implying I do not?' Nikolaos asked, the first threads of rehashed anger forcing through the words.

Gwydion locked hostile eyes on Nikolaos.

'Implying? No, Nikolaos. I thought I was being quite explicit. You are just as selfish and reckless as you were four centuries ago. Is this what power does to you? Does it send you into a state of madness where you lose all sagacity?'

'I would do nothing to harm Scarlet.'

Surprisingly, Gwydion responded with, 'I believe, Nikolaos, that you would never cause harm to your lover willfully.'

'What do you mean by that?' Nikolaos's French accent got thicker with anger, so much so it was almost hard to understand him clearly.

'I mean that your power is pernicious, and whether you like it or not, you have the typical vampire mentality of thinking with fangs before mind. Recklessness has no consideration for its iniquity.' It looked as though Nikolaos were about to respond, but Gwydion continued, 'You have no mind for consequences. This decapitated carcass leaves us all in a quandary. Did you spare a moment to consider how this would affect our innocent Scarlet? Your penchant for sin will consume her unsullied mind.'

'She is strong.'

'Yes, I do not deny that. But she is strong in ways you will never be. You are jaded with age; insensible to evil. She'—he motioned to me— 'has the clemency, compassion, of a human. I doubt you can recall what it means to tote the burden of empathy.'

'It is a burden you do not bear equally.'

Gwydion smiled woefully.

'I conceded to this many years ago.'

Kai, Adalia and I had become superfluous to the conversation. Whilst I couldn't deny Gwydion and Nikolaos needed some serious therapy, now wasn't the time to start delving into the death of their humanity, or lack thereof. When this was over, though, maybe I'd suggest couples counselling for the two of them. Lord knew if anyone needed some professional help, it was these two. The thought made me giggle. Probably an inappropriate response given the circumstances but the night had become so capricious I wasn't sure if I wanted to laugh maniacally or sob until I was dry. Maybe we could all do with some therapy.

The noise made the two men break their intense staring contest to look down at me. I swallowed back the next burst of nervous laughter. If I started laughing I didn't think I'd stop. Maybe ever. I'd become one of those people you see in straight-jackets, rocking back and forth in a soft cell laughing uncontrollably. Was this what it felt like to finally snap? If it was, it wasn't as unpleasant as I'd thought. I couldn't decide if it seemed better to be stuck in a perpetual loop of mindless hysterics or go back to that distant numbness I'd felt before.

I wafted my hand in the air, trying to physically disperse the strange tangents my mind was going on. There were much more important things on which to focus. We could all worry about our evanescing sanity later. Becoming a vampire was teaching me to push aside unwelcome thoughts. I kept telling myself they'd be dealt with at a later date, but so far it seemed the troubles I intended to deal with were mounting up much quicker than they were being solved.

'He's right, Nikolaos,' I said, finally. 'This'—I pointed

behind me to Maglark without looking—'is more than I can stomach. Let alone seeing what he did to those poor girls.' I hesitated for a moment, before whispering, 'To me.'

'You requested to see the images.'

I hung my head.

'You're right. That was my mistake.'

Nikolaos slipped a finger under my chin, turning my face up to look at him.

'This is the life of a vampire, *ma chérie*. What good does it do to obscure the truth of our ways? The bloodlust is a double-edged sword. It can be a beatific, sensual act, or it can be macabre and obscene. To relish the beauty of life means to appreciate the brutality of death equally. You shall learn to hunt, to kill, much the same way.'

I pulled my face away from his hand abruptly, giving him angry eyes. Laughter had been overcome with the stirrings of anger.

'No, Niko, I will not. I don't believe this is what it means to be a vampire. I think this is what it means to be'—I stabbed a finger into his chest—'you. You've spent two thousand years killing without a second thought. I will never be that way. I will never love this side of you.'

I had said the one thing I knew would cut deeper than anything. Nikolaos had opened the door between our two minds, and I had used it against him, twisting the trust into a knife aimed at his heart. It was petty, no it was cruel, and I would apologise, but right then I was too angry to feel remorse.

Nikolaos startled me with an abrupt, bitter laugh. Nothing like the using silken caress of his voice, or the rare joyous sound of the few times he had genuinely laughed around me, this sounded like nails down a chalkboard.

'Just like a nymph to be so sanctimonious. You are atop so high a horse you cannot humble yourself. Do not forget I saw inside your heart, Scarlet. It beat with the anticipation of his death.'

Such a poetic way to be called arrogant. And also highly ironic coming from him.

'Not like this! I wanted justice,' I replied bleakly. How can you argue with someone who's seen inside your soul and knows the truth?

'*Non,* you wanted revenge. As did I for what he did to you. Justice is tantamount to revenge if the sole resolution is death, Scarlet.' He sounded defeated by lassitude, saying my name with such hostile indifference it felt like shards of ice piercing my heart.

With the mental barriers torn down, I tried to reach out to him through the mind. At some point, they had been cast tightly back up, stronger than ever before. Trying to break through was like banging my fists against walls of impenetrable steel until my hands were bloody. I was well and truly shut off from him. Lonely, it felt so lonely, as if my soul had been trailed by the light silhouette of a companion, not to crowd me but as a reassurance. Now my soul felt cold without the presence to offer familiarity or warmth. There is nothing more heart-wrenchingly lonely than the solitude of losing something you hadn't even known was there. I was totally unprepared to be so suddenly isolated in my own head.

'This wasn't your justice, or revenge, to claim. You're acting so high and mighty as if you did such a great thing by killing him, but you didn't. You're just trying to rationalise a decision made in haste,' I snapped.

Nikolaos laughed again, that same nails-on-a-chalkboard racket.

'You have taught her too well, Gwydion,' he said,

looking at the man who still stood towering behind me. 'The voice is hers but the words are yours.' He turned back to face me. 'I thought better of you than to be so easily manipulated by the demon. The goblin is dead, thus what you do next is paltry to me.'

'Are you leaving?' I asked, anger drowned by woeful loneliness leaving my voice juvenile.

'My presence is unsought.'

With that, before anyone had a chance to say otherwise, Nikolaos fled into the darkness in a trail of whooshing air, leaving us to deal with the consequent imbroglio of his precipitous murder.

I fell to my knees, head encased in my hands as tears streamed steadily down my face. Blood, still so warm, seeped through the legs of my trousers in a sticky mess. There was no urge to laugh now. Instead, I choked on my sobs; mewling, whimpering.

⟩CHAPTER 26⟨

Two bodies wrapped themselves around me as I wept. The smell of large cat and amber perfume swarmed around me with their warmth like a comforting blanket. Kai and Adalai's heat chased away the coldness; their combined scents helped me breathe again, carrying through the autumnal wind to replace the stench of fouling corpse.

They both raised me, one on either side of me, still holding me close. The air felt particularly glacial where it whipped at my knees warmed by the blood that had pooled around me.

Maglark was dead. I didn't have the time to luxuriate in woe. He had gotten his comeuppance; however, the way Nikolaos had gone about it had, as Gwydion said, left us in a predicament. I didn't know what to do with a decapitated corpse. His death was not the end of our journey for retribution; it did not bring closure to the families who had lost their children. The people of Britchelstone could not sleep at night until they knew the murderer was publicly stopped. The problem was, we couldn't hand over a halved corpse without drawing unwanted attention to ourselves.

I rubbed my puffy, bloodshot eyes with the back of my hand.

'We cannot leave the body here like this,' Gwydion said from behind us, making me jump. He hadn't joined in the tactile comforts. Not that I had ever expected him to. Gwydion really wasn't the touchy-feely sort of person. 'Nikolaos has botched this entire plan.'

'What are we to do now?' Adalia asked quietly, her voice quavering enough to make me turn to her. Dried tears left a faded white stain down her cheeks.

Nikolaos's penchant for butchery bothered me as his lover, but I'd only known him for two months. Adalia had just watched her childhood companion show a side of himself that she had never seen before. When Nikolaos had fled from us, the battle of loyalty versus morality had played over her face like a performance. In the end, the latter had won, but again I had to ask myself at what consequence.

If Maglark had been kept alive for longer, we would have been able to frame his death as a suicide. A note would have been forged detailing his repentance for the atrocities he had committed. We hadn't known about the pictures before, but with them, they would have been all we needed to substantiate his involvement. In theory, it had been one of Gwydion's most clear-cut, easily achievable plans. Not only would it have publicly put an end to the murders, but it also could have offered some solace to the families of the murdered girls. My own could have had the closure they so readily deserved.

As usual with our theories, the reality was disappointing. Even by Gwydion's standard of machinations, making a decapitation look like suicide was virtually impossible.

'Could you not use your necromancy to bring him back to life? Like with the zombies,' I asked.

'I am afraid,' he replied, 'a body void of head or heart is definitively dead.'

'Is there a way to—' I paused, unsure if the idea was as ridiculous as it sounded. 'To reattach the head?'

Gwydion gave me a quizzical look, painfully thin lips contorting into a wicked smile. Adalia noticed the smile giving him wild, furious eyes.

'Gwydion!' she exclaimed. 'You cannot seriously be considering such a thing.'

Gwydion offered a perfunctory shrug.

'Ordinarily, no, but there is nothing ordinary about the situation in which we have found ourselves. Aberrant circumstances call for equally unorthodox methods of resolution.'

'You have no scruples to barter what is left of your soul! I will not so freely hand my power over to dark occultism.'

Soft lines formed in Kai's forehead, eyebrows furrowing together. Frowning, Kai looked older than I had ever thought. The quizzical expression aged him.

'You're talkin' about using black magick?' he asked.

'I, like most practitioners, do not subscribe to such ideals.'

I cast a glance at Adalia. The abhorrence had not drained from her eyes when she turned from glaring at Rune to meet my gaze.

Some of the anger drained from her as she explained wearily, 'He's correct. Magick is too ambiguous to be confined by labels. That's why we believe in the threefold law.'

'So what's dark occultism?'

'There are implicit rules in the occultist world,' Gwydion explained, 'that certain matters are not to be trifled with. We are to leave the soul and heart to rest without interference. Love and death are best left alone. To go against these unspoken laws is to practice dark occultism.'

'You're a necromancer. It's your nature to work with the dead,' I said.

'Yes, and as a necromancer, my magick seeks death. It is one of the idiosyncrasies of necromancy which differentiates it from many other abilities. My soul is safe from my own power as it runs through my veins, but if one were to try to learn such skills they would not be protected.'

'So you can use your necromancy to bring Maglark back?' I reaffirmed.

There was a pause.

'I could use my powers with the dead to aid the binding of Maglark's body once more, but it would be using necromancy in a way which goes against the natural purpose of my ability. I would, as you may say, be making a deal with the devil.' He didn't sound the least bit deterred by that. 'Thus Adalia is right, that would constitute dark occultism.' He shrugged again. 'Potentially, it is viable, but even I am not so impolitic to disregard caution despite what Adalia thinks of me. I can call on my power as a demon to aid us.' He hesitated for a moment, seeming to think about what had just been said, before nodding his head and continuing, 'Yes, in fact, I think it is quite possible, but I shall not lie and offer false promises of certainty.'

Adalia shoulders slumped in defeat, a frustrated sigh escaping solemnly pursed lips.

The sun would be rising shortly. Solid black sky was already fading to deep, ocean blue when Kai and I started our journey to their house. Gwydion had decided it would be best to perform the ritual at his abode. He said it was because of their home being built on enchanted lands; I had a sneaking suspicion it was because he didn't want me further distracted by my relationship turmoils. With dawn fast approaching, it would take too long to drive so Kai and I bounded through the woodlands together. Gwydion was left to collect the remnants of Maglark's corpse. Adalia had said she wanted no part in touching the body. Gwydion had agreed, saying he did not mind doing it alone, and had urged her to start the journey in her car without him.

Although fast, Kai wasn't speedy enough to keep up. I slowed to match his black panther pace. We tore through the opening of the trees where the stone cottage stood cold and bare. The sky was lightening with every passing moment, turning a deep turquoise with slashes of red, pink, and purple like claws ripping through the heavens. Slumber was pulling at me with ferocity, making my limbs weak and heavy. Rune and Adalia wouldn't meet us until well into sunrise. I couldn't wait up for them even if I wanted to.

Kai turned into human form with practised ease. He was totally nude, dark skin glistening with sweat and the remains of blood from the shift. Whilst he seemed comfortable wearing nothing but his skin and blood, I was having a hard time controlling the blush that burnt my face. I was grateful he stayed in front of me as we walked down the corridor. It was much less embarrassing to be faced with his tight backside than what lay at the front of his body. Kai stalked in front with feline grace, muscles rippling like water under the black satin of the skin of his back, arms, thighs, calves. He was built of pure solidity; everything about his naked body screamed strength and grace.

Kai told me to wait in the corridor whilst he quickly grabbed a pair of dark blue jeans. On his return, I was ushered through one of the old decaying doors set into the stone wall.

'It's the guest bedroom,' he explained with a coy smile. 'Not that we get many guests.'

Strangely, there were no windows. Kai lit a candle as he walked in, offering a dim light which flickered against the stone like an orange shadow capering through the room. The large candle was placed on a dark blue glass plate on one of the shelves of the navy farmhouse dresser. The dark paint was chipped and peeling to show the light oak wood below. The drawers and doors in the lower part of the furniture had white ceramic knobs, and navy flowers were delicately painted on the pearl white.

The shelves exclusively housed a collection of plants in pots of white, dark blue and grey. Spider plants with dark green leaves with a slice of paler green down the centre trickled down from the shelves like a verdant waterfall. Most of the plants I recognised: snake plants, Boston ferns, swiss cheese, and aloe vera. The one that caught my eye the most was a bush of dark purple leaves with a centre of shiny green almost silver. I walked over to the cream pot that housed it, running my thumb lightly over one of the soft leaves.

'Pretty,' I said. 'It almost doesn't look real with the silver.'

Kai turned from where he was fluffing the pillows to smile at me.

'It's a Wandering Jew.'

I fondled the leaf for a moment more before turning around, leaning my back against the dresser. With no windows, I couldn't see the sky, but I knew dawn was creeping too close for comfort. Kai was finishing off fluffing the last cushion on top of the pale oak bed. All of the cushions were varying shades of blues and grey, resting on top soft, white cotton bedsheets. The throw at the foot of the bed was a dark grey like the sky when it threatens a storm. I could feel the warmth of the candle by my head, coaxing tranquillity.

Hanging above the bed, where a window should be, was a painting of a black panther resting torpidly on a large stone. The panther's body was curled around itself, head turned up, eyes painted bright amber and staring out of the picture with surprising spirit. The background was a blur of dark grey clouds blossoming in the navy sky. Cerulean wood framed the painting.

'I'll get ya some pyjamas,' Kai said, looking me up

and down with a frown. 'I think those jeans are ruined.'

I followed his gaze down my body. Up to my knees was coated with thick, flaking blood. Luckily the sleeves of my top stopped at the elbow, so none of the fabric had been dirtied, but my hands and arms were covered in black blood from where I had fallen into the grass. Before then I hadn't even noticed it. To say I wasn't firing on all cylinders was an epic understatement.

I stared down at my hands as if I'd never seen them before. Blood coated all my pale skin like a gruesome glove. I held my hands out in front of me. Now I'd noticed the blood I could feel the tackiness of it as it dried, pulling on the light hairs on my arms. Dawn was too close to scrub myself clean of the mess. I couldn't risk falling asleep in the shower.

With a quivering lip, I said the only thing I could think to say. 'I'm going to ruin your clean bedsheets.' It was so trivial, but at that moment, it felt like such a huge burden. Enough that the first tears began and then did not stop.

I hadn't remembered falling to the floor, but I must have for Kai to scoop me up from the ground. He cradled me effortlessly against his chest the way you'd handle a child. Kai placed me on the bed, still wearing my bloody clothes and boots. Kai pulled the grey throw over my body. I curled into a ball, holding it to my face, feeling the coarse fabric prickling against my skin. Kai lay down beside me, pulling me close into his arms without moving the comfort of the cloth away from me. His bare upper body was so warm, like being cuddled by a heater made of flesh and muscle.

Kai wrapped one arm around my waist, the other he used to rest his head on, bending his arm enough to stroke my hair.

'The bedding, the bedding, the bedding...' I repeated over and over again between the sobs.

Kai made soft, comforting sounds trying to shush me but I couldn't stop the words from falling out my lips. I cried and cried until the break of dawn illuminated the sky, and darkness washed over me.

)CHAPTER 27(

Clouds concealed the stars in a canopy of grey, reminding me of the sky in the painting above the bed I
had fallen asleep in. I stood beside one of the battered
leather sofas, staring out the dusty window. Thunder rumbled through the night, lightning illuminat-
ing the darkness in sudden slashes of blinding white.
Rain beat at the stone like bullets falling from the
clouds.

I had woken alone, still covered in dried, black
blood. Feeding was usually my priority for the night,
but I had arisen feeling repulsed by the thought
of going anywhere near blood. By the time I had
showered, scrubbing the cracking residue off my skin
until it took layers of flesh with it, and changed into
a pair of Kai's black trackies, that repulsion had been
overshadowed by hunger.

Kai wasn't much taller than me, but the trousers
he had given me to wear were comically large. Even
with the drawstring fastened tightly, they were still
far too loose around the waist. The t-shirt was large
enough to be a dress. I'd debated just wearing the top,
but I wanted the comfort of clothing big enough to
swallow me whole. If I hadn't thought it would look
too childish, I would have taken the duvet cover and
wrapped it like a cape around me. I wanted to be consumed by warmth and comfort.

Instead, I found myself walking towards one of the
doors in the corridor where Gwydion waited for me.
Adalia was still asleep. Kai was off doing anything he
could think of to avoid being in the room with the
body. The fabric at my ankles was so baggy I almost

tripped over my own feet shuffling along the stone hallway. Cold ran up my legs in shockwaves from my bare feet hitting frigid stone.

The door was open to reveal an alchemy lab. Three of the walls were lined with wooden counters with high cabinets over rows of shelves. Varying sized and shaped glass apothecary jars were lined up along the wood. There were even some genuine calabash bottles amongst the glass, with cord handles coming out the top. The glass held a spectrum of ingredients: dried herbs of all kinds filling the room with an overwhelming sickly, dry smell; feathers in blues, greens, black, silver, purples; pink, white and black salts; different flowers, some dried and some fresh; and beautiful, twinkling gemstones.

In the centre of the room was a large, rectangular wooden planter. Flowers and vines grew up from the soil, leaves curling over the wooden barrier to slither along the floor. Bouquets of bright daffodils bloomed beside orange marigolds. The box was noisy with colour; purple lobelias grew beside crimson amaranth, both were almost hidden by the bushy rue which dominated one side of the box. In the centre of all the colour, was a bush of roses in a rich, velvety black. I had never seen a black rose before; it was stunning.

Space had been cleared on one of the wooden counters. Maglark's corpse lay wrapped in pale brown linen. Gwydion stood in front of the counter, hunched over the cloth package imbrued with burgundy blood. Three wooden bowls sat by Maglark's head. In the largest of the three, the white heads of hemlock flowers rested on a bed of pale purple mandrake and unbloomed poppies.

Gwydion gave no indication to if he'd noticed me entering the room. I leant against the wall watching him work. As usual, he wore a collection of fabric draped in disarray over his frame. They were all coarse and tan, hanging over him like an ill-fitting tunic and trousers. Old, soft leather boots in a darker brown contained his feet. There was a large, pointed hood attached to the tunic hanging loosely down his back.

'You know,' he said into the silence, making me jump, 'it is discourteous to stare, Scarlet.'

'I didn't think you'd noticed me.'

'I do not miss much.'

'Are those roses real?'

Gwydion looked over his shoulder to the black roses in the plant box.

'Yes, they are endemic to Halfeti, in Turkey.'

'Then how are they growing here?'

He frowned at me.

'Magick, of course.' Shrugging, he added, 'Also, they are the flowers of death. I find myself drawn to them as much as they are to me.'

My opportunity to reply was stolen by Adalia trudging through the door. Dark bags puffed under her eyes, making her look closer to forty than early thirties. Her soft brown hair was pulled back tightly, leaving her hollowed face bare and weary. When we had first met weeks ago, Adalia had been full-figured and vivacious. Now, as she walked into the room, she looked feeble and tired. The denim jeans she had worn exclusively for the past week were baggier on her than they had been before, the waistband slipping down to show the trickle of pale pink lace tracing the top of her knickers. I hadn't seen Adalia eat since we had started working together. I had assumed that she tended to those necessities during the day whilst I slept, but looking at her now, I wasn't so sure.

It hadn't occurred to me that the long, sleepless nights and excessive use of powers would be so draining on Adalia. I'd been so consumed by the hectic events of the last couple of months it had been easy to forget that Adalia was the most human of all of us.

Kai, trailing in moments later, took one look at her and frowned, turning straight on his heel to disappear back into the corridor. Kai returned with a steaming cup of coffee contained in a forest-green mug. Adalia took it from him graciously, offering an enervate smile.

Energy flared through the room in a wave, making me stumble backwards against the wall. The black coffee sloshed over the corner of the mug almost scalding Adalia's fingers. Gwydion's necromancy stirred something inside me, coaxing my flames to take a step towards him and consequently I was to follow their lead. I resisted the urge, knowing it probably wasn't intentional. We needed his powers of necromancy strengthened and had to accept the concomitant effects that would have on me as a vampire.

Gwydion raised a hand up to one of the higher shelves, his loose cloth sleeve slipping down his elbow to reveal the twig-like stretch of his arm. He wrapped long fingers around a pitch-black apothecary jar, pulling the glass down onto the table with a *clink*. He flipped the cork cap off with one finger letting the sweet aroma of blood fill the room. Without thinking, I was suddenly behind Gwydion, peering around his side to take in a deeper breath of the blood.

'Control yourself, Scarlet.' With his words came a sweeping force of power to dampen my hunger. The power cajoled me to step back from where he worked. Gwydion's necromancy didn't usually affect me this way. Either he'd been holding back, or the power he was calling was stronger than I anticipated.

Moving away to stand to Gwydion's left side, I got a closer glimpse of what he was working on. He was using a granite pestle to grind the blood into another bowl of flowers. This one had dried snowdrops, lavender, salt and a sweet-smelling clip of Cypress.

With no warning, Gwydion reached over to rip the cloth off Maglark's body, letting the fabric collapse in a pile on the floor.

The head had been crudely sewn back together with thick, scaly leather thread. It looked like serpent skin, but I wasn't going to take a closer look to be certain. Silky black feathers from a crow stuck out from between the stitches, with russet and white owl feathers peeking out between the black.

Nature's beauty was a stark contrast against the savagery.

'The clamorous owl, that nightly hoots and wonders. At our quaint spirits. Sing me now asleep,' Kai surprised me by saying.

'Shakespeare,' Adalia said weakly, with her cup pressed to faintly smiling lips.

He grinned. 'I ain't just a pretty face.'

'I am inclined to concur,' Gwydion said, with his back still to us although I could hear the smile in his voice.

'Seconded,' I said, grinning back at Kai.

We all stood in harmonious silence, the tension I hadn't even realised had been drowning us leaking from the room.

Gwydion was quick to ruin the mood. 'I will need your blood, Scarlet.'

I just nodded. Gwydion opened one of the lower cabinets, pulling out a chalice made of shining copper. Engravings of roses and vines slithered around the upper rim. The bottom of the chalice had been carved to look like scales. On closer inspection, the vines were actually snakes wrapping along the metal. Their metallic eyes stared at me, almost mockingly.

'Bite your wrist and let the blood fall into here.' He

handed me the chalice.

I did as was requested. Sharp and startling pain ran up my hand as my fangs sunk into my flesh. Without feeding, I was weaker and pain was more bothersome. There wasn't enough blood running through my veins yet to offer more than a few droplets.

'It will suffice,' Gwydion said, with his back turned to me. He'd gone back to mashing what was in the bowl. I placed the chalice on the counter beside him.

Gwydion stopped grinding the ingredients together. He sighed, shoulders hunching over.

'Just what is needed,' he said through gritted teeth.

I was about to ask what was wrong when I felt it. I could sense Nikolaos's presence moments before hearing the disturbance of air as he flew through the forest towards us. It didn't take long for Kai to hear, or smell, him as well. His head shot upwards, nose sniffing the air. That dissipating tension came back with force.

I departed to the room at the front of the cottage, swinging the door open before Nikolaos had time to knock. His right hand was curled into a fist ready to rattle against the wood, a lit cigarette hanging from between tightly pursed lips. Strewn over the dark silk of his shirt-clad shoulder was a limp body. Drenched hair clung in clumps to his cheeks. Nikolaos removed his hand from the air, holding the cigarette between his thumb and index finger and curling the rest of his hand over the lit part to protect it from the storm.

His shirt was the scarlet of old blood—suitably morbid under the circumstances, or maybe I was just reflecting—and was buttoned up lazily to show off the expense of his upper chest. The trace of black hair over his chest looked even darker against the whiteness of his skin and red of the shirt. As Nikolaos adjusted the body over his shoulder, I caught a glimpse of the mutilated skin of his left hand where his bare flesh had touched the crosses last night. I winced at the sight of the shiny, pink wound.

Nikolaos flicked the cigarette onto the woodland floor and sauntered past me in silence with the man stilled draped around him like a macabre scarf. Water sluiced off the two men, streaming to form a puddle at his feet.

'I could feel your hunger,' he chastised. 'You must have your strength for the night.'

Nikolaos carelessly let the body fall to the ground; it was luck alone that his head didn't smash into the stone.

'Niko!' I exclaimed, dropping to my knees to check the pulse at his neck. It was a valueless gesture considering I could hear the steady beat of his heart, but I wasn't dead long enough to lose all my human impulses.

Nikolaos looked down at me with something close to humour playing over his face.

'He is not injured.'

'Luckily,' I said dryly. 'Did you bring human food, too?'

Nikolaos held his hand out to help me up. I got to my feet without his aid. His face was puzzled as he asked, 'Why would I?'

'For Adalia. I'm worried about her.'

'I will return,' he said, stepping over the body on the floor towards the still-open door. I grabbed onto his arm as he passed me, fingers wrapping over the cold wetness of the silk.

'Nikolaos, wait—' I began, but the look he gave me made the words falter in my mouth. I had a moment of embarrassment: watching him damp and beautiful in blood-coloured silk and leather trousers, black hair slicked back from the rain, so it looked intentionally styled; and then me, in Kai's oversized trackies tied too high up around my waist, bulky under the jumbo top I'd borrowed. The embarrassment was overshadowed by indignation. The bond between us was still closed tightly, padlocked, the key tossed into oblivion. The heart-stopping loneliness had yet to fade. After the stunt he had pulled last night, I had every reason to be angry, but it was he who looked at me with ardent hostility.

Nikolaos uncurled my fingers from the grip on his arm. Skin on skin sent a jolt through my body that had nothing to do with amour and all to do with desolation.

'*Non*,' he said. 'Adalia's welfare takes precedent.'

Tears stung my eyes, but I let him ease my hand off his body. He was right. Whatever I had to say to him was not as important as Adalia. As quickly as he'd appeared, Nikolaos vanished into the night.

The man Nikolaos had brought to me appeared to be younger than I was. Golden hair in tight, fine curls waved around his face, framing cheeks that had never lost that baby softness. The word *cherub* came to mind. Nikolaos had allured him so heavily his eyes were rolling to the back of his head, white eyelashes fluttering against the glass of his round glasses. Glasses that shape don't usually suit round faces, but on him, they seemed to highlight the softness of his rosy cheeks, as if he weren't trying to look older but instead play to his endearing, infantile features.

His body was unfittingly gangly, with long legs clad in light-blue jeans. His trainers were off-white, and socks the same white with a dark blue strip matching the colour of his T-shirt covered his ankles. The bomber jacket he wore was a pale tan and much too big on his slender frame.

With my fangs locked around his limp wrist, I had

a moment of hesitation to wonder if the person I was feeding on was even old enough to go out to the pub legally, and then the first drop of blood spilt into my mouth. I hadn't realised how feeble I was feeling until that warmth trickled down my throat, breathing life back into me.

My senses heightened immediately. The world became suddenly clearer; the faintest cracks on the walls like black veins in the stone. I had never known storms had a smell until then: the night was filled with the scent of ozone, pungent and stinging like something acidic; petrichor from where the rain had fallen onto what was left of the flowers on the ground, casting pollen and sweetness into the air; and the clean, earthy scent of soil that had never been touched by chemicals or pollution. Underneath all of the rich scents of nature was something harsh and acrid. Not just the stench of Maglark's blood but something else; acidic and noxious.

I heard Kai's feet plodding lightly on stone, the noise should have been lost to the racket of thunder and rain, but I could hear it like an echo through a cave. I let the wrist fall onto the floor, wiping my mouth clear of any blood, and then turned in time to see him entering the room.

'I can smell vomit,' I said.

Kai nodded grimly.

'Rune asked Adalia to help him with something on the body 'n' she spewed everywhere.'

'Niko's gone to get her something solid to eat.'

'Good,' he said. 'I was gonna take her car to get 'er somethin' from town.'

'Do you not have food in? I'd just assumed wereanimals needed to eat like the rest of us.'

Kai failed to stop his gaze from wandering to the body I crouched beside. 'Like a human, I meant.'

'Usually, we do. There ain't been the time lately.'

'I'm sorry,' I said.

He smiled at me, but it didn't quite reach his eyes.

'Naw, don't be, darlin'. It ain't your fault,' he said. The words tasted of truth, but I didn't believe them.

Adalia was leaning against the wall in the alchemy room, sweat plastering all that brown hair to her ashen face. I really hoped Nikolaos would return soon with something nutritious.

'Niko'll be back soon. He's bringing food for Adalia.'

'That is wise. I will need her help this evening. I do not think I can bear the burden of tonight's power alone.'

'What are you gonna do with him?' Kai asked, nodding his head in the direction of the room where I had left my dinner slouched against the wall.

'He'll be fine. Niko allured him so thoroughly I don't think he even knows his own name right now.'

Kai frowned, opened his mouth to say something, thought better of it, and instead said, 'I'm gonna go'n put him on the couch.'

I thought back to the times Nikolaos and I had communicated telepathically. I didn't know if the connection between us had been severed enough to cut metaphysical conveyance, nor did I truly understand how it worked between us, but, looking at Adalia barely able to keep her back upright against the wall, I knew I had to try.

I closed my eyes, picturing myself sitting at the vanity in my bedroom. In my mind, there was a telephone sitting in front of me. It didn't exist in real life. In my head, I saw it as one of the old fashioned rotary landlines with a dial that had to be physically moved over each number individually. I don't know why that's what my brain had decided to picture. I had never used one of them before, but it was what felt most comfortable in my mental image and I knew better than to question it. Truthfully, it was probably a much more complicated method to reach out to Nikolaos than was necessary. I just wasn't comfortable enough with my powers to know how it worked. Adalia had taught me that visualisation made magick easier and so far it had worked. When we'd first started communicating this way I'd pictured it as writing a letter and sending it, but that process was slow and clunky. It's easier to imagine talking down a phone than writing each word as it's spoken.

I imagined picking up the phone and placing it to my ear. There was no number to call, no dialling or ringing tone, just the phone resting against my cheek.

'*Niko,*' I spoke into the silent telephone. No reply. '*Niko, are you there?*'

Again there was nothing but silence. Just as I was going to open my eyes, I felt the brush of power gently sweeping over me. I gasped quietly, goosebumps running over my skin.

'*Oui, ma chérie, I am here.*'

It was as if I could smell him. Faint floral aromas of musky rose, sweet saffron and earthy cinnamon danced around me. I wondered if the others could smell it.

'*Ma chérie, are you still there?*' he asked, no longer sounding hostile.

'*Yes, sorry, I was distracted by your smell.*'

He laughed, sending the sensation of warm velvet rubbing over my mind as if the sound were tangible. Such a peculiar sensation. Pleasant, but strange.

'*How long do you think you'll be? Gwydion seems anxious to begin, but truthfully I don't know if Adalia is up for this.*'

He paused for long enough I wasn't sure I'd get a response.

'*I shall not be long,*' he finally replied.

I opened my eyes to see Gywdion watching me knowingly.

'Niko said he'd be back soon,' I said.

'And how do you know this?' he asked coyly.

I frowned at him. 'You know how.'

Gwydion nodded.

'Will you humour my speculations?'

I explained it to him not entirely sure Nikolaos would be okay with me sharing our secret.

'I would not expect you to be able to communicate in such a way.'

'Nikolaos was surprised the first time, too.'

'I am sure he was. It is not only too soon, but Nikolaos lacks the power needed of a master for such skill. You are freeing him from the shackles of power-lessness.'

'The shackles you put on him,' I said.

Gwydion shrugged.

'Upon request. It took more from me than I would care to admit, at least not to him. I do not know if him knowing this truth would be ammunition to Nikolaos's resentment towards me or worsen his burden of regret.'

'I won't say anything if you don't want me to.'

'Perhaps,' he said cryptically, not really giving me an answer. 'I wonder if Nikolaos ever fathomed the slew of peculiarities that would escort you in the afterlife.'

I didn't know if that was meant as a compliment or not so I just shrugged.

Nikolaos was true to his word, arriving shortly after our conversation with food for Adalia. He walked in with a brown takeaway bag filled with burgers, chips and some other side orders. He'd brought enough for Kai, too, which surprised both of us. The brown paper was darker in patches where grease had leaked through in an oily stain. Holding the food in one hand, and a cup holder with two milkshakes and plastic straws in the other, he looked shockingly normal and totally out of place with the silk shirt and leather trousers. I had a moment to think that this is what it might look like if Nikolaos and I were human instead of creatures bound by darkness. In another life, would it be us sitting at the front room table, laughing and eating solid foods, instead of Kai and Adalia?

Technically, vampires can eat human food, the same way we can drink liquids other than blood, but it makes us sick. No one really knows why or how it works; liquids seem to be able to filter through our system, food cannot, so vampires end up vomiting to get rid of it. Apparently, there are some bulimic vamps out there who are not willing to give up the luxury of a hearty meal. They eat and then face the inevitable sickness afterwards. They still have to drink blood to survive, in fact, they have to drink more of it because of how much they lose when being sick. I missed food, too, especially smelling the sweet and salty fried potatoes, but it just didn't seem worth the effort.

When Adalia saw the food, she looked close to tears. I felt a wave of guilt that we had been neglecting her needs to such an extent. I hadn't been a vampire long enough to justify my lack of consideration for such basic necessities like food and sleep.

Adalia and Kai departed from the room to eat at the table. They thought trying to consume meat in the same room as Maglark's butchered corpse might kill their appetite. Couldn't blame them for that one, really.

That left Nikolaos, Gwydion, and I stuck in the room with Maglark. It was the first time Nikolaos had seen the corpse since Gwydion had stuffed him and sewn the head back on. He stood next to Gwydion admiring the work as if it were the most fascinating thing he'd ever seen. Admittedly, it was fascinating, if you could get past the urge to lose your dinner looking at it.

Leaning back in my spot against the wall by the door, I watched Gwydion explain to Nikolaos the process of binding Maglark's body. I tuned out—didn't need to know, didn't want to know. Nikolaos hadn't spoken to me since he returned, but the tension levels between us had dropped. That would suffice for now; I could handle being shunned if it meant the air wasn't overcome with animosity.

I wasn't sure what to expect for the night. I don't think anyone was.

⟩CHAPTER 28⟨

Gwydion instructed Nikolaos to carry the corpse-bearing parcel out into the storm carefully. If he'd asked me, it would have been a definite no. Luckily, Nikolaos was not so easily perturbed. Without arguing—a small miracle, if you ask me—he simply picked up the bundle and followed Gwydion's lead around the back of the house. I was particularly suspicious at this newfound compliance. Potentially he'd just realised that we wouldn't be in this mess if it weren't for his impetuous conduct.

Using a paste made of crushed chalk, mercury, salt, and a drop of his own blood, Gwydion began to draw a massive ankh on the ground.

'Why an ankh?' I asked.

Gwydion ignored me, focusing on the outline.

'It is a symbol of life, death, immortality and re-incarnation,' Adalia replied. Her voice was stronger than it had been, the food giving her much needed strength.

'Adalia,' Gwydion said, without looking up, 'that pentagram you wear around your neck. You must either remove or invert it.'

'Rune, I—'

'Just once could I make a request of someone without them battling me? I am offering you the choice of protecting the sanctity of it.' He looked up then. 'Although it would aid us further if you could invert it.'

Gwydion had completed the ankh; he was starting to draw a circle around it.

'What's the problem?' Kai asked softly. He and I were the two least familiar with magick, and his being mar-

307

ried to Gwydion hadn't changed that.

'To invert my pentagram would mean to become subservient to the evils we will call upon. The circle around it'—she traced the silver circle with a finger —'represents protection. I have blessed it with my intent, used it as a tool in countless rituals. All it knows is the touch of fire, earth, air, water and spirit. To invert, it would be like opening a door to a new world of magick, one that can breach the protection with no qualms. Usually, anything I would consider sinister would have to battle my power.'

'Could you not take it off?' I asked.

'Yes, but Rune is right. It would weaken our power. If I felt stronger then maybe I could risk it. But as it stands, I do not think I am able to do what is needed without the power held within my talisman.' Her fingers fiddled absentmindedly with the jewellery, tracing small circles over and over the delicate silver as she weighed out which choice was the lesser evil.

'I request you hasten to make a decision. We do not have the luxury of time for you to ponder. I wish to start before the storm passes on,' Gwydion called, he had almost completed drawing the bloody circle.

'I would have thought the storm would make it harder,' I said quietly to myself, but apparently it was loud enough for Gwydion to hear.

'Thunder silences the footsteps of spirits; they dance through the rain using it as a cloak. Demons and spirits use storms to walk more freely amongst us.'

Adalia undid the clasp at the back of her neck, letting the delicate chain pool into her palm. She stared at where the silver lay in her open hand, sighed, and began to unthread the necklace from the small hoop. Adalia flipped the pentagram upside down, so the two bottom points faced upwards, and then rethreaded the chain in between the points. There wasn't a hoop for the chain to go through, but the makeshift one worked just as well. Nikolaos, Kai and I were unable to help her reclasp the necklace as it was pure silver, but she managed it with fast expertise. If it were me, I would have been fumbling with the tiny bit of metal for ages. Claps that small are frustratingly fiddly to do up.

'Nikolaos, you must place the body in the centre of the ankh,' Gwydion instructed.
'Adalia, you need to be in here with me before I close the circle.'

Nikolaos scooped the body up into his arms and walked over with Adalia to enter the circle. He placed the bundle in the centre of the ankh as was requested and walked back out to stand by me. With Nikolaos free of the circle and Adalia safely contained, Gwydion finished the final line.

Power rippled through the air, forcing me to stumble backwards. If Nikolaos hadn't caught my arm, I would have ended up falling to the wet ground. His hand was shaking with tension, fingers gripping around my flesh with iron strength. It hurt, but the pain was grounding. Gwydion retrieved the ceremonial knife he used for all necromantic rituals. He had lined up an assortment of magickal paraphernalia including the copper chalice which still contained the few measly drops of my blood which he had diluted with his own.

Gwydion unbound the scraps that clung to Maglark's body. Raw, bloody symbols I didn't recognise had been carved into his naked torso. A small linen cloth had been placed over his pelvic area to keep the illusion of dignity. There really wasn't anything dignified about the scene in front of us, but I appreciated not having to see any more of Maglark's body.

Gwydion raised the chalice upwards, using a macilent finger to stir the gory concoction. He drew a line down from forehead to chin. If it weren't for his raised hood, the rain would have washed away the attempt. The blood dripped down his face in a thick line, running down his chin into the fabric of his tunic. With the blood in place, Gwydion began to rewalk the perimeter of the circle, chanting in an ancient language long lost to history. The language sounded sinister; even without understanding it, I knew it was a tongue that coaxed malevolent forces into being.

Black light flared from the engravings in Maglark's chest. Light should not, can not, be black. But this light was. It sucked in all the darkness around it as if emitting a light of shadow. Blindingly bright and harrowingly dark all at the same time. Gwydion's eyes were illuminated by the blazing blackness, emitting their own icy blue glare.

The air inside the circle picked up, whirling fiercely through the contained space. Gwydion's hood blew off, sending wisps of chalky hair whipping around his face. Adalia was standing with her heels pressed to the circle, as far back as she could without stepping free from the power. She watched Gwydion chant with wide eyes, lips parted. It was a gaze of horror, shock, and something else. Darkness, as if the power called to her, demanding more than she was willing to give of herself, but she wanted to. I saw the battle play over her face; her reserve fighting the temptation to give in.

I could feel the pull of Gwydion's necromancy. A minacious force was calling on something depraved deep within me. This power was perverse; tugging parts of me which I had never known were there before. Pulling on a darkness in my soul that Gwydion's necromancy had never previously touched.

Warmth flickered internally, the familiarity comforting in the face of devious and unwonted power. The circle of protection kept Gwydion's magick from escaping or attracting the unwanted attention of supernatural creatures that might be lurking in the shadows. I, foolishly, had thought that would mean we would be unable to feel the colossal deluge of power they conjured.

I could feel the power flowing over me, tasting my aura, spitting it out. It did not like me one bit. Nikolaos, however, it found very tasty. The power beat against my skin, flowed over me in waves of energy that were both scalding hot and colder than ice. It rushed straight through me into Nikolaos. He was suffocating against the pressure. I still had no idea what the rules were of metaphysics and how it worked. Honestly, I don't think even Gwydion really knew half of what he claimed, he had just mastered the pretence, and it seemed to work most of the time. You had to believe you knew what you were doing with magick—feign control, and, usually, it would obey your command. I knew that if the power realised the dubiety of my self-confidence, it would try and swallow us both whole. And it would probably succeed.

I knew how to fight against Gwydion's necromancy —sort of. Since I had first come into power I had thought of us as separate entities; my power was the leader, I followed blindly in its footsteps. But that wasn't the case. My power was an extension of me; I may not understand it, but I could try to control it. Part of that power was life; fire, energy. I had been a nymph before I became a vampire, that energy still flowed through my veins. Necromancy didn't want anything that had even the faintest embers of life. This power was feeding off Gwydion's necromancy; of death. We could fight it.

I gripped Nikolaos's hand in my own. I felt the coolness of his hand entwined in my own and thought of fire; of life. Fire, one of Mother Earth's elements. The giver of light to scare away the darkness. Warmth to fight the cold. A weapon against enemies. So much destruction in that one element and also so much life. Flame that feeds off oxygen like a living being, fueled by wicker and wood from the trees. Without air, we could not survive, without earth to grow the kindle we would perish, and without water, we would rage. In one blinding moment of clarity my place as a daughter of the earth, my role as an elemental deity, all fell into place, and I understood what it meant to be alive. More alive than I had ever been as a human.

I took that life and pulsed it into Nikolaos through my hand. I felt the heat run up his arm, shoulders, into his chest. Until finally the heat brushed over his heart. A heart that had not beat without stolen energy from a human for two millennia. It forced the organ to pound against his chest like a crazed animal finally awoken from a deep slumber. So wild, so afraid, so very alive.

Our hearts beat together in perfect unison, fighting the darkness that sought only death. My flames battled the iciness of the magick, melting the cage it tried so desperately to form. We stood together, hand in hand, and we were no longer what the power wanted. I could almost taste its disappointment; its surprise.

I had a moment to refocus my eyes, seeing the world clearly after gorging myself on my own power. Gwydion's clothes had always rested so uneasily against his back; before then, I had never known why, but now it was clear. He was extended in the air, huge white wings flapping gracefully around his body.

The arms of the wings were white bone with three downturned fingers. Hooked claws graced the ends of the bat-like fingers, pale tufts of soft hair growing around the claw. The plagio patagium was white skin stretched so thinly between the bones it was almost translucent, growing fainter in colour towards the lower part of the wing. Blue veins flowed along the surface like turquoise vines.

His tunic had been lost in the explosion of wings. Gwydion floated in the air, head thrown back, ivory hair defying gravity as it whipped around his face in a wind of power. Gwydion's torso was long and as painfully skinny as the rest of him. Ribs stuck out below his chest as neither muscle nor fat lay underneath the painfully stretched skin. Like the dead he raised, Gwydion looked like an animated skeleton with only the intensity of his own power keeping his heart beating.

The sensation of Nikolaos's hand in mine was fading away. Neither of us had moved, but suddenly my body was numb. My eyes unfocused, the world became a quavering blur, like watching through a veil of trembling water. Through the blur, I could make out the shape of white where Gwydion flew in the air, wings fighting against the wind of power. My last thought before the world faded into darkness was, *So beautiful.*

☽CHAPTER 29☾

Cold. Wet. I was lying on solid ground, freezing water soaking through my top into my back, and eternal darkness blinding me. Pellets of ice beat against my skin like tiny bullets. I thought, *I'm blind*, and then my eyelids fluttered open. Not blind, just forgot how to blink. Now my eyes were open it was as if all sound came back too. The heavens had opened, releasing a ferocious storm. Hailstones were hitting against my skin hard and fast enough it hurt, like tiny pinpricks bruising my skin. Hail pounded against the grass deafeningly. Thunder tore through the night, bellowing like an enraged scream.

'Lettie,' a male voice, American. 'Lettie, can you hear me?'

I rolled my head to the side to see Kai kneeling beside me. His amber eyes were dark with concern. I limply held my wrist out to him, making a thumbs-up gesture. He exhaled a deep breath of relief and grinned at me, taking my hand in his own.

'Can hear.' My voice was breathy. I swallowed back the urge to giggle but the slightest breath of humour escaped my lips. Kai's eyebrows raised into an expression of perplexion as if unsure whether to be relieved or concerned. Relief seemed to win.

'D'ya need a hand up?'

I thought about it and then nodded my head against the grass. The world still felt vaguely blurry. I was floating on a cloud, seeing the world through a haze of pleasant orange light. I didn't know why I was lying on the ground as the hail fought to draw blood from my skin and the storm tore through the skies.

There was something I was forgetting. Something important, but what? I giggled again.

Gwydion's face appeared above mine, cold blue eyes staring down at me. At some point, he'd found a new tunic. Seeing him brought back a surge of memories and all of that floaty joy was overridden with fear. Demonic wings like an albino bat. Maglark. The dark power trying to marry itself to Nikolaos's death. How could I have forgotten this? I felt myself frowning back at Gwydion.

So many things I wanted to say but the only words my mouth was capable of forming were, 'Bat wings. Beautiful.'

He smiled at me. Part of my mind was still panicked, the rest of it was back to floating in a haze of pleasure. I felt my eyelids fluttering closed again, lips spreading into a small, contented smile.

'Help her up, Kai.'

I felt hands wrapping underneath my arms, pulling me to my feet. Once standing, Kai used his grip on me to wrap one arm around my waist, steadying my body against his. My ankles felt weak, feet floppy. I would have fallen if it weren't for his solid hold. My eyes opened again, slowly, lazily. Gwydion wasn't smiling anymore. He looked at me impatiently.

'What's wrong with me?' It was the first full sentence I'd formed since regaining consciousness. I felt strangely proud of myself.

'You have gorged yourself on power. The effects will wear off shortly.'

'Where's Niko and Adalia?' I forced my head to turn enough to look around. The circle of power and ankh had been washed away in the rain. 'Where's Maglark?'

The power high was receding. Reality came crashing back; panic tightened my stomach into a knot.

'Nikolaos is too giddy with power to construct a

sentence. He is resting with Adalia.'

'Is she okay?'

'Exhausted, but otherwise well.'

Some of that tension eased.

'And Maglark?' I asked again.

I was feeling well enough to stand without Kai's help but I didn't pull away from his arms just yet.

'Follow me and see for yourself.'

I'd checked on Nikolaos and Adalia in the spare bedroom before joining Gwydion in the alchemy room. Nikolaos had been lying on the bed with Adalia curled in his arms. She snuggled her head into his chest with his hands tracing her wet hair absently. I had thought he hadn't noticed me in the room, but just before I had turned to leave, Nikolaos had half-opened his eyes and smiled languidly at me. I'd walked over to them both, sitting on the edge of bed beside Nikolaos to stroke his cheek lightly. He looked at me like the proverbial cat with cream. It was the most serene I had ever seen him as if a permanent tension had given way to joyous tranquillity.

'Mon coeur bat la chamade pour toi, ma petite feu.'

Not knowing enough French to understand what was said, I'd kissed him on the forehead and left Nikolaos to cuddle closer to Adalia.

Maglark was lying on the counter blinking up at the ceiling but not like he actually saw anything there. The wounds on his neck had knitted themselves back together like magick. No, not like magick. With magick. Thick, black drool poured from between his mouth onto the counter. The viscous liquid seeped into his hair, clumping it. It was too thick to be blood, and too dark. The smell was like something meaty and decaying. It reminded me of the smell of a butchers, if the butchers tended to rotting meat.

Maglark managed to muster enough energy to turn

his head. His cheek hit against the wooden counter as if his neck couldn't support the weight of his head. Although still unfocused and fluttering, Maglark's eyes darkened and I knew he saw me. Somewhere deep down the fires of sentience still burned, still understood what was happening. Maglark opened his mouth as if to speak but more of that foul-smelling slobber washed out of his mouth and he choked on the words.

I took a step further into the room. Close enough to see the engravings on his torso hadn't healed as wholly as the neck wound. The scars were bright, shiny pink. Linen cloth still covered his lower regions; short, beefy legs stuck out from the cloth, covered by a blanket of dark hair.

'What's wrong with him?' I asked, turning to face Gwydion. I was grateful he stood behind me. It gave me the perfect excuse to turn away from the scene without showing the cowardice I felt. 'He doesn't look like any of the zombies you raised.'

'Whatever magick you called broke the spell before it was consummated, hence the catastrophe behind you.'

Maglark made a sound of protest that almost made me turn back around to look at him, but I stopped myself in mid-motion. I couldn't take seeing any more of that bodily fluid leaking from his orifice.

'Natheless, I do not consider this such a tragedy.'

'What do you mean?'

For the first time, Gwydion looked uncertain, fretful even.

'The ritual,' he said, 'was unruly. It summoned a contumacious power. If it were not for your calling of magick, then I fear the consequence. The circle of protection should not have been so easily breached.'

'I felt the power like it was trying to taste me.' I

shuddered at the memory.

'We are fortunate you called on your power in such a manner. I confess without it I would have lost control. I do not think Adalia would have survived being drained by such force. Nor Nikolaos.'

'What about you? Would you have survived?'

Gwydion shrugged and smiled wryly.

'In body, yes. Soul, however, I am less certain.'

I didn't press him to explain further. For once I understood the meaning behind his ambiguity. I had felt the force of that power; even if Gwydion had survived being possessed, his mind would have been lost to something darker. Gwydion's necromancy gave him a natural affinity with the dead, but he understood the importance of balance between life and death. That odious power had known only death. If I hadn't managed to sever the spell then who knows what Gwydion would have done...I didn't even want to think about it. No point dwelling on what could have been, especially as there were always so many potentially adverse outcomes. I would quickly lose my sanity if I exhausted that much energy on the could-haves/would-haves of everything we did.

'What are we going to do with him now?' I asked, motioning behind me without looking.

'Tonight,' he replied, 'nothing. Dawn draws near. By dusk tomorrow I suspect Nikolaos will have recovered. You already have a succulent repast awaiting your awakening.'

It took me a moment to realise what he meant. The man I had fed on hours prior was still lying dazed and confused on the leather sofa where Kai had left him.

Whether I liked waiting for tomorrow or not, the sun would soon arise and oblivion would consume me until nightfall. Immortality as a vampire meant we were not confined by the ticking clock of transience, but still imprisoned by the light of day. Like most magick, it was a double-edged sword. We could walk the world forever but only guided by the glow of the moon. Untouchable by darkness, in daylight we were vulnerable. Sometimes it didn't feel like a worthwhile trade. Or maybe I was just tired and feeling cynical.

Kai gave me another oversized top to replace the soaked one I hadn't yet taken off. I declined the offer of trousers this time as the garment fell past my knees. This one was grey and soft and I promised not to keep ruining his linens. The bedding I had bloodied had already been discarded, replaced by white cotton sheets.

There wasn't enough space beside Nikolaos to sleep beside him so I walked to the other side of the bed beside Adalia. She was still curled into Nikolaos's chest, arms tucked up under her chin. Her face was peaceful, breathing deep and steady with sleep. Nikolaos's eyes were closed when I settled down next to Adalia. I thought he might have already been asleep, dawn was close enough for him to have slipped into slumber early, but he opened his eyes. The look he gave me was still lazy with intoxication but there was a tenderness to him. He reached his hand over Adalia's body. I took his palm in both my hands, cuddling it up against my chest. I settled my body very lightly against the back of Adalia, not quite touching her. I let the heat of her humanity blanket me and, still snuggling Nikolaos's hand, I closed my eyes.

)CHAPTER 30(

Nikolaos and I were standing in the exact spot this had all began.

Kai had fished through our meal's pockets and found his ID. I'd been relieved to see that Joey Smedley may have looked baby-faced but was, in fact, a year older than me. I don't think I could handle knowing I'd fed on a child. It was simply far too perverse. Nikolaos and I had found the address written on the provisional license and dropped him on the doorstep. It was a nice area, he'd be fine waiting there until someone found him. With the fang marks healed he'd probably just think a wild night had gotten out of hand.

When we had arisen for the night, Maglark had stopped 'bleeding' from his mouth. If it weren't for his eyes following us back and forth I'd have been sure he was dead. If his heart beat, I did not hear it. If he breathed, it was not visible to me.

Now Nikolaos stood beside me with a large rucksack slung over his back containing the body. The power high had faded from last night but there was still a newfound ease to him that hadn't been there before. It wasn't overt: a slight release around his shoulders, less tension around his eyes and mouth, an air of confidence that wasn't theatrical or forced. I didn't point it out, cautious that if he knew anyone noticed he would slip straight back into hiding.

It wasn't just the physical side effects that were so noticeable. Nikolaos's power floated around him like a living thing. The uncertain energy his power had before was now forceful and breathtaking. After so long free of magick, he didn't quite know how to control it yet. Gwydion said this time Nikolaos's power tasted different. He couldn't quite put his finger on it, but it had evolved into something newer, fresher.

This was the first time I had been back to the scene of my murder. I gripped Nikolaos's hand so tightly both our skin mottled. The pavement had been cleaned of any blood; there was no evidence that only two months prior a murder had taken place. I stood in the spot where my body had collapsed, almost able to see my figure on the ground like a shadow of the past come back to haunt me. So many feelings were fighting to the surface of my mind.

This was where I had died. Where Nikolaos had found me and given me a second chance. Without that, I never would have met Kai, Adalia and Gwydion. Without me, they never would have thought to put an end to the murders. Who knew how many more women would have fallen victim to his blade the way I had. Now I stood here and, although I was dead, I had not died. In some ways, I was experiencing more of life than I ever had before. Maglark, however, was about to face the true death. He would be given no second chances; any opportunity to make a plea of redemption had been ripped away from him when Nikolaos tore his head from his body.

In the end, the feeling that won was exhaustion. I realised I had been thriving on adrenaline. The adrenaline of seeking vengeance; of falling in love, not just with Nikolaos but the others, too, and with beginning to understand the potential of my power. The dawning realisation that this was the closing chapter of my life, giving way to a novel of death, hit me with a severity I had not anticipated. Once the sun rose, there would be no more murders. Closure would finally be offered to the families of the victims, including my own. The people of Britchelstone could go back to finding normality, a normal that was not tainted by the fear of peril.

Now the end was in sight I had no energy left to give. Depleted of vigour, I could not bring myself to feel the anger I hadn't realised was animating me. Despite all the agony Maglark had caused the people I loved and me, I could not bring myself to be the one who extinguished what was left of his life. It wasn't weakness. Maglark had robbed me of my life, family and dignity. It was the strength not to let him take what was left of my morality, too.

Across the road, an oak tree grew tall and proud. I watched Nikolaos cross the deserted road towards the tree. He jumped up onto one of the lower branches with the sack still attached to his back. The rucksack contained three things: Maglark's body; a braided polyester rope; and the polaroids of his victims sealed in an envelope with a letter detailing the atrocities of his crimes, and the contrition he could no longer bear to live with. My picture was amongst those of the slaughtered women. Nikolaos had refused to let me see them, and I had not battled him on it. My nerves were not that strong.

This suicide would seem like a public display of penitence. In his vegetative state, these final moments would be lonely and undignified. That thought made it feel like an almost satisfying requital for his crimes.

Nikolaos lay the bag onto the branch; it was wide enough to act as a table without the rucksack or its contents falling to the ground below. He opened the bag, pulling out the rope already fastened into a slipknot. Earlier in the night, Nikolaos had fashioned the noose with disturbing expertise. Next, he tugged the limp body free of the bag. He wrapped the noose around Maglark's scarless neck, placing the knot at the left-hand side of his jaw, just behind the ear. Finally, he pulled the letter from the bag and shoved it into Maglark's jacket pocket. We'd managed to find one that didn't fit him to illy. Nikolaos tied the other end of the rope around the thick trunk of the tree and then, without warning, pushed the body off the tree.

The body collapsed into the air, the rope bouncing as it caught his weight. I heard the snapping of bone as if it echoed through the night. The rope quivered under the weight of his suspended carcass. The only noise was the haunting creaking of the swaying rope.

Nikolaos returned to my side, engulfing my hand in his own. I buried my face into his chest, unable to watch the body swing back and forth any longer. He stroked my back in slow circles, resting his own head atop mine. I stayed clutching onto his body, trying to hide from what we had done, but the dramatically loud creaking refused to let me find sanctuary in blindness alone.

When morning broke I fell into deep repose. Wrapped tightly in Nikolaos's embrace, knowing that the battle was over and we had prevailed, I finally felt safe.

)CHAPTER 31((

I did not rise from slumber for three days. During that time all my dreams were haunted by the creaking of a hangman's rope. When I did finally arise I was given a copy of The Talus. My family were pictured looking solemn on the front cover, with a quote reading, '*The loss of our middle child, Scarlet, has been an immense grief from which our family will never recover. Knowing the man who did this to her is gone and unable to harm anyone else gives us the first glimpse of hope that we can begin to mourn our beautiful daughter and start healing.*' Detective Todd was also quoted saying how The Britchelstone Barbarian knew the police were close to finding him and was too scared to deal with the wrath of the law. It was a lie, but if it helped Detective Todd and the people of Britchelstone sleep better at night then who was I to destroy the illusion?

Nikolaos did end up travelling to meet the Empress. Whatever energy I called upon the night of Maglark's revival had forced new power on Nikolaos that he was required to divulge. I did not go with him. The Empress said Nikolaos is allowed to stay in Britchelstone as long as he vows not to turn any more humans. Seeing as that had never been his intention, he agreed readily. The Empress seems both cautious and intrigued by Nikolaos and has started requesting more frequent meetings with him. So far I've avoided the invitation but neither of us thinks that will last.

Gwydion suggested we continue working together as my powers grow. I accepted the offer eagerly. We've started meeting up on a weekly basis. Mainly I'm anxious to try and understand more about what it means to be a nymph, but I can't deny there's a part of me curious to uncover more about the enigma that is Gwydion. Gwydion also offered Nikolaos the aid of his expertise; Nikolaos, not so politely, declined. The two men quickly went back to their usual, supercilious selves. On the surface, you'd think they are enemies. I knew better. Nothing breeds hate like love.

Adalia and I never did get to have some time just the two of us. She fled back to London as soon as the ordeal was over, requesting none of us to contact her until she's ready. I was sad to see her go, but I couldn't exactly blame her. By spending time with Adalia, I had been hanging onto the last shreds of my humanity. She may not be truly human, but she was the closest thing I had to normality. By being around me, us, she had lost some of what she thought kept her human. I know all too well how that feels, so when she left, I wholeheartedly understood.

Unbeknownst to me, Adalia had continued working fortnightly with my family to help them through the process of losing me. She promised that she would not stop just because she needs space from us. It feels strange knowing that every other Tuesday Adalia is in town sitting at the dining room table with my family. It also feels like it's keeping a piece of me alive with them, and them with me. Little do they know just how strong a connection they are keeping open by working with her.

Nikolaos and I returned home from feeding one night to find a Wandering Jew plant waiting for me in a plum-coloured plant pot. Kai had left it for me beside a lone black rose that Gwydion had picked. I doubted it was actually Gwydion's idea, but I made sure to thank him anyway. The plant now lives on the coffee table upstairs giving some much-needed colour to the exclusively cream room. The black rose is in a vase on the vanity beside my bed. It has yet to die. Magick can be a wonderful thing in that way. Nikolaos bought me a bouquet of crimson roses the following night. They did die. But he replaces them every time the first petal falls. It's probably overkill but I love those roses.

The death of Maglark meant the closing of a chapter I wasn't fully prepared to let go of. With Adalia working with my family, I feel like I get to keep the part of my old life I had been too scared to lose. Besides, as the old saying goes, when one door closes another door opens.

I'm prepared to face the continuing changes and challenges in my new life—if you can call it that. I take solace in knowing I'm not alone. I have people who genuinely care for me as I do for them. There's no way to know what the future holds for any of us but somehow it all seems much less daunting now. I'm ready to dive into the unknown, safe in the knowledge that, if I begin to drown, there are hands who will pull me back to safety.

I was only twenty years old when I died. Who would have thought that with death came immortality?

AUTHOR'S NOTE

Hello!

I hope you enjoyed the first instalment of The Scarlet Cherie: Vampire Series. Book two of the series is currently being worked on (you can keep informed on the progress by following the social links below).

I started writing The Fire Within My Heart in April 2019, not necessarily planning on publishing it nor expecting how invested I would become in the characters and story as a whole. What started off as a novella being nonchalantly written during my breaks at work quickly evolved into something I poured my heart into. Over the last six months, I have spent every hour of every day writing, plotting, and editing this book and the future books in the series (currently, I've got up until book five planned out in detail—yay!). In April 2020, after countless rewrites, the original novella blossomed into a full-fledged novel with a greatly evolved plot and characters.

All of the writing, editing, and proofing have been done by me and several family members who graciously dedicated a lot of their time to help me (and to whom I am exceptionally grateful!). As a practitioner of Wicca, I have tried to incorporate some of my views on nature and the earth into my work, whilst also sticking to a world of arcane fantasies nestled into reality. Britchelstone is based heavily on my hometown, Brighton, and I'm hoping to explore some more places in future books, both in Britchelstone and across the UK (Edinburgh and Glasgow will make an appearance in book 2...)

Suppose you have any questions about the story and characters, or even just want to say hello, my social media will be listed below—I'm always happy to have a chat or answer any queries regarding my work! Equally, if you are inclined to leave a review, then I would be incredibly grateful to you.

Thank you, dear reader, for reading my novel. I hope you got as much enjoyment from reading it as I have done writing it, and that you are looking forward to seeing what book two entails.

Warm regards,
Ayshen Irfan

* * *

Follow me on social media to keep up-to-date with my work and The Scarlet Cherie: Vampire Series.

Instagram: Author_Ayshen
Twitter: Author_Ayshen
Facebook: Scarlet Cherie: Vampire Series
Email: ayshenbooks@gmail.com

Printed in Great Britain
by Amazon